About the Author

A father of two demanding daughters and married to a formidable woman, the author is nonetheless inordinately happy with his lot. An early passion for writing was savagely thwarted for twenty-five years by ill fortune, economic strife and a woeful lack of ambition. Instead, the author embarked on a torrid quest through the world's noble trades in an effort to find the one to which he was least suited. He found it in teaching. He's over it now and rehabilitating in the Lake District.

To my world, my wife.

Rosco Low

LIQUIDITY

AUSTIN MACAULEY
PUBLISHERS LTD.

A CIP catalogue record for this title is available from the British Library.

ISBN 9781787103139 (Paperback)
ISBN 9781787103146 (E-Book)
www.austinmacauley.com

First Published (2017)
Austin Macauley Publishers Ltd.
25 Canada Square
Canary Wharf
London
E14 5LQ

One

Even before he opened his eyes, he had a bad feeling about what would greet him when he did. Something to do with heat and pressure, space and time. Consciousness came to him in dull spasms and with it, nausea and nebulous images. A bar, incessant rain. The clamour of a hundred people shouting at each other above the din, closeness and sweat. A girl, "Don't leave…"

His eyes flicked open and pain spiked behind them like twin stilettos. He closed them again quickly, but the pain remained and took on a solid mass in his brain. He made a noise like an old man struggling to rise from a low sofa and risked opening his eyes again.

The light coming through the tall window opposite was grey and rain spattered. He squinted, reached over with his left hand to the drawer of his bedside unit, opened it and scrabbled for the packet of paracetamol. He put one in his mouth and felt for the glass of water he always took to bed. No glass. He got his vision as focused as he could and groaned himself up on to his right elbow. Saw the bedside lamp, alarm clock reading six twenty-three and a trashy thriller. No water. "Bugger," he said, then tried dry-swallowing the pill but it only made him gag, intensifying the throb behind his eyes. "Christ," he winced, closed his eyes again and managed to sit up. And saw he wasn't alone.

The carelessly abandoned black dress at the bottom of the white duvet made him glance quickly to his left. An unruly mass of dark hair and a thin pale shoulder protruded from the covers on the other side of the wide bed. He blinked and cast about in his mind for explanations and found only suspicions of feelings and heard only echoes of voices. Unconsciously, he breathed deeply through his nose and caught notes of spice, citrus, alcohol, and smoke and something he couldn't place.

A particularly sharp throb followed his deep breath and he shimmied carefully out of bed, across the smooth wood floor to the basin in the bathroom. Filled a glass with water and chugged the pill, then finished the glass before refilling it and draining it again. He held on to the sides of the sink, studying the little rivulets of water being sucked down the plug hole. The motion made him nauseous and he gagged a retch. He felt pathetically weak. An ancient part of his brain told him to take deep breaths, get the oxygen in, fuel the recovery.

From what? He looked in the mirror above the sink and saw that his normally bright, fudge-coloured eyes were flecked red and hooded more than usual beneath his strong brow and tousled brown hair. What other symptoms could he detect? His thin roman nose was intact, but there were grazes on both sides of his square jaw which was swollen angrily on the left. A lower left molar felt a bit loose and a small cut was healing on his full bottom lip. There was a hefty bruise on his left forearm. He inspected his lean torso, felt the wide bands and tight little knots of muscle. Okay.

A siren started up a few blocks away, causing his focus to switch to the bed reflected in the bathroom mirror. Why? There were neither movements nor sounds coming from his visitor. No little stretches nor sighs or grunts that sleeping people involuntarily make. Though the painkiller was kicking in and his head was beginning to feel somewhat habitable, he suddenly felt worse than he had at any time since he woke. Who the hell was she? As if approaching an unexploded bomb, he crept out of the bathroom to the edge of the bed. Listened hard but heard nothing above the growing siren. Suddenly he felt very cold. He grabbed a sweatshirt and pants from where they lay on an occasional chair.

Man up, McLeod, he said to himself as he shrugged on his top and realised he'd been holding his breath. "Uh, hello there," he ventured uncertainly. No response from the motionless form. The gloom in the room was lifted by a break in the cloud, and weak morning sunlight beamed through the window. The siren was very loud, then went quiet. He crept around the bed, his eyes following the outline of the woman's slender body beneath the covers. His hand found the black dress where it lay crumpled on the duvet.

What there was of it was very soft, silk maybe, thought McLeod. He continued round the bed and stopped suddenly and stared. He was looking at the most beautiful face he had ever seen. The flawless skin was clear and pale as alabaster, the cheek bones high and sharp. Her deep red lips were parted slightly, revealing even white teeth. Perfect features framed by wild waves of shimmering black hair. Only the woman's almond eyes detracted from this vision as McLeod stared into their dark-green pools. They were completely lifeless.

Two

Friday morning, 15th May, 2015

"This had better be spectacularly important, Constable," seethed Rosanna Wren into her cell phone.

There was a nervous cough on the line, then, "Just got an anonymous call tipping us off to a possible homicide, ma'am," replied the dispatcher equably. I'm not on a high enough pay grade to worry about the sensibilities of grouchy Detective Inspectors, he thought to himself. Especially at the end of a long and tedious night-shift and especially the sensibilities of a woman of DI Wren's volatile reputation.

"Is this *possible* homicide in my building?" DI Wren barked back.

"No, ma'am. The address given is Beaufort Street, SW3."

"Then why in sweet fuck are you calling me, at what...it isn't even six a.m., man? Get local down there, for Christ's sake."

The dispatcher smiled at the warmth of DI Wren's response and the huskiness in her voice. Plenty of character there. He thought of his own wife dozing away timidly at home and sighed.

"They're on their way, ma'am," he replied curtly. "The Chief requested someone from your unit attend and you're top of the list this morning...which has made my shift worthwhile, by the way."

"Lucky me, I guess," Wren replied sardonically. "Okay Constable," she continued brusquely, "why SO15 involvement, what have you got for me?"

Shock over, down to business, thought the dispatcher. Oh well.

"I caught something about the anonymous call. Apparently, it wasn't made from the UK."

"Shit...no getting out of it then."

And no getting out of the fact that this conversation was almost over, rued the dispatcher. Such brushes with law enforcement notoriety were all too rare in his day-to-day drudgery.

"I'm afraid not, ma'am. Do you want me to give you the address, or…?"

"No," said DI Wren. A muffled grunt.

The Constable imagined her removing a night dress. "Just text it to this number and SatNav'll…pick it up."

"Right you are, ma'am. Your local liaison officer at the scene will be DS Morewood of Kensington and Chelsea. I'll notify him of your ETA and status with your permission, okay?"

"Bollocks to that," she replied sharply. "You can notify him that I need a bacon and egg butty and a pint of hot coffee at the scene upon my arrival, both of which will enhance my status, with *your* permission, okay?"

Friday morning, 15ᵗʰ May

Before McLeod had a chance to draw breath, a loud pounding started up on his front door, followed by a short pause, and then a shouted, "Open the door, POLICE, POLICE," and more banging. He jumped at the sound, then instinctively his eyes were drawn away from the girl, towards his front door. He had heard the words, but they held no meaning for him. His treacle-filled brain was still struggling to process what his wide eyes told him to be true: an achingly beautiful girl, presumably naked, was lying dead in his bed, and he hadn't the slightest recollection of how such an appalling circumstance could be. His severely straightened physical and mental faculties were threatening to fail him completely. Darkness encroached the extremities of his vision which was otherwise afflicted by tiny pricks of dancing light. He was about to surrender willingly to the void, when his name being called dragged him back from torpor.

"Duncan McLeod, police, police. Open this door or we will be forced to break it." The words had the effect of a bucket of cold water, and he physically shook himself. On wobbly legs and with the mind of an automaton, he made it out of the bedroom into the dark hallway.

"Final warning, McLeod. Open this door NOW…"

"Please, I'm coming…please," he managed in a strangled wail. With the last of his strength, he made it down the hallway, using his hands for support, to his front door and opened it and saw the gun. The blackness came then.

Three

"You're sure you can't make it, Ken?"

"I literally can't move without puking, Andrew. This meeting is vital. Breathe no word of what's discussed to anyone but me, okay?"

Andrew Smith cut off the call with his boss as he heard him start another wretch. "Damn it," he said and sighed. He was a slight but sturdy man with thinning blond hair and sharp Scandinavian features. He'd known it would be useless to try to argue his way out of the assignment, but he'd had to try. He really hated flying. And that was regular big commercial planes. The company jet frightened the living crap out of him. You hit the trade winds and the wretched thing felt like it was in a food blender. He shuddered at the memory of his last journey to a subsidiary in Germany. That was only about an hour. This time he had to go to Washington DC. What was that, five hours? He checked the time on his phone. He'd be there in time for a late lunch.

He got dressed quickly without waking his wife who was whimpering and twitching and grasping the pillow. Smith hoped it involved him. He briefly contemplated jumping back into bed and finishing the job for her, but the plane was leaving in an hour and it would take him most of that to get there.

He knew these meetings were exclusively CEO affairs and were usually rearranged if one of the six couldn't make it. The fact that this one was going ahead without one of them spoke volumes to Smith about the gravity of the situation, whatever it was. Therefore, as second in command of the company, he knew it was his duty to attend. Why the hell couldn't it be done by video or something?

He quickly made up a thermos mug of coffee and ensured his briefcase contained everything he needed. Oh well, he told himself as he eased into the back of a company Bentley idling outside his door. It wasn't every day you got to meet with the US State Department.

Monday evening, 11th May

"How close is she?" Sir David Harris lowered his heavy frame into one of the sumptuous leather armchairs in his club's private lounge. The evening was cool for the time of year so a flickering fire crackled in the ornately carved hearth. It provided the only light in the room. Occasionally, the flames illuminated portraits of former Prime Ministers and other party grandees, glowering down from the dark walls.

"Our primary source employed the phrase 'touching distance.' It would seem she has everything she needs to ruin us but not in the right order," replied Sir Francis Argyll, pouring a generous tumbler of Laphroaig for each of them, before taking the adjacent armchair. They were the room's only occupants. They were the physical polar opposites of each other. Sir David was short, stout and dumpy. Sir Francis tall, gaunt and rangy.

"Shit," said Sir David. "Your health."

"Indeed, shit," said Sir Francis, "and yours."

The two men sipped in silence for a moment. The grandfather clock behind them chimed ten with muted bongs. A bit of unseasoned wood in the grate spat an ember onto the thick rug in front of the hearth.

"How old is that information, old chap?" Sir David murmured.

Sir Francis bristled slightly in his bony frame. "Yesterday," he replied curtly.

"Then she may have nailed it down today," mused Sir David. "Could have it ready for the public tomorrow."

"It's a possibility, old chap," Sir Francis replied gravely. "We'll have to move fast."

"Remind me of the economic implications, Francis," said Sir David, rising and stamping out the ember. He grabbed a poker and shifted logs with a practised podgy hand.

"Catastrophic, David, quite catastrophic."

"Hmmnn. Are we talking on a national level here?" Sir David stood with his back to the fire, poker in his left hand, glass in his right. Shards of black and grey hair were sporadically illuminated by flickers from the hearth. A bulbous snout and small dark eyes sat in a pair of jowly chops, his mouth a thin, grim crease.

"Well, yes, nationally it would hurt too," Sir Francis replied. "I mean, it wouldn't be ruinous, but with the state of the deficit, old chap... The point is, it could bring down most of our friends and disrupt the whole order of things." He poked the ends of his bony fingers together. "Pensions, stocks, shares, taxes, corporation tax, long-term financial stability for so many of us, everything...gone, practically overnight."

"I see," said Sir David. He replaced the poker and took a couple of languid paces to the humidor. Selected a couple of Cuhibas and got busy with the cigar cutter. "Of course there are other revenue streams we could..."

"But that might take years of highly complicated organisation," Sir Francis cut in. "You've got to think about the markets, old chap."

"Of course we must," Sir David replied, sitting heavily back down, handing Sir Francis a cigar and lit taper. This room of the club was one of the few places left in the West where you could still light up with impunity. They sat a while in silence until there was quite a fog between them.

"And there's no one else threatening us?" asked Sir David eventually, between puffs.

"How could there be? It's a complete fluke this woman's got where she has."

Sir David heaved himself again from his chair and walked to the room's only door, opened it and peered both ways. He closed the door noiselessly and crossed to the three large windows. He parted the heavy curtains of each and ensured they were all completely closed. Sir Francis watched impassively as Sir David came to sit on the arm of his chair and fixed him with a goat-like glare.

"Then for the benefit of all interested parties, the solution appears to be simple," said Sir David.

"Quite," said Sir Francis.

Four

Friday morning, 15th May

McLeod woke for the second time that morning and found his circumstances hadn't improved. In fact, they'd taken a turn for the worse. As his senses slowly returned, he was aware of many people moving around him, talking quietly. Strange metallic noises, buzzes and static. He opened his eyes and immediately wished he hadn't. The first thing he saw was the last thing he'd seen before passing out: an assault rifle, this time held across a uniformed officer's chest looming over him.

"He's awake, Sergeant," the officer called over his shoulder.

Immediately, all the other voices went quiet. There must have been a dozen people, mostly men, mostly not in uniform, in his sparse living room, and they were all now turned, looking at him. McLeod took stock of his situation. He was sitting on the brown leather sofa in his living room, a cannula in his right forearm was being fed by what he presumed was an I.V. drip and yes, the pain in his wrists was the result of them being strapped by plastic handcuffs. Not good. Lying on a gurney in the middle of the room was the sinister shape of a long black bag. Even worse.

"Can we talk to him now, Doctor?"

McLeod didn't see who'd spoken, but a tall, slender man, tending to the contents of the black bag stopped what he was doing, looked up briefly, then turned towards him and approached. He was wearing sea-green overalls and a medical mask which he now removed, revealing craggy, careworn features. McLeod guessed he was in his mid-fifties, drank a lot of coffee and took his job very seriously.

"Right then, Mr McLeod. I believe it's highly likely that whatever muck you put in that girl is affecting you as well. So you're on a saline drip for re-hydration." He paused and bent down to feel McLeod's pulse. "I've taken some blood which has gone for analysis. How do you feel?" asked the doctor archly.

Like I've been hit by a bus in a Kafkaesque nightmare on Black Monday, McLeod thought to himself grimly.

Out loud he said in his light Scots lilt, "Like I probably need a lawyer," as the doctor let go of his wrist.

"Oh, you'll be needing more than a lawyer, Mr McLeod…a priest maybe," replied the doctor without a ghost of humour. He wrote something on a clipboard, then shone a light into each of McLeod's eyes and did some more scribbling.

"Okay, Sergeant," he called over his shoulder. "His vitals have improved to a surprising degree. Five or ten minutes questioning shouldn't kill him…more's the pity," he said with a withering look at McLeod.

The doctor turned and made his way back toward the black bag and its stunning, dead contents. The horrible reality of his situation was beginning to take on a size and shape in McLeod's hamstrung brain. And he got the distinct impression that the approaching tall, broad man, wearing a long dark overcoat and brooding expression wasn't about to diminish it.

Monday evening, 11th May

"How do we go about it?" Sir Francis asked. He barely filled his evening jacket with his scrawny torso. A scraggy neck protruded awkwardly from his crisp white collar. Yellowing eyes sat in a long gaunt face topped with thin hay.

"Extraordinarily carefully," replied Sir David, who was pacing laps of the rug in front of the fireplace. His movement caused the thick cigar smoke in the room to swirl about him like a cloak.

"What's the PM's position?"

"He doesn't bloody well have one," Sir David snapped back.

"You mean he doesn't want any involvement."

"Can you blame him? 'I trust you to steer this business to a satisfactory conclusion, David, old man.' The self-serving bastard." Sir David threw his cigar stub into the fireplace where it died in a trail of sparks.

Sir Francis wheezed at his colleague's ire. "What's he got on you this time?"

"You know perfectly well what he's got on me. My only comfort is that he's got worse on you."

It was Sir David's turn to chortle as he watched the other jolt and stiffen as if a poker had been shoved up his backside.

"Is there no bloody privacy left in this country?" the bony man bristled, tossing back the last of his drink and slamming the heavy glass on the table.

"Apparently not. It's these wretched smart phones... everyone's got 'em. Even the ruddy woman who comes to clean."

Sir David slumped back down in his armchair and the two men stewed for a while, musing over the lunacy of the modern world. The grandfather clock behind them wheezed into life once more, chiming half past. Sir Francis suddenly grasped his scrawny thigh and leapt from his chair as though in the clutches of a giant fist.

"What is it man," said Sir David excitedly, "a stroke?"

"Ooof," spluttered Sir Francis. "No, it's my fucking phone. On vibrate. Can never get used to the bloody thing going off." He wrestled the device from his trouser pocket with long, bony fingers, peered at the display and frowned.

"Hmmnn, Lady Argyll. I'll let the answerphone deal with that. Tell her I lost it down the sofa again."

"Quite right, old thing. Now, what can you tell me about this Lane creature?"

Friday morning, 15th May

DI Wren, showered and dressed, made her way downstairs to the kitchen of her semi-detached house near Richmond Park. The crepuscular early morning suited her mood so she didn't turn on the light. Make-up could be applied adequately at countless red lights on the way to the presumed crime scene.

The photo of Finlay on the fridge, grinning out of a khaki tent somewhere in Scotland, reminded her that it was her estranged husband's turn to have him this weekend. She made a mental note to pick up milk and wine as she grabbed a water from the fridge, chucked it in her bag along with phone, keys and her puffer as Finlay called it; a largely pink, pen-like device that sometimes curbed her cravings for a cigarette. She wrote a hurried note to her son, instructing him to call her when he was up and doing, and left the house.

Where was the Stag? For years she'd had a map of the neighbourhood backed with cork on the kitchen wall by the fridge. Every evening, she stuck a pin in the map to inform herself the next morning where she had left the car. Parenthood and workload had robbed her, paradoxically, of the willingness to perform this time-saving routine so that now, she had to try to remember her walk home the previous evening.

It's human nature to keep one's possessions as close to home as possible, but with the paucity of parking opportunities in this part of London, Wren often found herself scouring the streets for her car for the best part of twenty minutes, longer if she'd had more than a bottle after work. Which never put her in anything other than a foul temper.

Gigi in the office told her smugly that she had an app on her phone that showed where her car was, her keys, her husband, her hairdresser and her dog. Shame it couldn't locate her brain. Fortunately, amongst the homogeny of modern dark and silver cars, Wren's was wildly obtrusive. The 1972 Triumph Stag V8 Convertible gloried in a mustard-yellow livery enabling it to be spotted in almost any street, given a little elevation. And there, some two hundred and fifty yards down the tree-lined road, was the familiar black soft top, shiny from the rain. Wren took a look at the sky in the west to see if she'd be needing a brolly. It was brightening, and she thought it might turn out to be a nice spring day. She was dead wrong.

Five

Monday evening, 11th May

Sir Francis recharged their crystal tumblers with more single malt from the Art-Deco drinks cabinet that an eccentric member had installed in the thirties. It clashed somewhat with the rest of the rather more staid furniture in the sitting room, much of which dated to the club's inception in the late eighteenth century. Then, as now, members were drawn exclusively from the highest echelons of the ruling classes. And then, as now, many of the most momentous decisions taken in the land were formulated not in the Houses of Parliament or the law courts, but in the hushed and darkened rooms of London's private clubs.

"How much do we really need to know, David?" said Sir Francis, handing him the whisky with a shaky hand.

"A fair point, Francis, but at the least, we need to be aware of the level of heat her sudden demise might attract. What of her family, that sort of thing?"

Sir Francis loosened his Windsor knot and undid the top button of a Gieves and Hawkes shirt. "Hmmnn, there's good news and bad on that front. There's very little close family, just a father and a sister of any consequence. The mother died of some species of cancer a couple of years ago. The bad news is that the father is the owner of a moderately large pharmaceutical company. Fairly well off, I believe."

Sir David leaned over to cast bulbous eyes directly at his companion. "Billions?" he asked.

"Oh no, nothing like that," Sir Francis blustered. "Well, not yet anyway. But he would be more than capable of funding quite a far-reaching private investigation."

"I see," said Sir David, taking a generous slug of whisky. They sat thinking quietly for a spell. From the street outside came the shrill squawks of a hen party making its merry way home.

"Bloody binge-drinkers," said Sir Francis, knees cracking as he loped to the cabinet once more. "Costing Alan's department a fucking fortune." This time he brought the bottle back with him and placed it on the rosewood table between them. Sir David laboured up to stoke the embers of the fire and put on another log. He turned around and gestured at Sir Francis with the poker.

"Any investigation, however profound, must come nowhere near us."

"Heavens no," said Sir Francis. "A D-Notice, are you thinking?"

"God no, Francis. This is nowhere near D-Notice territory. Besides, I believe they're known as DA-Notices these days, for issues of national security and nothing less."

"What about our national sodding security, David? If a whiff of this gets out, we'll be roasted."

Sir David replaced the poker once more, put his hands on the marble mantelpiece and stared over his belly into the fire. The log was beginning to take, and a sweet aroma of pine reached his nose. His lips parted in a triumphant grin as he turned to face Sir Francis.

"Who stands to lose the most if we fail to act on our information and this wretched woman works it all out?"

Sir Francis steepled bony fingers in front of glassy eyes. "Why, our friends in the industry, of course. But we can't afford them to be implicated either. It would cause a moral hysteria, man."

"But it's a further remove from us, Francis, in the unlikely event of it all going tits up." Sir David emphasised his point by moving his podgy hands from one imaginary place in the air to another. "Of paramount importance in all this is our personal immunity." He paused to marshall his words. "Who would ever dream of digging any further if they got to our friends in the industry first?"

They found their mark. A broad smile spread like a slug on Sir Francis' gaunt face. "Brilliant, David," said Sir Francis. "Quite brilliant."

Tuesday afternoon, 12th May

The flight had been as hair-raising as Andrew Smith had feared, not helped by the fact that there were no other passengers on board with whom to find solace. Nor was there the usual cabin crew member, such was the extreme urgency of the trip.

So he was in a shaken state when he was met at Dulles International Airport by two men almost indistinguishable one from the other. Both were clean-shaven, had short, dark hair, dark-blue suits and sunglasses against the bright day. Or perhaps they always wore them. They had a car right out on the tarmac, just off the runway where the small jet had landed. CIA, Smith wondered? FBI? Then the slightly taller of the two spoke.

"Mr Smith, we're with the Department of State." He and his partner flopped open their wallets long enough for Smith to see their photos and an official-looking seal. No names or anything. "We're going to need your phone and to check your person."

Jesus Christ, thought Smith, handing over his phone. What is this? The man's partner patted him down in solemn silence and then nodded his head. "Okay," said the first guy, "let's get you to your meeting."

The car, some sort of boxy, black Chevrolet, didn't look fast, but Smith found himself pinned back into his seat as it tore off toward the terminal buildings. He scrabbled anxiously to get his seatbelt on. Soon, they were screeching a left onto some sort of service road used by fuelling trucks, baggage carriers and the like. The car lurched as it weaved between them. Clearly, they were by-passing any kind of US border controls and that realisation made Smith uneasy. What the hell was he into here? They were headed toward a high steel fence at an alarming rate.

The man sitting in the passenger seat who'd spoken before, perhaps sensing Smith's discomfort said, "Just relax and enjoy the ride, Mr Smith. This is what we do."

A gap suddenly appeared in the fence and the car shot through it joining a proper road. Smith looked back and saw a man hurriedly closing a heavy gate. Then they were passing a large Marriott Hotel and seemed to be heading back towards the public side of the terminal buildings. Perhaps they were going to immigration control after all, thought Smith hopefully. But after a series of left turns, they were on a wide highway. Smith caught a glimpse of a sign: Dulles Access Road. He gripped his briefcase tightly as soon, they were accelerating toward Washington at more than a hundred miles an hour.

Monday evening, 11th May

"I suppose we give one of our friends a contact at MI5?" ventured Sir Francis. The two men had brought their armchairs and table nearer to the fire as the room continued to cool into the night. Dark shadows flickered on the walls around them as the flames rose and died back intermittently. Sir David prodded idly in the grate with the charred poker as he weighed his companion's words.

"I don't think the approach should come from us. I rather think this situation requires a little more circumspection, don't you, Francis? A little more finesse perhaps?"

Sir Francis bristled at the inference and narrowed rheumy eyes. "I thought we were clear the buck would stop with our friends in the worst case?" he said.

"Ideally, we don't want any possible investigation to get remotely as far as that, Francis. I think we need to lay down a few more buffers. A few more potential patsies if, for some reason, things do not go as smoothly as they ought."

"Interesting word, David," mused Sir Francis. "Are you thinking of our friends across the water?"

"Isn't it obvious, old thing? They co-ordinate the strategic meetings and stand to lose just as much as us in this, probably more given their history. Also, I should imagine they would be very grateful to us for the information. And you can never have too much American gratitude." He raised a size twelve and dashed another fizzing ember on the rug.

Sir Francis held his glass to the firelight and swilled its contents lazily. "But by involving more parties don't we increase the risk of exposure?"

"Normally I'd agree with you, but the Yanks are as good at this sort of business as we are, maybe better in certain areas. Isn't our primary source ex-CIA?" Sir David took a linen handkerchief from his breast pocket and dabbed briskly at his forehead. He knew it wasn't the heat from the fire making him sweat, but took another swig of whisky anyway.

"What about the actual, er…" began Sir Francis, before his companion cut in quickly.

"Enterprise, were you going to say, old chap?"

"Quite, thank you."

"Yes, that needs careful consideration," murmured Sir David.

"Based on the worst-case scenario?"

"I think that would be wise."
"Demum sacrificium ultimum solvit," whispered Sir Francis.
"Knock it off, old thing," Sir David glowered.

Six

Friday morning, 15th May

"Mr…er, McLee-od, I'm Detective Sergeant Paul Morewood, Kensington and Chelsea Response Team. I have some questions for you."

McLeod recoiled at the contempt oozing from the man's voice and demeanour.

"And I have one for you, Sergeant," replied McLeod, feeling the welcome return of his mental faculties. "Have you read many books?" Despite the peril of his position, McLeod was ill-disposed to ignorance and bad manners, especially from public servants.

"You what?"

"Books," McLeod repeated, "have you read any?"

"You're not best situated for making funny remarks, pal," the Sergeant snarled above him.

"I don't mean to be rude, Sergeant," McLeod replied, hunkering forward, elbows on knees. "The English language is a capricious and contradictory creature and mistakes, such as the split infinitive, are all too readily made." He cast a wary look at the bewildered officer before continuing. "Personally, I find that one rather pedantic. Lots of English words sound nothing like their spelling, right? My surname for instance. Not McLee-od, rather Muh-Cloud. I'd hate for you to be embarrassed in front of your superiors when you make your report later." A few sniggers broke out in the room.

The Sergeant looked behind him quickly and turning back, was clearly struggling with his emotions as McLeod observed him with a keen eye. His face looked like it was about to erupt. This could go one of two ways, McLeod mused: either he was going to spontaneously combust; or his hundreds of hours of interview training would win out.

Taking a deep breath and passing a hand through his short, dark hair, the Sergeant took the latter course. McLeod felt a glimmer of hope.

"Thank you for pointing that out *Mister McLeod*. I'll try and remember it for my report."

"Good idea, Sergeant. Am I under arrest?"

"Not yet, but I'd say it's a matter of time. Why, did you have plans?" Morewood smirked. "A hot date perhaps?" A grin smeared itself over the Sergeant's grizzled face. Was that meant to be funny, thought McLeod? Looking at the other faces he could see in the room, McLeod wondered if the ability to sneer was a compulsory requirement of the job.

"I do, as a matter of fact, but given the nature of the circumstances in which I find myself, Her Majesty will have to be disappointed." Puerile, McLeod admonished himself. Try to be the adult.

"Are you deliberately trying to wind me up, McLeod, 'cos I can make this pretty nasty if you are," Morewood spat.

"No, Sergeant." McLeod sighed and composed himself. "I'm in a highly stressful situation that I can't comprehend, and since the beginning of this interview, if you could call it such, I have found your manner deserving of contempt. I don't see how you can make this any nastier than it is."

"Oh believe me, Mr McLeod..." began the Sergeant ominously when he was halted by a minor commotion at the flat's front door.

"I'm DI Wren, SO15, let me pass or so help me, you'll be doing traffic 'til oil runs out." The anger and authority in the newcomer's voice struck fresh fear in McLeod's chest. This day just gets better and better, he thought grimly to himself as he cast a worried eye toward the door. A uniformed officer stood aside, revealing a petite woman, smartly dressed in a taupe trouser suit doing three things at once: replacing her ID in her handbag; scanning faces in the room to assess the situation; and barking "Bacon buttie and coffee, man, before I expire," at a hapless hi-vis jacket in her path.

As she strode purposefully toward Morewood, McLeod reassessed his initial impression of DI Wren. Humanity was unmistakable on her striking face. Her short blonde hair was stylishly cropped but gave her a slightly severe air. Her other features were somewhat elfin and her eyes were so vibrant, it seemed to McLeod that they positively glowed. With rage.

Monday evening, 11ᵗʰ May

The bottle of thirty-year old single malt was on its last legs, but the two men had several generations of strong constitutions behind them and were showing no signs of flagging.

"So the worst case would be that the, er, enterprise might be linked to our friends," said Sir Francis on his return from the club's kitchen. He placed a silver salver of smoked salmon sandwiches and a bowl of olives on the small table.

"Didn't you manage to find a drop of something decent with which to wash this lot down?" Sir David admonished his friend.

"You wrong me, old man," replied Sir Francis, producing an ice bucket with a flourish.

"Chablis, excellent, I'll fetch glasses." Sir David headed to the drinks cabinet. "Actually," he said, "I think we need to think about the situation prior to any potential investigation. What if the operative carrying out the enterprise were uncovered?"

"Surely that would depend on whom we employed, and I take it we shan't be using numbskulls, eh?"

Sir David placed large wine goblets on the table, which was becoming overcrowded, and poured the wine. He took one of the dainty sandwiches, sat down and began munching pensively.

"Obviously, we can't use our own people for the action. They could perhaps serve as conduits and facilitators. Batten down the hatches afterwards, that sort of thing."

"I suppose we can rule out the Yanks as having too close an interest?" Sir Francis mused.

"I'm afraid so," said Sir David, skilfully skewering an olive with a cocktail stick. "That leaves us with the second division."

"There's the time constraint to consider, don't forget. We've only managed to get her here for two days before she gets back to her infernal research. I understand she's scheduled a couple of meetings of her own as well as the things we've set up. Wouldn't leave much window, old chap."

"So, top of the second division and in town," said Sir David. "Doesn't give us a large field. I'd say it's time to get Urquhart on board."

Sir Francis took out his phone, found the number and hit call. It answered on the second ring.

"Are we secure, Urquhart, old chap? ... Good... Yes, he's here... Very well, and you? ... Excellent. I'm so sorry about the hour, but we have rather a pressing matter... That's good of you... Yes, that sort of matter. Who do we have at liberty in town just now? ... Just them? ... I see... No, that can't be helped. What might it take? ... We're hopeful it won't come to that, but yes, if necessary... I'm sure we could stretch to that... Yes, I think that would be in order... Very good... Thank you, speak soon."

Sir Francis put down his phone and picked up a sandwich. "Serbs," he said.

Sir David took a gulp of wine and dabbed the corners of his mouth with a napkin. "Thought as much. Could be a lot worse I suppose. The price?"

"Technical specifications."

"Hmmnn," said Sir David, rubbing his chin. "Okay, but nothing military. Have you got anything knocking around?"

"There are a few fiscal things they don't have that'll be obsolete in six months."

"Perfect. Is Urquhart going to secure a suitable intermediary?"

Sir Francis knew things were coming to a close and yawned. "As we speak."

"Then all that's left is a word in Washington's ear." He rummaged in several deep pockets, disturbing numerous bottles and strips of pills and top-secret memos before coming out with the latest iPhone. He raised his glasses and peered hopefully at the screen. "Damn and blast, my phone's dead," said Sir David. "Lend me yours, old thing."

Sir Francis tossed it over. Sir David found the long, encrypted number and prodded the screen, leaving an oily mark. The phone answered on the third ring.

"No, Bill, it's David... I'm using his phone... Couldn't be better, old chap, and with you? ... You'll be swinging too fast again. Remember, low and slow on the backswing... St. Andrews next week? It rather depends on how things progress here the next few days... Well, you know that situation we discussed the other day that was highly unlikely to ever arise? ... It bloody well has... I don't know, some woman working independently... Chance, we think, more than anything... No, no one else even remotely... We agree... Well, how about we get our friends to make the approach? ... Yes, we thought so too... We'd need that to happen tomorrow... I'm afraid that can't be helped, it's going to be tight as it is... Fabulous. Urquhart will be in touch with contact details in due course... Well, I'll try to arrange a provisional tee-time for after lunch... Oh, I dunno, the Old Course Hotel perhaps, or there's a decent seafood place, bit modern but... No no, our treat... That's grand... Cheerio, old chap."

Sir David handed back the phone and raised his glass. "To a highly profitable evening, old thing. Cheers."

"Cheers indeed," said Sir Francis, rubbing his phone on his trousers.

Seven

Monday afternoon, 11th May

Bill Marshall hailed from Louisiana. Old French blood masked by American spelling. Several generations ago, he would have been Guillaume Marechal. A mound of sandy hair sat on top of a broad, shiny face with robust, ruddy features. He wasn't enormous, but it was clear he didn't dodge too many pies either. He got off the phone with London and got down to logistics. Organising this kind of meeting at such short notice was going to be a stretch, even for someone with his power.

He knew three of the people he needed to assemble were currently in the US and could be in DC that evening. The other four would have to either travel through the night or have a very early start tomorrow. He didn't even know where the Japanese guy was.

He thought about the scores of processes that had to transpire for the meeting to take place, in order to work out which call to make first. Then he buzzed his private secretary.

"Martha, honey," he drawled in a thick southern accent, "I'm gonna need y'all to stay late tonight, okay? … Thank you darlin'. Listen, how do I go 'bout rustlin' me up a road crew and a buncha cones?"

Tuesday afternoon, 12th May

The Chevy hit I-66 doing better than a hundred and twenty. It was the only vehicle able to use the coned-off outside lane. Smith knew from his boss' strained tone that morning and the haste with which he was dispatched that time was precious in this venture. But equally he couldn't help thinking of his mother's words to him as a seventeen-year-old new driver: "Remember, Andrew, it's better to arrive late than not at all." At that age, you didn't think anything could kill you. Then you have children of your own and suddenly, the world becomes a very dangerous place. Nowhere more so than where he was right now.

"I say," he began uncertainly, "do you think we might…?"

"Mr Smith," the one who talked said, turning round in his seat, "this vehicle is designed to survive a direct hit from an I.E.D. That's as much protection as your army's Foxhound vehicles. My partner here used to race dragsters. Believe me, for him, we're barely moving. Plus, we have our own lane all the way to Foggy Bottom. Chill out, man," he concluded with a smile.

"Hmmnn, okay," Smith said weakly. Barely moving, he thought. The cars inside them didn't seem to be moving at all, and they were probably all doing fifty or sixty. Like someone on the brink of uncertain surgery, he resigned himself to his fate, laid back his head and closed his eyes. Better not to see it coming.

Fifteen arse-clenching minutes later, Smith stepped gratefully onto the safe haven of the pavement. Five and a half hours of travel terror. He needed a drink. Make that several, he thought to himself. And a lie down somewhere warm and quiet. But instead, he was about to go into what might be the most important meeting of his life. He set his briefcase down, closed his eyes, breathed in deeply through his nose and out through his mouth. Repeated it five times.

The two guys with the shades watched somewhat impatiently. Smith opened his eyes, feeling slightly better. He looked around at the bright, bustling street and suited office workers scurrying to and from lunch appointments. Then to his right, past the fountain and sculptures, the imposing south entrance of the Harry S Truman building towered over him.

"Welcome to Washington, Mr Smith. We're to accompany you to the seventh floor, if you're ready."

He breathed deeply once more, shot his cuffs, picked up his briefcase and checked his watch. Half past one. "Let's do this," he said.

Friday morning, 15th May

"Morewood, I'm Wren. SO15 are now in charge of this operation. Get that man's restraint off this instant." Her tone was sanguine, precise and even.

McLeod imagined she knew what she wanted and was very good at getting it. Her top teeth protruded ever so slightly and they rested provocatively on her bottom lip when she finished speaking. A uniform with scissors cut through McLeod's ties and he rubbed his wrists gratefully.

"Er, standard police procedure, ma'am..." began Morewood hopelessly. Wren's eyes blazed up at him and McLeod almost felt sorry for the Sergeant.

"Take what passes for your imagination out of my sight, Sergeant," she hissed witheringly, as she dragged a cushioned wooden chair next to a coffee table between her and McLeod. He took the opportunity to size up DI Wren in greater detail as Morewood departed, browbeaten.

Her clothes couldn't hide the fact that she was slender and she moved with effortless grace, suggesting a natural physical strength. Intelligence shone clearly from creased cobalt eyes that were looking McLeod up and down, assessing, questioning, before stilling as they lighted on his own.

A hand went to her lips and she looked down briefly, stunned somewhat by the rugged allure of the man sitting opposite her. When her gaze returned, McLeod felt positive for the first time that day, as her eyes hadn't glazed over as most women's did when they first saw him. Instead, they burned with integrity.

"I'm Detective Inspector Wren, Mr McLeod. In charge of this operation for the time being. Have they given you anything to eat or drink?"

McLeod was surprised by the softness of her tone. He jerked his thumb at the I.V. line in his right arm and said, "Breakfast."

The hint of a smile touched her lips before she continued, "I mean, would you like tea or coffee or..."

"A strong coffee would be good," McLeod replied. "There's a pretty decent machine in my kitchen." Once again, the absurdity of the situation was borne upon him.

"You heard the man," Wren barked at the officer with the firearm, whilst another approached briskly, bearing a large Styrofoam cup and a brown paper bag.

"Excellent work, Constable. See if you can track down a next of kin," said Wren, grabbing the bag and taking a gulp from the cup, then setting it down on the glass coffee table strewn with medical journals and sports magazines. She retrieved a cardboard box from the bag and held it toward McLeod.

"Bacon and egg?"

"No thanks," he replied, the thought of eating making him momentarily queasy.

"Do you mind if I eat while we do this?" Wren asked, opening the box and wrestling with a large bun.

"Go ahead. Do what?" McLeod shot back. Out of the corner of his eye, he noticed Morewood conferring with the doctor but couldn't make out what they were saying. Dark looks were being cast in his direction. A hi-vis brought McLeod's coffee in a mug and set it in front of him. He took a sip and nodded his thanks.

"Well, Mr McLeod, you haven't been charged with anything..." Wren managed between huge bites. McLeod couldn't supress a slight smile as she used a finger to scoop egg juice and ketchup from her chin. He noticed she didn't wear a ring.

"It appears I amuse you, Mr McLeod," she said, sucking her finger, eyes gleaming. McLeod welcomed a moment of levity, of normality amongst the bedlam of the morning.

He smiled grimly and said, "I'm sorry, Miss Wren. For a second, I forgot." He closed his eyes and sighed deeply.

"Forgot what, Mr McLeod? That there's a dead woman in that black bag over there? That until an hour ago she was in your bed? Or is there something else you've forgotten?"

McLeod was grateful that despite the meaning contained in her words, they were spoken calmly and without menace. Wren's eyes held McLeod's, searching for evasion, as she deposited the last of her bun in her mouth and wiped it with paper napkins. She saw only apprehension.

"Is that your usual breakfast, Miss Wren?" McLeod asked, desperate to avoid the weight of her previous questions.

"High metabolism, Mr McLeod. Why do you keep calling me Miss?"

"I'm sorry." McLeod thought for a moment. "Would you prefer Ms? I don't care for it myself."

"And why would you call me Ms?"

"Isn't that how you address divorcées?"

"What makes you think I'm divorced, Mr McLeod?" Who the hell is this guy, she thought to herself.

"Well, you don't wear a ring, yet you're thirty-seven, you're very attractive and have child-bearing hips," he observed, noting the stealthy approach of the doctor. "You seem to be highly personable and clearly successful in what you do. Ninety per cent right there," McLeod concluded.

"I might be a lesbian," Wren ventured. Christ, what's he doing to me, she thought.

"Oh come, Ms Wren," he replied laconically. The doctor would shortly be within earshot.

"That's very conceited, Mr McLeod."

"Maybe, Ms Wren. I prefer to think of it as an aversion to bullshit."

"Touché, Mr McLeod. And I think you're right, knock it off with the Ms. I prefer Miss too."

The doctor leaned to Wren's ear and whispered into it. McLeod watched her eyes carefully as she listened to the doctor. They gave precisely nothing away. Either the doctor's message was deeply unimportant, then why the need to whisper, or else DI Wren was the most phlegmatic person McLeod had ever come across.

"Excuse me a moment, Mr McLeod. Don't go anywhere," she said, rising and making to follow the doctor.

"Actually, I could use a trip to the bathroom," McLeod ventured, "I guess the coffee's got my juices flowing again."

"I'll accompany him, ma'am," volunteered the rifle-toting officer.

"Yes, coffee will do that to a man," smirked Wren. Turning to the doctor, she said, "Does he still need to be attached to that?"

The doctor checked his watch and gave McLeod a hard stare. "No, I'm afraid to say that I don't think I've ever come across anyone with such a strong constitution." He made the few steps to McLeod and pointed to the cannula, questioning. McLeod nodded and the doctor removed the drip.

"I'll be back in due course, Mr McLeod, probably to take some more bloods," the doctor said with cold satisfaction and followed DI Wren toward the gurney. McLeod stood up, feeling light-headed as he took in the faces of the ten or so remaining police officers gathered in his living room. He didn't like the sound of taking bloods, but it squared with his own feeling of something remiss with his system.

Accompanied by the officer, McLeod made his way toward the bathroom, giving the gurney a wide berth and avoiding the hard stares of the people in his living room and hall. The officer was right next to him as he reached the bathroom door.

"What, are you wanting to hold it for me?" he asked.

"Just leave the door ajar, McLeod," replied the officer sharply. Finally on his own and able to think straight, McLeod mused on his encounters with Morewood and Wren as he did his business. They'd both told him he wasn't under arrest, which struck him as odd. A dead woman in his bed, no one else living in his flat, no other persons of interest that he knew of, and yet, apparently, he'd been charged with nothing.

Clearly Morewood was just a local bobby, dispatched and arriving first due to his proximity. DI Wren was an enigma. Arrogant and domineering one minute, given to lashing colleagues with a throaty snarl. The next, she was waiting on him like he was a valued customer of some five-star hotel. He was fairly certain they were both acts designed to maximise his cooperation, but McLeod couldn't help wishing he could meet the real DI Wren.

He'd heard her mention SO15. Special Operations, maybe? McLeod seemed to recall much mention of it in the aftermath of the 7/7 tube and bus bombings. Something to do with terrorism. He wasn't a terrorist last time he checked. Perhaps that was why he hadn't been arrested. Was the girl a terrorist?

"You done in there, McLeod?" The question broke his musings.

"Just cleaning up," he said, washing his hands. He examined his face in the mirror. The grey pallor was gone and most of the redness from his eyes. He ran some cold water through his dark hair and let it fall where it wanted. Showtime.

Eight

Tuesday afternoon, 12th May

Smith was shown through large wooden doors into one of the building's diplomatic reception rooms by Bill Marshall himself. The man had shaken Smith's hand out in the lobby and still had hold of it. The room was clearly designed to intimidate foreign visitors. It was huge and sumptuously furnished with what Smith took to be priceless antiques. Oil paintings in gilded frames adorned eggshell-blue walls. Elegant chandeliers supplemented the sunlight pouring in through several windows and gave it a warm glow. At the far end of the room, a medium-sized oval table had been set up with seats for eight people, six of which were already occupied by four men and two women, all immaculately attired.

Marshall guided Smith to the table, on the way pointing out various antique vases and bureaux, desks and chairs. He felt tension hanging in the room just as palpably as the heavy curtains surrounding the windows and the stars and stripes around the hearth. Smith was pleased to see a copious quantity of sandwiches and other savoury snacks on the table but dismayed that there was nothing to drink other than a few decanters of water.

"Ladies, gennelmen," Marshall drawled as he finally relinquished Smith's hand and deposited his generous posterior in the chair at the head of the table. "As y'all know, Ken was unable to make it today. But given the severity and the, ah, nature of the, ah, situation that faces us, it was vital that we got a representative from the United Kingdom to be with us today. And we're sure pleased that Andy Smith here was able to come at such short notice."

Smith felt suddenly as though he were an exhibit in a museum display case as all the eyes around the table turned on him as he took the last seat. He barely heard the introductions Marshall was making as the desire for a calming drink overtook him once more. The hell with this, he thought.

"Excuse me, sir," he heard himself say. "I've had an extremely stressful morning. Right now, I need something a lot stronger than water to see me through this thing."

His words elicited intakes of breath and the odd nervous giggle from around the table. Marshall looked at him thoughtfully for a moment before a broad grin appeared in his round face. "Sure thing, Andy. What's your poison?"

"I'd like a whisky and soda please. Large."

Marshall nodded once and pushed a button on the phone beside him on the table.

"Martha, honey, can we get a bottle of fine scotch, some soda and some ice in here?"

There was a polite cough from the striking French woman. "Could we 'ave some white wine also?"

"Any sake?" added the Japanese chap.

"Did you get that, Martha? Good... Well, I guess it's been a long day already for some of our guests. Thanks, honey."

The mood in the room seemed to lift a little and Smith acknowledged warm smiles from several of the other attendees. The French woman even blew him a kiss. Martha soon appeared at the door, wheeling a heavily laden drinks trolley. Everyone other than the man from Indonesia helped themselves to various libations.

Marshall chuckled. "Well, we better get down to business folks before this turns into an AA meeting. Your very good health," he said and raised his glass. The others followed suit.

"Now, Andy, the only person I ain't introduced is Jack Loan here, from the Food and Drug Administration. Usually, he chairs this meeting, but given the, ah, global nature of the situation, your people came to me in the first instance. Showed mighty good judgement, yes indeed," Marshall said, helping himself to a samosa.

The warmth of the whisky was beginning to relax Smith. "It's good to meet you all. I understand from Ken that this meeting, whilst important for our continued success, is usually rather a ceremonial affair. Do I take it that some threat to our business has emerged?"

"Ladies and gentlemen," it was the FDA guy Jack Loan in a high-pitched Texan accent, wielding a gherkin. "We've received information about activity that threatens the very core of what we do here." He paused and looked at the faces around the table. A collective breath was taken. He continued, "It has the potential to wipe us out, practically overnight. From the trillion-dollar enterprise we enjoy today, to precisely squat tomorrow." No one moved and only two people were breathing as the words they'd never dreamed of hearing began to sink in.

"I don't believe it," the pretty African American woman almost shouted. Smith couldn't place her accent. Mid-west somewhere. "How could anything possibly do that?" Her incredulity was echoed in strangled exhortations from others around the table.

Marshall raised a palm and a heavy gold chain bracelet rattled on his wrist. "I'm afraid Jack's assessment is accurate, folks. We sure certain 'bout that." The timbre of his voice and manner of his speech seemed to have a calming effect. Canny politician, thought Smith. Then something else struck him.

"How reliable is the source of this information, if you don't mind my asking, sir?"

Marshall cast an appraising eye his way. "Would you consider me to be reliable, Andy?"

Smith didn't particularly like the diminution, but he let it go. He thought for a moment. Just how trustworthy was anybody in this game? And swarthy politicians in particular. Better go for a diplomatic answer. "I guess about as reliable as it gets," he said.

Marshall smiled, showing dazzling white teeth. "Well, that's just 'bout how much we trust our source."

"And the nature of zis problem is what?" the French woman said with her hands as much as her raspy Gallic voice.

"We understand that..." Loan began, before Marshall cut him off with a wave of his hand.

"Now Jack, I don't think these good folks need to be worryin' the'selves 'bout that. They sure have enough on their plates already, doncha think? What they need to hear from us is how we're proposin' to resolve the problem. And believe me, folks, thing this big, that's exactly what we're gonna do, don' nobody need worry 'bout that."

The room fell silent for a spell, the only sounds generated by thoughtful munching. The delegates looked anywhere but at each other as they wrestled with forms of words.

Smith dunked a chicken drumstick in barbecue sauce and aimed it at Marshall. "So you're telling us that we're going to the poorhouse but that you're not prepared to divulge the means by which that might happen? How are we to defend ourselves if we don't know the nature of the threat?"

Marshall was grappling with a lobster tail. "I understand your concern, Andy, believe me I do." He paused as a bit of shell cracked off, pinged across the table and hit the Indian guy in the eye.

"Apologies, friend," he said, chuckling, "feisty lil' critter."

The Indian guy dabbed at his eye with a napkin, not particularly amused.

"Aaah, as I was saying, folks, your concerns are quite understandable, yes indeed. But, thing like this, boils down to a simple question of rights and responsibilities." He paused and beamed a hundred-megawatt smile at everyone at the table. "Y'all have the right to carry on your legitimate and, might I say, highly lucrative business, and we have the responsibility to ensure you're able to do so. Now, we can all agree on that, right?" He sat back in his chair, arms outstretched.

There were general murmurings of approval. Smith picked pensively at his teeth. "So why the need for this meeting? I mean, if you're going to, how should I say, make the problem go away?"

Marshall leaned forward conspiratorially, elbows on the table, lobster tail in his paw. The smile was gone, replaced by a furrowed brow and a look of contrition. "We all want the same thing here, folks. We all stand to lose a great deal. Hell, we got a duty to posterity. Yes, we're going to make the problem go away. We just need your agreement that that's what we oughta do." He took a long, thoughtful swig of gin and tonic as murmurs of encouragement sounded around the table.

"Okay then, folks, this is the tricky part. It may be that in the process of solving your problem, some, ah, liberties are taken with national laws." He cast an iron gaze at the wary sets of eyes around the table. "As a sign of your gratitude to us for our assistance in this matter, and to ensure your equal involvement, we're gonna need y'all to perform a lil' task for us."

Alarm coursed through Smith's blood as Marshall fastened him with a steely look. He thought about saying something, then realised the futility of it. His phone and the body check. To all intents and purposes, he knew this meeting had never taken place.

Marshall saw the understanding hit home in Smith's eyes, nodded once and continued. "Okay, listen real close now, folks, we're nearly done. You'll all be given one time only contact details for an agent in your respective intelligence services. You're gonna give that agent the particulars of another person. You're then gonna destroy both sets of details. And that's it." He paused, looked around the table and saw expressions of relief. "Now, y'all clear on those points?"

He scanned the face of each delegate and got the affirmation he desired, and then broke into another wide, toothy grin. "Then we're 'bout done here folks," he said, rising. Martha appeared from a side entrance, holding a briefcase. "My personal secretary here has everything you're gonna need. I wanna thank y'all for your time," he said, rising, "and I hope we never have to meet again. Good day."

Nine

Friday morning, 15th May

McLeod returned with the officer to the living room suddenly bathed in warm spring sunlight streaming in through the large double windows. In normal circumstances, this would be his favourite time of year. In London's plentiful parks, plump dandelion suns were morphing into clocks and making way for pungent patches of bluebells and bright buttercups. It was the time of maximum green, nature at its most virile, before summer turned it dry and drab.

On the street below, he could see dozens of office workers juggling bags and keys and phones and plastic coffee mugs. Every species of delivery van was weaving through traffic, revving hard, trying to beat the next lights before inevitably slamming on the brakes. The drivers weren't paying for fuel or repairs, clearly. They were interspersed with black cabs and red buses and couriers on darting mopeds and weaving pushbikes. A worried-looking man emerged from the florist opposite, clutching a big bunch of red roses and talking heatedly into his mobile phone. Just another Friday morning in the great city.

The Bakelite clock on the mantelpiece above the large old fireplace read just after nine. He'd normally be an hour into his working day by now. No need to call in today, he thought ruefully. He sat back down on the worn sofa and drained his mug. Scanned the faces in the room again and detected a shift in the atmosphere. Something had happened.

Wren appeared at the living room door, approached and spoke quietly to several officers who shrugged their shoulders, then left. The man with the assault rifle wasn't one of them. She resumed her position in front of McLeod, a wary look in her eyes. A look that captured his full attention.

"You got my age wrong, McLeod," she said distractedly, kneading her thumb. "I'm thirty-eight."

"Oh…I beg your pardon," he replied.

"It was my birthday yesterday."

"I hope you enjoyed it," McLeod said and watched with mild amusement as Wren sighed deeply, frowned, then took a pen-like device from her bag and sucked feverishly at it.

"I'm sorry," she said, "do you mind?" Little clouds of vapour accompanied her words.

"Puff away," he replied. Wren had seemed so assured. What had changed, he wondered.

After another drag, she started in. "As you're probably aware, McLeod, we know a great deal about you by now," she said.

Where's my Mister gone, thought McLeod.

"All of it good, I hope," he replied, desperate to return to the easy tone of before.

Wren snorted. "Are you always this sure of yourself?" she said, her eyes shining once again.

"Not really," he replied. "You make me nervous." He saw her glance at his right leg which he hadn't been aware he was jiggling. He stopped. It was something he only usually did when he had itchy feet, in need of exercise. It didn't look like he was going to be getting much today.

"I'm aware I have that effect on people occasionally, Mr McLeod," Wren murmured. "I find it helps with their honesty."

McLeod smiled to himself at the return of his title and replied, "I don't think I have anything to hide, Miss Wren." As he spoke the words, he realised he might have something to hide soon if she continued to look up at him like that. He crossed his legs.

Wren smiled and said, "Oh come, Mr McLeod. I'm sure everyone has a secret or two hidden away in a dark place."

"I'm afraid I'll disappoint you on that front, Miss Wren."

"I'm equally sure you won't, Mr McLeod. I'm separated from my husband, by the way, not divorced."

"I'm sorry for your situation," he said and gave what he hoped was a nicely balanced look of commiseration.

"Yes, and I'm sorry for yours," replied Wren. "I believe that yesterday was the anniversary of your wife's death."

Tuesday afternoon, 12th May The little jet whined as it banked hard toward the darkening ocean. Andrew Smith could almost make out the faces of children playing on the wide beach as they raised their heads to see the low-flying aircraft. The combination of the pilot's antics and a greasy lunch were playing havoc with Smith's digestive system. One minute his intestines were being squashed down against his bladder, the next they were in amongst his ribs.

Focus on the horizon, he told himself. But there wasn't any damned horizon. He craned his head against the seemingly solid g-force, looked across the adjacent table and empty leather seats, but the far window was just a bright white patch of sky. His stomach gurgled and he closed his eyes. Cursed his feeble-bellied, delegating boss. However horrendous this day had been so far, Smith knew there was little likelihood of it improving when he got back to London. There had to be an easier way to make this kind of money, he mused. Then the intercom buzzed in the console above him.

"Sorry about the jock piloting, Mr Smith." It was the self-important pilot who didn't sound sorry at all. "We're clear of the Dulles stacking system now. Sit back, relax and we'll have you home for supper."

"Thank you so much," Smith replied as caustically as he could. Home. Shit. The plane levelled and began to climb steadily. He felt his stomach cautiously, groaned, then woke up his phone. Fired off a text to the girls' nursery to keep them on for after-school club again. Then a pleading message to his mother to scoop them up until Nicole finished work, whenever that would be. Then a grovelling message to Nicole ending <cu tmoz hpfly xxx>. Then his head started spinning. He leaned it back into his comfy seat and closed his eyes. Maybe next year they could afford a nanny like all their other friends. His mind drifted off into a swirling sea of astronomical numbers…mortgage repayments…car finance…school fees…holidays…health plans…insurance…clothes…phones…entertaining…gyms…

He was jostled awake suddenly and reached instantly for the wooden table in front of him. Clamped himself to it like a crag-fast crab. The cabin bucked and lurched and his head banged the hard table. His vision blurred and he couldn't tell which way was up. He heard ominous thumps and creaks and whines like from old war films. Then a deafening whoosh started up and his stomach felt as though it had been torn from him. It went on and on, growing louder and louder. This is it, Smith thought. This is how it ends. As the plane continued to plummet, he felt a strange calm and with it, a clarity of thought. All his money worries disintegrated and floated from his shoulders. He prayed that Nicole and the girls would be alright. Then he braced himself for whatever was coming. He'd always hated flying.

Ten

Friday morning, 15th May

Catherine. Even at the end, her spirit was indomitable. McLeod had met her during the last year of university, some party of a mutual friend. He'd fallen hard and fast, not his usual style at all. Of course she was good looking, but she was the first woman McLeod had met who was far more than that. His heart clenched as he flashed on her face and heard her laugh in his head, like the tinkling of a mountain stream. She was the nicest, kindest, funniest person he'd ever known and those ten years together, the last five as husband and wife, were the happiest he knew he would ever have. Wednesday had been a normal day. Thursday their world was over. Then months of pain and searching for information and treatments. Then more pain, then agony, then death. And then, she was only memories.

Once again, he wished that all the cancer cells in the world would coalesce like the molten cyborg in *Terminator*, into some sort of dark faceless fiend, so that he could kill it. So that he could stab it over and over and over again. Then he could take something brutal like an iron bar or railroad spike to its remains and pound it until his strength gave out. Then he could douse it in stinking petrol and set it on fire, watch gleefully as it turned to ashes.

But it didn't. Instead, it portrayed all the worst traits of the human condition. It hid and lurked, striking randomly like a spineless murderer. Seeking out shadowy, obscure places where it couldn't be found until it was too late. Then spread like an insidious idea, like Nazism.

But it was democratic. It took anyone, indiscriminately. It took all races and faiths. It took men and women, rich and poor. It took the hard living and the saintly. It took the very old and the very young. It took teenagers with huge hopes and dreams. It took his own hopes and dreams for a family. It just took.

"Last night was the first time I've been able to go out socially since she died," said McLeod, his voice cracking as he said the words. "I still wouldn't have gone had it not been for…" McLeod broke off wondering how wise it was to divulge any more.

But Wren knew. She cocked her head slightly and said, "Being made redundant, were you going to say?"

"Been a bit of a shit year, really," replied McLeod.

"And now this," Wren said quietly. McLeod looked her in the eye and was surprised to see compassion and empathy gleaming back at him. What wasn't she telling him? Did she know he had nothing to do with the beautiful girl's death? Christ, he didn't know he had nothing to do with it.

Wren sighed and chucked her device in her handbag. "Fuck it," she said standing. "I need a real one…Morewood!" she barked. "Who's got cigarettes?"

Tuesday evening, 12th May

"Well, Mr Smith," said the pilot, his teeth somehow gleaming in the darkness outside the terminal. "I hope that bit of *turbulence* hasn't put you off flying for good?" He stood next to his co-pilot at the bottom of the plane's little passenger gantry.

"On the contrary, you smug piece of shit," Andrew Smith replied serenely. "I think it's just become my favourite form of transport." He used his briefcase to brush past the flummoxed pilots and strode purposefully toward the brightly-lit customs entrance.

Fifteen minutes later, he was standing on the pavement fifty metres beyond the terminal's regular pick-up zone as instructed. He looked to his right, to the bright lights of the extensive terminal buildings. Strained to see the familiar shape of the company Bentley among the massed headlights of black cabs and minibuses. He checked his watch as another taxi roared past him belching diesel fumes. Eight thirty-three. She was late.

He thought about the brief conversation he'd had with the contact he'd been given by the American State Department. He'd phoned her about an hour ago when the plane was entering British airspace. When the euphoria he'd felt at realising he wasn't about to die, liquidised in the Atlantic, was beginning to dissipate. When he knew he couldn't live a day longer as the person he had been. Never again would he stretch every acquisitive fibre of his being in a soul-destroying struggle to stand still.

"Brennan," she'd said tersely.

Smith didn't know why, but he hadn't been expecting a female voice to answer the strange number he'd dialled.

"Erm, my name is Andrew Smith," he'd replied. "I've been given your number by the American St..."

"Stop talking, Mr Smith," the woman had said quickly.

Smith heard the 'line dead' tone in his ear for several seconds. He'd been about to hit 'end' on his phone when the woman came back on.

"Who do you work for, Mr Smith?" she had said. An accent in there somewhere, Scottish or Irish, thought Smith.

He'd told her who he worked for.

"And where are you now, Mr Smith?" Definitely Irish, he thought.

He'd told her where he was.

"Very good, Mr Smith. You will shortly receive a text message with instructions. Reply with the word 'yes' to confirm you have read and understood the message. It will then be deleted from your phone. Do you understand?"

"Yes," he'd said.

He looked at his watch again. Eight thirty-five. He began to wonder whether the whole thing was an elaborate hoax. Like that Michael Douglas film. But it wasn't his birthday. He passed an agitated hand through his thinning hair and scanned the slew of vehicles to his right again in vain. Began reaching for his phone, then stopped, hand hovering in mid-air, as his ears were assaulted by screeching tyres to his left. He gawped at the big black car as it bore down on him, scattering on-coming taxis as it skidded to a squealing halt at his toes. The rear-left passenger door opened and a woman's Irish voice shouted above the growling engine, "Get in please, Mr Smith."

He glanced about him and surreptitiously pressed the record button on his phone in his breast pocket before clambering aboard.

"Good evening, Mr Smith," said the attractive, auburn-haired woman comfortably seated to his right in the spacious rear cabin. She was thirty or thereabouts, Smith thought. Hazel eyes, pale skin and freckles around her shapely nose. "You might want to hold onto something for a couple of minutes."

For the second time during this day of ceaseless surprises, Smith found himself scrabbling for his seatbelt as he was squished into the plush leather by break-neck acceleration.

"How was your flight, Mr Smith?" the Irish woman purred.

Smith watched her closely as she leaned forward in her seat and tapped the black glass separating the front and rear seats. He knew he probably didn't have much time. But he also knew he couldn't afford to set the wrong tone. That would ruin everything. He just had to get her to say who she worked for. Then a quick call to his friend at *The Times* and he'd never have to work again.

"Fine thank you, Miss…er…" he blustered in as meek a tone as he could manage.

The Irish woman looked at him for several seconds. "I believe I gave you my name when you called me, Mr Smith," she said flatly. She reached into the small black briefcase next to her, came out with a phone and set it on her lap.

Shit, shit, shit, Smith thought. That hadn't been in his script at all. "I'm sorry," he said hastily, "I didn't catch it. You see, this is all a bit…"

"This, Mr Smith?"

"Well, quite, Miss…er…I mean, I don't even know what this is," he spluttered.

"My name's Brennan, Mr Smith," she replied icily. "And *this* is purely the offer of a lift to wherever you want to go. Home, I assume after such a busy day?"

Only if I can't get anything out of you first, Smith thought. "Actually, there are a few things I need to sort at the office, Miss Brennan. It's on…"

"I know where it is, Mr Smith," Brennan replied, picking up her phone.

Silence broke out in the rear of the hurtling car for a few minutes as Brennan continued tapping and swiping. This isn't what Smith had expected at all. The woman didn't seem remotely interested in the apparently top-secret information he was carrying. Perhaps it wasn't that important after all. In which case, his dream was dying right in front of him. He looked out of the window at the blur of semi-detached housing that marked the beginnings of the great city. "Is there a particular reason we're going so fast, Miss Brennan?" he said, to break the silence as much as anything.

"Yes, Mr Smith. The sedative we gave your regular driver only lasts about an hour," she replied without looking up.

Smith fought hard to betray no emotion. "I see," he said as calmly as he could. He thought about a nervous laugh, then decided against it. Just play it cool, he said to himself. "Does that have something to do with the information I've..."

"Yes it does, Mr Smith," she replied, fixing him with a nerveless glare. "I'll take it now, please."

He nodded briefly and bent forward to open his briefcase, his shoulder hiding the biggest grin his face had ever worn. He retrieved the A4 jiffy bag he'd been given by the US State Department and placed it in his lap. Made a face like something had just occurred to him. "This is a little embarrassing, Miss Brennan," he began, turning the envelope round in his hands. He registered the note of doubt enter her eyes and continued, emboldened. "You see, my boss is a bit of a control freak. He told me I had to be certain I was passing the information on to the correct...er...organisation." He held his breath.

Brennan's gaze seemed to harden momentarily, before she blinked and the hint of a smile touched the corners of her taut mouth. "Of course, Mr Smith," she replied and reached into her briefcase. Came out with a slimline wallet that she flipped open toward him. "I'm Field Agent Fran Brennan, Mr Smith. I work for UK Security Services."

Smith's eyes danced over the details on her I.D. card as though they were pound signs. He forced his smile into a weary expression of relief. One that hopefully conveyed that the strain he'd been under all day was finally over. "Thank you, Miss Brennan," he sighed, handing her the package.

She took it casually, flipped it over and placed it in her briefcase. "No, thank you, Mr Smith," she grinned, stretching her right hand toward him. He lifted his own to shake hers, but it was no longer there. It had dropped suddenly and was now pressing his seatbelt release button. Then the car braked brutally.

Smith's body flew briefly before smashing against the partition glass and panelling. Then it jerked back almost as forcefully and sprawled brokenly on the rear seats. When the car relaxed to a gentle idle, Miss Brennan unbuckled herself and reached calmly into Smith's breast pocket. She glanced briefly at the screen of his phone then down at the man with blood gushing from his nose. "Your country owes you a great debt, Mr Smith," she said, smiling.

Eleven

Friday morning, 15th May

The insistent tone of Penelope Lane's mobile drew her reluctantly from a particularly hot dream in which she was writhing wantonly in the clutches of several, glistening gladiators. She was just looking forward to the retiarius' next move, now that he had her in his net, when she was extricated by the banality of the modern world.

"Aaaww," she groaned, like a child denied sweets. She reached across her empty bed for her phone. Things were definitely more exciting in Roman times. She took a quick look at the screen to see who had the temerity to intrude on her fantasies but didn't recognise the number.

"Hello?" she said.

"Hello, Miss Lane. This is Lyn Tait in reception. There are a couple of police officers here who would like to speak with you."

The frustration caused by the sudden end to her dream abated, replaced by a sudden sense of foreboding. She searched about in her recent past for any occasion of wrongdoing. Couldn't think of anything worse than watching something edgy online.

"Er...right. Should I come down, or do they want to come to my room?" she asked, getting out of bed and searching for some underwear.

"I think it would be good if they came up to you, Miss Lane. I'll have someone bring your coffee. Will ten minutes be okay?"

"Um, could you make it fifteen? I haven't had a shower yet."

Precisely sixteen minutes later, there was a discreet knock on the door to her suite. Showered and casually attired in jeans and patterned shirt, Penelope opened the door to a maid with a trolley and two uniformed women police officers with pale, drawn faces. The maid arranged cups and pots on the coffee table while the police officers shuffled about nervously, looking anywhere but at

Penelope. She thanked the maid and saw her out, then turned with dread toward her unnerving guests.

"I'm Sergeant Wild, Miss Lane. Chelsea police. This is Special Constable Parrington," the officer said softly, indicating a slightly smaller version of herself. She had strawberry-blonde hair tied up and minimal make-up on what might have been an attractive face were it not so careworn.

Penelope made an effort to gather herself and said, "Please, sit down. Would you like some coffee?"

"No thank you," said Sergeant Wild as she and her partner sat uneasily in prim Edwardian armchairs around the coffee table.

Penelope wasn't very good at standing on ceremony. "Look," she said, a bit abruptly, "what's this all about?"

Sergeant Wild looked down and cleared her throat. When she looked back up, Penelope saw raw pain in her eyes.

"We tried to contact your father this morning without success. Afraid we had to use GPS from your mobile to locate you." She paused, closed her eyes and took a deep breath. "I'm sorry to report, Miss Lane... We, er, have reason to believe, your sister... We think she was killed last night."

Penelope heard the words, but they didn't make any sense. They just swirled around in her ears, her brain protecting her conscious self from the enormity of what she'd been told. The officers and the room were moving in and out of focus and she began to feel as though she were in an alternate reality.

"Miss Lane, are you all right?" Sergeant Wild asked, standing.

Penelope barely heard the words, but they were the only ones that could have prevented her from shutting down all conscious thought. The absurdity of them brought her round.

"All right..." she bawled in disbelief. "Are you off your rocker?" She stood up and started pacing around. "You've just told me my sister's dead. Of course I'm not fucking all right." She stopped suddenly, threw herself on the carpet in the foetal position and made a primordial sound that descended into violent sobbing.

By the end of their visit, the officers had earned a citation. It had taken a long time, but they had managed to calm Penelope and got her to agree to accompany them to identify the body. She followed the officers numbly through the magnificent hotel lobby and out into a maelstrom.

Tuesday evening, 12th May

Dragan Kurjac felt one of his phones vibrating in his jacket pocket. He got up immediately and left the room he was sharing with three other men. Because it was that phone. The one that only received calls from a single untraceable number. The General. His heartbeat quickened slightly as he held his finger over the answer icon. Then he hit it straight away because he knew the voice on the other end didn't tolerate delay.

"Kurjac," he said curtly. The voice that answered him was disembodied and metallic as he expected. Some sort of ancient scrambling device, he figured. It always sent a chill down his spine.

"Details of the subject will be available from twenty-one hundred hours today. Location six. Time is restricted. Forty-eight hours maximum. Method unimportant. Contact us by the usual means upon completion." The line went dead.

The sound of his mother tongue stirred dark memories as Kurjac contemplated the instructions. He massaged the stub that was all that remained of his right ear. Time was the only issue he could foresee, but that could be negated by the method employed. In his experience, restrictions almost always incurred increased exposure. In extreme circumstances, it might lead to the loss of one of his men. But then, they were his most readily replaced resource.

Location six hadn't been used for over a year, but he knew it was on top of an old-fashioned cistern in a Chinese restaurant in South Kensington. One where you had to stand on the toilet seat and reach up. Forty-eight hours from nine o'clock tonight. The ghost of a smile appeared briefly on Kurjac's otherwise impassive face. No problem.

Twelve

Friday morning, 15th May

"Better?" McLeod said as Wren took her seat opposite him.

"You've got no idea," Wren replied. He could tell from her eyes and posture that she was back to herself. She was more alert, aware of her surroundings without the need to look. Back in command.

"I thought your gizmo did the same job," he ventured.

"So I was led to believe," she replied bitterly.

"So how's it different?"

She thought for a moment, then said, "Do you like cheese, Mr McLeod?"

"You've got no idea," he replied. Wren hesitated and then flashed a toothy grin.

"Got a favourite?"

"That's a very difficult question, Miss Wren. Possibly the toughest you've posed. Give me a second." He trawled through the hundreds of cheeses he'd eaten. French, Italian, Spanish, Dutch, Swiss. Even Britain was producing the odd tasty morsel these days.

"Perhaps a very ripe Camembert," he offered finally.

"Okay. So, imagine the difference between your Camembert and that orange shit that they stuff in burgers in fast food places."

"Okay," said McLeod.

"On top of which, I feel like a shell of the person I usually am. Why are you interested anyway?"

His thoughts drifted back to Catherine and the only arguments they'd ever had. They were all started by him, all for the same reason.

"My wife smoked for years," said McLeod. "I nagged her fairly regularly to quit. She used to say, 'I do, twenty times a day'.

54

She finally managed about four years ago." McLeod paused and looked at the ceiling. "Then three years later she got cancer."

"Ain't life grand?" Wren said ruefully then shook her head, getting her mind back to the job in hand.

"We just got the initial toxicology report, Mr McLeod." That got his attention back too.

"The girl was poisoned?"

"And you apparently, though to a much lesser extent," Wren replied.

McLeod pondered for a moment. That explained a lot, he thought. Then he asked, "What with?"

Wren looked away. "Nicotine," she said.

Tuesday afternoon, 12th May

As Kurjac walked back into the main room, the other three men laid down their cards and looked up in unison at the slight, swarthy man. Expectation growing in their narrowed eyes. He was momentarily annoyed by the harsh smell of the men's Eastern European cigarettes, the smoke hanging in drifts in the sombre room. He walked past their table to the small fridge in the corner and took out a water. Took a long drink as he carried a wooden chair to the middle of the room. He sat on it, chest against the backrest, arms folded across the top. He looked into each man's eyes in turn and saw complete commitment.

In guttural Slavic tones laced with gravel he said, "We leave in fifteen minutes. Bartek, bring the Merc to the door. Ragnars, day and night field equipment in three bags. Karel, supplies for seventy-two hours. Move."

The men rose as one and headed out of the room in different directions. He watched them go with his dark, almost black eyes. Out of habit, Kurjac took another long drink of the cool, fresh water. He knew how important it was. Because of the countless times when he didn't know where his next drink would come from. When the sickly stench of death was all around him. In the woods north of Srebrenica.

Units of executioners hunted them by day, and food and water were very hard to find at night. The streams and rivers were most closely patrolled so the emaciated survivors in the woods were forced to drink from stagnant bogs and puddles if they could find them. Occasionally, in desperation, they risked exposure above the tree line to find a free-flowing mountain stream where they drank until their stomachs hurt. Then they hurried to another hiding place to try to sleep. As a boy before bed, Kurjac used to pray to God to keep himself and his family safe. He'd long since given that up. Probably the third time his parents sold his sister to pay for some food. Her screams still haunted him. She was ten years old.

Thirteen

Friday morning, 15th May

The clock on the mantelpiece read half past nine. McLeod could feel his headache returning. The doctor and two officers wheeled the gurney out of the apartment door. It jumped a bit over the threshold and then was lost to sight as the door was closed by the officer stationed outside. The living room suddenly seemed empty with just himself, Wren and the rifle-toting officer left in it. Wren was looking at something on her phone, flicking and tapping. A fresh mug of coffee sat steaming in front of her on the low table.

"Do you mind if I go and get some paracaetamol and a drink, Miss Wren?" he asked.

Without stopping her phone business, she reached into her bag and came out with an unopened plastic bottle of water and put it on the table. After a little rummaging, she pulled out a foil strip of pills and slid them across to him. McLeod couldn't supress a chuckle.

"I amuse you again, Mr McLeod?" A smile touched the corners of her mouth, but she didn't look up from her phone. McLeod swallowed a pill with some water.

"Just marvelling at the resourcefulness of the fairer sex, Miss Wren."

"Remind me to add patronising to your charge sheet, Mr McLeod."

He winced for a second, then countered, "About that, how come I haven't been charged with anything?"

Wren made a final swipe, then pressed a button on her phone and chucked it in her bag. Her piercing blue eyes found McLeod's and she opened her mouth to speak, then closed it again, her top teeth resting on her lower lip. McLeod's eyes darkened as he watched her wrestling with how to proceed. She raised a hand to her mouth and ran her fingers over her lips.

"That's a gesture often employed by liars, Miss Wren," McLeod observed dryly.

Wren looked startled for a moment, then gave a raspy chuckle. "Secrets, Mr McLeod," she said, eyes twinkling.

"I told you I don't have any," he replied making an open-armed gesture.

"We'll see about that, Mr McLeod," Wren said ominously.

Tuesday evening, 12th May

The S-class Mercedes purred past Harrods, heading towards South Kensington. In the front passenger seat, Kurjac surveyed the opulence surrounding him with contempt. He knew the streets around here were littered with Ferraris, Bentleys, Lambourghinis and Range Rovers. Liveried older gentlemen opened their doors and showed the impossibly stylishly dressed occupants to their porticoed doors. How many of these people actually earned what they had? How many would recognise a hard day's work if it punched them in their Botoxed faces? He'd seen his own father leave for construction sites at six each morning, sometimes not returning until eight at night, and still his mother had to work as a cleaner for the family to get by. He hoped tonight's subject lived in this neighbourhood.

She didn't. In fact, her address wasn't even in London. But she was in town for the next two days on business. As usual, the information Kurjac retrieved from the drop-off, tightly wadded in a plain manila envelope, was exhaustive. More than three quarters of it was superfluous, included merely as a demonstration of the depth of the General's power. By the Mercedes' cabin light, Kurjac found the woman's itinerary and the deep lines on his forehead creased into a frown.

"Problem, boss?" asked Bartek in a thick Polish accent.

"Eyes on the road," Kurjac replied. "There are never problems, only opportunities for deeper thinking."

As he studied the list of the woman's engagements more closely, clear windows for action didn't readily present themselves. Usually with this kind of assignment, the target would be completely exposed on at least a few occasions. But this was clearly someone whose time was extremely valuable both to herself and those with whom she was meeting. The only gaps between appointments appeared to be the time required to travel between venues. And she'd hired an ex-SAS corporal to drive her. Who the hell was this woman?

Fourteen

Friday morning, 15th May

Wren reached for her bag and came out with her phone again. Two taps and a swipe. "Duncan Clark McLeod, born Edinburgh, 5th of April 1981, age thirty-four, height six foot one, weight twelve stone. Eyes light-brown, hair dark-brown, no distinguishing features."

"Flattery, Miss Wren?" McLeod raised his brows in mock amusement.

"I don't agree with that one either," she said with a small smile.

"Please, don't let me stop you, Miss Wren. I need a new pair of shoes and I've forgotten my size," he replied with an answering smile.

"MI5, Mr McLeod," she said, grinning. "Apparently, you're a person of interest to them."

McLeod hesitated before asking the obvious question. This was getting weirder and weirder and once again he felt out of his depth. A beautiful dead girl, a beguiling interrogator, and now he found he was the subject of secret service snooping. He didn't need to search his past to know that he hadn't done anything to merit this last fact. A feeling of indignation fired in his chest.

"What exactly have I done to have interested the spooks?" His tone was angrier than he'd intended and his hooded eyes blazed.

It caused heat to fire in DI Wren's belly and she couldn't stop it reaching her mouth.

McLeod registered the increased huskiness in her voice as she countered, "I think it's more a case of what you haven't done."

She paused and wondered how much to divulge to the man with the smouldering gaze sitting opposite. The Thames House brigade would probably look askance at police officers discussing their methods with ordinary members of the public. Wren suddenly felt a bit of McLeod's resentment. She knew they had a file on her after all.

"A person of your expertise and experience, Mr McLeod, is known as a high-value target. That is, of high value to foreign governments interested in acquiring intellectual assets." She paused and forced herself to watch McLeod's eyes carefully, and saw a frowning bewilderment, then anger again, before humour finally won out.

He chuckled and shook his head.

"I see the irony isn't lost on you, Mr McLeod," she said.

"Well as my own government has no use for me, I think I ought to get MI5 to distribute my file as a CV, don't you?"

"Surely you don't believe your job was terminated yesterday, Mr McLeod?" Wren asked and took a long sip of coffee, followed by a drag on her puffer.

She would make an interesting biological study, McLeod thought to himself. The relationship between stimulants and increased metabolism was well established. Or was he thinking more about the effects of her stimulation on him? Dangerous ground.

"Very astute, Miss Wren. It was probably in March or April of 2009 when long-term budget forecasts were formulated following the banking bollocks-up. Smaller civil institutions like mine were easy targets, never mind that most of them worked in niche areas or with the most disadvantaged people in society."

"What exactly is it that you did, Mr McLeod?"

He eyed her quizzically before replying. "MI5 didn't tell you, Miss Wren?"

She glanced quickly at her phone before putting it back in her bag. "The file just says neuroscience. I understand that's a big field. Could be you're a psycho-babbling charlatan or a brain surgeon. You certainly have the hands for one." She stopped and smiled self-consciously, aware that McLeod's hands were in his lap. She saw him smile too and cursed herself.

"Mr McLeod, I didn't mean…" she began.

"Please, Miss Wren, I wasn't smiling at any discomfort you may have. The only surgery these hands undertake is on the strings of my Gibson Les Paul…and it's usually botched."

"Guitar-playing charlatan then?" said Wren, relieved.

McLeod grinned and said, "My last paper was on the extent to which superior cognitive development occurs in speakers of Koreanic and Japonic languages. Apparently, the government was keen to find out why kids in those countries out-performed ours by so much at sixteen." He paused and smiled to himself as he remembered the apoplectic reaction of the Junior Education Minister to whom he had delivered his findings.

"So, how superior was their development?" Wren asked, suddenly interested. Finlay was thinking about taking Japanese at GCSE.

"Not at all. I told them as much before they commissioned the research. The idea that growing up learning a particular language makes your brain develop better is deluded."

"So did you find out why kids over there are brighter than in the UK?" she asked and blew a stream of vapour towards the ceiling.

"They aren't any brighter. Not on a biological level anyway. Apparently in South Korea they have a saying along the lines of: if you sleep three hours a night, you might get into a top university; four hours a night, you get into another university; five hours a night, you don't get into university."

"Jesus, that's brutal. So you're some kind of brain and language quack, right?"

McLeod thought for a moment and chuckled. "I'll settle for that I guess, Miss Wren," he said and stretched.

Wren caught sight of some well-defined abdominal muscles as his sweatshirt rode up. She closed her eyes briefly, then said, "So tell me about the Olympic Games."

Fifteen

The Mercedes idled at the kerbside. With its tinted windows and matte paint job, it might have attracted unwanted attention elsewhere, but Kurjac knew that in this part of town, it was bordering on invisible. Hidden in full view. It was something he knew a lot about. The unwelcome memory of the first time he'd had to do it came unbidden to his mind.

Rumours had started circulating among the town's people of menfolk disappearing. Whispered bits of information exchanged at the market or the bakery or anywhere some food might be found. Under the savage glares of the men who were once their compatriots. So when the Kurjac family heard banging on the front door of their tiny house very early one July morning, they knew what to do. Mrs Kurjac and little Lejla would distract the soldiers, with their bodies if necessary, whilst Mr Kurjac and Dragan escaped out the back and into the forest.

Unfortunately for the man and his boy, such a flimsy plan had been tried by many others. They were marched to a large agricultural outbuilding and forced to strip naked. One of the soldiers smashed Dragan's father's nose with his rifle butt when he showed a sign of dissent. Soon they were joined by dozens more skeletal and terrified men and boys.

Most of the soldiers carried an AK-47 of some description. Some even had the latest 103 model. The two soldiers facing the line of twenty-five bare backsides had older versions. They had each fired over ten thousand rounds and the muzzles had metal fatigue. Wouldn't hit a barn door at two hundred yards, but then the filth they were tasked with cleansing was only fifteen yards away. They fired at chest height in one long, continuous volley, sixty rounds, until no one was left standing. Then they took out side arms and walked along the line of writhing naked bodies, silencing any wails with a single bullet to the head.

Warm blood from his father's heart was pouring over Dragan. His last act had been to pull his son in front of him as the deafening shots began. Despite the pain from his right ear, Dragan didn't move a muscle as the soldier walked slowly past him. Next to them, a man was still twitching. Dragan peeked out from below his father's lifeless body and saw the man's head explode. Bits of bone and brain splattered the thirteen-year-old's face. The soldiers' laughter was the last thing he heard as his brain shut down.

He didn't know how long he was out, but the blood covering his back was beginning to cake. The smell of death filled his nostrils. It was hot in the barn. He listened intently and heard no sound from within the building. In the distance, he heard a low rumble. Thunder? A tank maybe, or a lorry? It was growing louder. He risked opening his eyes and immediately wished he hadn't. The man next to him had half a face, a bloody pulp where the rest of it should have been. He gagged and the movement caused his father's corpse to shift heavily on his lungs making breathing more difficult.

The sound was definitely a big diesel engine, and it was definitely getting closer. He knew he had to run. If a soldier was standing guard, he didn't care. He couldn't bear to be where he was any longer. He put his hands on the blood-soaked bare earth and pushed and wriggled out backwards from under his father.

Dragan looked about him quickly. Plenty of daylight was coming through the barn's wide doorway and it showed him there wasn't another living soul in the building. He lifted a hand to his right ear and found only a ragged shred. The only other pain he felt came from his left cheek. He could feel something sticking out of it. It stung as he pulled it out. A piece of bloody bone. He remembered the man's head exploding as he ran to the ragged pile of clothes near the barn's opening and grabbed a t-shirt with Sarajevo Winter Olympics 1984 in faded orange writing. He poked his head out of the barn entrance, saw a yard and a low wall, then empty fields, and then the forest.

He found a water butt just outside the barn. It was half full of stagnant water. He plunged in the t-shirt and used it to wipe his face and bloodstained hands. The rest would have to wait as he could now feel the noise of the engine. He knew he didn't have time to look for his own clothes so just snatched up the first shirt and trousers that looked okay. His battered sneakers were there on the edge of the pile. He put the clothes on quickly and ran to his father's body. The engine roared toward the barn. Dragan bent down close to his father's ear and whispered through his tears, "I will find them, Father. I will find them, and I will kill them." With a little difficulty, he undid the leather strap on his father's watch and put it in his pocket. Then he ran out of the back of the building and crouched behind a milk pail. He watched as the monstrous tractor thundered through the barn's entrance and scraped up half a dozen bodies and began backing out. A bloody leg stuck out rigidly from the scoop. He closed his eyes briefly, took a deep breath and ran for the forest.

Sixteen

Friday morning, 15th May

McLeod had realised from quite a young age that the accident of birth was one of the world's most heinous iniquities. The life you would subsequently lead was fairly well mapped out at the moment of your conception. The likelihood of enjoying good health, happiness, love and prosperity all determined by the whereabouts and circumstances of your creation.

What chance of enjoying those gifts for a child born in war-torn Syria or in the slums of Kinshasa? What hope of a full and active life when struck by capricious fate with a condition like cerebral palsy or cystic fibrosis? How could you escape a life of misery and despair born to a raped or drug-addicted mother? Even worse, you could be a complete shit of a human being and win the lottery. He knew he'd never know what it was like to fly like an eagle or to swim and sleep like a shark. He knew life wasn't fair. He was aware he hadn't been dealt the best cards in life, but he knew there were far worse.

He thought back to his upbringing with his impoverished mother on a grey estate on the outskirts of Edinburgh. It was a time and place he'd spent the rest of his life trying to forget. Wizened men, young and old, wheezing into cans of Tennent's Super Strength as they hobbled off to collect their giros. Whey-faced young women pushing children against grey rain in plastic chairs, stripy shopping bags hanging off the handles. He recalled the sunken, dark-rimmed eyes staring out of the hooded faces of ghostly youths. They clustered noisily around park benches and bus stops, aiming foul-mouthed abuse at anyone more fortunate than themselves. Then they disappeared furtively down alleyways between the squalid rows of junk-filled back gardens. Did whatever they'd managed to get hold of to escape their pitiful existence. That was one way out of it, one many of McLeod's earliest friends had taken.

The fact that McLeod hadn't followed that path was largely down to his grandfather. He was McLeod's ace card, his one chance to escape his own accident of birth. A talented athlete in his day, he ran a club for local young people. McLeod remembered the trepidation he felt among the bigger boys when he first went, aged seven. He'd thought he would never be capable of any of the feats he saw them perform, but some eight years later, he had broken every club record.

Because he was good at running, jumping and throwing, he started entering decathlons. He was soon picked by national coaches to represent Scotland at the Commonwealth Games. He got a place reading biology at Loughborough University, Britain's premier sporting institution. He trained harder than ever and began winning national titles. People began talking about his medal prospects at the upcoming Olympic Games.

"Not much to tell, I'm afraid, Miss Wren. I came fourth," said McLeod. Where was she going with all this, he wondered?

"Actually, that tells me rather a lot." She looked away at a framed photograph of McLeod and his beautiful wife on the mantelpiece. She stood and walked towards it. "They say that's the worst place to finish. I've always thought dead last would push it fairly close, wouldn't you, Mr McLeod?" She turned and arched an eyebrow.

"I never enjoyed it," he replied quietly.

Wren studied the photograph for a long moment. "Fourth place isn't the whole story, though, is it?"

His mind wandered back to the stadium and the deafening roars of the crowd that accompanied each outstanding performance. He knew how it must have felt to be a gladiator in the Colosseum at Rome. It was the second day of the decathlon event and he had a handy lead after a blistering first day and a solid 110 metres hurdles that morning. The next event was discus, and it wasn't his favourite. Perhaps that was why he didn't focus properly during his warm up. As he entered the circle, the crowd's noise subsided to an excited murmur. He completed his one and a half spins and was unleashing the projectile when the excruciating pain struck.

"It was a long time ago, Miss Wren, another life, if you like."

Wren sensed McLeod's discomfort at talking about himself. If only more men were like that, she thought, as she recalled the hours wasted during recent dates with city-types, listening to their exploits on bloody FIFA and Grand Theft sodding Auto.

"As I understand it, Mr McLeod, before your shoulder popped out, you were cruising for the gold medal." She replaced the photograph on the mantelpiece and turned round. "You couldn't even take part in the javelin or pole vault events. And how you ran the fifteen hundred metres at all…"

McLeod gave an exasperated sigh. "Look, I'm more than prepared to help you with your investigation, Miss Wren, but I fail to see how…"

"I have my reasons, Mr McLeod," Wren replied. She paused and looked directly into his eyes. "I don't think you killed the girl," she said quietly. Watched as his eyes winced closed then opened again, bewildered. "But the more I find out about you, the more intrigued I am about your involvement in all this."

Seventeen

Tuesday evening, 12th May

Normally, for a thing like this, Kurjac would use his men in a stakeout of the target's residence and workplace. Clearly that was out of the question with this woman. The Savoy Hotel was impossible to watch conveniently from another building, and her meeting schedule covered most of Greater London. Tailing her wouldn't be a problem, but access opportunities were going to be slim at best. He thought about methods he'd employed on past assignments. Where access was tight. Thought back to his very first kills. To the men who'd gunned down his father.

He'd spent the rest of the day he was robbed of his childhood high up in the uncomfortable branches of a black pine. He felt numbed by what he'd seen, but instead of fear, he was filled with a quiet rage. It was a feeling that would never really leave him.

Hunger was starting to be a problem as he'd been taken before breakfast and now the sun was beginning to go down. Earlier, he'd heard a patrol of three men clatter along the path twenty metres away, then clatter back an hour later. The need for food overcame his fear of being found and he scrambled down the branches of his tree. He knew he couldn't risk going back to town to get something in daylight hours. But like all children his age from his background, finding food in the forest was second nature. Soon he was gorging on wild raspberries and cherries. Though he didn't like them, he sought out some safe fungi he knew of, as well as dandelion leaves, for vitamins and minerals. He knew these were important to give him the strength he was going to need for the grim tasks ahead of him.

In the cover provided by several large boulders, he thought about his home, his mother and his sister. Little Lejla. She had always been slow to grasp things, and people, even their own parents, were often impatient with her. But Dragan had always found a way to explain difficult things to her so she could understand. He was never upset or cross with her. As a result, he knew she looked up to him and wanted to emulate him.

Tears pooled in his eyes as he remembered the first time he knew he would do anything for her. She had just turned five and it was her first day at school. She was very pretty even then and caught the attention of some of the big boys. Dragan heard her screams from the far side of the ramshackle schoolhouse at lunchtime and ran as fast as he could. He turned the corner of the building and saw three boys much bigger than him dragging his struggling sister toward an area of waste ground. He roared and launched himself blindly at them. Rained punches, kicks and bites at whatever piece of any of the boys he could find. He felt no pain from their blows, and each one just made him fight back harder. He fought to the last of his strength until some grownups arrived and put a stop to it. Dragan was badly hurt but no one gave him or Lejla any trouble thereafter.

He searched his feelings for his mother and sister, but it was as though something inside him had died. Where before he had felt love and loyalty, now there was only a feeling of hollowness and futility. They had been defiled by the horror that had spewed into his town. He knew he would never see either of them again, and so he couldn't afford to waste his precious energy dwelling on them.

Dark was fast approaching. It was time to slay the soldiers whose faces burned in his retina. He knew where to find them and carefully made his way through the outskirts of town. He encountered no one in the deserted streets as he reached the hostelry the unit had requisitioned. Music, laughter and shouting came from within. He peered through the window, open to let in the night air. The first thing he saw was the back of one of the soldiers who'd soon be dead. Dragan recognised him from his shape. He was wearing fatigues and jerking wildly. Two other soldiers were facing him, holding on to something, laughing. Dragan moved to another window for a different angle. It was a girl who'd been in his class, naked and pinned by the arms to a heavy table as the dead man got to work. Her eyes were screwed up, tears trickling from their corners. He remembered her laughing and chasing him in the playground in junior school, letting her catch him and plant innocent kisses on his blushing cheeks. Another to avenge.

In the end, it was easy. It only needed patience and opportunity. And afterwards, he felt little emotion. Just the satisfaction of a job well done. He waited out the revelry, hiding behind empty beer barrels, then slipped through a downstairs window as a low moon rose over the distant forest. He found a sharp chef's knife in the kitchen and made his way through the bar room. The only light came from emergency exit signs and bits of neon advertising, but it was enough for Dragan to negotiate the bar's furniture. One of his targets hadn't even made it to bed. He was sprawled in a chair, his head back, mouth lolling open. The stench of stale beer reached Dragan's nose. He'd watched his father dispatch enough goats to know that he had to cut right through the larynx for there to be no sound. So that was what he did. Blood sprayed as the knife went through the carotid arteries.

He killed two more before he found the right bedroom. He was beginning to take a sort of pride in it. He decided to wake this one up so that he could watch the light go out in his eyes. And thirty seconds later it did. With a little difficulty, he pulled the knife from the soldier's chest. It was a good knife and he'd be needing it again. Dragan smiled grimly to himself. His calling had found him.

Eighteen

Friday morning, 15th May

A commotion in the street outside diverted McLeod's mind from dwelling too long on DI Wren's words. Another cyclist had been knocked off his bike at the junction. Chelsea would be grid-locked in ten minutes. McLeod watched people gather round, phones out. Some were taking photos, others making calls, possibly even to the emergency services. He saw that the rider wasn't badly injured and brought his focus back into the room and the blue steel of Wren's eyes.

"You say you were intrigued with my involvement with the, er…" began McLeod.

"Dead girl, Mr McLeod?"

"Yes, I mean…"

Wren cut him off again. "Well, clearly you had something to do with her," she said, retaking her seat opposite him.

"Yes, but not her death, you seem to think. How come?" McLeod's gaze intensified as he watched Wren pick at a loose thread on her skirt.

"In the same way that I presume you worked out my age, Mr McLeod." She paused and pointed a slender finger to her small, slightly upturned nose. "They can't teach you instinct."

"And yet now you're beginning to doubt your own?"

"I don't think I quite said that, Mr McLeod." She looked beyond him, to the world outside the window. "Why do you think that terror attacks, when they occur, are such big news?"

He thought back to the last one he could remember, some nut-jobs with a meat cleaver in Woolwich. And the more recent Charlie Hebdo business in Paris. Lone wolf attacks they called them in the media. He recalled wondering at the time what wolves had done to be associated with anything so depraved.

"Presumably because they are very rare, Miss Wren," McLeod replied.

"We're foiling plots every day, Mr McLeod, including... What do they call them? Spectaculars? Apparently, atrocities not happening is barely news worthy. A large part of that is down to instinct."

"Yours?"

"I'm a tiny cog in a huge machine, Mr McLeod, but yes, there are undoubtedly folk wandering around today who wouldn't be had I not followed my nose." She blew vapour through it as if to emphasise her point.

McLeod shook his head and said, "So what are you saying here? You're sticking with your instinct?" He watched guardedly as Wren got up smartly and started pacing little squares around the living room, trailing clouds of vapour. She stopped and retrieved her phone from her bag, did some rapid swiping and tapping, then looked at McLeod. In her eyes, he could see a decision being arrived at, a Rubicon being crossed. Where before he'd seen conflict, he now saw a cool certainty. He took a deep breath.

"As far as this case goes, Mr McLeod, you're all we've got. My boss is going to take a lot of persuading that you're not good for the poisoner. He said as much in the message I just read. My intuition will count for little without solid evidence putting you in the clear." She paused, drew on her puffer and saw relief working into McLeod's features. "Building a picture of your background and current circumstances will help me to do that, but my boss will only give me a certain amount of time," she concluded.

The twisted knots in McLeod's stomach unravelled with the strength of Wren's conviction and the sincerity in her gaze. The weight of the horror and persecution he'd endured all morning suddenly lifted, replaced by cautious hope. He felt like hugging her. Only the presence of the uniformed officer prevented him.

Instead, he released his breath and said, "I'm very grateful for your belief in me, Miss Wren. Ask anything you like, but first can you tell me why you're so certain?"

Wren found herself revelling in McLeod's gratitude like it was a warm coat. She sighed and reminded herself how difficult it was to prove a negative.

"You're aware of criminal profiling, Mr McLeod." It wasn't a question.

"I've done bits of work in that area, Miss Wren."

"I thought you might have. There are many characteristics that murderers have in common. Most, for example, are accomplished liars."

"You're saying I'm not, Miss Wren?"

"Oh, I'm sure you'd be capable of the porkiest of pies, Mr McLeod, but that doesn't make anyone a killer." She sat back down again. "You've demonstrated, however, more than once, the single characteristic that all pre-meditative murderers lack. Humility, Mr McLeod, is why I'm so certain. You have it, they don't, and it's impossible to fake."

"Yes, I know. I've tried."

McLeod's rakish grin made him look even more devastating and Wren covered her gasp with a nervous cough. The intensity in his eyes made her suddenly uncomfortable, and she got up to survey the chaos in the street below. Despite the fact that the cyclist only appeared to have a few cuts and bruises, two ambulances and several squad cars were muscling their way through the morass of stationary vehicles. No matter that a couple of mounted officers appeared to have the situation well in hand.

"My grandfather used to say the motor car would be the end of us," McLeod observed quietly.

"Does boundless optimism run in the family?" scoffed Wren, returning to her seat.

McLeod smiled, but it didn't reach his eyes this time. "Well, let's just say things are beginning to look up," he replied.

Wren frowned, then said, "Hmmmn, about that. Why was one of the country's leading young economists in your bed?"

Nineteen

Tuesday evening, 12th May

The name Kurjac used at the desk of the Savoy was Radovan Milošević. It was the same as the name on the card that he used to pay. It was a hybrid name of the two people he hated most in the world. One was already dead and the other was beyond even Kurjac's reach or he would be too. He used the name to help fuel his hatred. To remind himself of the thousands of his brothers and sisters who'd been butchered and mutilated during the Balkan Conflict. But he also used it to remind him that those two people had made him who he was today. Their policies turned him from an innocent thirteen-year-old schoolboy into a savage, nomadic assassin.

Living off the land with other exiles, he bore witness to the atrocities committed against his people in the towns and villages around Srebrenica. He and his brothers fought a guerrilla war against the devil, descending from the hills, striking in the dead of night. But his audacity and ruthlessness, born of an indifference to his own life or death, elevated him above his comrades. Stories of his deeds spread by word of mouth. By the end of the hostilities, he had slain more than two hundred enemy soldiers. He had become a valuable asset to a fledgling nation.

He took a key card from the woman with Lyn, Assistant Reception Manager on a gold badge on her lapel. No, he didn't need a porter, thank you. Loud, self-important theatre-goers were streaming back through the revolving doors. He overheard words that irritated him intensely: charming, wonderful, awfully, delightful. He made his way through the Front Hall to the wide staircase, musing on how much good he could do for the planet during his stay.

His room looked out over the river. To his right, the London Eye was a bright ellipse against the indigo sky. Something else he hated about this city. It never got dark enough. He remembered the countless nights he'd spent staring up through the trees at billions of stars. You were lucky if you glimpsed one in this town. He'd wanted a room facing the Strand, but there were none available— "You're very lucky to get any room at this hour, Mr Milošević."

He felt the bed. Good and hard. The best part of three years sleeping on the ground meant he had trouble sleeping on anything too soft. He'd sent his men back to their rooms in Battersea. They'd begin surveillance tomorrow morning at Paddington Station. Having studied the Lane woman's engagements in more detail, Kurjac identified Thursday evening's social meeting as the most promising opportunity. But there was also the slight possibility that he might secure a master key for the hotel. Perhaps a cleaner would be careless. He briefly contemplated breaking his rule about killing only his targets, but quickly dismissed the idea. Besides, he relished the added challenge.

He fetched a glass from the bathroom and got a bottle of Stolichnaya out of his backpack. Poured a generous measure and sat in an armchair. He thought about methods. Usually he liked to study the target's routine and identify specific moments of vulnerability, then a silent approach from behind with a knife. He didn't like guns. Not since that morning in the barn. Not since he learned how infallible they were. And noisy. There was nothing noisy or infallible about six inches of razor-sharp steel.

But an opportunity and sure location to employ his preferred method were impossible to ascertain to Kurjac's satisfaction. He considered transport scenarios. The woman would be spending a fair amount of time in the car. He toyed briefly with the idea of a small explosive device. It would be easy enough to procure one, but then he rejected the notion on the basis that the car would be secure at the Savoy and captured there and everywhere else by the city's countless security cameras. Not to mention the driver. Generating enough speed in London to cause a fatal accident was equally impossible to guarantee.

Then there was the issue of the target's gender. He'd never killed a woman. Not even during the war in Bosnia. The need had never arisen. He hadn't even contemplated the idea. He searched his feelings for a moment and knew he couldn't do it. Not physically, with a knife or something. Or even pulling the trigger of a gun. The job would have to be completed because this was the General. The consequences of failure were too horrific to think about. He thought about his men. Karel was a sadistic bastard, probably wouldn't give it a second thought. Did he trust Karel enough to do it? The fact that he needed to ask the question told Kurjac he didn't. He was fairly certain the other two would share his own reservations. And so the solution to the problem presented itself. Poison.

Twenty

Wednesday evening, 13th May

Penelope Lane sank into the deep, soothing waters of a steaming, foamy bath and took a long sip of Sauvignon blanc. The nasty taste in her mouth that she always got when she came to London was replaced by zingy citrus flavours. "Mmmmnn," she almost moaned. It had been a long, tedious day filled with long, tedious people. She shuddered as she recalled the man from the treasury with hands like a frantic octopus. One more day of it, she thought, then a tranquil downbound train.

She relaxed and gently stroked her slender thighs. Rubbed each forearm with the other hand and felt tension begin to abate. Put her hands over her breasts and felt a little ache develop.

No, shit it! She remembered with annoyance that her father had arranged for her to have dinner with one of his tennis buddies tomorrow night.

"Listen, Penny. I know it's been a tough couple of years for you, well for all of us. But don't you think it's time you put yourself out there again? There's someone I'd like you to meet. Frightfully nice chap, darling, and only a *few* years older than you. Worth a bloody fortune. He'll take you somewhere amazing, I'm sure. Do it for the old man, darling, and for Mum?"

That had been a pretty low blow, but how could she have refused? What was the creep's name? Nicholas something awful. Smythe-Achingly dull no doubt. Suddenly, she felt very aggrieved. Two days filled with a litany of stuffed shirts followed by a whole evening with another. And one to whom she had to be nice. Penelope Lane was skilled in many areas, but suffering fools wasn't one of them. The more she thought about it, the more certain she was she couldn't do it. She'd be sure to say something dreadful and that would upset her father, and she just couldn't lay that on the old bugger. Drat it.

She looked around the large bathroom and singularly failed to be mollified by the luxurious trappings and decadent décor. Polished marble tiles with Fleur de lis in gold accents surrounded the double sinks, above which, on glass shelves, thick white towels were lavishly layered. A huge array of toiletries by Le Labo were piled around the mirror units.

She finished her wine angrily in two gulps. It reminded her of illicit teenage drinking games with her sister, Nathalie. She stilled as the germ of a thought grew within her. Nathalie. Of course! A smile began to form on her alluring face.

Nat could do it. She'd recently finished with a man the last time they'd spoken, which was only a few days ago. Fast mover as Nat was, Penelope doubted she could be serious enough with any new chap to preclude the scheme. And Nat owed her big time for her help with the job, though she'd probably have got it anyway. What had she said at the time, 'How can I ever repay you, Pen?' Right now, sister. Hell, enough people confused each for the other that Nat could even go and call herself Penelope. Why not, she thought? It would mean she fulfilled her obligation to her father into the bargain.

She levered herself reluctantly out of the warm embrace of the opulent water onto the deep bath mat. She checked herself over in the full-length mirror on the wall and once again gave thanks for her genes. Tall and willowy, trusses of almost black hair met her ample bosom. Her pert bum gave way to long, svelte legs. You'll do, Lane, she thought, towelling herself briefly and reaching for a cavernous bath robe. She walked through to the big but elegantly appointed bedroom, found her phone on the dressing table and checked the time. Half eight, she'd probably be out.

"Hey, Pen," Nathalie answered on the fourth ring.

"Hey, Nat. Got a minute?"

"Just a sec… Okay. What's up? Everything all right? We only spoke Monday. It's not Dad again, is it?"

"No, er, well yes, but no, he's fine. There's nothing the matter, I just need to ask you something."

"Mmmnn… I'm all ears."

"Hang on, where are you?"

"At the pub with Gav and Gemma. Why?"

"It's not a warm night, Nat. How come I can't hear music but I can hear traffic? You're outside, aren't you? Nathalie Lane, you're smoking again."

"Only my third today, Pen. Please don't give me a hard time."

"After all we went through with Mum?"

"I know, I know."

"Right, well." A pause on the line. "Okay, so you remember a couple of years ago a certain somebody engineered a job interview for you?"

"I would have got the bloody job anyway, you know that."

"How can I ever repay you? Your words, I believe, Nat."

"That was histrionics, Pen, and you know it."

"You going to make this hard for me?"

"Oh…buggeration, Pen. Let's have it."

"It's just a few drinks, Nat, then dinner somewhere fabulous with a squillionaire friend of Dad's."

"Why aren't you going? What's the catch? Is he a banker?"

"Well…"

"Worse than that?! Spill it, Lane."

"One of his names might be Smythe."

"Oh, Christ… Wait a second…are you in town?"

"It was very last minute, Nat. I got a call late yesterday from the Treasury of all people, something to do with the business and tax."

"You could have texted, you know. Why don't you come over here? It's only early."

"No, I'm sorry, Nat, I'm shattered."

"Well, tomorrow then, meet up for lunch?"

"I'm scheduled to be in a working lunch with some plastics people. How about if you came here after work? Around seven maybe? I could fill you in on loverboy."

"Don't push your luck, Pen."

"He might be wonderful. Frightfully nice, Dad said."

"Jesus. You owe me now, Pen."

"I think you're probably right."

"Listen, thanks for not going on about…you know…"

"Sure, just look after yourself, okay?"

"Uh-huh. Where are you staying?"

"Oh, only at the Savoy, darling."

"Tra-la, what's that costing you?"

"Ha, ha, sweet FA. Treasury's paying."

"You're joking. Good work Pen!"

"Hmmnn, they're about to buy my supper too. Chateaubriand and champagne I reckon, after the shit they put me through today."

"Nice. See you tomorrow, Pen."

"Thanks, Nat. See you tomorrow."

Twenty-One

Friday morning, 15th May

Rosanna Wren had a rather old-fashioned nickname in the unit. The Blonde Bombshell, they called her. Not in the Jean Harlow sense of being a sex pot, though she was equally well put together. She earned her moniker for her ability to flummox interviewees with a casual precision.

The tale was told often of the occasion Wren was interviewing a senior politician who was involved with laundering money for a rich Bahraini family. The man was being very uncooperative so Wren asked suddenly, "Does your wife know you spend most of your waking life watching gay porn?" In front of his wife.

McLeod's hooded eyes were wide as he stared mutely at DI Wren. He knew the dead girl in his bed demanded some explanation on his part, but he had absolutely no answers. He cast around in his short-term memory and caught nothing. He wanted desperately to be able to give Wren something to repay the faith she'd shown in him.

"You know who she was then?" he asked, hoping that some detail about the girl would spark a memory. Wren was reapplying lipstick, then she reached across to the bottle of water between them on the table, pulled the nozzle between her teeth and took a swig. He noticed she hadn't wiped it since he'd used it.

She got out her phone and said, "Her handbag was on this table when the local team arrived at around half six. A work ID badge with a photo was found inside. The picture was probably a couple of years old, but I'd say she was fairly unmistakable, wouldn't you, Mr McLeod?" The coy smile was back on Wren's lips as she took another drink and placed the bottle back on the table between them.

"I remember thinking when I found her that she had an almost impossibly beautiful face," replied McLeod. He thought of his wife Catherine as he said it and felt a pang of guilt, but there was no point pretending he'd felt otherwise.

"Yes, I agree, there was something slightly other-worldly about her," Wren said absently, reaching for her puffer.

McLeod noticed a faint, dark red smudge of lipstick on the water bottle's nozzle. He reached for it and said, "Do you mind if I ask what her name was, Miss Wren?" before taking a long drink.

Wren smiled briefly, then said, "She was called Nathalie Lane."

A flicker of light sparked in McLeod's brain. He tried to catch it and pin it down before it went out, taking its meaning with it.

"She said, 'You can call me Nat,'" he breathed.

Thursday evening, 14th May

Bartek looked at his watch, a bulky imitation Rolex he'd picked up on the Khao San Road the last time he was in Bangkok. The woman had returned to the hotel fifteen minutes ago. It was now ten to seven and she was due to meet some man at Somerset House at half past. Lucky bastard, he thought to himself. She was one of the best-looking pieces of tail he'd ever laid his world-weary eyes on. Too demure for his tastes though. Too little make-up on her pale, gamine face. Too much poise in her demeanour. He did like the way her dark hair fell chaotically over her shoulders and the fact she stuck out in all the right places. With more war paint, longer boots and a whole lot less clothing, she would suit him fine.

He checked his watch again. Seven o'clock. Kurjac had told him to phone the second she left the hotel. How long did it take women to get ready? He looked back to the hotel's entrance in time to see the rear end of another cute piece of ass disappear inside the revolving door. He'd been on worse stakeouts, he reflected.

Nathalie Lane double-checked her sister's room number at the desk with a suave young man from Poland. It matched the one in the text she'd received at lunchtime. Yes, she was expected and would she like to be accompanied? Nathalie politely refused and the man's face fell. She made her way up a sumptuous staircase and cast an appreciative eye over the Art Deco and Edwardian décor. Found the right room and knocked loudly.

"Is that you, Nat?"

Nathalie smiled as she recognised their routine. "Who the hell were you expecting, Henry Kissenger?" she said and heard an answering giggle.

Penelope opened the door and they kissed and hugged. She took Nathalie's coat and whistled at the black satin strapless dress and matching heels.

"That's one lucky toff out there tonight."

"What, this old thing?" Nathalie swayed her hips provocatively as she walked into the suite.

"You've lost weight since last month, Nat," said Penelope. It was an accusation.

"Only a couple of pounds, Pen. And you look lovely too, by the way."

"Well, sorry, Nat. Just have a pudding or something tonight, eh?"

"Humf, depends if it's any good. Christ, this is a bit swanky," she said, admiring the view down the river to the Houses of Parliament. "Where am I going anyway?"

From a fussily decorated ice bucket, Penelope extracted a heavy bottle. She poured white wine in two glasses and set them down on a table between elegant Edwardian armchairs. They sat and clinked glasses.

"Mmmnn, stayed in worse places," Penelope murmured, replacing the wine. "You're meeting for a drink down the road at Somerset House…you know it?"

"Yeah, went to a concert there once."

Nathalie remembered a balmy summer's evening when she'd first moved to London, listening to Mozart's violin concertos in the vast neoclassical courtyard, sipping champagne. She felt like she'd conquered the world.

"It's a pretty big place, Pen, d'you know which bit?"

"Um, the River Terrace, does that ring a bell?"

"I'm sure I'll find it," said Nathalie, fidgeting.

Penelope got her phone from her bag and did some swiping and poking.

"You're eating at somewhere called Chez Bruce, over in Wandsworth. Sounds Australian."

"Ha ha. It's not." Nathalie stood and walked over to a painting on the wall. "But maybe your man has decent taste after all."

"Knock up something reasonable, do they?"

"That's the rumour. Bit out of my way though, Pen."

"I'm sorry, Nat. I really appreciate this, you know. I can't tell you the bullshit I've gone through the last couple of days. This thing tonight would have finished me off."

"Okay, don't sweat it, Pen. Just give us the particulars. Is that a real Monet?" Nathalie jabbed a thumb behind her as she sat back down.

"I imagine it probably is." Penelope studied her phone again. Grimaced.

"Nicholas Smythe-Hilliard is your congenial host." She paused and smiled gingerly at Nathalie. "Works in insurance, um, in the city. Owns a palace by all accounts, out near Esher." She could sense Nathalie's eyes glazing over. She continued quickly, "Plays tennis at the same club as Dad. Recently divorced, no kids."

Nathalie made a face like she'd recalled a nasty experience. "I know the type. They find out I'm an economist and start in on interest rates and inflation and blah bloody blah. I get enough of it at work."

"But you're going as me, remember, so you won't have to talk shop."

"That's even worse. You tell me bugger all about what you do."

"Just be vague about it. I always am."

Nathalie started scratching her wrist. "How old is he anyway?"

"Stop that, Nat, you'll make a mark. Early forties is all I could get out of Dad."

"What? Jesus, Pen, that's at least fifteen years." Nathalie took a large mouthful of wine. Started scratching again, brow furrowed.

Penelope could see her sister was having second thoughts. Time to lay it on thick.

"What's the worst that can happen, Nat? You'll have fabulous food and wine and have to suffer a bit of stodgy chit chat." She paused and looked imploringly at her sister. "You'll be keeping Dad happy and saving my hide…and making this fella's day."

Nathalie puffed her cheeks out, blew and smiled sardonically. "Well, when you put it like that."

Penelope answered with a beaming smile of her own. "Thanks, Nat. Listen, stop fidgeting, I know what you want. Have it out the window though, okay? And be quick, you're supposed to be there in ten minutes."

Twenty-Two

Friday morning, 15th May

McLeod ran long fingers through his dark hair, willing more to come.

"That's excellent, Mr McLeod," Wren beamed. "Now think, man, is there anything else?" He heard the pleading note in Wren's husky tone. He tried to find the spark again, but it was gone. He let out the breath he'd been holding in a long sigh. Wren answered with a pensive plume of vapour.

Then she said, "Okay, Mr McLeod, let's try something else. We know that yesterday was your last day working at the South London School of Advanced Studies."

"It was everyone's last day, pretty much, just cleaners and a site supervisor left. A hundred years of learning and cutting-edge research, bam." McLeod's fist struck his knee. He could tell from the intensity in Wren's gaze that she was considering her approach. Probably something conciliatory, thought McLeod.

So he was surprised when she said, "What were you doing at work, Mr McLeod, clearing your desk?" Her candour made him smile once more.

"Among other things, Miss Wren, yes. Have you ever noticed that the only inevitable eventuality following a death is the poor sods left behind end up carting around loads of crap?"

"The building's not dead though, Mr McLeod. What's going to happen to it?" McLeod could tell she was only asking out of courtesy.

"Given the state of the economy, I imagine it'll be sold to the highest bidder," he replied half-heartedly. He realised he neither knew nor cared.

"What about you?"

"Something'll turn up."

Wren made a grim smile and said, "I'd say something already has."

McLeod shifted uneasily on the sofa. His stomach growled and though the clock showed it to be nearly eleven, he didn't feel the hunger evident in his gut. Wren had obviously heard though, and she turned and addressed the armed officer lurking by the door to the kitchen.

"Constable," she barked, waking him from his reverie. "Could you run down to the deli over the road? Get a couple of subs, chicken or something and whatever you want," she said, handing the officer a twenty.

"I'm really not hungry, Miss Wren," said McLeod, rubbing his tummy in a vain effort to cease its gurgitations.

"That racket you're making would indicate otherwise, Mr McLeod. I don't need you passing out again."

The Constable who'd been shuffling uncomfortably made a noise reminiscent of an ancient sheep on a blasted heath.

"What is it man? Spit it out," Wren snapped.

"Well, it's just I've been given pretty strict instructions not to leave this position until relieved, ma'am," the Constable managed.

McLeod saw the almost imperceptible shift in Wren's comportment and felt sorry for the officer.

She squared her shoulders and took a deep breath. "What the fuck is it with your lot and bloody regulations? Has Morewood got you all brain-washed? I've never come across such a bunch of lily-livered pencil pushers. Either you go and fetch us something to eat, or I'll have myself put in your chain of command by this evening and your life won't be worth living tomorrow."

The Constable seemed to shrivel as he shifted from foot to foot, opening and closing his mouth like a skewered toad. McLeod watched with admiration as the slight figure of DI Wren bore into the officer, daring him to defy her.

He didn't. He gathered the remnants of his self-esteem and offered Wren his MP5, saying, "Then could you look after this for me while I'm gone, ma'am?"

Wren's posture relaxed. "With pleasure, Constable," she replied, taking the firearm with a practised motion. As the officer departed, she added, "Oh, and Constable, see if they've got any Camembert."

"Camembert, ma'am?" He looked bewildered for a moment. "You mean, like, the cheese?"

"I mean precisely the cheese, Constable."

"Very good, ma'am," he said and left the apartment.

As Wren sat back down, she unclipped the magazine from the gun and laid both on the floor saying, "I hate these things."

McLeod was watching with interest, this slight yet powerful woman with such easy control over people and objects. He wondered if it extended to other parts of her life. "You're against guns, Miss Wren?" he asked.

"How can you be against an inanimate object, Mr McLeod? That's like saying you're against toasters or trampolines, both of which injure far more people in this country than guns. They're just tools. And this one," she said, jerking a thumb at the dismembered weapon, "is useless at anything over forty yards. That's closer than I ever want to get to anyone dangerous."

"So you don't consider me dangerous, Miss Wren?" said McLeod, arching an eyebrow. He saw Wren's pupils dilate. With the Constable gone, McLeod could feel the tension growing in the space between them.

"On the contrary, Mr McLeod," she replied. "If you don't turn off the smouldering, I will have no choice but to do something that would cost me my job. So I consider you to be ruinously dangerous." She rummaged in her bag for her puffer, got up and started pacing again, avoiding McLeod's eye.

McLeod couldn't decide whether he preferred the front or rear view. He chuckled and said, "I can behave if you can, Miss Wren."

"I'm pleased to hear it, Mr McLeod. Now, how often do you get off your tits?"

Twenty-Three

Friday morning, 15th May

The phrase was not unfamiliar to McLeod. He'd been to university after all and had taught students for a couple of years. The connotation for him involved copious quantities of illicit substances as in, "I went clubbing last night and got completely off my tits." What was Wren inferring?

"I assure you, Miss Wren, that apart from a bit of weed at university, the whole drugs thing scares me shitless. Without a laboratory, there's no way of looking at a pill or powder and knowing what's in it."

Wren knitted her brow as she retook her seat and crossed her slender legs. "Then how do we account for the massive memory loss? The poisoning, do you think?"

McLeod puffed out his cheeks and replied sheepishly, "Maybe. Also, yesterday was the first time in months that I've had a drink, Miss Wren. For a few weeks following Catherine's death, I drank fairly hard for the first time in my life. Then it began to affect my work so I stopped. I was wobbling a bit after two pints last night."

"I see," said Wren, looking away. She knew that for her, two pints would barely raise a buzz. She pushed the unwelcome thought aside and said, "So were both of those pints consumed at Somerset House?"

McLeod stared in disbelief for a moment before realisation dawned. "My mobile?" he asked.

"Mmm, hmm. MI5 has most of your movements yesterday."

"But how?" replied McLeod incredulously. "My phone's ancient. It doesn't have GPS or anything else for that matter. The students giggle when I get it out." He recalled getting one of his classes to list the five most important features of their mobiles. Making calls didn't appear once.

Wren smiled. "Then you should keep it away where it can't be seen. Does it have Snake on it?"

McLeod was beginning to enjoy Wren in playful mode, safe in the knowledge she was on his side. "I believe that was on the model after mine," he replied. He thought for a moment longer, then said, "I was under the impression that with a phone as old as mine, it could only be traced when you made a call. I can't remember making any."

"You didn't," she replied. "But you took several. Including a call at 7.32 p.m. from your brother. Lasted two minutes, twelve seconds. What was it about?"

McLeod thought about his brother David. A couple of years older than him, similar height and build, but carrying a few more pounds. Quite good looking without approaching McLeod's chiselled allure. They'd seen each other more and more infrequently as the years went by, despite living a few tube stops apart. Despite being inseparable growing up. What was the phrase? Everyone has such busy lives these days. McLeod smiled mirthlessly as he realised it applied to him as much as the next person.

"He was calling to see if we could meet up at the weekend. Said he couldn't talk about it on the phone." McLeod remembered the edginess in his brother's tone.

Wren was tapping on her phone with several fingers, then stopped, and looked meaningfully into McLeod's eyes with her own intense, blue gaze. "Okay, your brain's not complete mush at half seven. Any other details of the evening you can dredge up? Where did you eat, what did you have, conversations with colleagues...anything?"

McLeod unconsciously assumed the pose of the Thinker, fore-finger and thumb pinching the bridge of his strong, straight nose. Wren resisted the urge to smile, trying instead for a look of earnest encouragement.

"Okay... David rang off quite abruptly and then I went to the bar," McLeod began.

"Wait, weren't you already in the bar?" Wren interjected.

McLeod paused for a minute, confused, before continuing, "It was a warm evening so we were sitting out on the terrace they have down there by the river. Because it was a private function, we had to go inside to get drinks and it was my round."

"I see," said Wren. "Go on."

McLeod thought hard. His eyes had been focused somewhere between Wren's shapely legs and her end of the table. When he brought them up to hers now, they had something in them Wren hadn't seen before. Dread.

Twenty-Four

Thursday evening, 14th May

The sky in the west looked like it might soon be administering a spring shower as Nathalie walked between two rows of splash fountains in the courtyard. It was a warm evening, but it was quiet for the time of year, just a few knots of tourists were taking pictures.

Having reconciled herself to the scheme, she was determined to have a blast. It was Thursday night after all, practically the weekend. She'd been working hard on an article that would put the cat among the pigeons in the economic world and she felt like celebrating. So what if the guy she was meeting was a thumping bore; there'd be other people out for a good time. You never know, the guy might even be all right. She lifted her chin, squared her shoulders and put a bit of sway in her hips as she walked up the steps towards the Terrace bar. She didn't notice the slight man with almost black eyes and a stub of an ear ghost in behind her.

There was quite a crowd in the place, plenty of laughter and loud voices. Perhaps the loudest was the one that bellowed at her as she approached the bar. "Hi, you *must* be Penelope. Robert's description fits you perfectly. Smythe-Hilliard. Nicholas to you, of course. I'm having a Pimms. Bit early in the season I know but there we are. What can I get you?"

Nathalie almost turned on her heel. The man oozed entitlement and self-importance and she knew he wasn't going to be all right. She'd read somewhere that it took about seven seconds to size someone up. With this bloke, it took Nathalie about two. He was tall, slightly rotund, with thin brown hair greying at the temples. Had the sort of face that would look good with a fist buried in it. He wore a salmon shirt with a pale sweater draped over his shoulders and loosely tied at the collar. If this was the sort of man that her father thought would suit her sister, then she worried about his mental health. But the old fella had always been terribly impressed by money.

"Erm, hello," she managed. Remember, you're doing this for Penelope, she told herself. Woman up. "Yes, I'm Penelope. I'll have a glass of Sauvignon blanc, please."

He grinned and Nathalie quailed as he took her hand and guided her to the bar. A waiter took her coat, but she kept hold of her handbag. It had pepper spray in it. The man was openly ogling her. She looked away, desperate to be somewhere else. Then he was waving a pudgy hand at the bar staff.

"Yes, yes over here," he shouted. "A large glass of your finest Sauvignon blanc." He smiled at Nathalie as though he'd clinched a deal. Just when she thought things couldn't get more dreadful, the man pressed up to her and put his hand on her bottom. That was it.

"What on *earth* do you think you're *doing*?" she bawled, reaching behind her and pulling the man's arm away.

"Now, hang on a minute," he began, pawing at her, before Nathalie cut him off.

"Don't you DARE touch me," she shouted. The boisterous conversation in the bar around them quieted and people began to watch.

"I was just..." he wailed before he was interrupted, this time by a dark-haired man coming between them, laying a hand firmly on Smythe-Hilliard's chest, pushing him back.

"I think you heard the lady," he said coolly. His voice was rich and had the lightest Scots accent. He was dressed in full evening attire but moved in it like a panther. He kept his palm on the other's chest as his pale-brown eyes bore into Smythe-Hilliard, daring him to reply. When all he did was open and close his mouth a few times, the stranger turned his head and said calmly to Nathalie, "Pardon me. Would you like this man to leave?"

Nathalie was trying to regain her earlier composure. It was shaken by the feeling of the awful man's hands on her but also by the savage allure of her would-be saviour. The crowd in the bar watched closely.

"Yes," she said huskily, "I think that would be a very good idea."

The stranger nodded once and turned back to Smythe-Hilliard. "Enjoy the rest of your evening, *elsewhere*, and I'll try to convince the lady not to press charges," he said menacingly.

Something about the man's assured movement, coupled with the look in his eyes, persuaded Smythe-Hilliard that this wasn't a battle he was likely to win. He drew himself together and brushed the cuffs of his shirt. The people in the bar nearby were giving him harsh looks.

"Yes, well," he huffed, "I must say the calibre of the people they allow in this place has deteriorated markedly." He got his coat, shrugged it on, emanating rage, and left to a smattering of applause. The noise level rose again as excited conversations about the incident broke out.

Nathalie was struggling with a range of emotions. Anger towards the departing creep; gratitude towards the man with the smouldering eyes; and a mixture of trepidation and downright hotness for the encounter she was about to have.

The man was regarding her with a quizzical look. "Interesting company you keep," he said in an even tone, indicating the door with his head.

Nathalie smiled nervously. "Well, I didn't keep it, thanks to you."

"Don't mention it," the man murmured, turning to the bar. "Enjoy your evening."

A pang of loss struck Nathalie's stomach. "Please," she almost wailed, a hand on his forearm, "don't leave."

A smiling barman approached with Nathalie's wine. "Thanks for getting rid of that, um, person. That's on the house, madam, as well as yours, sir. What can I get for you?"

The stranger paused, looked at the girl's hand on his arm and thought for a moment. He came to a decision and nodded at Nathalie. "What she's having looks good, thank you."

Nathalie took a big gulp of wine, put her glass on the bar and let out a long breath. "What are you," she said, smiling shyly, "some kind of knight in shining armour?"

He looked thoughtful for a moment, then broke into a rakish smile. Nathalie stilled.

"I'm afraid not. It was just my turn to get the drinks." He paused and thanked the barman who'd brought his glass. "I'm sure you could have handled that man, but I was interested to meet you." He answered her inquisitive look with a more tentative smile. "My name's Duncan McLeod, but most people call me Mac."

He raised his glass to Nathalie, a glint in his eye. The horrible incident over, she was suddenly very pleased that she'd agreed to come this evening. She raised her own glass and said coyly, "Pleased to meet you, Mac. I'm Nathalie Lane, but you can call me Nat."

Twenty-Five

Thursday evening, 14th May

Kurjac had witnessed the episode from his place at the bar a few seats away. He checked the photograph on his phone. Maybe her make-up was different. This new guy was an unwelcome complication. There was something about him that made Kurjac uneasy. Because it was something he recognised in himself. The more he thought about the new dynamic, the more he realised it was going to be at least a two-man job. His men were all close and on call. He thought for a moment about their qualities, stepped out of the bar and called Karel.

Nathalie finished a quick text to Penelope with: <I owe you a HUUUUGE favour!>

"Who was he anyway?" The effects of the alcohol were loosening up McLeod. He wasn't much of a drinker anymore, and this was his second glass of wine on top of the couple of pints of beer he'd had earlier.

He was sitting at a table in the corner of the bar, bowtie loosened, gazing intently at Nathalie. The function he was supposed to be at completely forgotten.

She twirled her glass by the stem, embarrassed suddenly. "That's a bit of a long boring story. Can we just say that he was a mistake?" On an impulse, she reached out and covered McLeod's hand with her own. She held her breath until McLeod smiled.

"I think I can live with that," he replied and took her hand in both of his. She was surprised by the muscle definition in his long fingers.

"Crikey, d'you work out a lot?" was out of her mouth before she could think about it.

McLeod grinned and the gleam in his eye disarmed Nathalie again. "Something similar I suppose," he replied. "I do martial arts a few times a week."

Nathalie's phone pinged. "Hang on a sec," she said, taking back her hand. She looked at the message and smiled. <NOT SMYTHE WHAT'S HIS FACE?!?!> Her smile widened and she hit reply.

"So I s'pose you'd have karate-chopped that moron if he hadn't left?" She made the motion with the hand that wasn't holding her phone and giggled. McLeod looked stunned for a second and Nathalie raised thick eyebrows.

"That's a lovely sound," he said wistfully. He cleared his throat. "It was never going to come to violence anyway."

Nathalie took a thoughtful sip while texting Penelope back: <Of course not. He was hideous. This guy, Mac, saved me from him. He is AAAAHHH!!> She pressed send and said, "You always so sure of yourself?"

McLeod shook his head and Nathalie liked the way his tousled hair bounced. "Not so much sure of myself as sure of certain human characteristics. That guy was so fond of himself, the slightest possibility of any harm coming to him was too great a consequence to ever consider." He took her hand again.

The faint callouses and deep lines on her palms intrigued him. "Guy like that, he'd want the odds heavily stacked in his favour."

"That's very insightful," Nathalie said. "Are you a quack or something?"

McLeod uttered a hollow laugh. "As of five o'clock today, I'm not much of anything, I'm afraid. Listen, would you like to get something to eat? This wine's starting to go to my head."

Nathalie looked around nervously for a moment. "Yes, I'm starving. I just need to pop out for a couple of minutes, is that all right?"

"Okay," said McLeod, standing. "I'll go and use the facilities."

Kurjac watched in wonder, in the mirror behind the bar, as the very scenario he was struggling to engineer with his man, Karel, transpired before his eyes. Both parties had departed, but were going to return to their half-finished drinks. Endgame, right there. Sometimes, the harder you tried, the luckier you got.

He sent Karel back to his surveillance position and took off his leather jacket. Underneath, he was wearing a generic London waiter's uniform. Black tie, white shirt, black trousers. He grabbed a bar towel and sauntered over to the table. London waiters rarely rushed. He took a glass vial from his pocket. As he was wiping the table, he deposited most of the contents of the vial into the woman's glass and the remainder in the man's. One dead, one in a very bad way. He returned to his seat at the bar to see it done.

Outside, on the steps to the elegantly lit courtyard, Nathalie's phone buzzed again. <Is that the noise you'll be making later? Am I an idiot?>.

She took a thoughtful drag and wondered if things with Mac would get that far. She realised that she hoped they would and flushed. He really was spectacular. She smiled to herself and felt the giddy rush that accompanies burgeoning lust. She replied to Penelope's text: <You're not an idiot but I will be if I'm *not* making that noise later! This is the best favour I've ever done, thank you. Please leave me alone. I have to be captivating>.

From nowhere, rain suddenly cascaded from the heavens. She got a piece of gum from her bag and headed back to the unknown with a fluttering heart.

In the men's room, McLeod was zipping up when he heard a 'Hey' from behind to his left. Human nature compelled him to turn towards the source of the sound. He briefly saw a round red object growing bigger. He flinched his head back, then he was sprawling, head and shoulders against the wall above the urinals. Pain ripped through his left jaw. Instinctively, he turned and raised his arms in front of his head. The next heavy blow dashed against his left forearm, but he was able to get a hand on the object. Opening his eyes, he saw it was a fire extinguisher. He pulled it hard to his left, the motion exposing his heavy assailant's right shoulder. Driving off the wall, McLeod aimed a precise, hard punch at it with his right fist. His attacker cried out in shock as his right side went slack. The fire extinguisher clattered to the floor, followed quickly by the guy as McLeod hooked his right leg away with his own left.

McLeod breathed hard and rubbed his singing jaw, relieved it was mostly intact. Might lose a tooth or two. He felt his left forearm carefully. There was going to be a mighty bruise but nothing broken. He looked down at the keening figure, inert on the chequered floor. It was the creep who'd been harassing Nathalie. Smythe something or other. McLeod needed him out of action for a while.

"Guess it's just not your night, pal," he said and delivered a hefty size ten to the man's groin. Doubled him right up. McLeod left the men's room, massaging his chin, and made his way to the bar. He summoned the friendly barman from before.

"That guy I asked to leave earlier?" he said, rubbing his arm. "He came back. If he's not out of the gents in ten minutes, you might want to look in on him."

The barman shrugged, nodded and carried on polishing glasses.

Nathalie was standing by their table when he returned. "What the hell did you do to your face?" she asked, alarm in her voice.

"Your friend from earlier fancied himself as a fireman," McLeod replied, dabbing at a cut on his lip with some tissue.

"Eh? What do you mean? Does it hurt?" She raised a hand to his swollen cheek.

"Doesn't matter," he said. "I'm all right."

"I know something that'll make it better. Here," she said, grabbing both glasses and holding McLeod's out to him.

"To an eventful evening," he said and smiled. They clinked glasses.

"Hopefully," Nathalie said, smiling up through dark eyelashes. They drained their glasses and headed out into the building storm.

Twenty-Six

Friday morning, 15th May

The tension in the living room was relieved by the noisy return of the Constable. He carried two brown paper bags and an air of unease. As if holding a couple of unexploded bombs, he approached Wren with the bags outstretched.

"Just pop them on the table, Constable, and I could use another coffee. Mr McLeod?"

"Water's fine," he murmured. He watched the incredulity in Wren's face as the Constable handed her some change.

"Bloody King's Road," she muttered as she put a few coins into a small black purse in her handbag.

"Closest they had to camembert was brie and grape, ma'am."

"I thought that went out with the nineties," Wren replied, passing McLeod a small carton. He opened it and found that he was indeed hungry. They ate in silence for a while, the only sound coming from the Constable making coffee in the kitchen. McLeod took another bite of his stodgily bland sandwich and looked up to see Wren depositing the last of hers into her wide mouth.

She smiled and he realised he must have been staring. "I'm sorry," he said. "You must spend a lot of time at the gym?"

"None," she replied. "I sometimes go for a run if I have the time, which is very rarely." She gathered up empty cartons and put them in the bag. "You recycle these?" she asked, heading for the kitchen.

"Box under the table," he managed between chewing. He knew he didn't have long. How to tell her? McLeod got a good view of Wren's slight but agile figure as she returned carrying more coffee.

"You're keeping something from me, Mr McLeod," she said, setting down her mug, bright eyes fixed on his. McLeod couldn't hide from the image of the man's hand on the woman's bottom. Try as he could to avoid it or see beyond it, nothing more would come. If he told her this, what else might she believe him to be capable of?

"When I got to the bar, the girl, Nathalie you said, was standing there." He paused, ran agonized fingers through his hair. Wren could see him debating something in his mind.

"Well," she said, "we know you must have met somehow. What's the problem?"

He blew out the breath he'd been holding. "I'm sorry, Miss Wren. She was there with another man," he said finally and looked away, ashamed.

"I see." She thought for a second and got her phone. "How do you know?"

McLeod looked again at the image in his head. "Because his hand was all over her behind," he said disconsolately.

"Hmmnn. That would seem to be fairly conclusive." She got up and paced a while, vaping and composing a quick text. McLeod vigorously rubbed his face.

She stopped suddenly, turned to McLeod. The beginnings of a smile on her face.

"But this is good, don't you see? We have a possible motive. We know she wasn't married, but what about a jilted boyfriend? Happens all the time."

McLeod was hopeful for a second, then he thought a bit more.

"Those are almost always crimes of passion, spur of the moment jobs with blunt instruments, kitchen knives and the like. Poisoning is more, what did you say…pre-meditative."

Wren's smile broadened. "Not anymore," she said, pointing to her puffer. "You can get the stuff that goes in these things everywhere. All sorts of warnings and a skull and crossbones on the bottle."

McLeod wasn't convinced. "Surely they wouldn't allow it to be sold if it was that dangerous?"

"Plenty of other everyday things are," replied Wren. "Solvents, bleach, petrol, all lethal." She counted them out on her fingers. "Knives, guns, golf clubs, gardening tools, hell anything in the wrong hands."

McLeod had been sitting down for a long time. He stood and stretched, affording Wren another glimpse of his taut abdomen, muscles disappearing in a V to his groin. She looked away quickly and her phone vibrated once. It was the mail she wanted.

McLeod looked out of the window at the day the girl he'd gone to bed with would never see. A beautiful young woman with a full life ahead of her all sketched out. A million possible experiences torn from existence. The human cobweb everyone creates had unravelled and its strands could never be reconnected.

He leaned his head against the window pane and closed his eyes tight. Despair and guilt overwhelmed him in waves. Why couldn't he have prevented it? How could he not remember what had happened? And then, what could he do to atone in some way for his failure? Dispassionately, he withdrew from himself and the circumstances. Looked closely at each in turn and came to an irrevocable conclusion: he would do whatever it took.

Twenty-Seven

Friday morning, 15th May

Sir David received the details first. His phone buzzed during a brunch engagement at Royal Wimbledon Golf Club. He looked at the caller ID and frowned. Brian Urquhart. As far as he was aware, everything had been taken care of. Why was the head of MI5 calling him now? He rose reluctantly from his eggs and sausages and apologised to his guests for his breach of the club's etiquette. Walked over to the large windows overlooking the eighteenth hole. It was a bright spring morning. Overnight rain had left dew sparkling on the grass and a light mist wafted through the avenues of vibrant green trees.

"Good morning, Brian, how are you?" said Sir David, picking a bit of gristle from his incisors. He anticipated this was just a call to confirm the fallout was being dealt with and he could have a carefree round of golf this afternoon. The familiar voice that answered him had a worried note in its Etonian timbre.

"Been better, old chap, to tell the truth. Bit of a funny morning."

Sir David wiped his mouth with a napkin. "Really, Brian, how so?"

"Well, as you know, about nine o'clock last night, I received word that the necessary steps had been taken."

"Mmn hmn, yes."

"We were monitoring all calls from the Savoy this morning and had the clean-up personnel on standby."

Prickles rose up Sir David's back. He took a deep breath. "Go on," he said.

"No call has come from the Savoy."

"But it must have by now," Sir David said hoarsely, "it's nearly half eleven."

"I know. So about an hour ago, I started checking calls to all London emergency services. Hundreds of the bloody things. A message was received from an untraceable foreign number at around six this morning. It said that a murder had taken place at an address in Chelsea."

Sir David was struggling for breath. He opened the veranda door and went out into the fresh air. "What the fuck is this, Brian?" he barked.

"We don't know exactly, but we're beginning to build a picture."

"We? Who the hell's *we*? This needs to be tighter than a nun's snatch, man." He looked about himself nervously.

"I'm fully aware of that, David, but I can't manage it on my own. As well as the liaison girl, I have another highly dependable person briefed on certain aspects of the situation."

Sir David nodded at a couple of frowning ladies in a passing buggy. A greenkeeper trundled off on a mower towards the fairways. Chattering Jackdaws were squabbling by the practice green. Otherwise he was quite alone.

"Okay," he said, "keep it to that. How do we stand?"

"So, a local team was dispatched to investigate. Apart from a couple of officers, they've been taken off it and are being debriefed. Unfortunately, because the call originated abroad, SO15 was also notified."

Sir David passed a shaky hand over his forehead. "Sweet Jesus, Brian, we can't do much there."

"Ordinarily no, but that's the one bit of good news. I'm quite friendly with the Commander. Put a word in for him for his post. He ought to be open to any suggestions we might have."

"That's good." Sir David thought for a second. "Does the press have it yet?"

"Not that we're aware of. No request for information from the public has been issued by the lead investigator. But she has requisitioned CCTV footage from the Terrace bar at Somerset House."

"She?"

"I know. Quite a maverick by all accounts. Detective Inspector Rosanna Wren. One of the best they've got, I'm afraid."

"Shit," said Sir David, kicking a stone on the path. "Can we stop her getting the footage?"

"'Fraid not. GCHQ says it went to her phone direct in an e-mail. Copy to her boss at SO15."

"Bollocks." He thought some more and realised something was wrong with the picture. "Hang on, Brian. How the bloody hell has the Lane woman ended up in Chelsea?"

"You've got to ask a question even more basic than that, I'm afraid, David. And that's the really bad news."

A cold fear gripped Sir David's heart. "You don't mean… It's not her…is it?"

"The deceased is listed as Nathalie Lane."

Twenty-Eight

Friday morning, 15th May

McLeod came back into the living room, showered and changed into an old pair of loose jeans, pale-blue shirt and dark-red pullover. His hair was still damp and the whole look distracted Wren from her phone conversation.

"Um, sorry," she recovered. "I'll be there shortly. I just have a couple more things to sort out here first, okay? … Yes, I'm positive… Right, I'll tell them now… Yes, bye."

She watched from her place by the mantelpiece as McLeod crossed the room like a cat and took his seat on the leather sofa. She smiled and said, "I've got something interesting to show you, Mr McLeod. Do you mind if I come and sit next to you?"

McLeod grinned at her choice of words. "By all means, Inspector," he murmured. He was surprised when she didn't come over but went instead to the armed officer. He didn't catch what was said, but the officer swiftly left the room. Wren was walking back towards him, then he heard his front door shut.

"I've convinced my boss you're our only witness," she said, bumping hips with McLeod as she sat. "Do you think we could knock off this Mr and Mrs lark? My friends call me Anna." This close to him, she could see the dark stubble on his angular jaw.

"Nice to meet you, Anna. I'm Mac to the few I have."

Wren looked at him inquisitively. "I've only known you for a few hours. You seem like decent friend material to me."

McLeod looked down. "Catherine was always the sociable one. I have three or four good friends. Don't really need any more." He looked at Wren tentatively.

She wallowed in his intense brown eyes for a second, then nodded. "I understand, Mac." She unlocked her phone. "Take a look at this. It's footage from Somerset House last night. From different cameras in and around the building."

Wren tapped a thumbnail and it expanded into a wide-angle view of a vast cobbled courtyard. The remains of the evening sun flared the buildings on the right of the image. A couple of groups of people were visible in the shadows to the left, taking photos, looking up. A dark-haired woman in a coat and heels approached slowly. She stopped and drooped her head. She looked like she was taking deep breaths. Then she lifted her head high and walked purposefully towards the building's entrance. McLeod recognised her and winced. "She was so beautiful," he said quietly.

"I know, Mac," said Wren.

As the woman disappeared from view, a slight, dark-haired man in a black jacket and trousers broke from a nearby group of people and hurried to the entrance with a hand cupped to his forehead, hiding his features.

McLeod shot a look at Wren. "The next sequence is from a camera behind the bar," she said.

There must have been fifty people in the shot. McLeod strained to make anything out. "I can't recognise anyone," he said.

"Wait a second." Wren used a finger and thumb to zoom in on an area in front of the bar. It centred on the back of a large man with a pale jumper hanging from his shoulders, arms outstretched, glass in hand. The woman from before came into the frame. It was a bit blurry, but she seemed to be smiling uncertainly. Then they were both facing the camera leaning against the bar. The man had put his drink down and had his arm aloft. Seemed to be shouting. The woman put a hand over her eyes. McLeod saw himself come into the frame some ten feet behind the couple at the bar. The large man moved closer to the woman and his arm went down. The woman suddenly reached behind her and reeled away from him, a look of horror on her face. She seemed to be shouting.

Wren paused the action. "Still think you did something wrong?" she asked, eyebrow arched. McLeod looked at her nonplussed.

"The next bit'll make you feel better," Wren said.

She hit play and McLeod saw the man put his hands on the woman's shoulders. Then he watched in amazement as he saw himself come quickly between them, his right arm thrusting the bigger man away, holding him by his shirt at chest height. Saying something. Then he was turning to the woman and she was replying and nodding. Bystanders were staring, mouths open. A barman's head and shoulders came into view. Then the big man was straightening up, talking. Then he took a pale trench coat from the barstool and stomped off out of the frame.

McLeod felt disembodied as he watched himself and the young woman chatting and drinking wine at the bar. There was no mistaking the chemistry between them. Then the sequence stopped.

"Quite revealing, wouldn't you say?" Wren slapped McLeod's thigh. "Who said chivalry was dead?"

McLeod was struggling to process what he'd seen. Why couldn't he remember any of this? "Is there any more?" he asked.

"You don't recall any of that?"

"I told you. The last memory I have is of that man in the video's hand on Nathalie's bottom."

Wren looked at him pensively for a moment. "The next bit explains your swollen jaw and cuts. It's from a camera in the men's room." She tapped another thumbnail. The image that came up was grainier and in black and white.

Bathroom only needed a cheap camera, McLeod figured. A dark shape on the left was just about discernible as a man presumably doing his business at the urinal. Another figure wearing a long pale coat came into view in the lower part of the screen. He seemed to be holding something in his right hand, supporting it with his left. He moved quickly towards the other man and seemed to thrust the thing he was carrying at the man's head. McLeod watched himself sprawl against the wall. Then he saw himself turn to his assailant, arms across his face. There was a blur of limbs and the man with the coat was dropping something, then falling. McLeod watched himself lean over the man on the floor briefly, then deliver a kick to his middle. Then he was walking toward the camera, hand on his jaw and the playback stopped.

"We're fairly certain it was the big guy from the first video. We figure he was pissed off, came back for revenge. The thing he hit you with was probably a fire extinguisher." She paused and looked away suddenly, feeling a little shy. "Do you want to tell me about those moves, Mac?" She turned to face him, a trace of awe in her eyes. "I mean, he was a big guy, with a fucking fire extinguisher."

McLeod was processing the sequence of events from the two videos. He leaned against the sofa back, closed his eyes and let out the breath he'd been holding. "I do judo and taekwondo," he said simply. He risked a glance at her. She was looking at him expectantly, not quite drumming her fingers.

"That wasn't on your file," she said.

"I took it up when I was no longer able to compete as an athlete."

Wren looked at him with an 'I wasn't born yesterday' expression.

"I tend to pick things up quite quickly," he said vaguely.

Wren gave him a stern look. "My boss is an advanced self-defence instructor for the Met, Mac. One of the best in the country. Said those moves were about as good as he's ever seen. He reckoned he could have done what you did. One time out of ten."

"So I guess I was lucky," McLeod countered.

She was still looking at him dubiously.

"Okay," he said, standing, facing Wren. "I don't remember what I did obviously, but it looked like I hit his shoulder, right?"

"Looks that way," she said, taking the opportunity to get her puffer out.

"So a little knowledge of human physiology goes a long way." He put a finger to his right shoulder. "The brachial plexus in here is the hub of loads of other nerves. You strike it with enough force, you can pretty much shut down that side of someone's upper body. The shock is fairly intense. I guess that's what I aimed at and got lucky."

Wren searched his eyes, looking for any sign of deceit, and saw none. "Well, whatever," she said finally, "the guy had it coming."

McLeod was thinking.

Wren put her head on the side. "What is it?" she asked.

"You know," he said introspectively, "I've never been attacked like that before. Sure I've had a lot of practice bouts in the gym, but that's completely different. Until you're actually placed in a situation like that, you don't know what you're capable of." He looked at his hands, looked at Wren.

She nodded her understanding. "You always wonder whether you'd have the ability to do something like that when it mattered," she mused quietly. "I guess now you know you do."

McLeod sighed. "None of this helps us with finding out what happened to Nathalie, does it?"

A tentative smile touched the corners of Wren's lips. "Sit back down. That was just the curtain-raiser."

McLeod joined her again on the sofa and he saw that her eyes were filled with animation. Like a terrier on a scent, she swiped to find the right thumbnail. Hit it and pressed play. "Time's the important factor here," she said.

It was the same camera angle as before from behind the bar. It wasn't as busy. "See at the bottom right," said Wren. "Eight thirty-eight. Lots of folk will have gone off to dinner." She paused and pointed to the left of the screen. "That guy is the one who followed Nathalie into the bar. The bigger one next to him arrived a minute previously."

It was quite dark on the edge of the camera's field of view, but McLeod could make out a man with sharp dark features, looking away from the camera to his right. The big man just stared ahead.

He saw Nathalie come into the picture from the left, walk past the bar and out the entrance. The guy on the left turned his back to the bar and watched her go, briefly showing his right profile. "See his ear?" Wren pointed.

McLeod squinted. "Doesn't look right," he said.

Then the slighter man said something to the bigger guy who followed Nathalie. The smaller one unzipped and took off what looked like a leather jacket, looked around briefly, then grabbed something from the bar and disappeared out of shot to the left.

"Check the time, Mac," Wren murmured.

"Eight forty," he replied.

Some thirty seconds went by with nothing happening, then the wiry man was back at his seat at the bar, putting on his jacket and looking to his right again. Wren moved the slider on to eight forty-three and some seconds. The man was still sitting, looking away from the camera. Nathalie came back through the entrance to the bar, walked back past it to the left and out of shot. A minute went by, then McLeod watched himself with a hand at Nathalie's back, guiding her through the bar and out. The guy in the leather jacket got out his phone and spoke into it for maybe three seconds. Then he got up without finishing his drink and left the bar. The footage ended.

McLeod looked at Wren. Excitement shone in her eyes. McLeod didn't get it. "Time was important, you said?"

Wren nodded briskly. "Nathalie was outside between eight thirty-nine and eight forty-three, yes?"

"I saw that," replied McLeod uncertainly.

"That footage from the men's room, you planting the big guy?"

McLeod got it.

"Eight forty," said Wren.

Twenty-Nine

Friday morning, 15th May

"I'm afraid he's in a meeting, Sir David." It was Jennings, Sir Francis' straight-laced private secretary. About as inventive as a dung beetle. Sir David passed a feverish napkin over his brow. The events had withered his faculties and he needed a keen mind to help steer a course through the mire.

"Well get him out of his sodding meeting, Jennings," he snarled into his mobile, all thoughts of club rules forgotten. He'd been sitting on a bench under the elegant veranda, but the approach of two middle-aged ladies, wielding trollies with huge golf bags, forced him to walk out onto the practice green.

"I'm afraid he's with the Chinese, Sir David. Highly important."

Sir David took aim at a worm-cast with a hefty brogue and made a divot in the green instead. "I don't care if he's with the bloody Queen," he shrieked. "I need him on this phone now as a matter of national importance." He could almost hear the cogs turning in Jennings' mind. He suddenly felt an overwhelming urge to pass wind. He looked about him stealthily, bent over slightly and let it go. The unmistakable warmth of a follow through pooled in his best boxer shorts. He blanched and jolted back upright.

"Er... Very well, Sir David. I'll go and see what I can do. Will you hold?"

"Yes, you by the throat if Sir Francis isn't on this line in thirty seconds," Sir David bawled, eyeing the advance of some wretched juniors. He minced gingerly back over to his spot on the veranda and sat down uncomfortably with a grimace. Then he felt something moist on the back of his thigh. Got up and saw a white splat on the bench and a corresponding stain on the back of his trouser. "Holy Jesus Christ all-fucking mighty," he yelled.

"No, it's only me, old chap," came Sir Francis' mellifluous voice in his ear. "Jennings used the words national importance. Is everything all right?"

"No, everything's not bloody all right. Everything's all bloody wrong. I've just shat myself and sat in pigeon poo."

"Hmmnn, nasty, but hardly of national importance, old chap. I've got the Chinese on the cusp of signing here," replied Sir Francis.

"Hrrrrrr, the sodding Serbians managed to get the Lane woman's sister instead of her and we weren't on top of it."

"What? How?" Sir Francis shooed Jennings out of the office.

"We don't know. And what does it matter, frankly?" Sir David sighed heavily, shifting stickily on the bench. Mrs Holmes was going to have the devil of a job.

Sir Francis swivelled in Jennings' leather office chair and cast an eye over the walls of books and dark oak panels. It smelled fusty and he thought it was high time the room had a makeover.

"Who's investigating the sister's death?"

"A local team initially, but then SO15 got involved. Some abominably proficient woman, it seems."

Sir Francis was stunned for a moment, then leaned forward in the chair, elbows on knees. "That's fucked, David. We can't go there."

"Well," said Sir David, trying to get more comfortable, "Brian says he might be able to. Knows the Commander apparently."

There was silence from the other end for a spell. Sir David pondered a shower and some fresh clothes before returning to his engagement.

"Right," said Sir Francis. "This is an unholy mess, but we need to remember what's of paramount importance here. That the Lane woman must be prevented from continuing her God-awful research. To that end, this thing ought to hold her up for a bit." He paused and his words worked like balm on Sir David.

"You've got it, old thing," he said, galvanised. "She'll be obliged to stay on in London for a few days at least. Plenty of time to arrange something else."

"We'll need Urquhart to get SO15 taken off the investigation somehow," said Sir Francis.

A troubling thought occurred to Sir David. "The press'll have a bloody field day with it, you know? Two sisters in suspicious circumstances in a matter of days?"

"What's the bloody alternative, David?"

"Yes, you're right, of course." Sir David caught a whiff of himself and knew he had to push things along. "Okay, I need to, er, get sorted here. Can you call Urquhart? Get him to pull SO15 and issue fresh instructions to the Serbians? To do it *right* this time?"

Sir Francis looked at his watch anxiously. "All right. But it'll have to be quick. Can't keep ten billion pounds of Chinese investment waiting much longer."

Thirty

Friday afternoon, 15th May

"It'd be quicker to walk, you know," said McLeod, climbing into the passenger seat of Wren's quirky car. It had the musty smell of old leather. Wren pulled out of the leafy square and into heavy traffic. Warm sunshine lit the gaudy shops and cafés on the north side of the King's Road. People walking on the busy pavements were carrying bits of discarded winter clothing.

As the lights were changing from amber to red, Wren blasted through a junction heading west. "I know I can park at the hospital and I might have to have a car later."

"Careful!" warned McLeod as a van loaded with precarious ladders broke sharply in front of them.

"All right, all right," said Wren testily. "Why am I even allowing you to come anyway?"

"Lots of reasons," said McLeod, removing his hand from the dashboard. He looked at her profile framed by the window. A blonde quiff descended to spiky tendrils over her elfin ears. A smooth, pale forehead led to a small nose turned up daintily at the end. Piercing blue eyes scanned the road and slightly protruding teeth rested on deep red lips. Delicate features that belied the steel beneath. He returned his focus to the state of the traffic.

"Nathalie's sister is going to be there and you need me as a point of reference for her," he said, relieved that the van was turning off. "Maybe Nathalie spoke to her regarding me. Then there's the possibility Nathalie told me something that's important in some way, maybe even a link to why she was killed. Who knows, my memory might get better." He paused as they made a right turn. "I'm your only witness and the person or people who did this are out there somewhere." He went quiet for a moment. "Then there are my own reasons," he murmured, waving to an Estonian builder who'd done some work on his flat.

Wren glanced at him, but he was looking out the window. "I don't think you need to be feeling any guilt over this, Mac," she said quietly "You're just as much a victim here."

Anger flared in him suddenly. "Yeah, but I'm not cold on a slab with a ticket on my big toe."

"You say that as though you'd rather it was you than Nathalie," Wren said, shooting him a look of alarm.

"Maybe I do," he said quietly. He was about to add, 'She seemed to have a lot more to live for,' but thought better of it. He had to make Wren understand or he was going to get nowhere. "Listen, Anna. I know I wasn't responsible for her death. I even realise there was probably little I could have done to prevent it. But it happened on my watch, you know?"

She heard the anguish in his tone. "I get it, Mac," she said. "I know you feel a duty to help her, but what can you do practically?"

"I don't know" he glowered. "But I know I won't be able to rest until I find out why this happened to her and who's behind it."

"That's my job, remember?"

He sat brooding for a minute. "Well, I hope you're bloody good at it," he said finally.

Wren killed the engine in the last remaining reserved space at the hospital. "Are you allowed to park here?" McLeod asked.

"That badge allows me to park this car anywhere in London," she said, indicating the windscreen. Wren checked her phone as they made their way through an avenue of parked cars to the entrance. "I don't fucking believe it!" she hissed and stopped dead, ten yards from the sliding doors.

"What's the matter?" McLeod said warily. Wren had gone pale with fury. Over her shoulder, McLeod saw a woman carrying a young child walking toward them. He put a hand on Wren's shoulder and a finger to his lips. The woman passed them and disappeared inside the building.

Wren composed herself with an angry sigh. "I sent CCTV stills from the bar of the guy in the leather jacket and his partner to MI5. They say they have nothing on either of them. Not a fucking thing." She stabbed the screen and looked as though she was about to smash it on the ground. Then she went quiet in frustration, shoulders slumped, staring at her phone like it was a snake. It dawned on McLeod how much she cared about this as well.

"I'm sorry, Mac," she said disconsolately, looking at the ground, "that was my best shot."

McLeod lifted her chin to look straight into her moist blue eyes. "No, Anna," he said with as much conviction as he could muster, "that was your first shot."

She lost herself for a moment in McLeod's searing gaze, then looked away and sighed. "Okay then. The hard way it is." She put her phone back in her handbag and took out her puffer. "Maybe the sister, Penelope, can throw some light on things. She should be waiting for us inside."

Friday afternoon, 15th May

Penelope Lane sat in lonely purgatory in a small grey windowless waiting room. Generic prints of dahlias and irises littered the walls and three-year-old copies of special interest magazines and *Reader's Digest* sat unread on a low table. The room was filled with cold, stark light from a strip on the ceiling and calm, muffled voices from other parts of the building reached her ears.

In the last hour, she'd gone through every human emotion on the scale between rage and horror. Memories came like so many right hooks to her mind. Just now, she'd recalled a silly fight she'd had with her sister over a hairbrush as eight- and ten-year-olds. They'd made up making jam sandwiches together. Each thought was like a fresh dagger twist in her aching heart, increasing the size of the hole in her core. A steady flow of racking guilt further fuelled its growth. Why had she coerced Nathalie to go to the date in her place? She'd asked herself the question a thousand times and the answer was always the same: selfishness. Whatever had happened to Nathalie was all her fault.

"Miss Lane?" She was startled from her bleak reverie by the voice of a striking petite blonde with piercing blue eyes. Following her into the small room were a doctor of some description in protective green overalls and a dark-haired man who made her breath hitch. She quickly dabbed at her puffy eyes with a handkerchief and tried to find some composure.

"Yes," she said, standing weakly, "I'm Penelope Lane."

McLeod stared at her green eyes flecked red, dark eyebrows and raven hair. Exquisite nose, prominent cheekbones and full red lips. All the features he'd seen first thing this morning, all subtly different. Numb grief gripped him afresh.

"Miss Lane, I'm Detective Inspector Wren and this is the Assistant Coroner who'll be overseeing things." She paused, trying to remember some training from years ago as Penelope nodded vaguely at them. Some anodyne method of managing bereaved relatives. Then thought, to hell with it.

"I'm sorry to be meeting you in such circumstances, Miss Lane. There's really no nice way of doing this, I'm afraid. Shall we?" Wren indicated the only door in the room with an 'after you' gesture. Penelope cast a horrified look at the door and she reared a shaky step back from it. Her mouth was working, but it produced nothing audible. Wren walked two brisk steps to Penelope and put a gentle hand on her left forearm. Penelope saw the tears welling in Wren's eyes. Then she buried her head in Wren's shoulder and let it all out.

McLeod clicked off his phone on the tenth ring. It was unlike his brother not to answer. He slumped back in his uncomfortable chair in the waiting room and stared up at the strip light, willing it to shine into the dark corners of his mind where answers might lie. But it just made his head hurt, so he sat hunched on his elbows instead. He was beginning to wonder where they were when the door opened. Where before Penelope's face was pale, now it was ashen, like she'd aged suddenly. Her eyes reminded McLeod of her sister's this morning, there was so little life in them. Wren guided her to one of the chairs opposite McLeod. "I'll go and find some tea," she said quietly. "Coffee, Mac?"

He nodded absently at her departing figure.

Penelope was staring, unseeing, her eyes having shed all the tears they had. Her brain was struggling to process what she'd just seen. She couldn't get the appalling image of the black bag that held her vibrant, beautiful, brilliant sister out of her mind. Distantly she was aware there was a man in the room. Her subconscious latched on to Wren's last words. Something meaningful in them somewhere. She delivered them to her thinking brain. McLeod saw Penelope's eyes come into focus and narrow on him. She pulled a phone swiftly from her bag and did some feverish tapping. When she looked back up at him, there was murder in her eyes.

119

Thirty-One

Friday afternoon, 15th May

Kurjac looked out over the lime-green spring leaves and garish pink cherry blossom in Battersea Park. Early lunchtime joggers were weaving between late-morning dog walkers in the warm sunshine. Swathes of purple and yellow tulips danced in the occasional breeze. Kurjac failed to be uplifted by the scene.

He knew that the land he was surveying was once a popular site for duelling. The Duke of Wellington, no less, had settled a matter of honour here in 1829. As was customary by then, both the Duke and his adversary fired high and wide. Tradition observed, honour was restored through an exchange of letters. Kurjac thought of himself as a man of honour. And the painful conversation he'd just had called that into question.

The fact that they'd killed a woman was bad enough. That it was a completely innocent woman caused Kurjac's hardened heart to be wrought with guilt. Something he'd witnessed as a boy during the conflict had given him a similar feeling. A baby crying in a camp somewhere, Potočari, was it? A Serb soldier telling the mother to make it stop. It wouldn't. The mother desperately trying to soothe her tiny child with soft murmurings and caresses to no avail. Young Kurjac willed the baby to be quiet but it continued wailing. The Serb marched over to the woman and took the baby. He slit its throat and walked off laughing.

Kurjac closed his eyes on the memory. Thought back to how his life today had all begun. The General. At the end of the war, the General saw a huge opportunity. He was effectively in a new country surrounded by several others. Brand new markets for all sorts of products and services and the most profitable of those were all illicit. He needed someone to strike the fear of God into his competitors.

Word had reached him of an audacious guerrilla fighter operating in the hills and woods around Srebrenica. So he sought out the young Kurjac and took him into his home. The General got doctors to heal his wounds and sores and nutritionists to nourish him back to full health. He had skin grafted onto his ear. He saw to his education and instructed him personally in military history and tactics. "Remember, Dragan," he'd intoned forcibly one day. "Never plan in hope."

Kurjac paid careful heed and began to forget the horror of the past few years. Then life became valuable to him once more. When the General called him into his study one day and asked him to assassinate one of the old Serbian regime, Kurjac jumped at the chance to repay the kindness he'd been shown. He would have gladly killed any of them for nothing, but the General paid him handsomely. Soon, offers for Kurjac's services from other rival factions within the former Yugoslavia started flooding in. It brought the General wealth and power. Then the Russian Mafia came calling.

"It's a huge opportunity, Dragan. These people are drowning in money."

"I have no interest in money, General." Kurjac was glowering at his benefactor across the wide mahogany table in the General's study.

"It's nothing that you haven't done before. These people are scum, Dragan. They deserve everything coming to them."

Kurjac thought of the life he'd led with his family before the war. The long hours of work and meagre food. It had been hard, but he'd been happy. "They haven't done anything to me or my people," he said.

"Neither had the Macedonians, but that didn't prevent you carrying out an assignment over there."

"That's not true," Kurjac railed. "They offered safe haven to those who killed and raped my brothers and sisters." He paused and took a deep breath, controlling his anger. It would not serve him here. Recalled the mantra he used to justify what he did. "I have no right to kill anyone who has not earned their own demise through their actions against me and my people."

The General rose and strode to the bay window. He looked north to the verdant valley, the pine woods and rolling hills for which he'd fought so hard. It wasn't enough.

"Then you leave me no choice, Dragan," he said and took a couple of steps to a walnut cabinet. Though he had always been good to him, Kurjac knew how ruthless the General could be. His senses spiked, adrenaline priming fight or flight. But it was a plain brown envelope the General came out with. He retook his seat and pushed the envelope across the table to Kurjac. "Open it," he said disdainfully.

Kurjac calmed his heart rate and cautiously took the envelope. It had no words on it and was unsealed. He parted it carefully and extracted the contents. Two photographs. The first was a weathered and crumpled Polaroid. It showed a family of four enjoying ice creams at a summer fête, eyes screwed up against the sun. Kurjac froze. That was the first time he'd ever tasted ice cream. The photograph had sat for years on a shelf above the wood burner in their tiny sitting room.

"Where did you get this?" he snarled.

The General's eyes were like slits of obsidian. "War is a complicated business, Dragan," he said with no trace of emotion.

Kurjac's mind raced and he felt his world collapsing all over again. Tears pricked his eyes. He blinked them away and instead let the ice enter his heart once more as bitter realisation took hold.

"You were one of them." Each word was a study in hatred. The General's grizzled features contorted into an uneven sneer.

"Yes, Dragan, I was." He leaned forward and looked into Kurjac's murderous eyes. "Until I found out which way the wind was blowing." He paused and Kurjac thought about the number of ways he could kill the man he had come to trust so deeply without a weapon.

"NATO airstrikes were starting to cripple us. There was only one possible outcome."

"So like a coward, you swapped sides," Kurjac spat.

The General's sneer disappeared, replaced by a look of cold disgust. "It wasn't to my liking becoming one of your kind. But it was easy at least." His voice took on a matter-of-fact air. "I summoned the men in my unit and gunned them down. Took the uniform from a dead Bosnian major nearby and waited for the UN troops." He grinned. "They gave me a medal."

Kurjac put his hands on the desk and prepared to vault it. "STOP, DRAGAN," the General shouted. "Look at the other photograph."

Kurjac stilled at the words and he was gripped by a cold fear. He looked ominously from the blank back of the second photograph to the General. A nine millimetre had appeared in his right hand. "This is in case the photograph doesn't have the effect I hope it will," the General jeered.

Kurjac's fear turned to awful resignation as, with a shaky hand, he flipped the second photograph. It showed a young woman, maybe sixteen or seventeen. Years had passed since he'd last seen her, but he would never forget those eyes. He retched. She was tied naked to a wooden chair in a dark room with just a table and bare bulb in a wire cage. She had a deathly pallor and her sunken eyes were filled with terror. Kurjac looked closer and saw small round scars, some pale and some dark, all over her torso. There was a preponderance of them on her breasts.

"The spoils of war, Dragan. I burn her if she fails to please me. You should hear the screams."

Kurjac closed his eyes, but the image of his beloved scarred sister was seared onto his retina. In blind fury, he leapt with out-stretched arms across the table. The General had been a fearsome soldier and his reactions were still fast. He stood with a backwards step, then delivered a vicious blow with the gun to Kurjac's left ear.

"And I'll burn her even more if you fail to please me," were the last hissed words Kurjac heard before he passed out.

Thirty-Two

"You," Penelope hissed. Her anger brought colour back to her face. "You're Mac." It was a condemnation.

"I am," he replied quietly. He'd been half-expecting this situation. He was worried about how it might pan out and hoped Wren wouldn't be gone too long. "Miss Lane, I don't have the words to say how sorry I am about your sister." He paused, agonising over how to proceed. "I don't know how or why it happened, but I woke up this morning next to Nathalie's body."

"How dare you say her name," Penelope fumed. She jabbed a slender finger at him. "I know how and why: you killed her!"

"No, he didn't," said Wren, breezing into the room from the hallway. She handed Penelope a steaming mug of tea and put a reassuring hand on her shoulder. She looked into Penelope's impassioned eyes. "We can't be sure of much in this case, Miss Lane, but of one thing I'm certain." She paused and let her words sink in. With searing conviction, she continued, "Mr McLeod had nothing to do with Nathalie's death. In my opinion, he's lucky he didn't share her fate."

Penelope eyed Wren dubiously. "Really? Well, how do you explain this?" She held up her phone angrily. Wren put down a mug in front of McLeod and took the phone from Penelope. She read a couple of messages and shot a worried glance at McLeod. He replied with a questioning look.

"Do you mind if I show this to Mr McLeod, Miss Lane? You see he has no memory of last night beyond about seven thirty. These may help him to remember, which might help me find answers to your sister's death."

Penelope cast a glance at McLeod. Saw the earnest expression on his alarmingly handsome face. She understood

Nathalie's attraction at least. She sighed and said, "Okay. I would certainly be fascinated by an explanation."

McLeod took the phone from Wren like it was a priceless antique and looked at the screen. There were a series of boxes of varying size in two shades of blue filled with writing. He quickly worked out that it was an ongoing, punctuated conversation between Penelope and her sister. He'd seen enough of people using modern phones to know that you had to swipe down to see previous messages and up to see the most recent. The message in the middle of the screen alluded to noises Nathalie hoped to be making later in the evening. He blinked a couple of times and looked at Wren.

"Seems like you made quite an impression, Mac," she said, sitting in an adjacent chair.

He scrolled down to the next message which was in a darker box, so from Penelope. It was sent at twenty minutes past nine.

<I'm bored. What's hot pants like? How's he treating you? How much trouble am I in with Dad? Take care, Pen.>

The answering message from Nathalie was sent three minutes later.

<Hey, I always take care. You're in no trouble with Dad. I think that Smythe freak attacked Mac in the gents. Won't talk about it. He'd cringe to hear you call him hot pants. I can't describe him. He's other. Our food's come. Feeling woozy, need to eat. Luv Nat.>

"Looks like the poison was starting to work. Roughly forty minutes after you left the Terrace bar." Wren looked thoughtful for a moment. "Sounds about right."

With a weird sense of déjà vu, McLeod scrolled to the next message from Penelope.

<OTHER? What the hell does that mean? Dish it, Lane.>

Nathalie's reply was sent at nine thirty-one.

<Not felling great Mac takinf me home hop he hasn druuged me ha luv nay>

McLeod had to reread the message a couple of times to work it out. A feeling of abhorrence overcame him. He was reading the words of a dying young woman and it felt sacrilegious.

"I'm sorry, Anna," he said, handing the phone back to Wren. "I can't read any more."

"That's all right, Mac. There is no more from Nathalie, just a message from Miss Lane to give her a call."

McLeod stood up quickly and walked to the water cooler in the corner of the room. He couldn't bear to be where he'd read the beautiful girl's last words. He filled a cone with water several times.

"You still don't think he had anything to do with it?" Penelope's voice cut harshly through the silence.

"No, Miss Lane, I don't." Wren's tone was imbued with authority. "Your sister was drugged all right, but not by Mr McLeod. The same poison was present in his blood but in a much lower quantity." Her phone started ringing. She checked the screen, hesitated and shut it off. "The most decisive factor in Nathalie's tragic end, Miss Lane, is that we were tipped off as to her whereabouts by a call from outside the UK."

"What?" Penelope's eyes grew in disbelief. "I don't..." she began and put a hand over her mouth, thinking. "How is that even possible?" she said finally.

McLeod was feeling equally stunned. "You could have mentioned that earlier, Anna," he said perturbed.

She looked at him and nodded. "I know, I'm sorry, Mac. I had good reasons." She paused and addressed Penelope again. "I'm afraid we don't know why, Miss Lane. I was hoping something might occur to you."

"To me?" Penelope asked incredulously. She looked away and saw McLeod looking hopefully at her. She suddenly felt horribly ashamed. "Um, I'm sorry for earlier, Mr McLeod. I hope you can see how it looked from my point of view?"

McLeod waved a hand. "Don't give it a thought, Miss Lane." Something occurred to him. "It seems Nathalie was able to call me Mac. I'd be pleased if you would too."

She was almost undone by the look on McLeod's face. Earnest, humble and brooding in equal measure. Other, she thought. Maybe Nathalie was onto something. She tried a small smile. "In that case, Mac, I'm Pen."

Wren's phone pinged. She looked at it briefly and stood. "I have to make a call, Miss Lane. Can I leave you in Mac's capable hands for a minute?"

Penelope nodded and cast a wary look at McLeod as Wren walked off down the hallway. "So you don't remember meeting my sister, Mac?" she asked, pain etched on her forehead.

McLeod retook his seat opposite Penelope and swigged some coffee. "I remember very little of last night. Miss Wren showed me some CCTV footage taken in the bar where we apparently met. It was like watching an actor playing me."

"I see," she said. "Then, forgive me, but I don't quite understand why you're here."

McLeod felt the room's grey walls close in around himself and Penelope as he pondered a response. He flashed back to the banalities he was served up in the wake of Catherine's death. All the well-meaning phrases that don't mean anything to someone in the throes of loss. He needed to try to give Penelope something to hold on to, something positive to start the process of moving forward. He looked into her dark-green eyes.

"There was a point in the video from the bar last night when I was looking at Nathalie." He paused for a moment, derailed suddenly by the force of his emotion. He coughed and continued uncertainly. "She was giggling and the look I saw on my face is one I've only seen in old photographs of me and my wife." He looked away with a hand over his mouth.

"I beg your pardon," said Penelope aghast, "you're married?"

McLeod returned his hooded gaze to her. "I was. My wife died a year ago."

Shit it, thought Penelope, not again. "Oh...I'm sorry, Mac," she murmured.

McLeod sighed. "So am I, Pen." He looked away. "She filled my life with joy and wonder. I haven't experienced either since she died. But those emotions were all over my face when I was with your sister in the bar last night."

Penelope winced, screwed up her eyes and put a hand to her mouth. Dry sobbed a few times before taking a deep, alleviating breath. "Thanks, Mac," she said sincerely. "That's how she made most people feel."

McLeod nodded and fixed Penelope with his warm brown eyes. "That's why I'm here, Pen. I failed your sister last night. Miss Wren won't have it. But there must have been some point when it was clear Nathalie needed a hospital."

"I don't think you can be that hard on yourself, Mac. Who's to say what condition you were in. Didn't the Inspector say you were poisoned as well?"

Mac thumped his thigh. "I just wish something would come back," he blared. The sound of muffled footsteps made them both look to the hallway. An apparition emerged through the entrance. It had DI Wren's body, but it was as though the life-force had been sucked from it. Her normally bright blue eyes were unseeing and the rest of her body looked like it was bearing a great weight.

McLeod rose and walked to her, and put gentle hands on her shoulders. "Anna, what's wrong?" he said.

Wren buried her head in his chest. "I think I've put you in terrible danger, Mac," she sobbed.

Thirty-Three

Friday afternoon

A distinctive mixture of smoke and perfume accompanied Wren into the driver's seat of the Stag. She took her phone from her bag which she chucked between McLeod's legs in the passenger floor well. She sucked hard on a mint imperial, thinking feverishly. The car was parked, rear in, under the boughs of a bright green beech tree. It gave a good view of the rest of the car park and the people walking to and from the hospital entrance.

"Don't you think you're reading too much into this, Anna?" McLeod was turned toward her in his seat, looking for anything in her face. She dashed a palm on the steering wheel.

"I wish to hell I was," she replied mournfully.

"Just because they've put local police back in charge doesn't mean we're in mortal danger."

Wren heaved a weary sigh. She had too much else to think about without worrying over how much to divulge. "After I got off the call with my boss, I knew that everything about this...whatever it is, was wrong. Normally he'd say, I don't know, 'I've got something more important for you to work on, Anna.' Just now, the words he used were, 'You're being taken off the case.' You see the distinction?"

"That's just semantics, surely," McLeod replied.

"It didn't feel like that, Mac. I know my boss. It felt like he was warning me." Wren was looking intently at the faces of hospital visitors. Satisfied for the moment, she brought her phone to life. "I wanted to have another look at the footage of that guy at the bar last night. See if I could get a better still off it." She held her phone screen to him. "It's gone, Mac. It's all gone."

He was looking at a list of e-mails with subjects and dates. The most recent was from yesterday, the fourteenth of May.

"Not just my e-mails, Mac. All the attachments I saved in different apps, like the stuff about you. The bits I had on Nathalie." She paused and looked at the road out of the car park. "All my call history and text messages from today have been erased as well."

There was silence in the car for a moment until Penelope said from the back seat, "I don't understand. How can anyone other than you have done that?"

McLeod suddenly fathomed Wren's fear and he too started scanning people's movements around the car.

"GCHQ in Cheltenham, Miss Lane. Probably via MI5. They can root about in your personal information like a rampant badger. Which means whatever this shit is has just gone national." Wren put the key in the ignition. "I don't know what your sister was into, Miss Lane, but it had her own government against her."

Wren gunned the throaty V8 engine. "I need to get you both somewhere safe until I find out what this thing is," she said, winding down her window and accelerating hard towards the hospital exit. She threw her phone into some shrubbery, headed west out of the exit and then took a right onto a quieter street. "Chuck your phone out the window, please, Miss Lane. Doesn't matter where."

"What? But I've got people I need to speak to, Miss Wren. My sister's dead...my father doesn't know yet... There must be a hundred things I need to organise..."

"There's nothing you can do for your sister now, Penelope," Wren snapped, checking the rear-view mirror. "I'm sorry, but that's a cold fact. You've got to think about yourself from now on. Please get rid of your phone."

Penelope copied a couple of numbers hurriedly on the back of an envelope before throwing the phone into someone's basement flat entrance.

"Thanks, Penelope. Better you didn't have yours either, Mac. I know it doesn't have GPS, but they can still triangulate your calls." In the mirror, she saw a matte black Mercedes, tinted windows, two cars back.

McLeod didn't need to write any numbers down. He still rang the few he used from memory. "What about this car, Anna?" he said, dropping his phone out the window.

"It doesn't have GPS and they won't be looking for it unless I fail to report to my station within the next twenty minutes." Wren slowed the Stag as she approached the next junction.

"Where are we going?" asked Penelope.

The light ahead was changing from green to amber. "I don't know, but hold onto something quick."

Wren dropped the gear, floored the accelerator and the Stag tore through the red light. A black cab must have taken off early from the left as they were headed straight for it. Wren looked at its cabin. Knew the driver wouldn't see her and threw the wheel hard left. The right-wing mirror smashed on the back of the cab. She pulled the handbrake then accelerated hard. Just missed the pavement and made the entrance to the road north. Wren kept the hammer on to the next junction and screeched a left. She crossed two more junctions with the traffic and turned left again, heading back south on a residential street. Three quarters of the way down, Wren mashed the brakes and parked up on the opposite curb, facing north, then let out the breath she'd been holding.

"What the hell was that in aid of?" Penelope shrieked from the back. "I'd feel safer going to the police."

"I am the police, Penelope, and right now, I'm the only officer you can trust." She got out of the Stag and scanned the street behind them before ducking her head back in. "Okay, grab my bag, Mac. We've got to move fast."

Thirty-Four

Friday afternoon

Kurjac cursed as he clicked off the call with Bartek. The imbeciles had lost the targets in Fulham. The torn photograph from another life shook in his hands as he contemplated his next move. He traced his little sister's smiling face and his vision misted. The smile forced onto his father's face couldn't mask the strain in his dark eyes. It was the look on his mother's face that always wracked his body with shame. Her mouth was a thin, unsmiling line set in a taught, square jaw. Her eyes were narrowed against the sun, accentuating the feeling that they bored into his soul. That they knew all his secrets. That they didn't think he was doing enough to protect his sister.

He'd tried to find her once. The General allowed him to speak with her on the phone each time he completed a job successfully. It was the only payment he got anymore. It was awkward speaking to her and more than anything in the world, he longed to see her, to hold her. She had become his only reason for living. Ten years into his bondage, and after a particularly challenging assignment, the General finally relented to his repeated requests. Blindfolded, handcuffed and accompanied by three of the General's best men, he was driven at night in the back of an old Land Rover. Kurjac tried to keep a mental picture of where they were going, but sitting with his arms behind him made concentration on anything other than relative comfort impossible. He reckoned they'd been driving for about half an hour when the vehicle slowed and rumbled over a cattle grid. Then they were on a rough farm track for a while before coming to a halt.

Kurjac's hearing and smell were heightened by his lack of vision. He could smell goats and could hear the distant rumble of a goods train and he knew exactly where he was. He heard the same sound from the prison that was his bedroom. At night, he often held the bars across his window and watched the lights from the train's carriages as they blinked between the trees in far off woods. Lots of people going somewhere. He wished he could take his sister on the train far, far away.

They were at the tiny farm beyond the southern edge of the General's compound. It was rented by a middle-aged couple with two young children. They must have driven in an elaborate circle.

Rough hands grabbed his right shoulder and pulled him from the vehicle. Then more hands were on his left shoulder and the unmistakable feel of a gun barrel was at the small of his back. He moved his head slowly left and right, trying to find the source of the goat smell, but it was all invasive. He was being turned to his left. If they'd stopped outside the farmhouse to go there, he would have expected to be going straight on. Therefore, they were going to one of the outbuildings. The evocative smell of straw grew stronger, and then they stopped walking. The gun left his back and he heard the jangle of a bunch of keys. Then loud knocking on hard wood.

"Lejla, take your position." It was the gruff voice of Goran, the General's chief enforcer. Then Kurjac heard his sister's voice.

"It is done," he heard her say, faintly. Kurjac was trembling with anticipation. He was really going to see her. He'd believed her to be dead for years. Knew that she'd been held captive and tortured for the last four. Butterflies filled his stomach as he thought about what to say. Then he heard a sharp crack and an ascending creek as the door to the barn was opened. He was bundled forward onto hard stone flags. Something he hadn't smelled since he was thirteen punctuated the strong straw and its familiarity made him gasp.

"Lejla," he cried as his blindfold was removed. Although the light in the barn was scant, he flinched and screwed up his eyes against it. He looked over to a dark corner of the room and squinted. Saw an old mattress on the stone floor. A dog-eared copy of a woman's magazine lay open on the worn blanket. As his eyes became accustomed to the light, he moved their focus slowly to the centre of the room and froze. The barest trace of his beautiful sister was apparent in the figure sitting before him on a small wooden chair. Her tear-strewn eyes were filled with pain. Her cheeks were hollow and lines creased her eyes and forehead.

Her dark hair was lank and matted. She was wearing a long grey pinafore. It couldn't conceal her huge belly.

"Is it really you, Dragon?" she quivered.

"Yes, I'm here, Lejla," he managed, fighting back tears. The rage that fuelled his existence and helped him deal with difficulties had abandoned him. Hope crept into his heart. "Please take off these handcuffs," he said quietly.

"The General made it clear…" Goran began.

"What, you're AFRAID OF ME?" Kurjac yelled. "With your three canons on me?"

He turned and looked at Goran imploringly. "I need to hold my sister, Goran, please."

The General's henchman was torn for a minute before machismo won out. "I don't need a gun to bring down filth like you," he spat.

Kurjac felt his arms pulled back harshly. Then a gun nozzle was at his temple. "One false move, Kurjac," Goran warned.

"I understand," Kurjac replied. He felt the mechanism click and the handcuffs come off. He rubbed his wrists and took tentative steps toward his sister. He stretched out his arms and lifted her off the chair. Turned her round and sat down with her nestled sideways across his thighs. He cradled her face in his wiry hands. Her smell transported him back to his childhood as they held on tight to each other.

After a while, he held her face away and looked into her glistening eyes. "Whose is it?" he murmured.

She pursed her lips and tried to turn her head. But Kurjac held it firmly. She dropped her eyes. "I don't know," she whimpered.

Kurjac was quiet for a minute as he felt the rage build back up. "I see," he said eventually. She looked back down at him.

"There are two more, Dragan." The tears came again. "They don't let me see them. They live here with the old man and his wife." She screwed her eyes up in agony. "I hear them playing in the yard, Dragan, I hear them…"

"ENOUGH," Goran shouted. Kurjac felt the gun muzzle between his shoulders.

It took him three more jobs to acquire the four things he needed. He was routinely strip-searched at the rendezvous, usually a hotel room, after each assignment. Therefore, anything he wanted to take back could only be secreted safely in one place. The job on the Hungarian drug dealer supplied the first item. A small plastic bag came from the airplane meal tray on the way back. He worked a fraying strand of cotton loose from his own pillow case. From the dying Russian oligarch's desk, he took a large, sturdy paper clip. Put it in the plastic bag and tied it with the cotton. Put it where he had to.

The last item was going to be a gamble. This third job required the use of a small torch. When it was completed, he dropped his pants and gritted his teeth. He would say it got lost in a struggle. Stranger things had happened before. Then it was a question of reining in his impatience for the right weather conditions.

They came two weeks later, a wild night in mid-October. A wolf wind lashed squally rain and hail against his barred window. No one would be venturing outside tonight out of choice. Kurjac wasn't allowed any stationery in his bare room so he had to make a mental map of the General's grounds. His en-suite bedroom, to which he was confined when not on an assignment, was on the third of the house's four storeys. Getting out of the building wasn't going to be easy.

The farm was situated about a kilometre to the south, across mostly flat, open ground with an occasional copse and a few drainage channels. Two further buildings lay in that direction. Most of the General's men were housed in a modern, three-storey block about a hundred metres south-east of the main house. Fifty metres closer on the same concrete road was a large motor pool and armoury, on the roof of which sat the General's helicopter.

He knew there were a minimum of three armed men guarding the compound against the General's many enemies at any time. One, sometimes two patrolling the perimeter fence with savage dogs. One on the ground floor in the main house, wandering between the various points of entry. The last was the most pivotal to Kurjac's plans. A room on the first floor of the main house was what the General liked to call the brains of his operation. From it, he was able to communicate with, and to a certain extent, conduct the criminal underworld in Eastern Europe and beyond. His business interests extended to every conceivable vice and racket, all built on the pay-offs and fear generated by Kurjac's unerring work. The main computer network was located in this room as well as a wall of screens showing live images from twenty or more cameras around the complex. Usually one, but sometimes two men were stationed there at all times. One click of a mouse from the brain room would bring a dozen heavily armed ex-soldiers running. That wasn't part of Kurjac's plan.

During his time living in the wild, evading the death squads, he'd developed the ability to shut down for long periods in a trance-like stupor. It conserved energy and he came out of it with heightened awareness in a state of nerveless serenity. It was in this condition that he rose from his mattress at two a.m. and went to his tiny bathroom. He unscrewed the rose from the shower head and retrieved the torch and paper clip. Screwed the shower back together.

For once he was grateful that all his clothes were black. Over his t-shirt he layered up with a thin polo-neck, a warm fleece and a waterproof shell. He slipped the torch into the back right pocket of his jeans. Inspected his footwear. Trainers would be best for speed and stealth but would be useless in a fight. His army-issue boots were the best option for that scenario but were about as furtive as a couple of bricks. He went with a comfortable pair of lightweight climbing boots.

The old house had old heavy locks. Kurjac had broken more than one ordinary paper clip trying to pick them. With some difficulty, he worked a hook into the stout paper clip, held his breath and inserted it into the mechanism. He wiggled it until he felt it catch. There was no going back from his next move. He slowly let out his breath as he simultaneously turned the doorknob and flicked the paper clip. He eased the door back and slipped into the dark wooden corridor, listened hard for a minute and heard only the ticking of the clock in the lobby two floors down.

The first problem was the camera that pointed down the stairs that he needed to take. But disarming it would hopefully bring about the solution to his second problem. It all depended on who was watching the screens tonight. If he was really lucky, it would be one of the few slack guys in the General's crew, dozing on the job. More likely it would be one of the ex-soldier guards who'd come to investigate the camera himself. If he was really unlucky, one of the two tech guys would be on duty. They would radio to the guard downstairs to investigate, remaining in position, watching the screens behind a locked door.

Grasping the power cord at the back of the camera, he rolled the dice. Five seconds passed. Nothing. Kurjac waited at the top of the stairs, back against the wall, looking into the camera's lens. Ten seconds. Then, from the floor below, came the sound of a door opening and being locked. Not a slacker or a tech guy. An armed guard. Could be ex-special forces or cannon fodder. Either way, he'd be dead in twenty seconds.

"Just checking a camera upstairs," the guard called down to his colleague on the ground floor. A grunt came back.

Kurjac kneeled and judged the height of an average man standing on the penultimate step as he heard the guard start climbing. Then he raised his fist a few centimetres higher to take account of the fact that the General's men weren't average. He practised the moves in his head and pulled back his left arm.

Speed was everything. The guard's right foot hit the step and Kurjac whipped his left fist into the man's groin. His last breath left his chest as he creased up. Kurjac grasped the guy's chin and the back of his head and pushed hard with his left and pulled hard with his right. Cushioned his fall. Less than three seconds and practically soundless.

He didn't bother looking at the guard's guns, looked instead for keys and a knife. He also found a decent amount of cash, at least enough for train tickets and a night in a hotel. He thought briefly about Lejla's children, then put them out of his mind. That was another battle for another day. Kurjac left the guard's body where it was and descended the stairs to the first-floor landing. If there was more than one man watching the screens tonight, he'd be seeing Kurjac in two cameras right now. Would he come out himself or radio to the guy downstairs? Human instinct for self-preservation suggested the latter course, so Kurjac positioned himself against the wall at the top of the stairs leading to the ground floor.

Nothing happened. There hadn't been a second man in the brain room. He tried three keys in its door until he found the right one. He entered the room cautiously and went to the bank of screens and saw the ground floor guard in screen one. He was eating a sandwich at the great table in the lobby, facing the main entrance with his back to the stairs. Kurjac checked out the other screens. Only one depicted any human activity. A guard was kicking a pebble aimlessly in the rain outside the front of the motor pool's huge roller doors. Kurjac grinned. This was going to be easy.

In the mansion's penthouse suite, the General's alarm woke him at two fifteen in time for an important call with an ambitious Los Angeles politician. If it went well, the whole western seaboard of the United States might open up to his goods and services. He went to his own, smaller brain room, his study, and looked in a drawer in his desk for his book of contacts. Movement on his computer monitor distracted him. The screen displayed a composite of all the camera feeds. The movement was caused by a negligent guard in screen twelve outside the motor pool. The General made a mental note to sack him in the morning.

Then he noticed that screen four was dead. That got his attention. He quickly scanned the other screens and then double-clicked screen one so that it filled the monitor. It showed most of the grand oak-panelled lobby and the bottom of the wide main staircase. A dark figure was just discernible, descending it slowly. The General bristled. It disappeared behind the wide back of one of the great table's chairs. In it sat one of his guards eating something. He suddenly flinched and looked behind the chair back to his left. Then the guard's hands were at his throat as the dark figure reappeared beside him. It grabbed the guard's head by the hair and smashed it into the table. It bounced once and settled in the unmistakable attitude of death.

The General recognised the figure's deft movements. He followed Kurjac's progress on various screens as he exited the building north before heading west around it and then south. The General smiled. Only one thing in Kurjac's interest lay in that direction. He picked up the phone and dialled the three-digit extension of the farmhouse. It answered on the tenth ring. "Be in the barn in two minutes with a shotgun in Lejla's mouth. I'll be there directly."

Three things changed after the incident. Firstly, Kurjac's bedroom door was fitted with the latest keypad locking system. Secondly, a wide-angle camera was installed high up in his room. And thirdly, all contact with Lejla was indefinitely suspended.

One thing didn't change. Kurjac had to carry on completing assignments if he wanted to keep Lejla alive and well. It became his sole aim in life. He began to crave the jobs, as they were the only occasions he escaped the slow death of his room. As the years went by, the hope that he could one day escape with Lejla withered to a tiny speck of light, and then died.

Thirty-Five

Friday afternoon

"Do either of you have a cheque book?" Wren asked. She was looking east and west from where they stood at a busy crossroads. She almost had to shout above the roar of big diesel engines as they lurched from one grinding halt to the next as profligately as possible.

"I have a couple," Penelope said, patting her handbag, "Lloyds and Santander."

"Okay, there's a Lloyds over there," Wren said, pointing. "I hope I'm wrong about this thing, but if I'm not, your card numbers will be flagged as a means of tracing your movements. Let's go," she said as the green man came on.

They dashed across four lanes and circumnavigated the street furniture and groups of tourists and reached the bank. "You're going to have to withdraw cash and use a driver's licence or passport as security," said Wren.

"Don't they usually ask for a card?" Penelope replied, looking for items in her bag.

"They do, but you can't use it. Say you don't have it with you. MI5 can trace a cheque withdrawal, but it usually takes a day or two to process." Wren was looking back to where they'd come from but there were hundreds of people in the street. She did some quick maths. "Can you get four thousand?"

"Uh-huh. Why not five?"

"Make it five, then," said Wren, checking her watch. "Please be as quick as you can. We'll be in the back of that café," she said, pointing at a generic coffee house a couple of units along the high street.

Wren found a table in a dingy corner from which she could see the rest of the relatively quiet room and the entrance. The morning rush for caffeine was over and the afternoon refuel was yet to begin. McLeod brought mugs and a pastry for Wren and sat next to her on a leather banquette. "Have you ever worked out how many calories you eat a day?" he asked, pushing across the confection.

Wren was lost in thought. "Accident of birth," she muttered, sipping cappuccino. Her eyes darted to the door each time it opened or closed. "Listen, Mac," she said, turning to look him in the eyes. "I'm going to have to check in with my station house soon, then you're on your own." She looked away quickly as she heard the door go again. A gaggle of Chinese tourists came in laughing. Wren relaxed.

"I still think you're reading too much into this, Anna," he replied.

"But what if I'm not, Mac?" Her eyes were back on his and they were full of anxiety. "For someone to have gone to the lengths they did with my phone, this is serious shit." She put a hand on his forearm. "Think about it, Mac. That information being out there was too much of a loose end for someone." She paused and looked down. "I'm afraid I've put you into that category as well."

The door opened again and this time, the entrants increased Wren's apprehension. McLeod caught the expression in her eyes and followed them to see two uniformed police officers walking toward the counter. He could tell from their body language they were only here doing community relations, and he concentrated instead on Wren's words. Serious shit. He'd been in it since he woke this morning. He sighed heavily. "What do we actually know about this thing, Anna? Apart from a beautiful girl being murdered? What facts do we have?"

The anxious look in Wren's eyes was replaced by a gritty resolve. "We know that she was poisoned and that you were too. Possibly to incapacitate you or render you useless to help Nathalie."

"Wait, Anna. That's not a fact."

"No, it's not, but it just occurred to me now and it's a possible reason for something happening which we're shit short of in all this." She paused and munched the last of her pastry. "I'm as certain as I can be that the wiry guy in the bar is the poisoner."

Something struck McLeod as he flashed on the shadowy figure from the CCTV footage. "What nationality d'you reckon he was?"

Wren made a weary face. "You're pounding the wrong flounder, Mac. MI5's behind this...whoever that guy was. They have no rules. They'll use whoever they can to do their dirty work."

McLeod furrowed his brow, struggling with the idea that his own country's secret service would kill one of its subjects. "How sure are you about MI5, Anna? I mean, the implications..." Words failed him as he contemplated their enormity.

Wren saw the realisation in McLeod's blazing eyes. "I'm sorry, Mac, I'm about a hundred per cent certain. My phone? It was like a direct warning to me. They could have just wiped the lot and I'd have thought I'd been hacked or that it had had a fit." Wren watched the police officers carefully as they left. "By deleting only the files relevant to this case, they were as good as saying: stay the hell out of this."

Despite the coffee, McLeod suddenly felt tired. It had been a long day on top of having being poisoned and waking to the nightmare he was living. He thought back to the morning. Something felt wrong there, but in his weary state of mind, he couldn't catch it. He thought about the hospital and the look of foreboding on Wren's face when she came back from her call. She couldn't have faked that. Or the antics in the Stag. "So you think MI5 were following us from the hospital?" he asked.

An uncommon look of uncertainty entered Wren's eyes. "No, I don't," she replied hesitantly. "Matte black Mercedes with tinted windows? That's too overt for those shady buggers." The door went again and Wren was relieved to see Penelope making her way over to them. McLeod saw no trace of a recently bereaved woman in her purposeful stride. Red-rimmed eyes told another story though as she took a chair opposite Wren and McLeod. Wren rehearsed the things they needed to do in her mind.

"Can I get you something, Pen?" McLeod asked, before Wren interrupted.

"No time for that, Mac. Did you get it?" she asked, chucking back the last of her coffee.

Penelope took a thick brown envelope from her bag. "They had a bit of trouble believing I had my cheque book and driver's licence but not my bank card. Asked me loads of questions."

Wren was scanning the street outside the café over Penelope's shoulder. "Okay good. Keep hold of it, Penelope. We need to move."

She led them out onto the bustling street, heading west. Every black car that passed was a cause for concern as they crossed a couple more junctions until Wren found what she was after. A pop-up street vendor was hocking touristy chintz and cheap electrical goods. She bought three throw-away mobile phones and a couple of chargers. They kept heading west and stopped outside a newsagent.

"Okay, you're on again, Penelope. This place will have a camera, but I don't think they'll be looking for you yet. Three pay-as-you-go SIM cards, twenty quid on each should do it."

When it was done, they took the next tree-lined residential street south and exchanged numbers and loaded the cards. McLeod played back Wren's words in his head and came to a worrying conclusion. "You got Penelope to go into the shop because you think they're looking for me right, Anna?"

Wren was looking up and down the street. "That's right, Mac."

"Why, because I'm a loose end?"

Wren turned and looked up at him. He saw the conflict between anxiety and cool professionalism in her expression. "I think it's more than that, Mac. I think that whatever Nathalie was into was so big, it's nationally sensitive, maybe even of international importance." She stole a quick glance at Penelope who was deep in thought. "I think that maybe you were supposed to die too, Mac. That maybe they didn't figure on your constitution or they got the dose wrong." She paused, considering what to say while a young couple walked by. "She may have told you something they don't want you to know, Mac. Maybe the something that got her killed."

McLeod was weighing the significance of Wren's words when he was halted by a gasp from Penelope. They both turned and looked at her expectantly. Anguish was written deeply into her features. "I've just remembered something Nathalie said in passing a couple of weeks ago." She took a deep breath and passed a hand over her brow. "I didn't think anything of it at the time, just thought it was Nathalie's bravado." She winced and closed her eyes. "She said something like: 'This paper I'm working on will make the shit hit the fan.' But she was always saying things like that..." She broke off as fresh tears welled in her almond eyes. Wren rummaged in her bag and came out with some tissues.

"Thank you," Penelope choked.

McLeod saw the gleam return to Wren's eyes and a spark of hope ignited in his overwrought stomach.

"All right," she said, "that's what we've been missing, Penelope. Something to go to work on." She smothered a sudden feeling of panic but not before McLeod registered it. "What is it, Anna?"

She shook her head, annoyed at herself. "Doesn't matter," she muttered. She looked south down the street and then back at McLeod. "Okay, head that way, Mac. Buy clothes for two days for both of you and a bag to put them in. Find a hotel or guest house that'll take cash up front and stay there. Don't answer the door to anyone."

"But what about my sister, Anna? I can't just abandon her," Penelope pined, dabbing her eyes.

Wren shot her a worried look. "You have to for now, Penelope. I'll try to get hold of your father... Wait no! This is fucked." She threw her hands on some railings and her head between them. McLeod followed her train of thought and looked quickly at Penelope who was staring at Wren, mystified.

"If Anna tells your father, Pen, what would he do? What would any father do?"

Penelope was still appalled. "Why, he'd go to the authorities of course," she railed. Wren spun around and desperation haunted her eyes.

"There are no authorities left to you, Penelope, don't you see that?" Her voice quivered as she continued. "Who tells MI5 what to do?"

Penelope stared at her, not understanding. Then not believing. Then McLeod was holding her up as the enormity of their predicament hit home. A matte black Mercedes with tinted windows cruised slowly along the high street, past the entrance to the residential street.

Thirty-Six

Friday afternoon

"I think we've found them, boss." Only six little words, but they were life and death to Kurjac. Not his own. Lejla and her children's. They were all that mattered in the world to him.

The General didn't allow Kurjac to see his sister for more than a year following his thwarted attempt to free her. But a job came up that required Kurjac to have greater freedom of movement and men to assist him. It was a huge pay-day; one the General wasn't prepared to forego. And the paymaster was the most powerful organisation in the world: The United States government. An election was looming and the media was in a foment over a perceived crack cocaine epidemic. The importance of a positive news story on the issue was impressed upon the CIA. They couldn't be seen to be acting directly against another foreign government, so they made some noises across the pond and were taken with the General's operation.

He now needed even more leverage over Kurjac than the threat of injury to his sister. He worked out the best way to achieve that was to increase the attachment between the siblings, to make Lejla's health and the wellbeing of her children directly dependent on Kurjac's compliance in all matters. But the General wasn't blind to his assassin's fundamental desire for freedom. He thought hard about that, then put his plans in action. When they were complete, he sent for his killer. Under heavy guard, Kurjac was taken to a new building on the General's estate. It was a tiny, white, two-storey house with a zinc roof, sitting in a small garden within a thick wall topped with rolls of razor wire. A small steel gate was built into the wall and was operated via a keypad. There was a similar arrangement on the only door to the house. Kurjac was pushed through it and it locked behind him. The scent of his sister once again transported him to the happy days of their childhood. He was standing in a little sitting room painted magnolia with a sofa and a television and bars on the window. On the sofa sat a little boy and a smaller girl reading a book together. They turned and stared at him with huge eyes. He was equally in shock.

"Dragan!" Lejla cried, running into the room and into his arms. Kurjac nuzzled in her thick black hair. When she let him go, she smiled and wiped her cheeks. Kurjac looked her up and down carefully. There was more colour in her skin than he remembered from the barn. The sallowness was gone. He saw no fresh bruises or scars on her slender arms or her smooth cheeks. Her dark eyes gleamed with life once more. He smiled back at her. It felt strange on his face. Lejla beckoned to the children on the sofa with hands out-stretched. They got up tentatively and each clung to one of her legs, peeping out with one eye. "It's all right, children. This man is good. He's the one I told you about, my brother. He is your Uncle Dragan."

Kurjac stared at the beautiful infants in wonder. They were so similar to himself and Lejla in the old torn photograph. He squatted down to their height and held out his right hand. "I know I have a funny ear, children, but if you're really good I'll let you feel it."

The little boy looked up at his mother and she smoothed a hand through his floppy black hair and nodded enthusiastically. Slowly, the boy left his mother's side and shuffled toward Kurjac. Stretched out a cautious hand. Kurjac took it ceremoniously in his forefinger and thumb.

"This is Tarik." Lejla's voice shook with pride. "He had his sixth birthday last week."

Kurjac looked shrewdly at Lejla and nodded.

"Tarik, you are named for your grandfather. He was an amazing man. I'm sure one day, you will be too."

The little boy smiled shyly at Kurjac and then looked at his ear. "What does it feel like?" he ventured.

Kurjac smiled and pulled the boy's hand to the stub of his ear. "You tell me," he said.

The boy giggled and his eyes shone. "It feels rough. How did it get like this?"

Kurjac's smile dissolved and he looked down. "Ask me again when you're older," he said quietly.

Lejla walked the little girl over to them. She had skin like porcelain and huge dark eyes with thick lashes. Kurjac thought she was the most beautiful thing he'd ever seen. "This is little Hana," Lejla said. "She'll be five in January." Kurjac smiled shyly at her and held her tiny hand in both of his. The little girl looked up into his eyes and Kurjac felt like she saw through all the conflict and violence in his soul to the hopes and dreams of the boy he once was. He realised he wasn't breathing and looked at Lejla who was kneeling and smiling between her children. Tears streamed down her pale cheeks.

"These last weeks have been like heaven, Dragan. Please help us to stay together," she pleaded.

He nodded slowly to himself. Looked at the walls of the little sitting room. Here and there, Lejla had stuck Tarik and Hana's colourful drawings. He looked at the TV and the little sofa and the lamp in the corner. "One day," he breathed, "we're all going to be together." He paused and looked into each pair of glistening eyes. "This is my promise," he said and he felt his heart explode in his chest.

"What do you want us to do, boss?" Bartek's voice shattered his reverie. Brought him back to what had to be done. The General had made the consequences of further delay clear and the thought of one hair on Hana's head being harmed focused Kurjac's mind. Strategy and logistics. They were so ingrained he barely had to think about them.

"They are on foot, yes?" His mind conjured up the sequence of events following his men's failure to stay with the yellow car.

"Yes, boss, all three of them."

Kurjac briefly toyed with the idea of sacrificing his men by having them gun down the targets in broad daylight. But the level of heat that would bring would be too much for even MI5 to suppress. He tried to put himself in the shoes of the police woman and lost the picture. He knew she'd been pulled from the case over half an hour ago. She ought to be long gone. She was either stupendously stupid or incredibly astute. Kurjac went with the latter as a default to which he added the area of town the targets were in. A vision crystallized in his mind.

"The police woman will be gone soon. The Lane woman and the man will look for a hotel around Fulham Broadway. See them do it, but do not be seen. Then call me with the location."

Thirty-Seven

Friday afternoon

The hotel they chose rejoiced in the name 'Serendipity'. The only happy accident about the place for Penelope and McLeod was that the monosyllabic owner was more than pleased to take cash up front. They left the dated brown décor of the small lobby and climbed four flights of an old wooden staircase to find their room. The door felt good and solid as McLeod turned the weighty key in the lock and walked into a much larger space than he would have imagined. A short hallway had storage on the left with ironing equipment and surplus bedding. An adequate bathroom was on the right. There was plenty of room to walk around the large bed. A vanity unit sat in front of two tall windows that gave good views to the south-west over rooftops toward the river. A television was mounted on the wall in the corner above a tea and coffee chest. There were a couple of comfy armchairs and a handsome pair of old wooden wardrobes on each side of the bed.

"Not too shabby, eh?" said McLeod, chucking their rucksack of newly purchased clothes on the bed. Trying things on hurriedly in shops and giving opinions and casting judgements had been a welcome relief from their predicament, whatever it was.

"No, it's fine," said Penelope, inspecting the fraying pillows. She thought about the luxury of the Savoy and the things she'd left in her room there, and the enormity of everything pole-axed her afresh. She collapsed, sobbing, on the bed. McLeod was lost for a moment. He'd never been told how to deal with a complete stranger grieving over her dead sister whilst being pursued by her own security forces. So he thought about what his grandmother would do. She was the wisest person he'd ever known. She instinctively knew what to do in any situation. He needed to get her talking so he went to the bathroom and found a box of tissues.

"Tell me about Nathalie," he said, moving the rucksack and sitting on the edge of the bed.

Penelope opened her eyes and saw McLeod's hand holding the tissues toward her. She switched her focus to his face and was struck by the warmth in his eyes and the sincerity in the line of his mouth. She managed a faint smile and took a couple of tissues.

"Thank you," she said, wiping her eyes and sitting up. "You must think I'm completely useless."

McLeod dropped the box on the bed between them. "What was she like, Pen?" he asked again.

Penelope looked into his eyes and saw only a genuine desire for knowledge. She sighed heavily.

"She was a beautiful conundrum," she managed eventually. Her eyes glazed as she lost herself in the busy pattern of the green and beige wallpaper. "She had a mind as sharp as a tack, but she could come out with the most inappropriate comments at times." She closed her eyes and couldn't supress a snicker. "We were in a restaurant a couple of months ago and Nathalie was starving. The waitress came over with some menus. Nathalie said, 'I don't need that, thank you. Just get me whatever that large girl over there's having.' I must have gone crimson, but Nathalie didn't bat an eyelid." Penelope looked over at him nervously, but his eyes were smiling. McLeod cast his thoughts back to the video from the bar and a familiar feeling of disquiet accompanied them.

"I don't understand the whole business of Nathalie at the bar and the Smythe bloke and how I came to be involved," he said, grabbing a bottle of water from the rucksack and passing it to Penelope. Her fingers lingered on his for a second longer than they needed to. Her heart fluttered slightly as he turned to refasten the rucksack. She took a long cathartic drink and tried to gather herself.

"That was all my fault," she said harshly. "This whole thing is my fault." She stood up suddenly and crossed the room to the wall and thumped it with the side of her fist. McLeod was encouraged by the shift from tears to anger and knew he had to push harder despite what she might think of him.

"Why, Pen? Why was it your fault?"

Penelope turned around and leaned back against the wall. She shot McLeod an unpleasant look. "Because she was there instead of me, okay?" Frustration built in her stomach. "I should have been meeting that Smythe creature but I... I couldn't face it." She paused and fought against the urge to cry. Channelled her frustration into anger. "She'd be alive now if it wasn't for my selfishness," she spat, a wild broken look in her eyes.

The rawness of her emotion and the sight of her heaving chest stirred something in McLeod that he hadn't felt for a long time. Without thinking about it, he went and stood in front of her. She looked up into his eyes. Her anger turned to fire. She reached up and pulled his mouth to hers, sought his tongue desperately as she lifted his shirt and felt for his belt. His hands were tentative, then warm at the base of her spine. They travelled up and took her blouse with them. He pulled away and tossed it on an armchair. His breath was ragged as he turned back and searched her eyes. "I need you," he breathed. She buried her face in the soft dark hair on his chest.

"I know," she said and thrust a hand through the waistband of his jeans.

McLeod woke sluggishly and opened his eyes with a sense of déjà-vu. Long dark hair filled his field of vision for the second time in a long day, but the body lying next to his was warm and soft. He ran a finger down her slender neck and along her shapely shoulder.

"Uuurrrhhh," Penelope groaned. He knew exactly how she felt.

"Doesn't get any better, does it?" he murmured. She rolled toward him and lost herself in his warm brown eyes.

"Hold me," she gasped. He consumed her in his long arms. For a minute, he forgot everything and nourished himself with the feel of her skin against his. "That's quite a body you've got going on, Mac." Her voice was muffled in his embrace. "You work out a lot or something?"

McLeod's eyes flicked wide open and he let go of her. He leaned on his elbow and looked into her olive eyes.

"Nathalie said that to me last night," he said quietly.

Penelope struggled with the notion for a second and then a look of hope entered her eyes. "Is your memory coming back?"

McLeod shook his head and Penelope liked the way his hair danced. "Just flashes. Triggered by images or things people say." He sighed and brushed a lock of hair from her face.

She smiled a thank you.

"Who's the Beatles fan?" he asked, raising an eyebrow.

Penelope rolled her eyes. "My father. He still insists on calling me Penny." A look of alarm crossed her face. "He doesn't know, Mac. He's somewhere in the wilds of Scotland." Her breath hitched. "His daughter's dead and he doesn't know." She buried her head in his chest again and McLeod felt her warm tears. "Oh, what are we going to do, Mac?" she keened. "What are we going to do?"

Several miles away, Kurjac's phone pinged. Worried that the General might take pre-emptive steps against his sister and her children, he'd pleaded that the McLeod character was a mitigating factor in the previous night's failure. He'd requested any relevant information on the individual now that he needed to be negated to complete the assignment. His hand hovered over the e-mail icon. He took a deep breath and pressed it. The subject of the message was: collateral damage. The first things it contained were two photographs. He stared at them in horror. One was a close up of Hana's right ear. Kurjac recognised the earrings he'd got for her on a job in Paris last winter. The second was of a crude hunting knife. Under the pictures were two words: don't fail. He breathed again. It was a threat rather than a fait accompli.

There were two attachments. The first was a word document, probably a résumé, but the second was a video file. He frowned and opened it. Grainy footage from a CCTV camera in a toilet somewhere. There was a flurry of action between two men, then one was on the ground doubled up and the other was walking toward the camera rubbing his jaw. Kurjac recognised the annoyingly handsome features of McLeod from the bar last night. His dark eyes grew as wide as they could. He replayed the video, not quite able to believe what he'd seen. The speed and precision of the moves were beyond anything he'd ever heard of. And that was without being hit in the head first. He played it back again in slow motion. Thought about his men staking out the hotel, waiting for the word to act. Then the germ of an outrageous idea drifted like a speck of pollen into his mind.

Thirty-Eight

Friday afternoon

"Never mind, she's just walked in. Yes, all right. Bye." Chief Inspector John McKay smashed the receiver back on its cradle. He was wiry with the energy of a man twenty years younger than the forty-nine he'd lived. A furze of steel hair topped a narrow, angular face from which grey eyes bore into DI Wren as she closed the door behind her. "Where the fuck have you been?" he shouted in a fairly thick Yorkshire accent, leaning on his desk.

Wren was equally full of indignation. "Why the hell did you pull me from the case?" she shouted back. She'd learned long ago that if you didn't fight your corner in this place you got nowhere. Her hair was freshly primped and her make-up reapplied because she'd also learned to make the most of the advantages her femininity afforded her. Instinctively, she scanned the large whiteboard on the wall of the office to her left for details of the case. Saw none.

"I'm serious, Anna," McKay's tone was still harsh, but more measured, "the Commander's been going bat-shit for this." He made a chopping action with his hand and arm.

His words did nothing to alleviate Wren's growing sense of alarm. If the Commander was directly involved, her worst fears were all but confirmed. She thought about Mac and Penelope holed up in their hotel. About the collaboration the man fuming in front of her had provided only this morning. Then she began to think about her own safety.

"What's the Commander got to do with it?" She wasn't sure she wanted to know the answer. McKay glowered and sat back in his roomy office chair. Debated with himself about how much to tell the best operative he had. How to prevent her further involvement. He sighed, realising it was probably useless and motioned for her to sit. He forced himself to look into her eyes.

"I dunno what this thing is, Anna. Okay?" Not for the first time, he found her gaze too distracting. He picked up his mobile phone from where it sat on his desk. "Has yours been wiped too?"

Wren pictured it languishing in a bush outside the hospital. "Only the stuff related to the Lane case." She thought about saying more but decided to leave the statement hanging like a baited hook. McKay shot her a sharp look.

"So you know what that means?" Wren swivelled in her chair to look at the right-hand wall of the office and the countless framed citations and awards. Each one represented many lives saved. She knew at least two of them were for preventing incidents potentially worse than 7/7. The common denominator behind each success was information from MI5.

"A woman's dead, John." She closed her eyes and turned back toward him. Anger flared in her stomach. "A beautiful, brilliant woman with her whole life ahead of her." She rose and put both hands flat on the desk and leaned in. "Cold on a fucking slab, John." She banged the table and McKay looked away. "Who speaks for her, for Christ's sake?"

An A4 notepad on McKay's desk was covered with dozens of intricately constructed doodles. He took a pencil and began a new one. Precise little strokes, each meaningless without the proximity of others. Might become a feather or a leaf or a rainforest or nothing at all.

Wren sat back down to await the Chief's verdict. "There's nowhere for this to go, Anna. Commander's made that very clear." He turned the notepad thirty degrees. Started making longer concentric curves. "Where are they?"

Three barely audible words but their portent caused Wren's eyes to widen and her heart to hammer in her chest. He'd laid his cards on the table with another clear warning. One that screamed to her that she'd been right. That Mac and Penelope were in terrible danger. That she would be too if she continued to help them. She thought fast. How far did her trust in her boss extend? She needed to ascertain his degree of complicity and decided on a blatant lie. "They gave me the slip in Islington."

The Chief's pencil hovered over the pad for a second before continuing its precise strokes.

"I see," he said thoughtfully. He leaned further over his doodling, avoiding Wren's eyes. "Then we're out of it. Take the rest of the day off, Anna. The weekend too. File nothing. Breathe nothing." He opened the top drawer of his desk, took out a cheap mobile phone, pressed a button and peered at the screen. He wrote something on a corner of his notepad. Tore it off and handed it to Wren. "Call me on this number if you get anywhere." He finally looked up at Wren. His expression was bleak. "There's bugger all I can do on this, Anna. The Commander hears, it's your neck. Look after yourself, okay?"

Wren weighed his words and their thinly encrypted messages: SO15 has no jurisdiction, but I can't be responsible for officers' actions in their own time; I'm here for advice if you want, but no more than that; don't get killed.

She smiled grimly and McKay nodded her out.

Friday afternoon

"THE BLASTED CHINESE BAILED ON US!" The combination of Sir Francis' volume and his own hearing aid squealing caused a spasm that nearly led Sir David to drive his golf buggy into a bunker. He transferred his phone to the other ear and corrected his course.

"Steady on, old chap," barked Sir David, aiming the buggy at a spinney of oaks where his errant drive had come to rest. "I'm not actually *in* China, you know."

There was a pause on the line, some muffled cursing followed by a clear "JENNINGS," then Sir Francis was back on. "Billions of pounds just hauled its sorry arse out of my office, David. All manner of kickbacks and dividends up the shitter. What do you want, fucking poetry?"

Sir David parked his buggy in the rough and gesticulated with his phone to his playing partners further up the fairway. "Calm down, Francis. We've bigger boils to lance today. Hang on a minute." Sir David put his phone on the vacant seat beside him and selected a nine iron from his bag. By some miracle, he found a ball straight away a few yards into the trees. Didn't bother to ascertain that it was his. With his third attempt, he squirted it out of the rough, across the fairway and into a welcoming bunker. "Little bastard," he shouted after it. Heaved himself back behind the wheel and set off in pursuit. He heard a tiny, tinny voice and looked all around him. Then remembered his phone on the other seat.

"Yes, yes, I'm sorry about the Chinese. Listen, I've just got off with Urquhart," he said conspiratorially. "His operative reports that the Lane woman had help escaping the planned pick-up at the hospital."

"Not the ruddy Special Branch woman?" said Sir Francis, alarm in his Harrovian drawl.

"Hmmnn, it appears she must have disobeyed a direct order. Not one for following the rules, apparently. But there's worse. I've just got to take a shot."

"Don't leave me…"

But Sir David had already gripped his sand iron and was lowering himself into the pit. Four blows later, he was thirty yards closer to the green.

He quieted Sir Francis' protests as he climbed back into the buggy. "It seems this Wren woman ditched her phone at the hospital and the Lane woman's was retrieved nearby. What does that suggest to you?" Sir David heard a sharp intake of breath.

"Shit, David, she's onto us."

"No need to over-egg it, old thing," bristled Sir David, casting an anxious look at his partners up at the green. "But it is worrying on one level. Won't be a minute."

"Damn it, man, will you stop…" he caught as he pulled a seven iron from his bag. He aimed into the trees to the left to give himself some privacy. Made an action reminiscent of an octopus trying to escape a bag and connected perfectly with the ball. Then he watched in wonder as it sliced unerringly toward the green, bounced twice and nestled close to the cup. He danced back to the buggy and retrieved his phone.

"I wish you'd seen that shot, old man. Like a bloody Exocet it was."

"Never mind your damned pogo sticks," said Sir Francis, warmly. "What's worrying on one level?"

Sir David steered the cart proudly to the side of the green. "Well," he said, lowering his voice, "the Wren woman wasn't intimidated by the threat inherent in Urquhart's, um, manipulation of her phone. And that was after being pulled from the case. She's going out of her way to involve herself in our business and may cause us trouble down the line."

"In which case, she's put herself in harm's way." Sir David could hear the strain in his old friend's voice.

"We've got to see this thing through, Francis." He cast a glance at his playing partners who were finishing their putts and marking cards. "Listen, I'm going to have to leave you. Everything should be sorted by tonight, old thing. Have you got the fiscal stuff ready to go?"

"Upon completion." Sir David heard him wrestling with something. "What about this chap with the Lane woman, what's he called… McKenzie?"

Sir David took his putter from his bag. "McLeod. Urquhart says he's just some harmless academic. Nothing to worry about. We'll speak later, okay?"

Sir David clicked off and walked toward his ball, a bounce in his step. "No need to putt that, Sir David," said one of his partners.

"That's very good of you, old chap," he said, picking up his ball. "Put me down for a five."

Thirty-Nine

Friday afternoon

DI Wren walked through the open-plan operations room and conversations died in her wake. She avoided the stares of her strait-laced colleagues and support staff and made it through the door at the far end. She closed it and heard the inevitable hubbub erupt behind her.

"Hey, babes. I hear you've got the weekend off, you lucky moo." It was Gigi, one of the secretaries, emerging from the photocopying room with reams of stuff that nobody would ever read. Wren stifled a groan. She was about the most indiscreet person in the building but perversely acquired gossip like a magnet.

"Oh, Gigi?" Wren looked around theatrically. "What do you know about it?"

Gigi looked like she was about to self-combust. Her frizzy hair quivered and a coy smile appeared in her broad, heavily made-up face.

"Well, I heard the Commander unexpectedly called a halt to his brunch meeting this morning." She inched closer to Wren and bent to her ear. "Shortly after, there was a mahoosive row between him and the Chief, mostly about you. My source tells me the Commander was pushing for your suspension." Gigi broke off to revel in Wren's reaction. A slightly quizzical look was all she got. "Anyway, apparently the Chief threatened to resign, isn't that fabulous?"

That got Wren's attention. Her lips parted and her breath hitched. Gigi beamed back at her.

"Where the hell did you get this, Gigi?" Wren's eyes blazed in the dark corridor. A troubled look crossed the secretary's face and she pursed her lips.

"Gigi, I've got people's lives at stake here." Wren paused and let her words sink in. Wrong tack. She thought about a gossip's motives. "I don't believe a word of it," she said and made to walk off.

"Anna, wait," Gigi squealed.

Wren turned around with 'well?' written in her glare.

The coy smile was back on Gigi's face. "I'm, er, sort of seeing Sarah." Her fingers fiddled an earring. Wren thought through any meaningful possibilities. Came up with only one.

"What, Sarah the Commander's P.A.?" A furtive smile touched her lips. "What about Philip?"

"Oh, Anna, please. Being straight is *so* last century. Later, babes," she said with a wink and sashayed off. Wren watched her return to the ops room thoughtfully. If her boss was prepared to resign on her behalf, perhaps he would provide more assistance than she'd anticipated. She got her new phone from her bag as she walked the corridor to the stairs and hit Penelope's number. She answered somewhat breathlessly on the sixth ring.

"It's me, Anna. Is everything all right, Penelope? … Are you sure? You sound shocked or winded or something… Okay, good. Listen, I need Nathalie's home address." She paused on the stairwell between floors and wrote an address in Camberwell on the back of a depressing mortgage statement. She needed to get Penelope thinking positively if she was to be of any help. "We're starting to make a bit of progress, okay, Penelope? What I need you to do now is try to think about what Nathalie might have used for passwords… I know, but unless she used some sort of program, it's always something someone close can work out… Good. Call me when you've got anything."

Penelope tossed the phone to the bottom of the bed. "That was amazing, Mac," she breathed, lying her head next to his on the pillow. He smiled and his eyes flicked open and met hers.

"What, talking to DI Wren?"

Penelope grinned and slapped him on the shoulder. "Seriously, I never thought that was possible for me," she said shyly. "Where did you learn to do that?"

His smile waned slightly as his hand rubbed the length of her arm and rested on her pale hip. "My wife was a very sensual woman, Pen," he said quietly.

"Oh… I'm sorry, Mac." She screwed up her eyes and cursed herself.

McLeod drew her close and hooked a leg over her soft behind. "Don't be, Pen. This has been really helpful." He paused and looked into her eyes. "Thank you," he murmured. The ache built again in Penelope's groin and her breathing became shallow.

"Want to show me again how thankful you are?" she said, lowering her head and looking up through thick lashes.

McLeod grinned and said, "What about thinking of passwords?"

"To hell with that," she said, rubbing the taut muscles of McLeod's abdomen. "Plenty of time later. This is what I need right now." She rolled McLeod onto his back and stilled above him, searching for and finding the same hunger in his eyes.

Forty

Friday evening

The London Underground was the world's first rapid public transport system when it opened as the Metropolitan Railway in 1863. The bit of it that Wren was riding was originally excavated in the 1880s and she could feel the years in every bump and lurch of the carriage. She hated the tube, but it was the only practical means of getting anywhere fast in the city. Late afternoon on a Friday, it felt like the least private place on earth. She was fairly certain that the actions of at least two of the people she was herded against would be classed as sexual assault were they taking place in an office.

She was spewed out of Kennington Station like one of a thousand ants leaving the nest to forage in the concrete jungle. She stood on the pavement and surveyed the surrounding streets and saw the same geography that littered every other tube station. Fast-food outlets, newsagents, florists, hairdressers and betting shops. A boarded-up pub and a mobile phone dealer were probably the only changes in a hundred years. She always lost her bearings coming out of the tube and she tried to find where the sun was going down behind the terraced houses to her right. Straight ahead was south-east which was where she wanted be.

She walked for a while through pleasant streets of post-war red and brown brick housing, then under a railway line until she reached a row of elegant Georgian houses. Most of them were split into two or three flats surrounding a little green with mature chestnut and cherry trees. A white van was making a delivery, but otherwise the short street was deserted. Wren couldn't help looking in the downstairs windows of each smartly painted building as she walked the row. She saw fine art on the walls, elaborate mirrors and antique furniture. Very nice if you liked that sort of thing. Wren didn't. Everything in her house earned its place through solid practicality and a minimum of upkeep.

Nathalie's apartment occupied the lower two floors of the last building on the row. A bright yellow 1970s Beetle sat on the curb outside. There were four buzzers, but only two had names next to them. Lane was at the bottom and Singh was neatly printed next to the third one up. Wren pressed it and held her breath. Checked her watch in the early evening sunshine. Nearly eight o'clock. "Hello," came a woman's cheery voice on the intercom.

"Good evening," said Wren, relieved, "am I speaking to Mrs Singh?"

"Yes, you are."

"I'm a police officer, Mrs Singh. Could I come in please?" There was a muffled buzz and the door came off its latch. That's how easy it was to get into most homes in the city, Wren lamented. She pushed through into a short porch area. There was a robust door with no handle to her right and stairs in front. She took the stairs and was met at the top by a short, attractive Indian woman somewhere around forty. She wore a contemporary ochre and gold Bengali saree and minimal make-up.

"Sorry to disturb your evening, Mrs Singh. I'm Detective Inspector Wren. May I come in?"

Mrs Singh looked confused for a moment before politeness took over.

"Please, Inspector," she said, pulling the door wide. A heady aroma of garlic and rich spices made Wren's tummy groan.

"That smells amazing, Mrs Singh," she said as she entered a formal drawing room. The low sun streamed in through two large windows and gleamed on the modern silk tapestries adorning pale green walls.

"Thank you, Inspector. Please have a seat." Mrs Singh indicated a couple of sleek, beige leather armchairs facing a wide fireplace. "I'll fetch my husband. Would you like some tea?"

Wren fancied something a lot stronger at this time on a Friday evening but smiled and said, "Yes please, just as it comes." Mrs Singh nodded and disappeared through the far door. The hyperactive babble of Friday night television blared briefly. Wren took a seat and fished in her bag for her phone. One message from Penelope.

162

<Hi Anna. Try 'valdisere'. Not sure about any numbers but she was born in 1988. Pen.> Wren frowned and fired off a quick reply. The far door opened, this time without the accompanying racket, and admitted an immaculately dressed man, slightly older than his wife. He crossed the room with a confident stride.

"Please, don't get up, Inspector," he said, shaking Wren's hand warmly. He sat in the chair opposite. He had the rakish look of Omar Sharif about him which Wren had always found alluring. "What can I help you with?"

Wren leaned forward in her chair, elbows on knees, hands clasped. "I'm afraid I have some bad news, Mr Singh." She paused as Mrs Singh appeared with a tray bearing a cosied teapot and best china cups.

"You better stay, Meena. She says she has some bad news." Mr Singh's look of concern was echoed in his wife's eyes.

"Yes, please, Mrs Singh. I'd like to speak with both of you."

Mrs Singh put the tray on a low table and stood by her husband who took her hand in both of his. Wren bowed her head briefly, then looked at them uncertainly. "We believe Miss Lane, your neighbour downstairs... We believe she was murdered last night."

Wren shuddered as if the room had suddenly become colder. Somewhere outside, a car alarm started up.

"No... dear God... NO," Mrs Singh cried, a shaky hand to her mouth. Mr Singh's eyes were wide in disbelief. He shook his head.

"This can't...this can't be true, Inspector... Not Nathalie...please... It's not possible..." Mr Singh stood, tears in his eyes, and put his arms around his wife who leaned, sobbing, against his chest.

"I'm sorry, Mr Singh, Mrs Singh," Wren murmured, somewhat overwhelmed. She stood as well, feeling awkward being the only one sitting. "You say it's not possible, Mr Singh. Do you mind telling me why?"

Mr Singh dabbed his eyes with a thick white handkerchief. "Because everyone loves her...loved her, Inspector." He paused, stifling a sob. "She has only lived downstairs...about two years...and already she is like a daughter to us." He held his wife tight as his words caused her more grief. "Who would do such a thing?"

Wren walked to the window and watched a crescent of red sun melt into the black skyline. Finally, Mrs Singh sat down wearily and Mr Singh perched on the arm of her chair. "Who would do such a thing?" Mr Singh repeated.

"I don't know, Mr Singh, but with your help, I will find out." She put all of her resolve into her voice. "And I will find them and bring them to justice."

"You do that, Inspector." He paused and took a deep breath. "Now please, how can we help?"

"But, Sunil." Mrs Singh looked up at her husband tearfully. "No justice is strong enough for whoever put out such a light."

"Tell me about her, Mrs Singh," said Wren, retaking her seat. "Tell me about the Nathalie you knew."

Mrs Singh looked uncertain for a minute then screwed up her eyes. "She was an impossible girl, Inspector. Forever forgetting her keys." Wren felt like getting up and doing a cartwheel.

"Go on, Mrs Singh," she said, just managing to keep the excitement out of her voice.

"She was like the sun, Inspector. You felt like dancing when she was near. She was never down or grumpy or moody, even when her mother died." She sobbed again. "She had a way of speaking that made you feel so alive. I can't explain it. Even when she would say terrible things, and she did often...always you would end up laughing."

Mr Singh pulled his wife's head to his chest as her tears came again. "Once or twice a week there'd be a knock on the door around nine in the evening." Mr Singh paused and smiled grimly. "Nathalie would be there with a bottle of wine, having been working late or having burned her dinner again." He looked up to the ceiling. "Our children would hear her and leap out of bed. She would eat our leftovers and listen to our girls' gossip from school and give advice about boys. Then she would do impersonations of the teachers and the girls would howl with laughter." He took his wife's cheeks in his hands and wiped her tears. "Oh God, Meena. How do we tell the children?"

Wren suddenly felt a desperate need to be elsewhere. She grabbed her bag and stood. "Thank you both. You've been very helpful."

"But you haven't had your tea, Inspector," said Mrs Singh, dismayed.

"I know, I'm sorry." She put her bag over her shoulder. "Do you have a key to Nathalie's flat that I could borrow?" She didn't need to hold her breath this time. Mr Singh took a couple of steps to a bureau, opened a small drawer and came out with two keys.

"Shall I come with you, Inspector?" he asked, handing Wren the keys.

"No thank you, Mr Singh. You stay with your wife."

Mr Singh walked with her to the door. "Thank you for your time, and I'm so sorry," Wren said, shaking Mr Singh's hand.

"Please make whoever did this sorry, Inspector," Mr Singh said and closed the door.

Forty-One

Friday evening

"You hungry?" McLeod murmured, running a finger along Penelope's collar bone.

"Starving," she replied, rubbing her taut tummy. An indigo sky was darkening above black rooftops out the window. Traffic noise had subsided to an occasional taxi. McLeod's leg across the top of her thighs sent little surges of electricity through her chest.

"When did you break it?" he asked, finding an almost imperceptible bump. Penelope shifted her head to look in his eyes. They were dark in the weak light from the bedside lamp.

"Know your anatomy, don't you?" she said, gently biting his lower lip. "When I was twelve. Me and Nat were swinging on a rope in a hay barn." She moved her head to his warm chest. "I held on too long and went over the edge of the bales. Must have fallen twenty feet to the ground." She paused and McLeod felt the familiar warmth of tears on his chest. "She was usually the adventurous one," she whispered.

McLeod smoothed his fingers through her silky dark hair. "Misadventurous, d'you think?"

Penelope was quiet for a spell. "What are you saying, Mac? Nat got herself killed?" The edge in her voice caused McLeod to think over his next words carefully.

"I'm sorry, Pen. I just hate being in the dark like this. Not knowing why someone would want to kill Nathalie. Not knowing if we're in danger ourselves." He lifted her head from his chest, laid it on the pillow and leaned on an elbow above her. "You can't think of anything…"

"We've been over this, Mac." Penelope couldn't keep the frustration from her voice. She reached a slender hand to his rough jaw. "Please believe me. Nathalie and I hid nothing from each other. The only thing we never talked about was work."

McLeod looked away, a frown hooding his eyes. "Then maybe that's the thing."

Penelope scoffed. "She was a bloody economist, Mac. She used to say the reason she had such a big personality was like an antidote to her work. Yin and yang kind of thing, you know?"

McLeod nodded pensively. "You never told me what you do."

Penelope smiled ruefully. "Because it's deathly boring too. I run a tiny research lab, an offshoot of my father's pharmaceuticals operation."

McLeod lost himself again in her eyes. "But that sounds very interesting. Mixing potions, blowing things up, exotic items of clothing…"

"Yeah, right, Mac. The most exotic thing I do at work is trial and bloody error. Almost always error." She reached over to her bedside table and grabbed a plastic-coated file. Opened it and skipped through a myriad of touristy options to a clear plastic wallet containing fliers from local take-out restaurants. "What do you fancy, Mac? There's Thai, Chinese, Indian, Mexican, Lebanese, Malay, Jamaican…"

"I think I've had enough spice for one evening," he said, cocking an eyebrow.

She disarmed him with a shy grin.

"How about a pizza?" he said. "There's a place that does a good tomato sauce five minutes from here. I know the number."

"Fine, Mac. You order, there's nothing I don't eat. I'll jump in the shower, if that's all right." She placed a tender kiss on McLeod's full lips and eased out of the covers with a moan. McLeod was floored by the sensational sight of her departing figure. He sighed and wondered if there was any future for them beyond whatever this thing was. Wondered if he'd live long enough to find out. Had it been the same with Catherine? No, that was love. This was necessity and lust driven by the thrill of danger and the ache of stress. An escape for both of them from grim reality. McLeod resolved to make the most of it and reached for the phone.

Four and a half minutes later, they stood panting and spent against the wall of the shower. They blinked at each other through the torrent of warm water. "Jesus Christ, Mac. My legs don't work," she gasped, holding him tight round the neck.

"Pen," he breathed heavily, "that's the coolest thing I've ever heard."

She looked at his fervent eyes, shocked for a moment, before they both collapsed in laughter on the shower floor.

Forty-Two

Friday evening

"He just left the hotel, boss. She's on her own up there." Kurjac heard the excitement in Bartek's voice and felt bile rise from his stomach. He did this shit because he had no choice. People like Bartek did it because they enjoyed it. He thought about what might be happening at his sister's little house. Would the General have taken Hana away from Lejla yet? Surely he wouldn't do it at her house? He closed his eyes and sighed wearily.

"Do it," he said and clicked off. Then he reached for the bottle of vodka on the floor beside his chair.

McLeod's brain couldn't compute the sight that greeted him as he turned at the top of the stairs toward his room. Three figures, darkly dressed, were visible in the low light outside his door thirty feet away. Two were standing, one bigger than the other, holding something behind their backs. The third was kneeling and grunting by the door handle. Horrible realisation hit him like a haymaker in the stomach. He felt cold and sick. This was real and it was really happening now. It was as bad as Wren had feared. Worse.

Standing frozen, he thought fast. They hadn't seen him yet. Penelope, Jesus. He had to get them away from her. Three men, probably armed. Impossible. He had to get them on their own. To do that, he had to run. "Hey," he shouted. They turned toward him. The two men standing grimaced and bolted for him. McLeod threw the pizza boxes at them and took off down the stairs.

He knew the brain works best in threes, so that was how he took them. He wasn't as fast as he used to be but could still do the hundred in close to eleven seconds. He was two flights down before his pursuers had reached the second. He scanned the deserted lobby as he descended the final flight and saw what he wanted by the hotel entrance. He hid in the shadows hard against the staircase, panting as quietly as he could. As his first assailant was nearly level with him, he shoved the umbrella through the old wooden spindles. Caught the guy's back leg. Sent him flying through the air, arms windmilling desperately. There was a sickening crack as his head hit a big old iron radiator against the wall of the lobby. McLeod didn't have time to check him as the bigger guy was thundering down the last few stairs. He dashed for the door one step ahead.

McLeod knew that the humble human foot was one of nature's most remarkable structures. Capable of bearing forces upwards of two thousand pounds per square inch and subjected to constant abuse on a daily basis for eighty years or more. Yet its hundreds of bones, ligaments, muscles and tendons were extremely fragile in isolation. He thought about this as the pressure he was exerting on his own feet was propelling him thirty yards ahead of his pursuer. The tree-lined pavement was dark between pools of street light and devoid of anyone else. He thought about his footwear. Lightweight sneakers. Good for running. Useless at protecting tarsals, metatarsals and phalanges. So it would have to be the heel.

He slowed, turned and accelerated back toward his surprised would-be attacker. Leapt to head height and thrust his left leg straight out. The last four inches of its journey coincided with the arrival of the big guy's chin. It snapped back and the rest of his body followed in a perfect backward somersault. He landed flat on his face and went limp. A vicious-looking knife skittered across the pavement. Two down, but McLeod saw no sign of the third man in the empty street.

Heart pounding in his chest, he sprinted a hundred yards back to the hotel, through the lobby, past his other inert attacker and hammered up the four flights of stairs. He saw slices of pizza smeared everywhere and light spilling from his door. "No... Penelope..." he gasped. Warily, he approached the open doorway. He was conscious of his heavy breathing but could do nothing about it. Something dark was splattered above the light switch on the wall to the right. Not pizza.

With mounting dread, he pushed the door fully open with his left hand, his right pulled back poised to strike. Sprawled on the floor level with the bathroom door on the right was a dark-haired figure. Wearing a black leather jacket. A dark stain was spreading on the pale carpet next to its mouth. McLeod's eyes flicked up to Penelope, standing above the figure in a black satin nightshirt, clutching a hardback book. Tears filled her eyes, then they were flooded with relief when she saw him in the doorway.

"Mac, I..." she stammered, "I think...I've..."

McLeod knelt and put two fingers to the swarthy guy's bristly neck. "No, there's a pulse, Pen." He looked up at her in admiration and heaved huge gulps of air. "What happened?" he panted.

Penelope steadied herself with a hand on the wall. McLeod leapt to catch her as her legs began to give. "You're all right, Penelope." He carried her to the bed and sat her up and held her. "We're both all right. But we're not going to be safe here for long."

She nuzzled on McLeod's shoulder. "I was so frightened, Mac," she whispered.

"So was I, Pen," he said, rubbing her back. "Deep breaths, get the oxygen in."

She did so for a spell, then said, "Two minutes after you left, I heard scratching at the door." She grabbed a bottle of water from the bedside unit and took a big drink, then passed it to McLeod. "It stopped for a bit then started up again louder." The ghost of a grim smile touched the corners of her wide mouth. "Dad always made me and Nat carry pepper spray. I got it from my bag and hid behind the bathroom door. Then there was a click and a creaking sound."

She shuddered. "Just like in the bloody movies, you know?" She glanced at McLeod who nodded impassively. "Anyway, I darted out and emptied half the can in the man's face. He was screaming and scratching at his eyes. I looked for something heavy to hit him with, but all I could find was the room's bible."

McLeod grinned. "Slayed by the word of God." He put a hand on either side of her head and gazed into her dilated eyes. "You're amazing, Penelope Lane," he said fervently. Her lips parted in anticipation, but McLeod pulled her head to his chest and ran his hands through her hair. Penelope undid the top buttons of his shirt to find the soft dark hair. "This day has been the worst of my life," McLeod said with a weary sigh. "But you know what, Pen?" He lifted her chin to look in her eyes. "I wouldn't have missed it for the world."

Forty-Three

Friday evening

The insistent tones of the slow section of Vivaldi's Spring concerto had just started in the elegant dining room of Royal Wimbledon Golf Club when Sir David's phone buzzed in the breast pocket of his dinner jacket. His third gin and tonic was starting to take the edge off the catastrophe of the sixteenth hole. He excused himself from his guests and stepped out into the cool evening air. The raucous hubbub died as he closed the door behind him.

"All ears, Brian," he said, heading away from a gaggle of smokers huddled under the veranda.

"Sorry to disturb your evening, David."

"That's alright, old chap," replied Sir David, squinting keenly at the veranda seat. "I could use some good news," he continued, sitting cautiously. There was a momentary pause on the line. Sir David took a big gulp of his drink.

"Then I'm doubly sorry, David. I think we may have an unforeseen issue." Sir David rose sharply and stomped round the corner of the building.

"By Christ, Brian," he seethed, "is this wretched woman not flesh and blood?" He drained his glass and hurled it into the night. Staggered slightly and remembered with annoyance that he had to take his pills. "What fucking issue?"

"This chap the woman's with. Seems we underestimated his, um, potency."

Sir David took his phone from his ear and stared at it in apoplectic disbelief. "POTENCY, MAN?" he bellowed at it. "What is he, a fucking sperm donor?" He wheezed a couple of calming lungfuls and returned the phone to his ear. "Spare me the bloody psycho-babble, okay, Brian?" he said more evenly.

"Sorry, David. Capabilities doesn't quite seem to cover it."

"I see," said Sir David thoughtfully. "All right, what's he done that's so damn potent?"

"Well, as you know, we often have one of our people shadowing the actions of outside agencies. Our man, Stones, reported that a little after nine p.m., three of the Serbian's foot soldiers entered the hotel. Apparently, the McLeod character had gone out to collect pizza."

"You can knock off the culinary asides as well," Sir David muttered warmly. "I've yet to have my dinner."

"Right, well, McLeod returned shortly after at a fair rate. Our man started filming when McLeod left the building again a minute later, closely pursued by a real meathead. I've just watched the footage, David."

Sir David passed a weary hand through lank, grey hair. "Well?" he barked.

"It's like nothing I've ever seen."

Sir David furrowed an already wrinkled brow. "What does that mean?"

"It's the movement...the agility...the speed, I don't know. Our man was in a car on the opposite side of the street and it's dark and there are trees and parked cars in the way. But all that can't hide the guy's..."

A pause on the line increased Sir David's frustration. "The guy's what, man?" he snarled.

"I can't explain it, David. I have nothing to compare it to. McLeod put thirty yards on his pursuer in a hundred. Turned on a sixpence. Took four strides and launched at the big guy's head. It's like he took all the momentum from the initial sprint and reversed it into his attack. Like quicksilver or something." He went quiet.

Somewhere in the dark, an owl hooted mournfully. A slight gust of wind ruffled Sir David's trousers and sent a chill up his spine. He wished he was inside with a steak and a decent drop of red instead of listening to Urquhart's drivel. "Okay, McLeod can handle himself. You said there were three of them. And what about the Lane woman?"

"We don't know. Clean up team's dealing with the big guy, a Pole, Bartek Budzinska. Stone-cold killer. Worked for the Russians for a while before being recruited by the Serbians. Won't walk again. Another man, Ragnars Bogdans, Latvian knife specialist, was retrieved from the hotel lobby floor. Major blood loss and likely brain haemorrhage. We don't know how yet. They've been taken away."

Sir David rummaged fruitlessly in his jacket pockets for a Montecristo and remembered he'd left them at his table. "Damn and blast it, man, what about the woman?"

"Two possible scenarios, neither of which involve her demise because the third foot soldier hasn't left the hotel yet."

"Wait…your man's still in place?"

"He's watching the hotel entrance from his car."

"Good. Carry on with your riveting narrative," Sir David chafed.

"Best-case scenario is that the third guy has Lane and McLeod trapped in the room or is playing some sort of game with them. Quite a sick bastard by all accounts."

"The order was clear," bristled Sir David, "despatch her and get out."

"Which is why we think it's more likely that McLeod's done for the third guy as well."

The name was beginning to wear thin on Sir David. "I thought you said this man was a harmless academic?"

"I got the other person I have working with me on this to do more digging. Turns out my predecessor was thinking about approaching him. Agile mind and an international athlete. Perfect material. Background checks were impeccable. Colleagues, tutors and the like were spoken to. Not a bad word from anyone. That was the problem. It was felt he wasn't ruthless enough for fieldwork."

"Try telling that to your three East Europeans." Sir David snorted.

"But that's different, don't you see? McLeod was acting in self-defence."

Clouds were descending once more on Sir David's brain. The gin wasn't helping much. A little voice was nagging at him from recent memory. He cast his mind back to the beginning of the enterprise. The clouds parted and indignation rose like a boil in his belly. "We weren't supposed to be involved in any of this, Brian. The plans were laid. There was to be no come back on us."

"There still isn't, David. But McLeod and Wren have brought us to the point where that may no longer be an option." He went quiet for a moment and let the words sink in. "We can walk away from this now and no investigation from local police

174

forces will get any further than our friends. Highly unlikely it would get that far. McLeod, Wren, Lane, hell even her father could make as much noise as they wanted. Nothing would touch you or me or Sir Francis or the State Department."

Sir David suddenly felt very tired. The weight of hundreds of years of privilege and possession were bearing down on his shoulders. The millions of experiences of countless lives that owed everything to the financial security whose fate rested in his hands. "There must be another way, Brian?"

"Nothing we could put in place in the timeframe we have."

The happy, exhilarated faces of his grandchildren, splashing in his pool in the Dordogne flashed in his mind. Then he saw the faces of his friends in the city, in dozens of cities around the world. He saw them turn hard against him. He felt the force of the global shockwave. He sighed deeply. "It is my duty," he said and screwed his eyes up. "Whatever it takes, Brian," he murmured and clicked off his phone.

Forty-Four

Friday evening

Wren turned the key in the second lock half right and the door to Nathalie's flat eased open. A thought occurred to her and she put the keys in her bag and came out with a compact pistol. She checked the safety and used the muzzle to push the door all the way open. She stood still and listened intently, felt her heart beating hard in her chest. She took long deep breaths as she scanned the gloomy hall in front of her. There was a trestle table on the left, under a window. On it were a shaded lamp, a Wi-Fi hub, a landline dock and a load of post. No computer, no laptop, no tablet. In the weak streetlight from the window, she could also make out a spiral staircase beyond the table and three wooden doors to the right, all partially open. Wren flinched as the car alarm suddenly stopped. She took a step into the flat, pistol in both hands out in front, and listened hard for two full minutes. She heard a tick from a clock somewhere. An almost imperceptible hum. A fridge? Nothing else.

She was fairly certain there was no one else in the flat, but she closed the front door cautiously behind her. A sign hung from a nail on the back of the door. In Pythonesque script, it read: 'Always look on the bright side of life.' Coats for all occasions hung from a rack on the pale wall to her left. The flat had a musky, feminine smell. Wren took a couple of soundless steps to the first door. She saw a light switch on the wall just inside and knew immediately that it was a small bathroom. She flicked the switch and nudged the door. A toilet, a low cupboard housing the sink, a mirror and a few items of make-up and bottles of perfume. She left the light on, turned left and listened again. The hum was slightly louder and she guessed the next room would be the kitchen.

It was actually the rest of the downstairs living space. To her right, a range of sleek white kitchen units and appliances merged via a breakfast bar into a living room with sleek white sofas and armchairs, a wide modern fireplace and a huge television. Straight ahead of her, a large rectangular dining table was practically invisible beneath an unruly mess of thick files, random pieces of paper, stationery, iPads and a laptop. And resting on the laptop was the left hand of the man sitting calmly, legs crossed, in the dining chair beside it. He was staring directly into the barrel of Wren's gun. His dark, snake-like eyes flicked up. "Detective Inspector Wren, I presume," he said in a deep, home counties accent. "No need for the weapon, Inspector."

Wren didn't lower her gun as she looked him over more closely. Somewhere around thirty, she guessed. Not unattractive. Light from the spots in the ceiling glinted off his slicked back, jet-black hair. Narrow eyes and a broad nose sat symmetrically in a recently tanned, bemused face. He was slightly larger than average build but looked to be in good shape beneath a black polo neck, blue jeans and a short navy trench coat, buttons undone. Definitely MI5, thought Wren.

She lowered her gun and clicked the safety on but held onto it as she took a few steps to her right and leaned back against a kitchen worktop. She saw a glimmer of admiration in the man's eyes as they followed her movement. He wasn't here to kill her.

"You have me at a disadvantage, young man," she said as huskily as she could. She hated the form of address, but she had to try to project a sense of authority and calm.

"Nice try, Inspector, but we both know that's not going to happen," he replied, a gleam in his eye.

Confirmation, not that Wren needed it. So what was he here for? The laptop she craved lying beneath his palm? She was more than happy to let the silence build between them. She had nothing to do until Monday. She presumed he did. She remained impassive as the amusement left the man's face, but inside she was pumping a fist. "Breaking in to private people's homes a hobby of yours, Inspector?"

"I didn't break in, I had a key from a very concerned neighbour," she answered, an edge in her clipped tone. "I can't imagine how you got in." The gleam returned to the man's eye and a feeling of dread suddenly gripped her.

"The same way I got into your lovely house over in Richmond," he said, nothing in his voice. "I was sorry not to catch Finlay." A bored expression in his eye as he flipped up the lid of the laptop. "I understand he's with his father in Guildford this weekend. Shame you two don't get along anymore." He flashed her a cold, hard look.

Wren had been prepared to expect a certain level of threat, but this was way beyond anything she could have imagined. She couldn't keep it from her face.

The man continued to look at her as though she were something he'd trodden in. "I see you're unfamiliar with our remit, Inspector," he said, typing something on the laptop and hitting <ENTER> on the last word. He looked at the screen non-plussed for a second, then took a phone from his coat pocket. Started tapping and swiping.

With a huge effort of will, Wren smothered the fear and hatred that had built in her chest. "I'm familiar with the fact that if you touch a hair on my son's head, I will hunt you 'til your last breath," she seethed. It only succeeded in returning the amusement to the man's face.

"Can I let you into a secret, Inspector?" he chuckled. Then he switched off the mirth as quickly as it appeared. A murderous look replaced it. "I've got no idea why I'm here. I couldn't give a shit what you've done. Planning, tactical bollocks, fucking strategy. People far more qualified than me take care of that shit. Because they're the best in the fucking world at it." He uncrossed his legs and leaned forward. "Like I'm the best in the world at what they use me for."

Wren observed the look in the man's eyes. She'd seen the same look once before. In the eyes of a suicide bomber as he tried to detonate his faulty belt. Not psychotic, but incapable of fear or any hint of empathy. "You're forgetting that I have the gun," she said. And then she didn't. She'd barely registered his movement and started raising the pistol before it was wrestled from her hand. Pain shot up her right arm as the man placed the gun carelessly on the table, retook his seat and crossed his legs.

"Rub your arm, Inspector. The discomfort should wear off in a minute or two," he said calmly. Wren stared at him in abject terror. Fifteen years of close-quarters training undone in the blink of an eye.

"What…?" she began.

"Party trick, Inspector," he said languidly. "Made easier by the knowledge that you'd never shoot an MI5 operative."

Wren rubbed her forearm and the pain was replaced by pins and needles. Would she have shot him? Probably not, she conceded. The clock ticked and the fridge hummed. Wren's restless brain reassessed the new dynamic as the man eyed her with thoughtful distaste. It wasn't good. The reason she was here was being tapped on by a remorseless killing machine. Her only means of protection gone. The safety of the most important thing in her life in jeopardy. Her home compromised. She focused on that for a second.

"What were you doing at my house?" she asked, trying to keep the strain out of her voice.

His mouth contorted into a sneer. "Someone, probably a worthless strategist, thought you'd take your boss' warning. To stay out of whatever it is you're into that has warranted my deployment." He paused to let the implication sink in. "I was there to reinforce the message. I waited half an hour before I was sent here. Plenty of time to get acquainted with your stuff." The bored tone was back.

It raised hackles on Wren's neck. But she knew what this was now and she knew she had some difficult decisions to make. She also surmised that whoever was behind this thing didn't want it escalating. Someone had an acute aversion to exposure. She cursed silently. The knowledge was useless without an identity. The man's eyes flicked from the laptop like a snake's and narrowed on her hand as it moved slowly into her bag and came out with her puffer.

"Afflictions of the weak," he snorted and went back to typing.

"I suppose you're trying Val d'Isère and 1988 in some combination?" she said as placidly as she could.

His eyes zeroed in on her again.

"I wouldn't waste your time," she continued brusquely. "It's rarely a place other than a house name." She looked away and saw a cork board on the wall, dozens of random photographs stuck to it. Many of them were of Nathalie and Penelope together. Under the Eiffel Tower in Breton shirts. On a gondola with ice creams. At the top of a mountain, somewhere in the Lakes maybe. Sweaty in a crowd at a gig. Love, life and laughter poured from the images. Each was like a Kitchener poster, pointing an angry finger at Wren: What are you going to do? How are you going to right this terrible wrong? She closed her eyes. But she knew that was futile. She was suddenly very angry and beyond care. "Let's get this over with, shall we? Then you can crawl back under your grubby rock."

The man glared at her for a moment and then shut the laptop. He stood up and walked to the board Wren had been looking at. "Very pretty aren't they?" he murmured to himself. "I assume they have something to do with this business?"

Wren thought hard for a moment. Is he playing a game with me? "You really don't know what this is about?" Her gun was on the table in her peripheral vision to her left, equidistant between them. He was facing away from her, studying the photographs.

"Would that help me perform my work better?" he asked, not turning round.

Wren was shocked by the seriousness in his tone. She cast about in her mind for a suitable response. Couldn't find one. Then she thought about Mac and Penelope and she knew she had to try something. "One of those beautiful girls was killed last night." She let her softly spoken words hang. The man flexed his neck a couple of times. "For no reason that I can fathom," she continued in pleading tones. "Her sister is equally innocent."

He spun round suddenly, eyes blazing. "INNOCENT OF WHAT?" he roared at her. She flinched and recoiled against the unit. He took a slow pace toward her. She felt rage emanating from him like heat. "I bet you had a happy childhood," he snarled.

Wren didn't think. Wren ran. Straight into the man's palm which tightened around her throat. "So predictable," he hissed into her frantic upturned face. He pressed harder and Wren couldn't breathe. Animal instinct overtook. Flight wasn't an option so she lashed out a leg which the man met with a sharp heeled shoe. Adrenaline and the lack of oxygen prevented her feeling the full effect of the pain that seared into her shin. Nothing could have prevented her feeling the pain from her left kidney that followed the man's precise punch. She fell to the wooden floor as he let go of her throat. Instinctively, she gasped a lungful of air and agony ripped through her body. She writhed in vain against it, arms wrapped around her middle. She felt his hot breath on her neck and tried to turn her head away. "Imagine me doing this to Finlay, Inspector," he spat. "And not stopping until he was a vegetable."

"NOOOOO," she howled through the pain.

"That's what *will* happen," he breathed, "if I'm contacted about this again." The hot breath disappeared and Wren curled into a ball on her side. But the expected blow didn't come. She felt his deliberate footsteps through the polished floor, and then her brain gave it up.

Forty-Five

Friday Evening

McLeod poured cold water on the face of the man on the floor who coughed and spluttered and tried to sit up. McLeod pushed a size ten on his chest. The man's puffy eyes were bright red as he struggled to see where he was. He brought his bound hands to his face and rubbed desperately at his eyes.

"That will only make them worse," said Penelope, "which I'd be quite happy about. Alternatively, you could let me bathe them with this flannel."

The man was writhing his head from side to side. "Please," he wailed, "anything."

"You're going to have to lie nice and still," she said, kneeling beside his head. McLeod checked that the pillowcases binding the man's knees and ankles were tight. Then he rested a toe on the man's forehead to prevent him head-butting Penelope whilst she gently bathed his eyes with warm water from the room's fruit bowl.

McLeod was inspecting the items they'd recovered from the man's pockets and laid on a side table. He picked up an object like a penknife and pulled out a couple of its extensions. They were quite short and thin with little hooks on the end, pointing in different directions. "This might come in handy," he mused. "Gets you in most places, does it?"

The man on the floor grunted as Penelope softly massaged his eyes with the flannel. McLeod put it in his jeans pocket and picked up a black handle about six inches long. He pressed a tiny button near the top and six inches of blade flicked out. McLeod felt it with his thumb. "That's a nasty little piece of work," he said, rehousing the blade. "Aren't these things illegal?"

Again, the man did no more than grunt. Penelope finished up and took the bowl to the bathroom.

McLeod took his toe off the man's forehead and noted that his eyes were less red and puffy. "My friend did a good job. I'd like you to say thank you when she returns," he said evenly.

"Fuck you," barked the man on the floor.

"I see," said McLeod and sat in one of the room's armchairs. Penelope walked to the table and picked up the man's wallet while McLeod inspected the phone and frowned.

"Which one are you?" said Penelope, holding two credit cards. "Pavel Maksimiuk or Karel Kowalski?"

The man just glared up at them murderously. Penelope found a driver's licence. "Kowalski it is."

McLeod handed Penelope the man's phone, saying, "I'm not very familiar with these." She hit the 'on' button and a touch pad appeared. She tried one, two, three, four and shook her head at McLeod.

"We don't have much time, Mr Kowalski, and we need the code to your phone." McLeod checked his watch. Ten minutes had elapsed since they'd revived the man. He was fairly sure that the other two were in a much worse condition. But were there more of them? "Your code please, Mr Kowalski," he repeated.

The man sneered up at him. "Fuck you," he snarled savagely.

"Yes, I thought you might say that," said McLeod, standing wearily. He was fairly sure it was going to come to this. The big man in the bathroom at the bar that he knew nothing about, the guy on the stairs and the one in the street. All self-defence. Violence born of necessity. Now he had to do something he'd never contemplated. Something abhorrent to him in his normal existence. He was going to have to injure another human being in the full knowledge that that was his intention. So he'd been preparing himself mentally for the last ten minutes. Telling himself over and over that the man on the floor was here to kill him and Penelope. That he'd still be trying were he not trussed up like a turkey. More than anything, he drew the necessary steel from the searing image of Nathalie, lifeless in his bed, and from the deep attachment he was developing for her sister.

Penelope looked at him uncertainly. His posture was different, menacing, and there was something in his eyes she hadn't seen before. A dark look, a look that frightened her and sent her pulse racing.

"I'm quite new to this torturing business," McLeod said, stalking around the prone man's head. He flicked the knife out and Kowalski and Penelope both stared in horror at it in his hand. "I suppose you just…" With no warning, McLeod drove his right foot into the man's left side. Kowalski screamed. Then he bucked and brought his knees up toward his chest and howled as the pain spread out through his body.

McLeod closed his eyes briefly and took a deep, calming breath. "Let me know if I'm doing it right, Mr Kowalski," he said, pacing round the shaking man's legs. "Now I can't be certain, Mr Kowalski, but I think I've broken a rib and may have ruptured something." The man on the floor was trying to keep an eye on McLeod, but he kept having to close them against the pain wracking his body. "I'm fairly sure that if I do the same on this side, you'll probably spend the rest of your life needing help to take a piss." McLeod danced to follow the man's squirming efforts to put his right kidney out of his reach.

"NO, PLEASE," Kowalski screeched, "it's one-nine-seven-seven."

McLeod kneeled down to Kowalski's level. "Thank you," he said. "I'd consider another line of work if I were you because I'm a complete novice at this sort of thing." He shifted his right elbow in front of the man's contorted face just as Kowalski screwed his eyes up and threw all his remaining force into a head-butt. The jar of the impact of the man's head on his elbow caused pins and needles to shoot up McLeod's biceps. Kowalski's head smashed back onto the carpet and his eyes rolled over.

McLeod stood and physically shook himself all over. Then he cast a fearful eye at Penelope. Saw the shock in her face and prepared himself for the worst. Instinctively, Penelope knew what she had to do. She had to run. She took two quick strides and launched herself at McLeod, threw her arms around his neck, her legs around his middle and held him tighter than she'd ever held anyone before. "God damn it, Mac. That was amazing," she choked, fresh tears burning her cheeks.

McLeod was dumfounded. "I just hurt someone, Pen. Really badly," he said, incredulous.

Penelope pulled her head back to look in his bewildered eyes. "I know, Mac. But we really needed that." She closed her eyes and kissed him deeply. Then bit his top lip gently as she reluctantly withdrew. "I think I know how hard that was for you," she murmured.

McLeod grabbed a tissue from the box on the side table and dabbed at her cheeks. Smiling wearily, he said, "You're a wise owl, Penelope Lane." Then something of the look she'd seen in his eyes before returned. "Come on," he said. "We've got to move. Take this guy's legs, will you?" Together, they heaved him onto the bed. Penelope filled a glass with water from the bathroom and put it on the table beside the unconscious man as McLeod stuffed everything in their rucksack. Then she picked up her new mobile and called Wren. McLeod was adjusting the sheet round the man's wrists. He looked up at Penelope and saw fear etched once more in her beautiful eyes.

"No reply, Mac," she said.

Forty-Six

Friday evening

Kurjac stared in horror at the phone in his hand. How was it possible, he thought numbly, for an inanimate object to be the source of such despair and pain. His face twisted into a look of undiluted hatred as he smashed his left fist into the screen again and again and again until the remains of the phone lay in a twisted mess of glass and plastic and metal at his feet and his knuckles were grazed and bleeding.

He hadn't cried since that day in the barn beside his dead father despite all the death and heartbreak he'd endured since. He'd thought he was no longer physically capable. That his heart was just a cold, hard lump of granite. But he was sobbing uncontrollably now. He threw his head back and howled at the ceiling. Eventually, the weight of the pain transformed into a rage more devastating than anything he'd ever felt before. It seared every fibre of his being and gave him a feeling of all-consuming omnipotence. Like nothing mattered anymore. There was a small, sturdy table beside the armchair. He picked it up by two of its legs. He strained every sinew and snapped off three of them one by one. The fourth one was harder. He had to use his feet to help him smash it. As it came off, a wave of bitter euphoria washed over him. He collapsed, panting, to the floor.

He lay there for a while until a strange peace descended on his tortured mind. Until he felt like he was above himself, looking down. He could just make out a dark figure lying on the lushly carpeted floor of a room in one of the grandest hotels in the world. It was barely recognisable as a human being. Hadn't been for years. Not since the day the soldiers broke it for the first time as an innocent young boy. It had been broken repeatedly ever since, each time a mark was left like the rings in a tree trunk. So that now, its soul was like a shattered mirror, scattered into tortured, twisted shards. It lay there dying, like the last embers of a fire. The words of his favourite British poet came to him. 'Rage, rage against the dying of the light.'

His eyes flicked open. Wearily, he hauled himself across the floor to the bed and sat with his back against it. Leaned his head on the mattress and looked bleakly up at the ceiling. He closed his eyes. This was it. Did he have the strength and the will to mend his broken self? To bring back to life the boy who'd been killed all those years ago. To be the person he was meant to have been. Or was he beyond repair? Wouldn't the world be a better place without him in it? He thought about all the people he'd killed. Only one troubled him. The beautiful girl last night. Remorse struck him afresh and he reached for the bottle again. Took a swig and spat it out. He threw the bottle against the wall opposite, where it smashed, leaving dark trails on the wallpaper.

He dragged his knees up to his chest and wrapped his arms round them and tried to envision an outcome that could possibly make him whole once more. Thought about all the things that would have to happen to make that outcome possible. The enormity of what he had to do almost made him give it up. Then the terror in Hana's eyes in the awful picture flashed in his mind and he knew he had to do whatever it took. It was his only chance. If it meant his life, so be it. He reached a nervous hand for his other phone.

Forty-Seven

Friday evening

Penelope had Kowalski's unlocked phone on her lap as she rode next to McLeod near the front of the top deck of a lurching night bus. The display read nine thirty-two p.m. and at this time on a Friday, heading in to central London, there were only five or six other occupants upstairs. They'd found no trace of their other two attackers on their way out of the hotel. They had discovered the hotel owner in a pool of blood behind his counter as they used the lobby's phone to call the police. They neither saw nor heard the darkly dressed man who got out of his car and followed them in the shadows as they made their way to the high street.

McLeod was flung against Penelope as the bus made a sharp right. "Sorry," he said, grabbing the rail on the vacant seat in front.

"I'm not," Penelope replied, smiling, and gave his thigh a squeeze. She frowned and McLeod couldn't decide whether he preferred her happy face or her serious one. "Why can't we get hold of Wren, Mac? I'm really worried about her."

McLeod looked uncertain for a second, then said, "I'm not, Pen. She's one tough cookie."

The concern didn't abate in Penelope's eyes. "Where are we staying again?"

"A private club owned by a friend from my university days." He smiled briefly as he recalled the batty décor. "Funny place tucked down an alley. Might have to sleep on a sofa, but it's safe. You need a code to get in."

She seemed slightly reassured. Then the fearful look returned as she looked at the phone in her hand. "Are you really sure you want to do this, Mac?"

McLeod glanced behind him at the other occupants on the top deck. Four had their eyes closed, earphones in, and the other

188

two were involved in a heated discussion. Penelope's eyes were momentarily lit by a streetlight. He saw the worry in their corners. "Absolutely, Pen. It might be our only chance to get whoever's behind this nightmare to leave us alone." He knew it was bullshit before the words left his mouth. Penelope wore a 'yeah, right' look on her face. "Okay," he said, "but I don't see how it could increase the danger we're in and whoever it is might let something slip that could help us."

Penelope looked at him doubtfully but brought up the phone's call register, tapped on the most recent contact just marked 'K', hit 'call' and passed it to McLeod. It answered on the second ring.

"Kurjac," said a deep foreign accent.

McLeod said nothing for five seconds.

"Karel, talk to me," the voice said.

East European, thought McLeod. Probably Slavic. "I don't think your friend will be saying anything for a while," McLeod replied calmly. There was only heavy breathing for a few seconds. Then a strangely quiet, disembodied voice came back at him.

"I don't have any friends, Mr McLeod."

There was another pause as McLeod pondered the slightly incongruous words.

"So," the man continued, "you put all three of them down, Mr McLeod. That's very…impressive. Are you with Miss Lane?"

McLeod thought about the safest way to answer that. Then decided not to. "If you are," the man continued, "I want you to do something for me." Another pause.

"Go on," said McLeod.

He heard the strain in the man's voice as it intoned, "Please tell her I'm very sorry about her sister."

McLeod put as much venom into his response as he could. "Bit fucking late for that," he seethed and glanced warily at Penelope. She shot him a questioning look.

"I know," the man said morosely. "I'm sorry about that too."

The guy didn't sound much like a cold-blooded killer. More like someone confessing their sins to a priest. The bus came to a jerking halt and the arguing couple took to the stairs. A young man in waiter's uniform came up them. McLeod frowned. Wasn't it a bit early to be coming off shift on a Friday night? But he was engrossed in a game on his phone.

"Are you the guy from the bar with the funny ear?" he said into the phone, not worrying about the man's sensibilities. McLeod heard the heavy breathing again.

"My name is Kurjac and part of my right ear was shot off when I was a boy." The man's tone was indifferent. Why the embellishments, wondered McLeod. The use of his name? What else could he get him to divulge?

"Listen, Kurjac. Neither Miss Lane nor I know of any reason why you're doing this." He paused, thinking about his next words. How to make them as convincing as possible. "We don't have the slightest clue about whatever it was Nathalie was into and have no interest in finding out. You have absolutely nothing to gain by continuing to pursue us." McLeod couldn't keep the note of desperation from his voice. The line was quiet. "Did you hear me, Kurjac?" The man's silence was disquieting. "Why are you doing this to us?" McLeod practically pleaded.

"Because my niece has only one ear left." A pause and then, "You'll need to watch your back, Mr McLeod." The line went dead. A frown hooded McLeod's eyes as he handed the phone back to Penelope. It had started to rain and the droplets on the window gave a fly's eye impression of the bright street below.

Penelope looked at his sharp profile. Thick, furrowed brow, straight nose, deep-set eyes. A wide mouth and a strong chin. "Well?" she said as he continued brooding.

"Confusing," McLeod answered finally.

"So I gather," she replied, slightly exasperated. "Confusing how?"

The bus shuddered to a halt again outside Victoria Station. McLeod felt the handbrake come on and heard groans from the other passengers. Changing drivers never seemed to take less than ten minutes. An attractive redhead around thirty came up the stairs, chatting on her phone in a clipped Irish brogue. She glanced at McLeod as she walked past. He followed her progress to the back of the bus. He could tell from her body language as she sat down that she was gossiping with a girlfriend. He turned back to Penelope.

"When I asked this Kurjac why he was trying to kill us, he said it was because his niece only has one ear."

Penelope looked at him as though he were speaking in tongues. "What the hell's that got to do with anything? You can't have heard him right."

Her words made him think again. "No…sorry, Pen." He took a deep breath and tried to recall the man's exact words. "He said she had only one ear *left.*"

She continued to look nonplussed. "I still don't see how…" She broke off at the look in McLeod's eyes. They were gleaming.

"I wish you could have heard how the guy sounded, Pen. It was like he was deeply conflicted or something." McLeod paused and chewed over Kurjac's words. "He said for me to tell you that he was sorry for Nathalie's death."

Penelope felt like the world had turned upside down. That the man for whom she was beginning to harbour serious feelings was beginning to be affected by the strain. "I…I…" she began before words failed her. She couldn't even begin to comprehend why the man who'd killed her sister would say such a thing. She felt numb. The bus revved briefly, then lumbered out into the light traffic.

McLeod was still deep in thought as they approached Westminster. The rain had eased to spits and spots. He half-turned to face Penelope. He noted her look of uncertainty and thought carefully about his words. "I think this guy Kurjac has problems of his own. The conflict in his voice? The reference to his niece? Somehow I get the feeling he's not acting from free will." McLeod paused as the bus veered into perhaps the most influential street in the modern history of the world. He cast a baleful eye at the Treasury offices, then the Foreign and Commonwealth buildings. They passed the Cenotaph, edifice to the glory of Britain's war dead. McLeod failed to see what was glorious about dying face down in some putrid, blood-soaked field. Especially when it was the greed and intolerance of your own forefathers that put you there.

"It's the apology bit I don't get," he said quietly. "Why would you say sorry unless you didn't mean…" McLeod froze. They were level with Downing Street and he turned away. What had Penelope said to him in the hotel room?

"What is it, Mac?" Real alarm in her voice now. Her words came back to him and their implication took the wind out of him. No, that couldn't be possible, he tried to tell himself. Why would anybody…? He opened his mouth to try to breathe.

"Mac, you're beginning to scare me," she gasped.

Shit, shit, shit he thought to himself. That's the last thing he wanted. Their stop was approaching fast. He mustered all the will

191

he could find and aimed for a look of worried composure and made a mental note to think about this again later. "I'm sorry, Pen," he said, taking her hand. "I guess it's the stress of not knowing what's going on or who to trust or where to turn next." He sighed and took heart from the look of sympathy in Penelope's eyes. "I woke up this morning as an unemployed academic, for God's sake." Now I'm haring around town with an impossibly beautiful woman pursued by faceless fiends, he thought. "Come on, Pen," he said, grabbing the rucksack, "this is us."

The only other passenger who got off with them was the young waiter still playing games on his phone. Which struck McLeod as being odd. He looked around at the Friday night hubbub back toward Trafalgar Square and couldn't think of anywhere a young waiter could live round here. Penelope saw his look of unease and followed his gaze. She watched the young man saunter along the pavement toward the Strand. "What, you think…"

"I don't know," McLeod replied. "I just want to be sure." They followed him at a discreet distance for a few minutes. Relief flooded him as the guy climbed a couple of steps and entered a late bar. He hadn't come off shift, he was just starting one. "Okay, we're safe, Pen. Let's go."

The young man watched through the glass door of the bar as McLeod put an arm round Lane and navigated the broad street. Then he dialled the number he'd been told to. "They're on foot heading west. Charing Cross, maybe." He smiled and clicked off. Easiest hundred quid he'd ever earned.

They weren't heading for Charing Cross, but that made no difference to the man standing on the steps under the elegant façade of St Martin-in-the-Fields as they passed right in front of him. He tapped his phone as he pressed himself off the wall of the ancient building. "I have them," he said, quartering the church and following them toward theatre land. He smiled as they ducked into a tiny alleyway. Perfect, he thought. It was dark, but he could make out their silhouettes easily from the light at the other end of the alley. They were twenty paces ahead of him. He took five quiet steps further into the dark and raised his silenced Glock and then sighted it on the girl. He put pressure on the trigger and took a slow, deep breath. It was his last. His head was pulled back sharply and he felt a second of searing pain across his throat. Then he fell like a sack of bones to the grimy floor of the alley.

The sound of the gun clattering and the man's head hitting the cobbles caused McLeod and Penelope to look round quickly. Instinctively, McLeod pushed Penelope behind him. He caught a glimpse of a dark shoulder and leg darting out of the alley's entrance. His heart beat fiercely in his chest as he turned to face Penelope. "Are you all right?" he breathed. He used both hands to touch her cheeks, her shoulders, her waist.

"I'm fine, Mac," she said shakily. "What was that?"

McLeod drew her to him in a tight hug. She smelled musky and warm. "I don't know, Pen," he said, adrenaline coursing through him. "I think there's someone on the ground back there."

She pulled out of his embrace and peered around his broad shoulders, and could just about make out an incongruous shape writhing near the alley's entrance. She took a couple of quick steps in that direction before McLeod put a hand on her shoulder.

"Wait," he whispered frantically, "it might be a trap."

She stopped dead, unzipped her handbag and came out with Kowalski's phone. "I think these things have a torch," she said, bringing it to life. She hit the camera and volume buttons before she found the right one. She looked at McLeod and saw her anxiety reflected in his eyes. "We need to know, Mac."

He knew she was right. Cautiously, they made their way back the way they'd come. McLeod was amazed by the amount of light the phone generated and they hadn't taken ten small paces before it was evident that the dark shape wasn't going anywhere soon. No one still breathing would choose to lie like that. As they inched closer, they saw the shock still captured in the dead man's eyes in a head that was twisted toward them at a grotesque angle to the rest of his prone body. His face was already white as blood continued to seep from his gaping neck. Penelope buried her face in McLeod's chest. "Jesus, Mac," she whimpered.

He put a hand through her thick hair. "Wait here, Pen," he said. "You don't need to see any more of this."

She looked up at him in the eerie light in the alley and saw again the look in his eyes that unnerved her. The image of Nathalie's greying lips in the black bag at the hospital came unbidden to her mind and a grim resolve settled in her core. "Yes, I do, Mac," she said, taking his hand and pointing the light towards the body.

The blood had sprayed mostly on the walls of the alley, but there was still enough of it on the ground that McLeod and Penelope had to pick their way carefully around the man. He was white, somewhere around forty, McLeod guessed, and dressed in jeans, a dark pullover and a lightweight jacket. Penelope's eyes widened as she saw the gun still gripped in his outstretched right hand, finger taut on the trigger. Gingerly, and trying to avoid looking at the horrible face and throat, McLeod knelt to feel in the man's jacket pockets. He found a phone and a wallet and a piece of A4 paper, folded twice. He stood and handed Penelope the phone. "Can you get this to work, d'you think?"

"I'll try," she said as McLeod opened the dead man's wallet. "No, it's another code, Mac, and I can't see this guy giving it to us." She shone the light on the wallet in McLeod's hands. It was a simple brown leather affair. The left-hand half of it was for credit cards and the like. The right half was clear plastic. Nestled behind it was a card which displayed the man's photo, the Queen's insignia and the words 'MI5 Security Service.' McLeod dropped it as though it were burning his fingers.

He looked at Penelope and the disbelief riven on her features. With a shaking hand, he unfolded the piece of paper. Penelope shone the light on it. Two colour photographs made by a good printer. The one at the top was a close-up of Penelope from the chest up. A woman's hand was resting on her right shoulder. McLeod guessed it was half of a photo and surmised the hand belonged to Nathalie. It was the other picture that caused his blood to run cold. He'd expected to see himself gurning up out of the paper. He didn't. He saw Detective Inspector Wren.

Forty-Eight

Friday evening

"Sorry I'm late, old man," said Sir David, lowering himself into the familiar contours of his favourite leather armchair in the study of his Mayfair town house. A dying fire wheezed in the ornately tiled hearth opposite. Muffled sounds of feminine laughter were just audible from somewhere above.

"Hhhrrruummfff," gurgled Sir Francis, jerking to life.

"Oh, I didn't realise you were asleep, old thing," Sir David said, fishing a small plastic container from his jacket pocket. He placed it on the antique oak table between his chair and his companion's.

"Huurrr, must have dozed off," said Sir Francis, rubbing his long, thin face and taking a hearty draft from his cavernous brandy glass. "It's these wretched pills I'm on."

Sir David groaned out of his seat and hobbled to a cabinet. Eighteen holes was getting to be a serious proposition, even with the buggy. He sat back down heavily with a glass of his own and filled it generously with twelve-year-old cognac. He opened the plastic container and rattled ten pills of varying colours and sizes into his palm, chucked them in his mouth and washed them down. "I know what you mean," he said, swirling the liquor in his glass. "And the cost! Seventy thousand a year for this lot." He shook the empty container at Sir Francis and set it back on the table.

"What, you don't pay for the stuff, man?"

"Good Lord, no," he said vociferously. "I don't think so anyway. The Party does, I s'pose, or the taxpayer more likely."

They sat sipping in silence for a spell in the dimly lit room. Old books lined the walls in heavy oak shelves around the hearth. A shaft of weak streetlight ghosted through a gap in the heavy curtains. Occasionally, a vehicle's headlights caused it to brighten and swish across the thick carpet. There was a dull thud from the floor above. Sir David cast a dark, yellowing eye at the ceiling. "How many's she got up there?" he said irritably.

"I popped my head in when I arrived," said Sir Francis, stretching in his chair. "Like a bloody viper's nest, it was. What is it tonight?"

Sir David snorted. "I dunno. What is it, Friday? Book club maybe." He took a large gulp of brandy and his phone from an inside pocket. "Urquhart send you news of the latest arse-up?"

"Hmmnn, fairly nasty by the sound of it." His own phone pinged and Sir Francis grunted as he retrieved it from the floor. "Must have dropped it when I fell asleep," he said absently. He did the fingerprint thing, hurriedly shut down the unwholesome website he'd been perusing and opened the picture message. "Very nasty, here take a look."

Sir David pushed his glasses up and peered at the screen. "Christ, Francis," he said, rearing back from the ghastly image. "Give a chap a bit of warning." He took a few laboured breaths and glanced at the fire. "I suppose we'll be needing another log on," he said, heaving himself up again.

"And another bottle of brandy, old man," said Sir Francis, pouring a stiff measure. "This one's nearly done for."

Sir David emptied the remnants of the bottle into his glass and crossed to the cabinet. "I don't want to have to deal with Lady Harris' biddies," he said, rummaging. "This'll have to do, I'm afraid." He deposited a bowl of cashews on the table along with the cognac.

Sir Francis grunted, took a handful and began munching thoughtfully. "Something's not right with this," he said, pointing a finger at the gruesome picture on his phone.

"You reckon?" Sir David snorted.

"That's not what I mean, David. What was he called, our fellow... Stokes, was it?"

"Stones," said Sir David, reaching for the nuts.

"Stones, right. Did you see his file?" Sir Francis made his points on his long bony fingers. "Sixteen years in the field, seven of them with Section Six, for Christ's sake." He paused and found the file on his phone. "Assignments in Moscow, Istanbul and Cairo. I wouldn't go within a hundred miles of any of those places." He drained his glass again at the thought. "Highly skilled in close combat, top marksman, specialist in side-arms." He held eight opaque fingers up to Sir David and an apoplectic glare.

Raised a ninth. "He had his gun drawn, yet our erstwhile academic left him with his head hanging off?"

Sir David felt a chill and looked morosely at the log wilfully refusing to ignite in the grate. He groaned and hauled himself up from his chair again. He coaxed the smouldering wood into a more favourable position with a sooty poker. "How sure are we that this was the work of the McLeod man?" he said, resting a stout elbow on the mantelpiece between framed photographs of himself with the Prime Minister and the President. "Didn't Brian say they found a knife in the hotel room along with the tied-up Polish chap?"

"My point entirely, David," said Sir Francis, stretching his long, scrawny legs. "I can just about accept that this McLeod character is some sort of martial arts fiend, but this?" He held his phone toward his friend.

Sir David flicked an ember from his fresh trousers. "Remember that Yank, Rumsfeld?" he murmured. "That God-awful guff about knowns and unknowns?"

"Actually, I always thought that was rather clever," replied Sir Francis, primly. "Got the media in such a stramash that they forgot whatever it was he was trying to cover up."

"Whatever," said Sir David, shortly. "What we actually know is that for all he's a mild mannered, recently redundant professor of mumbo jumbo from some minuscule university, he's put four men in hospital. Three of them highly skilled, cold-blooded killers." He retook his seat and began wrestling with the bottle. "I mean, who else could have done it?"

Sir Francis cast an impatient eye at his companion's fumblings with the corkscrew. "Well, not the woman, we take it. What do we know of his associates?"

"Damn this infernal thing," Sir David blared. "Blasted wire and foil and cork. It's as if they don't want you to get at the bloody stuff. Have a word with your chap in Paris, won't you, old man?"

"Pass it here, you old coot. You'll hurt it like that."

Sir David handed over the duties gratefully. "Associates you say?" He dabbed his forehead with a handkerchief. "Not many that we know of. There's a brother and a few work colleagues. A couple of friends from university and that's it." He swilled the glass Sir Francis handed him. "Not the sociable type, apparently."

"Not much scope there, then."

197

"Urquhart says he doesn't have a sausage on any of them." A sudden crackling in the hearth met with Sir David's approval.

"Bah, this is just pointless speculation, don't you think, old chap?" said Sir Francis, dashing his phone on his scraggy thigh. "What's it matter who killed the fellow?"

Sir David cast him a pregnant look. "Precisely that, Francis. We now have two dead people. Two sets of friends and relatives and colleagues to circumvent. Not that anyone knows about either yet, but we can't sit on them forever."

"No, I suppose not," said Sir Francis gloomily. "But how could anyone ever make a link between them?"

"They bloody-well will if the idiots ever get the right sodding woman," Sir David replied, taking a prodigious swig. "I've half a mind to do it myself." He checked his watch. Half ten. The weekend was approaching fast. Things always became more complicated then. He lifted his specs to his forehead, rubbed his eyes and sighed heavily. "The Polish man's phone still where it was?"

"Urquhart said he'd call if it moved," Sir Francis answered with a yawn.

Sir David looked at his phone with a feeling of annoyance. Then a brighter thought struck him. "All work and no play doesn't make the world go round, old thing." He glanced at his friend and saw a gleam enter his eye. "I'll give Brian the go-ahead to sort this thing out tonight. Launch the heavy artillery. You see what entertainment you can rustle us up."

"Boys or girls?" asked Sir Francis, swiping his phone.

"I rather fancy a bit of both," replied Sir David, hitting call.

Forty-Nine

Friday evening

Wren felt cold. Then she felt terror. Then she felt something calling her. Then she woke. She tried lifting herself from the hard, wooden floor, but she was struck by an intense pain in her side. She gasped and reached awkwardly behind her and felt for the insistent phone in her bag.

"Hello," she said weakly, hitching herself across the floor to rest against the back of the kitchen unit.

"Anna, thank God. We've been trying to reach you for ages." Something in Penelope's voice cleared the clouds in Wren's brain. The terrible threat from the monster repeated in her mind. She needed to get Finlay somewhere safe. Where the hell was that? She inched her bottom backwards and winced at the stab from her left side, felt it carefully with her hand. She looked around her warily, listening hard for any trace of the fiendish man. She heard only the hum of the fridge and the tick of the clock on the wall. It read ten thirty-five. She looked across the dark wood floor to the dining table, her eyes coming to rest on the slim edge of the laptop still sitting there. Why hadn't he taken it?

"Penelope, where are you? Is Mac with you?"

There was a pause on the line, some muffled noise. "Yes, Mac's here." Again she caught the apprehension in Penelope's inflection. "We're at a private club near Covent Garden. A friend of Mac's."

Wren brought her legs up to her chest and planted her free hand against the unit behind her. She pushed painfully with both and worked her way upright. She must have made an awful racket because Penelope came back on. "What's the matter, Anna? Are you all right?"

"Been better," she replied, hobbling a few steps to the table and sitting in front of Nathalie's laptop. The effort made her head spin. She rooted in her bag and came out with paracaetamol, a bottle of water and her puffer. She availed herself of them all and detected a slight improvement. "Listen, Penelope. This thing is just too big. You have to get out of the country or something."

The anxiety in Penelope's voice went up a notch. "We've been having the same thoughts...but Mac's passport is at his flat. We think someone from MI5 followed us here." Her voice cracked. "He was killed, Anna."

"What?" Wren cried. "How?"

"We don't know." She could hear Penelope stifling a sob. "We heard a noise behind us in an alley and found a man with his throat cut."

Wren heard heavy breathing as her brain raced. "He had a gun drawn, Anna." There were more muffled noises, and then Mac's warm voice was on the line.

"Anna, where are you?" he said, urgency clear in his tone.

Wren lifted the lid of the laptop and hit the power button. "At Nathalie's apartment. Mac, none of what Penelope said makes any sense." She couldn't keep the disbelief out of her voice.

"I know, Anna, but it happened just as she described. I think I got a glimpse of someone running away, but it was so dark..."

Wren thought about her own recent experience and tried to equate it with what Penelope and Mac were saying. It confirmed only one thing. "This is completely fucked up, Mac. You've got to get as far away as you can right now."

"I know, Anna, but where? How? They must know where we are. There's more..."

"Wait, Mac, how must they know where you are?"

Wren detected a touch of impatience in his reply. "I don't know, cameras or something." There was a pause on the line and then, "Oh shit, Anna. I think I've done something stupid."

The painkiller was starting to work so that a dull ache was all Wren could feel down her left side. She watched the laptop screen powering up with growing irritability. "Go on, Mac," she said with a sense of foreboding.

"We were attacked at the hotel. Three men. East European. We took one of their phones. Thought we could call whoever's behind this and persuade them we didn't know anything."

Wren closed her eyes. It was as bad as she feared. "You've still got the phone, right, Mac?" She took a deep drag on her puffer.

"I'm sorry, Anna. We didn't realise the lengths they could go to."

Wren detected a definite note of resignation in Mac's voice. Not good. She needed him thinking positively if they were to have any hope of finding a way through this thing. Problem was, she couldn't think of a single positive thing to say. MI5 were trying to kill them and knew where they were to the nearest couple of metres. Probably had the place staked out, front and back. Private club or not, they could probably walk in whenever they wanted. She wondered why they hadn't done so already.

"Are you still there, Anna?"

His words disrupted her train of thought. "Damn it, man, let me think for a minute," she said, a little more testily than she'd meant. McLeod didn't apologise. Very literal man, Wren mused briefly before returning to her previous thoughts. She knew little of MI5's methods beyond a vague understanding that they were often unpredictable and always ridiculously meticulous. She tried to put herself in their position. Couldn't do it. Then something else Mac had said jarred in her mind. "You said you were attacked by three men, Mac? What happened? Are they still out there?"

"I don't know, Anna." She heard a soft scraping sound and imagined him scratching his chin. "I'm fairly sure two of them won't be doing much of anything for a while. The third guy was a Pole, Kowalski. It was his phone we took. We left him tied up in our hotel room."

Wren's head was spinning again. "Jesus Christ, Mac. You're like a one-man army or something." Her own words got her thinking again. She thought about the possible connection between three incapacitated East Europeans and MI5. Thought about the dead MI5 agent. None of those people were less than extraordinarily competent. She put it all together and came up with the face of the demon who'd visited her earlier. "I think you've got them in a bit of a spin, Mac." She thought some more and motives became clearer. They were thinking that Mac had dispatched three hired help and one of their own. She thought about her own small unit. Had someone done that to them, she'd be scared shitless. She tried their tactics again and her thoughts were more fruitful. She looked at the clock on the wall. "Listen, Mac. I think you've got a window to get out of there, but it's closing fast." She debated telling him about the man who was probably on his way but decided that it couldn't possibly help.

"Okay, Anna, what should we do?" Hope back in his voice. Wren smiled to herself.

She thought harder still, her mental faculties fully restored. The phone was the problem, but might it also be a possible solution? A scenario began to take shape in her mind. Could it ever work? It might just and she had sod-all else to go with. The laptop had finally powered up. She ignored the password entry and instead hovered the cursor over the battery indicator. Thirteen percent or sixteen minutes available. It would have to do. She thought about the geography around where Mac and Penelope were as she closed the laptop and rummaged on the table for a carry case. She found it and loaded the computer. "Okay then, Mac," said Wren, walking along the hallway to Nathalie's front door. She paused as she caught a glimpse of a VW badge attached to some keys on a hook by the door. "Here's what I need you to do."

Fifty

Friday afternoon

Miles Gatuso cast a cursory eye over the bright lights of the London night. From five hundred feet above, they stretched almost to the horizon in every direction. The earlier rain made all the surfaces glisten with reflected light so that the whole of the great city seemed to shimmer. Gatuso could feel its energy coursing through him as he sat in the co-pilot's seat of the rattling ex-RAF Gazelle. This is what he lived for. The anticipation. The job on the Wren woman was all right, but he'd known it was only going to amount to one small act of violence. This time he had carte blanche.

He'd always known he was different, years before he heard of the term sado-masochism. He didn't know whether he was born weird or whether his childhood had fostered the condition. Probably both. His face hardened as he thought of his parents. His absent father, always away on business. Bringing back presents as a substitute for any form of affection. Disappearing, stony faced into his office room and slamming the door. At night, he would often hear cries from his mother, but he didn't know what they were. Her life was mostly spent zonked out on gin and sedatives or attending endless society engagements. The sight of him always caused a pained expression to cross her face.

He'd been packed off to boarding school at seven years old. The bullying started then. He hadn't developed much language and had no idea how to form friendships. He was singled out as being odd and was beaten up almost every day. He started banging his head on the wall until he knocked himself out. Then he began cutting himself. He didn't know why.

The next year brought children smaller than himself to the school. He found ways of getting them on their own and hurting them. It made him feel alive. Soon he was threatened with his parents being summoned which was the last thing in the world he wanted. He needed another outlet for his torment. He found it in animals. He started pulling legs off spiders. He visited the school's gardens and smashed slugs and snails to a pulp. Slaughtered any insects he could find with a ping-pong bat. One day he spotted a cat hiding in the shrubs. He stole a vegetable knife from the canteen and used a bit of his lunch to lure it behind a groundsman's shed. He plunged the knife in over and over. His euphoria lasted the rest of the day.

In senior school, he discovered a new form of relief. One night early in his first term, three older boys came to his tiny room. Two of them pinned him face down on his bed by his arms and legs while the other went to work in his behind. It was incredibly painful and the two boys holding him punched him to try to stop his wriggling. The combination of the painful blows and the sensations below were amazing and he had his first orgasm. When he became too big to be bothered with, he began inflicting the same treatment on smaller boys and that was even better.

A few years later, he left school with few qualifications and went straight into the army. It was the perfect environment for him. He was told on a daily basis that he was worthless and any necessity to think about anything at all was removed. The discipline and no-nonsense of army life was what he craved and he began to excel. Guns became an obsession. He trained for a couple of years on the range and became one of the infantry's best shots.

Then the second Gulf War came along, which, like the first one, had absolutely nothing to do with oil. Gatuso didn't give a shit what it was about. He just wanted to kill people. And on the third day of his first tour, he did. Lying prone on the roof of an abandoned apartment block in searing Baghdad heat, he had the head of an Iraqi insurgent in a building half a mile away in his sights and a massive hard on. He pulled the trigger and a couple of seconds later, the man's head exploded like a watermelon in his scope. He came spontaneously in his fatigues.

By the end of his third tour, he was highly decorated with over thirty confirmed kills. It was during this tour that he learned via a strained letter from his mother that his father was dying of prostate cancer. Gatuso wrote back saying he hoped it was slow.

It wasn't. He was forced to attend the funeral by his squadron's Captain. He hadn't seen his mother in three years and she was frail with a grey pallor. She couldn't look at him as they stood solemnly around a big hole in the ground, a shapeless mound of dark brown earth beside it. The November morning was cold and blustery, the wind whistling in the twisted black yews. A gust caught his mother's coat sleeve and it rode up, revealing scores of angry red puncture marks on her forearm. Gatuso focused a murderous gaze at the heavy coffin poised above the cavernous pit.

That night he slept in his old bedroom for the first time in years. He woke in a sweat from a nightmare in which his father was flogging his mother. He switched on the bedside light and saw his duffel bag on the floor. A cold calm descended on him. He got up and reached into the bag for his hunting knife, carried it to his mother's bedroom. He switched on the wall light. She was out cold, snoring weakly. He got on the bed and pulled the covers. A pair of white silk pyjamas couldn't conceal the emaciated state of the body they covered. He rolled her onto her back. She remained lifeless. Then he thrust the knife repeatedly into her broken heart.

He was sent by the army to a psychological facility while the case against him was being prepared. A few days later, he was visited in his private hospital room by a doctor and a high-ranking MI5 operative. He answered their questions and filled out evaluations for several hours. By the end of their visit, he was told that the case against him would never be heard for as long as he worked for them and remained under their strict control.

"What's the work?" he'd asked.

The doctor had looked at him with disgust. "What you were born to do," he'd replied coldly.

The sudden descent of the helicopter brought him back to the mission. He clicked off the GPS map on his phone that charted their progress toward the target area and opened the message again. He savoured the words. <...by any and all means necessary...> Reluctantly, he deleted the message. He rewarded himself by thinking of all the things he could do given time and a suitable location. He tapped open the images of his victims again and felt like pinching himself. The man was magnificent and the woman spectacular. This could well turn out to be the best night of his life.

Bob Cannon was bored. He had only one task to perform tonight and it had begun to grate a long time ago. He'd been staring at a stationary dot on a grey map on a computer screen for over an hour. All he knew about the dot was that it was a phone and it was in the interest of national security that its location was monitored. It hadn't been exciting previously when the blasted thing was actually moving, but at least he felt as though he were achieving something. Fair enough, it was only keeping his section head informed of its progress from Chelsea, where they picked it up, to its current location a little north and east of Trafalgar Square. But it had been some form of activity.

He rubbed his eyes for the umpteenth time. Rolled his neck and flexed his shoulders. A nerve was painfully trapped somewhere. He looked around the stark, sterile monitoring room and received sympathetic nods from a few of the other poor sods still working at quarter to eleven on a Friday night. With a deep sigh, he looked back to the screen. Had the dot moved? He blinked his eyes and looked again. Definitely. He adjusted his headset. "Sir, it's on the move, heading east," he breathed urgently. He watched, mesmerised, as the little object of such interest jumped three metres at a time. "Looks like it's entered a building…it's gone through the building…it's continuing to head east towards the Strand…now it's moving north on Bedford Street."

Gatuso and his pilot got the feed through their earphones. A different voice came on. "Are you sure? I didn't see them leave the front."

"They didn't come out the back either," said another operative.

A more authoritative voice came on. "Interconnecting cellars. Got to be. Move now. Bedford Street, heading north."

"Roger that," the disembodied operatives said in unison.

Gatuso ground his teeth and cursed. He'd wanted them in a room by himself with a variety of implements and his imagination. Now it had turned into a footrace. He knew from experience that they never ended in the circumstances he desired. Usually a blockade or siege and a hail of bullets. Well, the least he could do was to ensure it was his gun that fired them.

"We'll be coming up on Bedford Street in ten seconds, sir," the pilot's static-heavy voice said in his earphones.

Gatuso zoomed out a little on the map on his phone and studied the area for a couple of seconds. "Okay, looks like they're headed for Covent Garden. Safety in numbers. Set me down in the grounds of that church," he said, pointing for the pilot. "Should put me thirty seconds ahead of them." They went into a near vertical descent.

"It's stopped moving."

Gatuso recognised the voice of the guy watching the phone's progress back at HQ. Shit, the helicopter. "It's entered a building and it's stationary, I repeat, stationary."

Gatuso envisioned what had happened. They'd heard the helicopter, seen its searchlight as it approached from the east and dived into the nearest bar or pub. That was going to make things more complicated. Or, Gatuso mused, more interesting.

The helicopter hovered over a small area of grass in front of the church. The downdraft sent confetti flying and spinning off into the night as Gatuso abseiled the short distance to the ground. He waved to the pilot who wheeled off over the rooftops to the north. He attached his earpiece and tiny microphone and checked that his gun and knife were secure inside his lightweight jacket. He saw the way out of the church grounds to the street his targets were on, and he moved through a gap in the buildings with the ease of someone much slighter than himself. "Do you have me?" he said, reaching the busy pavement and looking south. The dark street was illuminated by taxi headlights and neon signs and spill from kebab outlets and bars.

"Affirmative," came a voice in his right ear. It was Urquhart himself. This was a big deal.

"Have they moved, sir?" he said, scanning the buildings and people milling on the pavements.

"Negative. Looks like they're in a bar about a hundred and fifty yards south of you. East side of the street."

Gatuso's dark eyes found the range and zeroed in on the sign for the bar. "Okay, I see it," he said. "Who else have you got?" He made his way steadily down the street, eyes fixed on the sign. People coming toward him stepped out of his way, unnerved perhaps by the look on his face.

"Two men moving north towards the bar. I'll put one out front and one on the side entrance." A pause on the feed. "Listen,

Gatuso, don't take these people lightly. We think they may have a knife."

Gatuso grinned. "I hope so," he said and felt another jolt of adrenaline. Forty yards. Twenty seconds. "Extraction?" he said, flexing his fingers.

"Plain white panel van, two minutes away."

"Good," said Gatuso. Ten yards. Four seconds. He felt a heavy bassline coming from the bar. "I'm going in," he said.

Gatuso pulled the solid wood and glass door by its brass handle and moved smoothly into the large, noisy room. The air was hot, the décor staid and filled with the babble of a hundred conversations competing with the boom of Swedish House Mafia. He didn't care how dangerous this McLeod dick was supposed to be. He was Gatuso. He scanned animated faces as he moved through throngs of happy Friday nighters. People began shying away from him as he strode menacingly between them. Then he stood stock still. A tall, smartly dressed man standing at the shiny bar was grinning at him and waving. Gatuso knew the trick and didn't look round. Instead, he took two lightning steps to his right and whipped around ready to strike. But there was no one there. He looked back to the man at the bar. He was beckoning him over with his hand. Something was wrong. Gatuso took a few cautious steps toward the man.

"You were right," he heard the guy say, "I did recognise him." The man held out the phone to him. "It's for you," he said.

With a sickening feeling, Gatuso took the proffered phone. "Who is this?" he said, coldly, a finger in his left ear against the music.

"I thought it might be you," came a familiar voice. The Wren bitch. He hadn't hit her hard enough.

"Your son's a vegetable," he said without emotion.

"Not where I've put him he isn't. I've got people too, freak."

Gatuso paled. "Don't call me that," he said with quiet rage.

"Tell me your name, then."

"You know you're just as dead as they are, bitch," he hissed. People in the bar were staring at him and moving away.

"Enjoy your drink, freak."

"I TOLD YOU…" he roared. But the line was already dead. He dropped the phone to the floor and looked emptily at the man who'd given it to him. He was pointing at a drink on the bar. The top half of the glass was a sort of beige colour and the bottom half was dark brown.

"It's called a slippery nipple," said the man jovially. "Compliments of Miss Lane and Mr McLeod."

Fifty-One

Friday afternoon

Wren rolled down the window of Nathalie Lane's bright yellow 1976 VW Beetle 1600 and threw out her phone. Pain flared briefly in her side, but she was taking no chances from now on. Having picked up Mac and Penelope at the rendezvous at the top of Whitehall, they were now making good progress through light traffic in south-east London. Although the car was nearly forty years old, it had only done thirty thousand miles and the engine gave a distinctive throaty splutter as Wren worked the gears. A previous owner had fitted it with a tiny racing steering wheel, and coupled with the lack of power steering, it made for an exhilarating ride.

"Can I ask you something, Anna?" said Penelope from the front passenger seat. She'd changed before leaving the club into black skinny jeans, brown ankle boots, a grey cashmere sweater and a brown gilet.

Wren checked the mirrors and accelerated hard through a junction. "Fire away," she said.

Penelope worried the quick of a thumbnail. "I'm very grateful that you are, but why are you doing this for us? I mean, you've become a target yourself."

Wren eased into the inside lane of a dual carriageway and thought about Penelope's question. Why the hell was she doing this? A gap appeared in the outside lane and she moved into it and floored the pedal. She could be curled up on her sofa watching mindless crap on TV with a nice bottle of something cold for company. Nothing to worry about or anything bothersome to do until Monday morning. Instead, she was hurtling through Lewisham with two people marked for death by her own secret services. Herself too probably. Didn't make much sense. Was it because of the injustice of Nathalie's death? Or the intrigue of finding out what was behind it? She knew she was deluding herself. The enigma of the man sitting on the back seat was all the motivation she needed. She felt a kind of unquestioning compulsion to help Mac, perhaps because that's what he was doing for Penelope.

"Lots of reasons," she said out loud. "It's my job to solve crimes and bring criminals to justice. And I've got a feeling this case could be the biggest thing I'll ever do." She flashed her headlights at the car in front resolutely refusing to move into the vacant inside lane. "I wish I had my bloody siren," she said, undertaking the vehicle. She turned her head briefly from the road and looked into her beautiful passenger's wide eyes. "You're two good people, Penelope, and it feels like the right thing to do."

Penelope smiled at her. "Thank you," she said.

"Don't mention it," said Wren, "now get your thinking cap on. We need that password. Any ideas, Mac?"

McLeod was sprawled all over the back seat of the Beetle. He'd changed his red jumper for a figure-hugging navy-blue one. The staccato strum of the engine behind him had been sending him to sleep. Only Wren's startling manoeuvres prevented it. He thought back to something he'd written for a science journal once. "Human beings are incredibly simple creatures of habit. It's in our nature to look for patterns and to avoid things that don't make sense to us." He shuffled his sturdy frame on the leather seat to get more comfortable. "For all that we're told to use random words or letters and numbers to increase online safety, hardly any of us actually do. Nine people out of ten choose something that's relevant to them. Nicknames, pets, children's birthdays, football teams, house names, that sort of thing."

"That's the problem." Penelope sighed. "Nathalie had none of those things."

"What about the house you two grew up in?" said Wren, easing the Beetle reluctantly over eighty.

Penelope gripped the handle on the door. "It was just number eight Salisbury Road."

"That's worth a try," said Mcleod.

Penelope shook her head slowly. "I don't think so, Mac," she said, looking down at her hands. "Our Mum died in that house."

"Oh…sorry, Pen," he said.

Other than the racket from the engine in the back, there was silence in the car for a few fast miles. Penelope wracked her brains for a way into her sister's erratic mind.

McLeod was doing the same on a more general level. "It must be something else significant to her, like a favourite band or song or a film or…I don't know…a funny little catchphrase she used."

Penelope froze her own thoughts. Could it be that simple? She focused again on Nathalie and took a breath. "My sister had many wonderful traits," she murmured. "She was highly intelligent, had a wicked sense of humour and was a really good friend." She sighed. "But like everyone, she had things to work on. Her flightiness used to drive me potty. She got bored of things so bloody quickly, you know? Boyfriends came and went so regularly, she often forgot their names. Not that she slept with many of them." Penelope smiled to herself, recalling Nathalie saying one time, 'You know what, Pen? To hell with it. I'm going to be like Holly Golightly. I'll call them all Fred.'"

"Then she was always on the latest diet or exercise regime. Pilates, Hatha Yoga, Tantric Yoga, she did all of that stuff." She turned in her seat and found Mac's eyes. "Other than her work, I think I was about the only constant thing in her life."

McLeod closed his eyes briefly and then nodded at her. "Go on, Pen," he said.

She took a breath. "Growing up, Nat and I used to love watching Monty Python and Fawlty Towers together. Then, when I went off to university, we developed a little routine on the phone." She paused and winced. "Whoever answered the phone had to say, 'Is that you, Nat?' or 'is that you, Pen?' And the other would have to say, 'Who were you expecting, Henry Kissenger?'" She looked out the window as they passed a road sign. Dover was listed at the bottom. Sixty-five miles. "Stupid, I know…but it was our little thing."

McLeod thought for a second. "I think that's worth a shot," he said.

"I agree," said Wren. "Fire it up, Penelope."

She took the laptop from the case on the floor, opened it on her knee and hit the power button. They were approaching a mass of signs. Wren slowed a bit to try to assess the information. How there weren't more accidents was beyond her. "Okay, we've got some decisions to make very soon. Do we want to stay on this road or take the motorway? Do we want Dover or Folkstone?"

"None of those," said McLeod. "Think about it, Anna. You're police, so are they, more or less. If you think those are our best bets, so will they." He looked at his watch. Just after eleven fifteen. "They may have this car by now. They could be setting roadblocks as we speak."

Wren shook her head and slowed considerably. "I said those places because they're the only options for a fast way out of the country, Mac."

"I'm sure I got a ferry from Ramsgate to Dunkirk once."

"You might have done once, Mac. They shut that route down a few years ago."

Penelope had half an ear on their conversation as she waited for the laptop to power up.

"Then we're shit out of luck," said McLeod. "Portsmouth's too far, surely."

Penelope threw her memories back to her childhood. Recalled the many happy years she'd spent around the south-west coast with her father and Nathalie. "What's the weather doing?" she said, looking out the window again. The trees at the verges of the road seemed to be bristling, but in the dark, she couldn't work out in which direction.

"What the hell does that matter, Penelope?" said Wren, pulling on to the hard shoulder and coming to a stop, engine idling. She knew Mac was right and she was angry with herself. Of course they'd have the Beetle and they'd be concentrating their resources on ports, airports and train stations.

"Maybe everything, Anna." The laptop was up to speed. She tapped on the password box. Typed in 'henrykissenger,' held her breath and hit enter. It came up with a dialogue box saying 'password incorrect.'

"Shit," she said. "I can't think of anything else it could be."

"Have you tried capitals, Pen?" said McLeod.

"Doing it now," Penelope replied. "Nothing doing." Two minute's battery remaining.

"Okay," said Wren. "What about adding 1988? Wasn't that when she was born?"

Penelope tapped away and was again greeted with the 'password incorrect' box.

"Try splitting it," said McLeod. "'19henry88kissenger,' something like that."

Penelope tried. Nothing. "Down to one minute's battery," she said.

She tried 19henrykissenger88. The screen went blank for a second, then changed to an old photograph of herself and Nathalie jumping into a loch on Skye with fearsome mountains and a bright blue sky in the background. "YES," she exalted and pumped her fist. Penelope was momentarily transported back to the camping holidays with her parents that she and Nathalie always dreaded but ended up loving.

"Good work, Penelope," said Wren, smiling broadly, craning her neck to see the screen. "What's so important about the weather?" she asked again.

Penelope hovered the swirling blue ring over the documents icon. "Come on, wretched thing," she barked at the screen. "Can we get to Rye?"

Wren thought quickly. "Rye...near Hastings?"

"The same," Penelope replied, clicking on the documents folder and then on recent files. The battery icon went red.

"Shouldn't be a problem," said Wren, noting Penelope's feverish manipulation of the laptop. "What's in Rye?"

A lorry with two trailers thundered past, rocking the small car. McLeod leaned between the front seats and rested a warm hand on Penelope's left shoulder. She nuzzled her cheek against it and then looked back to the screen as a list of files appeared. Quickly, she double-clicked on the first one, a word document titled 'Credit Crunch.'

"My father has a yacht moored there," she said as the blue circle wheeled round again. "Sailing and skiing were our things growing up. I've got a tidal coastal qualification."

Wren switched her gaze from the screen to Penelope's face and watched her eyes carefully. "You're saying you can sail us out of the country?"

Penelope's eyes remained assured as she said, "Given a half-decent prevailing wind, we could be in France before morning."

Wren's eyes flicked back to the screen where the file was still loading. The red battery icon was now flashing. She wound down her window and licked her forefinger. "We're pointing south, right," she said, holding her finger out the window.

"More like south-east," said McLeod, studying a battered road map in the weak ceiling light. He plotted the route to Rye.

Wren moved her arm round until it was almost against the side of the car. Brought her hand back in. "Okay, it's not strong, but it's from the north-west."

Penelope smiled as the file finally opened. It was in print preview layout, each of the seventy-two pages a tiny white rectangle with blocks of black lines indicating paragraphs. "Then it's a straight reach east or a slightly longer run depending on how far south we want to be."

Wren clicked her tongue. "Bloody sailing talk. What the hell does that mean?"

Penelope gave her an apologetic smile. "Sorry, Anna. It basically means we can sail a fairly straight course depending on traffic." She double-clicked on the first page of the document. It was the title of the paper. They looked at it in stunned silence. In a large Times Roman font, it read: 'Credit Crunch – Crime of the Century.'

"Could this be it?" Penelope asked, scrolling down to the next page.

"Depends who she implicates," Wren replied.

The next page was a short précis. Penelope ignored the flashing battery warning and adjusted the laptop to make it easier for the others to see and started reading.

'This paper presents the findings of a two-year investigation. It was conducted solely by myself and is in no way reflective of my employer's position or opinions, nor was any of it undertaken on their time. The main focus of this paper will be the collusion between the right-wing political movement and corporate banks in Western countries in order to manipulate economic factors and market forces which gave rise to the Credit Crunch. It will identify in detail those who gained politically and economically from the fallout and how recompense from such organisations and groups of individuals could be achieved. Some names have been changed to protect…'

The laptop died.

Wren blinked. "Jesus Christ. That's it, all right." She crunched the gearstick. "M25, right, Mac?"

"Right. Then the A21. What about this car, Anna?"

"A little obtrusive, you think? It'll have to do for now, but I'm beginning to like it."

215

She slammed the accelerator and the bright yellow Beetle tore off into the night.

Fifty-Two

Friday evening

"I suppose I'd better call off our entertainment then, old chap?" said Sir Francis, when he finally had a chance to speak.

Sir David's breath came in ragged wheezes as he stood, hunched over, hands on knees. His vision was coming in and out of focus as he surveyed the mass of dismembered first editions at his feet, the floor ankle deep in pummelled pages. In a final fit of rage, he turned and hurled the poker at the far wall. It embedded itself in the bosom of a fine portrait of his wife.

"Nice shot, old chap," Sir Francis said, draining his glass. "Feeling better?"

Sir David worked his way upright and steadied himself against the now empty section of bookshelf as the blood rushed to his head. He felt tingles in his arms and his heart was racing. His phone pinged once over by the curtain where he'd thrown it a couple of minutes ago. Wearily, he hobbled his heavy frame through the morass of books and bent to pick it up. Glanced at the message and immediately wished he hadn't. He put a feverish hand to his forehead and massaged his temples.

"There was me thinking it couldn't get any worse," he said, making his way back to his chair. He flopped into it like it was his last resting place. "That's the PM wanting confirmation that the business has been *satisfactorily concluded*." He seethed with ferocious indignation. "I mean, why can't he just write 'sorted out?' The pompous arsehole."

Sir Francis eyed his companion warily. "How will you reply?" he murmured.

"I know how I'd bloody-well like to reply." Sir David poured more brandy with a shaky hand, took a gulp and closed his eyes. He prayed that things would look better when he reopened them. They didn't. "This is a stinking arse of a mess, Francis. Now we have three of them to get rid of. One of them a highly decorated police officer with a son for Christ's sake."

"I agree, it's not ideal," Sir Francis replied, "but consider the alternative."

Sir David did for a moment and came to the same horrible conclusion. "Damn all researchers to hell. I mean, why can't they just leave things as they are? Were we not happier in the fifties without all the shit that surrounds us today?"

"Leaving aside the fact that I know you have shares in most of the shit, things never stay the same for long, old chap, except in areas like this. Where it is in our interests and those of our friends that they do so." He paused and tapped his knee with a long finger. "Our duty is clear, David."

"I know, I know," he replied irritably and wafted a weary hand at the fire. "Bung another log on for me, old thing. That bout of exercise has taken it out of me somewhat."

Sir Francis groaned as he rose. "Shall we be requiring the commode again, old chap?"

"Not with the pants I'm wearing," Sir David muttered.

"You're a lazy old bugger," said Sir Francis, waggling a log at him. "I suppose Brian's put out an all ports warning?"

"He's hopeful it won't get that far. It appears they're probably travelling in a yellow Beetle. At least, that was the other Lane woman's car and it's missing from her premises, which was also the Wren woman's last known whereabouts."

Sir Francis was wrestling the poker from the wood panelling behind the painting. "Roadblocks?"

"On all routes to the ferry ports," said Sir David, scowling at the empty bowl of nuts. "Superfluous really with their passports flagged."

"Brian's sure they'll try to leave the country?"

"Jesus Christ, man, wouldn't you?"

The fire spat at Sir Francis as he jostled a log. "OUCH! You evil swine!" he shouted at it, and then gave it another poke for good measure. "They're no less vulnerable in France or Belgium or wherever they try to get to," he said, creaking back into his chair.

"But they don't know that, old man." They both cursed as the old clock standing against the wall behind them began chiming midnight. Another thud came from the ceiling.

"Dropping like flies up there," mused Sir Francis, rubbing his scrawny tummy. "Might be able to risk a dash to the kitchen before long."

"Don't count on it," his companion replied darkly. "Lady Harris can hold her juice better than a milk tanker."

The prospect of some late supper galvanised Sir Francis' mind. He caught the thread of an idea and began fraying at it, narrowed his yellowing eyes and steepled his veiny fingers. He examined the notion from several angles and failed to find a flaw.

"Well?" said Sir David, fixing him with a watery eye.

"Call off the roadblocks and unflag the passports."

Sir David looked his friend over for other symptoms. "Hmmnn," he said finally, "it's not like you haven't given fair warning."

"What's that?" bristled Sir Francis.

"That last marble you've been clinging to all these years has finally rolled away."

"Well at least I had a full set to start with, old chap," Sir Francis retorted. "Hear me out on this, David. You might just learn something."

"Oh I never stop learning, old thing," said Sir David, charging their glasses once more. "That'll always be the difference between us."

"Your wit fails you, old man. Now see if you can pick any holes in this." Sir Francis swirled his glass, swigged and marshalled his thoughts. "Our problem essentially remains the same: The Lane woman. But it has escalated due to the infernal meddling of Wren and McLeod. They are credible people and could expose us."

Sir David banged a podgy fist on his leg. "Exactly why we should eliminate them at our earliest convenience, man."

Sir Francis favoured his friend with a sympathetic smile. "The big picture continues to trifle with you, David. Think about the fallout from the, um, demise of these three people. On top of the two we already have."

Sir David waved a hand over the tattered remains of the bookcase on the floor. "What d'you think I've been doing, you old goat?"

"You haven't thought about it, old chap, merely reacted...petulantly, I might add."

"Hrrrmmmff," growled Sir David. "If you ever have a day like I've had, *then* come and talk to me about petulance."

"Not securing ten billion quid of Chinese investment was hardly my finest hour, old chap," Sir Francis re-joined.

They exchanged irascible pop-eyed glares in silence for a few minutes before Sir David finally relented. "Right then," he said, doubtfully, "let's hear it."

"Think about it, David. Who else besides us wants rid of this woman?"

Sir David thought briefly and grasped his friend's train of thought. "Why, the government of every developed country on the planet, I should think," he said, eyes alive with hope once more.

"If they were to disappear in another country," Sir Francis continued, "preferably one as far away from here as possible, it wouldn't add to the shitstorm in the media we're going to have."

"In fact," said Sir David, doling out the last of the bottle, "it would focus bothersome minds elsewhere. You've hit it, old thing…in your own way." A frown etched more lines on his haggard face. He ignored his companion's haughty glare. "We can't afford to lose track of them in the meantime, though. She could restart her wretched research practically anywhere."

"A few words and some photographs across the Channel should do it." Sir Francis yawned and his belly gurgled. "My bet is we'll be hearing from Sécurité Intérieure tomorrow."

It was Sir David's turn to have a flash of inspiration. "What if it is the French and they were able to implicate Wren and McLeod in the Lane woman's tragic end? It would turn the potential scandal we'll have here into all manner of intrigue." His eyes glazed over as he imagined the tabloids' reaction. "It'd be like Bonnie and Clyde. Editors will think they'd scooped a rollover."

Sir Francis looked down his long, thin nose at him. "I think you're worrying overly about them. It's the girl we need to focus on," he said, making a chopping motion with his arm.

They were interrupted by a sharp bang on the sturdy library door. "Shit," said Sir David, closing his eyes.

A tall, elegantly attired woman with greying blonde hair and an angular face breezed into the room. "Don't tell me you two are still… WHAT THE HELL HAVE YOU DONE NOW, DAVID?" she shrieked as she took in the carnage on the floor.

The two men rose as their breeding demanded. "What are you doing down here, Genevieve?" Sir David asked irritably.

Lady Harris strode imperiously to the edge of the pile and rummaged for a thick cover. "Heaven forfend I should visit my own library, David." She held up a battered wooden book jacket. "*Principia Philosophiae* by Decartes." She thrust the cover toward her brooding husband. "Any idea how much these are worth, you old fool?"

"No," he replied caustically, "have you read it?"

A look of cold hatred entered his wife's eyes. "Don't be facetious, David. It took my father years to collect this lot."

"That's funny," Sir David replied breezily, "it took barely thirty seconds to do that to it."

She tossed the cover back on the pile and put her hands on her hips. "We've run out of gin upstairs. The key to the wine cellar. What have you done with it?"

Sir David patted his pockets. "I haven't had it, Vieve, I swear," he blustered.

"Well," she replied crossing to the sturdy cabinet, "we'll just have to drink your brandy then, won't we?" She extracted a couple of bottles and strode to the door. "And David," she said as though addressing a child, "*try* to be discreet if you're having *entertainment* tonight. We don't want a repeat of last time, do we?"

The men retook their seats with the sound of the door reverberating in their ears. "Old girl seems to be mellowing," Sir Francis mused.

"Hrruummf," replied Sir David. "What were you saying? Some guff about Wren and McLeod being unimportant?"

Sir Francis wriggled in his chair and adjusted his jacket. "Not unimportant, old chap. I just think they've distracted us unduly." He eyed his empty glass dolefully. "Threaten her with the sack, she'll soon keep shtum. And I imagine he'll be more than happy to go back to being a nobody."

"You don't like my scheme, then?" Sir David said peevishly.

"Oh no, it's admiral, old chap," Sir Francis replied. "I just think we need to get the girl at all costs and then worry about the others."

"Then tomorrow," said Sir David, heavily, "we shall."

Fifty-Three

Saturday morning

Wren pulled the handbrake and killed the engine. The sudden silence was unnerving. She looked at the analogue clock on the dashboard. Half past midnight. They'd made good time. A brief stop to buy some milk for the long night ahead only cost them a couple of minutes. A feeling of trepidation overcame her as she realised this was actually happening. "Okay, Penelope, you're on," she said, scanning the empty little parking area. Weak light from a chandlery building to the right caught in the low sea mist swirling near the ground. "I'm going to be next to useless, I'm afraid. Can't stand boats."

Penelope felt a familiar tingle she'd missed for too long. For a moment, she forgot the enormity of their situation and felt exhilarated by the prospect of the crossing. "Relax, Anna," she said, seeing the tension in her eyes. "The yacht is joy to sail. About the hardest job we'll have will be getting the covers off."

Wren sat on the wall of the river dock, vaping pensively as Penelope and Mac worked nimbly with cleats or sheets or whatever the hell they were. She recalled the last time she'd been on water a couple of years ago. A foul-mouthed day of kayaking on some boiling river in southern France. Finlay had spent most of it in tears as she and his father vented their frustrations with their marriage at each other's handling of the small boat. It wasn't long after they'd got back that her husband told her one shitty morning that he was seeing someone else.

She sighed and switched her focus back to her current, equally unhappy situation and tried to find any positives in it. Finlay was safe. That was the main thing. Her boss and his wife had kindly scooped him up. Nobody would try anything against them. That was it for anything concrete. Their only hope of extricating themselves from the danger they were in lay in

Nathalie's document. But what to do with it? Could they somehow use the information it contained as leverage against the forces pursuing them? Threaten to publish it if they didn't stop? What about getting the damn thing published? She stilled. Could it be that simple? The more she thought about it, the quicker her heart beat in her chest. Yes, why should anyone continue to hunt them down if the terrible secrets the document contained were freely available for anyone to read?

She winced a bit as she hopped down from the wall and hurried to the boat's berth or mooring or whatever it was. It bobbed gently against the wooden walkway and Wren's grin turned to a frown as she inspected her footwear. Low-heeled ankle-length boots with bugger-all grip. She squinted at the deck in the light from the cockpit and cabin. It looked dry at least, and the pale wood wasn't shiny. Mac was passing a rolled-up boat cover down to Penelope in the cabin below. A deep rumble came from the engine idling at the back of the boat. "Could you give me a hand, Mac?" she called.

McLeod climbed agilely out of the cockpit, took Wren's forearm and steadied her on the deck. The slight motion of the boat made her legs wobble. She leaned against him and then gratefully sat on the cockpit housing. "How come you're not floundering all over the place?" she asked with an arched eyebrow. McLeod had untied a rope at the stern and was curling it into a tight spiral on the deck.

"My honeymoon was a week's cruising round the Caribbean," he replied. Light reflecting from the water rippled across his dark features.

"Christ, is everyone made of money?" said Wren, reapplying some make-up.

McLeod cast her a rueful smile. "Well, I don't know about Penelope or her father, but I'm still paying for the honeymoon." He leaned past Wren and called down the hatch. "Shall I do the other ropes yet?"

Penelope's disembodied voice was barely audible from deep within the hull. "Yep, just sorting the gas."

McLeod caught the gleam in Wren's eyes. "Gas, did she say, Mac? Do you think that means food?"

McLeod grinned as he walked past her to the beam.

"What?" she said, aggrieved. "I'm starving. Haven't had a thing since the pastry in that café." God, that seemed a lifetime ago.

McLeod was leaning precariously over the side of the boat. "You go ahead, Anna. Penelope and I had something at the club."

Wren swung her legs into the cockpit and carefully negotiated the four steps down to the main cabin. It was bright from spots in the ceiling and side panels and surprisingly spacious. The interior was all finished in expensive-looking dark wood. There was a large wooden table with a pale leather corner sofa built in. There was further seating on the left and a panel of screens, dials and buttons. Two doors led off to other parts of the boat. To her left was what she was after. A small kitchen area had an oven and hobs and a sink and several interesting looking lockers. A couple of minutes later, she had about a week's worth of tinned and jarred and dried food up on the counter.

Penelope came through a door to the left of the steps. She smiled at Wren and said, "The wine ought to be cold in the fridge by now, or there's red if you prefer."

"This place is amazing, Penelope," Wren replied, opening a drawer to find neatly stowed utensils.

Penelope nodded briefly. "Just root around for anything you need. We've got about ten minutes of smooth motoring before it gets rougher. There are heads fore and aft."

Wren's smile faded, replaced by a look of alarm. She wondered briefly whether Penelope's father was a serial killer before realising it was must be more sailor speak. "Heads...toilets, right?"

"Yes, sorry Anna," Penelope replied. "It just comes out when I get on a yacht." She paused on the steps. "You still sure about Boulogne?"

"Mmm hmm, you still sure you can get us there?" said Wren, wrestling with pans and a kettle.

"Absolutely. It'll be fun with this breeze." Penelope went above to check on Mac and left Wren to her cooking.

McLeod held the yacht by the painter, a short rope at the front of the boat, while Penelope made sure the tender they'd be needing was securely fastened to the stern.

"Okay, let her go, Mac," she called, opening the throttle. McLeod hopped on and tied off the final rope. "Knots and everything. I'm impressed, Mac," Penelope said when he joined her in the cockpit. They navigated the narrow channel before joining the wider estuary.

"Went on a sailing holiday once," he said quietly.

Penelope was startled by a pang of jealousy. "Here, put this on," she said, handing him a lightweight windcheater. The night wasn't too cold, but what clouds were visible in the half-moon light were scudding along briskly. "It's Dad's." Saying his name reminded her again that he knew nothing of all this. She sighed, knowing that there was no alternative. "Might be a bit tight in the shoulders, but it'll do."

He put it on and wrapped his hands around her waist as she held the wheel. "Thank you," he nuzzled in her muskily perfumed neck.

"Don't harry the helm. You'll have us aground," she giggled.

McLeod sat on the cushioned bench and admired Penelope's assured handling of the vessel, making minor adjustments with throttle and wheel to keep them in the middle of the dark waters.

He looked at all the instruments and screens in front of Penelope and couldn't remember seeing so much kit on the yacht he'd stayed on six years ago. He surveyed the wide expanse of teak decking and immaculate fixtures and fittings. "It was too dark to read the name on the hull," he said over the growl of the engine.

"Blackbird," she replied and poked a couple of screens. "It was Mum's favourite song."

What the hell must it be like to wake up as Paul McCartney every day, McLeod mused. "Does she have a class or something?"

"She's an ocean-going yacht, Mac. Hallberg-Rassy Forty Mark two, if that means anything to you."

He looked up at her ghostly profile against the black sky. "Is your father very rich?" he asked warily.

Penelope wrinkled her nose. "Yes, Mac," she murmured, looking down, "he is."

Her discomfort was clear in the stiffening of her back and her massaging of the wheel. A couple of white and brown seagulls were following them, juveniles, scowling faces illuminated briefly in the light from the cockpit. Maybe they could smell Wren's cooking below. McLeod thought about all he knew of Penelope and encounters he'd had with other rich people and couldn't square the two. "Then how come you're so...?" he began uncertainly.

"Nobody's normal, Mac," she cut in, flashing him a look.

"I was going to say humble, Pen, but that didn't sound right either." He paused and watched the two seagulls arguing over the best position with squawking beaks and webbed feet angled at each other. "How come you're you?" he asked finally.

She glanced down at him, expecting to look into his eyes. But his head was quartered away, hooded eyes brooding. Other, Penelope thought again. "You're a piece of work, Mac," she said and bent to plant a quick kiss on his broad lips.

He grinned up at her, light twinkling in his eyes.

She thought for a moment and then said, "Why's anyone how they are? I'm the product of two wildly different people." She paused and did some tapping on a touchscreen panel beyond the wheel. "Isn't it every son or daughter's duty to try to rebel against their parents? I love my dad, but he's flashy and avaricious. My mum came from a poor background and used her looks to get where she wanted to be." Her eyes met his thoughtful gaze. "I'm not judging them, Mac, that's just how it is. They gave me and Nathalie an incredible childhood."

He nodded once and looked beyond the bow to the white horses just visible in the near distance.

"Better set the sails," Penelope said.

"Okay," replied McLeod. "What do you want me to do?"

Penelope smiled and pressed a couple of buttons. "Absolutely nothing," she said. "Having too much money should be a crime, but it can have its advantages."

McLeod watched in amazement as Penelope let go of the wheel and hit another button. The main sail and genoa started unfurling and swinging to port. She killed the engine and came and sat astern of him on the bench. The sails suddenly filled and the yacht lurched forward, thrusting McLeod into Penelope's waiting arms.

"You did that on purpose," he breathed, then kissed her, a hand cradling her head. He pulled back and saw a carnal look in her up-turned eyes.

"That's why you couldn't say humble before," she sighed and sought his welcoming lips.

Fifty-Four

Saturday morning

McLeod took the first watch, having slept for most of the car journey. Something about rhythmic engine noise always sent him off. Out in the vast blackness surrounding the cockpit, the only sounds came from the lapping of the sea on the yacht's hull and the luffing of the sails and metallic straining of the mast. Occasionally, the wheel would turn and the sails reset in response to course changes plotted by the boat's navigation system or by something called the Automatic Identification System. AIS, Penelope explained, was fitted to the majority of sea- and ocean-going vessels these days. It was a system that used data from land-based and satellite sources which plotted the course and speed of every other vessel in the vicinity. The yacht's computer used the data to adjust course if necessary to avoid any possible collision. Penelope had said McLeod's only real job would be to keep an eye out for the unlikely event that there would be a small craft that didn't have the system loose in the Channel.

He'd closed the hatch against the light from the cabin. His eyes had become accustomed to the dark, and aided by the weak light from the moon, he could see reasonably well. The twinkling lights of England's southern towns were receding behind and to his left. Far off to the south-east, he could make out the dark silhouette and bright lights of a large vessel, probably a ferry of some description. He breathed in the salty air and felt the cool breeze at his back and realised he was enjoying himself. He felt at one with the gentle pitch and yaw of the boat. Somehow, their desperate situation floated away from his mind like all the bits of plastic he kept seeing on the rippled water, like he was in the calm in the middle of the tempest.

Then the worrying thought that struck him on the night bus made an unwelcome return to his mind. Had the Kurjac nutter apologised because he hadn't meant to kill Nathalie? He could think of no other reason for it. McLeod forced himself to consider the implications of that possibility. Had Kurjac instead meant to kill Penelope? His knees suddenly felt weak and his whole body began to shake. The reaction confirmed two things to his scientific mind as he sat heavily on the cockpit bench: it was definitely a possibility that was worth giving thought to; and he was definitely falling for her.

Below, Wren was considering doing something she hadn't done since she was ten years old. Eating jelly. She'd washed down a reasonable jar of bolognaise and pasta with half a bottle of Montrachet and was eyeing the little, brightly-coloured plastic pots on the cabin's table in front of her. The boat gave another lurch and she decided against it. She put her plate in the sink, then jerkily retook her seat at the table and poured more wine. Then she looked again at the screen of Nathalie's on-charge laptop and the notes she'd scrawled in pencil on the back of a sea chart. She unplugged the pen drive Penelope had found in a gadget drawer and put it in her bag. Took out her puffer as Penelope emerged through the little door to her right and plonked down in one of the two comfy seats opposite.

"Can't get off," she grumbled, rubbing her eyes. Wren could tell that she'd been crying again.

"Listen, Penelope," she began contritely. "I know I've been quite abrupt with you at times today." She paused and took a pensive drag. Penelope observed her with interest.

"Partly because that's how I am and partly because the situation required it." And partly because you're jealous of her, she admonished herself. "I just want you to know how sorry I am about Nathalie and I understand this business hasn't allowed you to grieve properly."

Penelope nodded sadly. "Thanks, Anna. I guess it'll hit me more when all this is over." She smiled grimly. "Something to look forward to."

A particularly large swell caused Wren to lurch against the table and her pencil and puffer to roll off. Penelope picked them up and rolled them back across the table to her. "How's that working out for you?" she asked.

Wren looked at her sharply but saw only a look of keen interest in Penelope's eyes. "Not very well, I'm afraid," she sighed. "All too often, it's just not enough."

Penelope nodded thoughtfully, glad to be talking about something other than their circumstances. "You put juice in it, right?" she said, indicating Wren's gadget.

"Mmm hmm," said Wren, between drags. "Something called 'Ice Blast' at the moment. I'd happily blast it into outer space for a real one."

Penelope rose suddenly, a purposeful look in her eyes. "Empty the juice and clean it out," she said, heading for the door she'd come from. "I'll be back in a sec."

Intrigued, Wren did as instructed. Penelope came back out of the stern cabin holding a small clear plastic bottle, filled with a beige liquid. She sat next to Wren at the table and took the clean tank from her. "My mum died from cancer a couple of years ago. Probably smoking related. So I switched part of my research facility from 3D printing to e-juice development." She unscrewed the little bottle and filled the tank with a practised hand. Screwed the tank to the rest of the device and handed it back to Wren. "This is my latest mixture. Give it a go."

Feeling slightly embarrassed, Wren sucked on her puffer and inhaled deeply. "Jesus Christ," she cried, vapour spewing from her nose and mouth, "that's…" She took another drag and closed her eyes. A smile started to spread across her face. "That could almost be the real thing," she said, exhaling. She looked in wonder at Penelope whose hopeful expression turned into an answering smile. "How's it so much better than my stuff?"

Penelope held the plastic bottle between forefinger and thumb and looked thoughtfully at its contents. "Smoke from tobacco contains something like four thousand chemicals, right? Loads of carcinogens in it."

Wren nodded, savouring another hit.

"Most producers of e-juice try to put as few chemicals into it as possible to make it seem harmless. Usually just water, nicotine, flavourings and glycerine to make the vapour. I thought why not put something else in? That's the result."

"What was it?" Wren said, grabbing the table as the boat lurched again.

Penelope screwed up her shapely nose. "Bit of a trade secret, I'm afraid, Anna."

229

"Oh…of course. Sorry, Penelope." Wren thought for a second. "Won't kill me, will it?"

Penelope smiled. "Tests so far have detected one carcinogen added to the vapour, but it's not remotely as harmful as any of the dozens contained in smoke from tobacco." She looked out of a porthole at the dark outside. "It's all to do with the mysteries of umami," she murmured.

Wren frowned. "Isn't that the stuff in cheese?"

"It's not so much a stuff," Penelope said, unscrewing the bottle and sniffing the earthy mixture. "I'm not sure that it's even a flavour, but the brain has powerful receptors for it." She screwed the lid back on. "You find it in all kinds of food. Cheese, chocolate, meat, crisps. Anything tasty and not particularly healthy, basically." She paused and looked at Wren's plume of vapour. "And in smoke," she said.

Fifty-Five

Friday evening

They're crazier than I am, thought Kurjac as he watched the Beetle tear off down Whitehall. He scanned the still bustling streets for any signs of pursuers. Satisfied there were none, he stepped out of the late shop's awning and marched purposefully toward the Strand. He tried to forget the knowledge he had and imagined what he would do in their position. Get as far away as possible as quickly as possible. And if they were heading south, that meant only one thing. And that suited him fine.

He waited impatiently at a pedestrian crossing. A seemingly endless stream of growling black cabs roared past him. Ferrying people home or to hotels after a Friday night bender or on to other venues or God knew what.

Kurjac had never given much thought to how other people lived. Free people. Ordinary men and women who were able to get up each morning and choose what they wanted to do that day. He glanced at the pretty woman waiting next to him and saw twin Burger King logos on the collar of her shirt under her coat. The bored-looking man in a suit beyond her was tapping away furiously on his phone. No, he thought. Everyone's a slave to something. Money, work, position, family. All forms of bondage almost as suffocating as his own.

Then he smiled to himself as he recalled the decision he'd made. It had only two possible outcomes, both of which would result in him finally becoming a free man. The lights changed and he hurried across the road. He never used to have to worry about on-coming pedestrians. They used to give him a wide berth, perhaps sensing in his features the darkness in his soul. Now he had to use his forearms to fend off people glued to their phones.

Back in his unlit hotel room, he stuffed his few clothes into a small backpack. In the bathroom, he rinsed the blood from his flick-knife and dried it carefully. He washed his face with cold water and filled a two-litre plastic bottle from the tap. He looked in the mirror and saw something in his eyes he'd not seen since he was a boy. Hope. Then it faded back to emptiness as he thought again about everything standing in his path. He thought about phoning his contact at MI5, then dismissed it as he realised he probably knew more than they did. The fact that he hadn't been contacted by them meant he was probably out of the loop anyway. That suited him fine too.

Down in the lobby, he settled his account and bought a thousand euros, and ordered his car to be brought to the front of the building. He thought about MI5's position while the nervous receptionist counted his cash. Surely they'd be happy to have the woman leave the country. They had enough to clean up in London as it was. The police woman was good. She'd probably switch transport after the crossing, assuming her status afforded them freedom of movement. Flying wasn't a feasible option and buses were too slow. Haste would be important for them, but it was critical for him. He thanked the receptionist brusquely, put the cash in his wallet and headed for the lobby doors and a rendezvous with his quarry at Gare du Nord.

Some thirteen hundred miles south-east, the General hung up with his liaison at MI5. The Irish woman seemed to have little doubt that Kurjac was involved in the killing of one of their operatives. At first, it made no sense to the General. He picked up another phone from his wide office desk and opened the call register. He'd rung Kurjac's phone twelve times in the past couple of hours without reply. He thought about the pressures and forces that motivated his most important asset. About the hatred he harboured that was always ready to explode into murderous assault upon himself. Had the photograph he'd sent been the final drop that forced open the floodgates? Was all that rage now aimed blindly at him?

The General levered his sturdy frame from his swivel chair and took a couple of steps to the large bay windows that pointed north. It was pitch black outside, and only the compound's main gate was visible a couple of hundred metres distant, lit by arc lights on either side. Somewhere out there was a demon he'd lost control of. He strode purposefully to the console on his desk and hit a button. "Goran…double the guard on the perimeter fence and put two more men downstairs." A thought occurred to him. "Bring the girl to my suite and leave a good man guarding her house." He crossed the room to a wooden bureau and opened a large cigar box. Selected one that ought to last a good hour and smiled to himself.

Fifty-Six

Saturday morning

"You two seem pretty close," Wren said, passing McLeod a mug of gratefully accepted coffee. They took a few steps from the galley and sat at right angles on the L-shaped sofa. Penelope had taken over watch duties from him in an exchange that had left them both frustrated. He thought about Wren's statement and could find no argument with it.

"I think it's an entirely rational response to the circumstances," he replied, blowing on his brew.

Wren cast him a sharp glance. "This isn't a time for games, Mac. I know you're not that cold." The boat heaved as it altered course and McLeod had to grab the left edge of the table and raise his mug. He was ambushed by a sudden sense of fear of losing something he'd only just found.

"You see it too?" he murmured.

She flashed him a 'wasn't born yesterday' look.

He smiled ruefully and Wren had to look away. "I suppose some things are just too strong to fight," he said and reached for Wren's notes. She nodded slowly to herself.

He read some names and numbers and their relative acclaim and wealth was dumfounding. "Have I got this right?" he said, passing a hand through his thick brown hair. "Nathalie's suggesting that much of the money that was artificially created after the crash was being secretly siphoned into the coffers of right-leaning institutions and then to groups of private individuals?"

Wren drew tensely on her puffer and felt an immediate sense of relief. "Quantitative easing, I think they called it," she said, exhaling from the corner of her mouth. "Something to do with increasing the liquidity in the markets."

McLeod sipped his coffee and thought about his previous fears for Penelope. They didn't add up any more now that he knew how explosive Nathalie's paper was. Then he thought about the attempts on his and Penelope's lives. They'd happened before any of Nathalie's research had been discovered. He looked again at Wren's notes. Most of the money seemed to flow through Switzerland and the Cayman Islands. "We're headed for Zurich?" he asked.

Wren eyed him warily. "You and Penelope don't have to, Mac." She paused and went over the words she'd rehearsed that she didn't want to say but knew were for the best. "You two could go and stay in a little hotel in the wilds of Brittany or somewhere. There's no need for you to be exposed to more risk."

"You know I can't do that, Anna," he flashed back. The look on his face was one she hadn't seen before and its iciness made her pupils dilate and her heart beat faster in her chest. Events had changed him so much from the man she'd met barely a day ago. Then he looked away, uncertainty in his expression. Wren recognised that look all too well.

"Okay, Mac," she said, "let's have it."

Was it pointless to be dwelling on his previous fears? Perhaps Wren could give him the confirmation he craved. "Remember I told you we tried to get hold of whoever was behind this thing on the Polish guy's phone?"

He arched his eyebrows.

"Well, we succeeded. Spoke to a man calling himself Kurjac. He's the guy with half an ear. The poisoner."

Wren frowned. Was that name familiar? "Go on, Mac," she said.

McLeod tried to recall the man's exact words. "It was strange. Like he was torn...or repentant even. He asked me to tell Penelope that he was very sorry about Nathalie." He watched Wren's expression carefully. It ran a gamut of incomprehension, disbelief and derision, before settling on uncertainty.

"You're sure you heard him right, Mac?"

"Penelope had exactly the same thought," he replied. He saw her asking herself why a professional killer would say such a thing. Saw the worry creep into her eyes as realisation took hold. "There's more," he said quietly. "Just before he hung up, he said for us to watch our backs."

His words added more doubt to the worry already in Wren's cobalt eyes. He watched them as they darted from one place on the table to another, weighing different scenarios. When they flicked back to his, the anxiety was gone, but the hesitation remained. "Don't you think you're reading too much into this, Mac?"

"Those words sound familiar," he replied, the trace of a gleam in his hooded gaze.

"That was different, Mac. I had solid proof back then."

McLeod drained his mug and set it on the table with a weary sigh. "I wish you could have heard how this guy sounded, Anna. It was like he was in pain or something." He raised his hands and let them fall back on the sofa. Something else about the Kurjac guy nagged at him, but he couldn't catch it. He put his head back against the wood panelling and looked to the hatch, focused his mind on the beautiful woman on the other side of it. "I just can't think of any reason in the world why anyone would want to kill Penelope," he said in exasperation.

Wren took another hit on her puffer and revelled in the sensation. She cast a grateful eye at Penelope's magic juice in her tank and was struck with a sudden thought. Could it be that simple? Her eyes widened as a realisation took hold.

"What is it, Anna?" McLeod asked alarmed.

"Shush a minute, Mac," she said. She thought back to her initial homicide training years ago. Nearly all murders in the UK were the result of love or money. Nathalie's had nothing to do with love. She held her device toward him. "Twenty-five years I've been smoking off and on. Probably thousands in profits to the tobacco companies. Thousands more to the exchequer's coffers." She pointed to the little tank on her gadget. "Penelope gave me a liquid she's developing for these things. It's so good, Mac, I swear I'll never have another cigarette."

McLeod looked at her bewildered for a moment, then caught her drift and thought about a previous conversation. "Are we talking a ripe Camembert here?"

"As close as makes no odds, I think," Wren replied, warming to her theme. "Certainly a bloody strong Cheddar."

McLeod weighed the implications with a growing sense of alarm. "How many smokers are there worldwide?"

Wren cast her mind back to an article she'd read a couple of years ago. "Over a billion, ballpark," she replied.

"And how many of them would want to quit?"

Wren frowned. "I wouldn't know, Mac. All kinds of cultural and social issues involved in different countries." She took another thoughtful puff and marvelled again at the feeling. "Don't you see though, Mac? I've been trying to quit for years. Patches, gum, hypnotherapy, even this puffer. None of it's good enough. Penelope's stuff isn't like quitting though. More like switching to something just as good with none of the harmful effects."

The hatch opened and Penelope's face appeared. Light was visible in the sky behind her. "I'm going to have to switch off the electrics in a couple of minutes, so if you want a last brew..."

"Thanks, Penelope," Wren called up to her.

McLeod had a far off look in his eyes. "A billion people," he said quietly. If they were all put together in one place, they'd be the third biggest country on Earth. And the numbers fell off a cliff to the fourth. What would the financial repercussions be?

As if reading McLeod's thoughts, Wren said, "Trillions in future pounds, dollars, euros and yen, literally up in smoke. Who would take that shit lying down?" The realisation hit them at the same time. "Christ, Mac," Wren breathed. "She isn't safe anywhere in the world."

Fifty-Seven

Saturday morning

Miles Gatuso fastened his seatbelt as the pilot prepared to land. Sitting across the aisle was the small cabin's only other occupant, the Irish woman, Brennan. He'd been told her Christian name once but had forgotten it. Wasn't important. She was damn good at surveillance. That was important. Especially for the job ahead of them.

Tactical dicks back at the House had decided on trains and, therefore, Paris. He didn't give a shit about the reasoning behind it. That it was all about the Schengen Agreement and freedom of access to over one and a half million square miles of hiding places in twenty-six countries. That Paris was one of the key hubs of the transport network that serviced the four hundred million people living in it.

All he cared about was the anticipation. It had been ungratified in the debacle in Covent Garden and his hunger to have it fulfilled this time was almost unbearable. The small jet touched down at Base Aérienne 107, eight miles south-west of Paris. He breathed in deeply through his nose. The Irish woman glanced at him and looked away quickly. Her pretty freckled face was contorted in shock.

Kurjac turned up the volume on his phone. It was tuned to a local French radio station and his earbuds filled his head with the remorseless riff of Led Zeppelin's 'Kashmir'. The car's stereo and other electrical equipment including, most importantly for him, the GPS system, were smashed to pieces. He'd taken the vehicle's jack to them just outside Calais. He was now off grid. He didn't delude himself that the General wouldn't work out he was heading to Paris and alert his man there, but it was a mighty big city.

Traffic on the autoroute was light at this time on a Saturday morning, but he was keeping to the speed limit, conscious of the Mercedes' visibility. The French police wouldn't be a problem, but he could ill afford any hold-ups. He checked the time on his father's watch. Nearly seven. He looked out of the windows at the vast flat farmland. Some of the enormous fields were a freshly-ploughed dark brown, steam rising from the rich earth in the early morning sunshine. Some wore the bright green of young crops and some rejoiced in the dazzling yellow of oil-seed rape. He was approaching a large road sign. Paris was at the top. 180km was next to it. Kurjac scanned the road ahead and nudged his foot down on the accelerator.

The inflatable tender's little four horsepower motor was being helped by the flood tide as it spluttered toward the wide sandy beach just south of Boulogne's harbour. McLeod looked back to the 'Blackbird' anchored a few hundred metres off the calm turquoise shoreline and wondered if he'd ever sail on her again. He allowed his mind to wallow in the possibility of a romantic holiday with Penelope, cruising the Western Isles maybe. Or the Mediterranean. Then the reality of their plight returned and smashed his fantasies to smithereens.

Penelope killed the engine and they drifted the last few metres to the beach. McLeod hopped over the bow and hauled the little boat further onto the shore. Penelope and Wren got out as he scanned the sands to the harbour wall. A lone distant figure jogging with a dog in a mirage was the only sign of life. He grabbed the rucksack from the boat and checked his watch. Just after seven. The low sun glinted off the grey town's Basilica to the north.

"Better get the tender up to the dunes, Mac," said Penelope, pointing.

They managed with a little difficulty, then found a coastal road behind the sandhills and headed toward town through a drab housing development. They walked silently in single file, each weighing their hopes and fears.

McLeod was torturing himself with Wren's theory and the fiend Kurjac's haunting words and wondering how the hell he could keep Penelope from the same fate as her sister.

Penelope was staring through blurry eyes, agonising over how to get a message to her father about Nathalie. And his boat. Then about how she could get some alone time with Mac.

Wren was thinking about proper French bread and croissants and pain au chocolat.

They just made the quarter to eight Paris train thanks to a ride in a battered Citroën from a jovial local who had been heading in the opposite direction. A smartly dressed waiter was serving them breakfast in the sparsely occupied first-class coach, courtesy of the hefty wad of euros Penelope had liberated from the yacht's strongbox.

"What?" she'd said indignantly in answer to Wren's mild look of shock. "I'd happily do the same with the rest of my father's millions along with the trillions gathering dust in other rich people's bank accounts. World poverty would be solved overnight. How we live in a world where billionaires are free to walk around is completely beyond me."

McLeod took a sip of what would be called espresso at home and was immediately transported to his year of studies in Paris. Wren was slathering apricot jam inside her third croissant while Penelope was re-reading the summary of Nathalie's paper they'd written. "You know," she said, folding the sheet and handing it to Wren, "we don't even need to try and find a publisher for Nathalie's work. Just upload it to the internet. Wikileaks or something."

Wren cast a quick look of warning across the table at McLeod who turned his bleak stare out the window at the featureless farmland that stretched as far as he could see. "That's an interesting idea, Penelope," Wren replied between mouthfuls. "But I've been thinking. Surely the Swiss authorities should see a copy of it first. Nathalie makes a strong case that jurisdiction lies with them if there are cases to be made."

McLeod turned his head to Penelope in the aisle seat next to him. Dark patches were starting to show under her big green eyes. "Switzerland's also about the safest country in Europe for us to be," he said with as much conviction as he could. "They take civil liberties very seriously there."

Her sad eyes remained on his and he knew he was doing a bad job of keeping the worry from them. She put a slender hand to his cheek and stroked it gently. "Thank you, Mac," she said, a solitary tear rolling to her pale jaw.

"What for, Pen?" he murmured, wiping it away.

"Everything," she said simply. She took off her thin brown gilet. Folded it twice and put it in McLeod's lap. Ten seconds after her head hit, she was fast asleep.

The phone in Gatuso's jacket pocket began ringing. The buildings lining the streets they were being driven through were getting taller as they entered Paris proper. He looked at the caller ID and felt a buzz of excitement. "Gatuso," he said.

"We have an unconfirmed sighting at Boulogne train station." Urquhart's usually calm voice was strained. Gatuso guessed he hadn't been to bed.

"CCTV?" he said.

"The French are working on it."

"What else are the French doing, sir?" Gatuso bristled.

"Don't worry. They don't want anything to do with the operation beyond containment."

"Okay. They take a train, sir?"

"It's scheduled to arrive Gare du Nord at ten fourteen."

Gatuso checked his watch. Ten past nine. Not good. He scanned the street outside their vehicle, then looked out the rear window and saw what he wanted. He pointed urgently at Brennan sitting next to him on the back seat, then at the driver, then at the floor.

Brennan nodded once. Tapped the driver on the shoulder. "Arretez la bagnole," she said. The driver performed an expert emergency stop.

"Okay, we're going to be gone for a while, sir," he said, following Brennan out of the car.

"Understood. Call us when you can."

Gatuso clicked off and sprinted after Brennan, briefcase flailing. Pedestrians scattered in alarm as the pair pounded down the tree-lined pavement and dove into Balard Métro Station.

Kurjac cursed himself for twentieth time in as many minutes. He'd killed the SatNav with the jack and run his phone out listening to music. Horns blared all around him in the outskirts of northern Paris. He checked his father's watch again. Twenty past nine. He leaned his head out the window again and saw the same sea of stationary cars. He dashed his hands on the steering wheel and looked murderously at the back of the car ahead. His dream was dying in front of him.

"NO," he roared and grabbed his backpack from the passenger seat. He left the car where it was, keys in, engine running, hit the pavement and took up a fast, steady jog. One that he could maintain all day if necessary. Ten minutes later, he was running under an elevated section of railroad. Five minutes after that, he boarded an RER train which terminated at Gare du Nord. He sat panting heavily in a bucket seat. The man next to him got up and moved away. From his backpack he retrieved the rough prints he'd made of Lane and McLeod. The train rattled as he seared their faces into his brain.

Fifty-Eight

Saturday morning

Wren's mind was working as furiously as it could on four hours' sleep. She knew they were hurtling into danger as she made out the Stade de France off to her left. The image of the man's face from Nathalie's apartment kept intruding on her thoughts. She concentrated on exposure, maximum and minimum. Getting out of the station and into a taxi would be the minimum. No one would be foolish enough to risk an attack in the heavily policed concourse. There would be a brief period of exposure to a sniper's bullet between station and taxi doors, but that was all. Therefore, that's what they'd be expected to do. Maximum exposure would be to plunge into the winding corridors, endless escalators and long platforms of the Métro system. Plenty of opportunities to be ambushed or chased down, but very limited scope for using firearms. Too many corners, too many bystanders and way too many cameras on the platforms. That swung it for Wren. She looked up as McLeod returned and took the seat next to her. Penelope was still asleep, curled up on the two seats opposite.

"Okay, there's a train from Gare de Lyon at ten fifty-seven," he said.

The icy look was back in his eyes and Wren tore her own away. "Can we make that by Métro, Mac?"

McLeod thought about it. "It'll be tight. Depends how the network's working, how busy it is, how quickly we can get tickets at the other end. Probably another couple of variables I've missed."

"One of those is the make-up of the welcoming party we've been sent."

McLeod looked at her nonplussed for a moment. "You think they'd try something in a public place?"

"There's no second-guessing anything these people will do, Mac."

The train slowed as the number of tracks adjacent to their own increased. An old engine languished on the sidings covered in years of graffiti and bird droppings. McLeod glanced briefly at Penelope and then back to Wren. "Don't you think we ought to tell her that she could be the target, Anna?"

Reflected sunlight caught her irises, making them an iridescent blue. For a second they were uncertain, before being filled with resolve. "I don't see how that could possibly benefit her, Mac. It would only add to her worry. And her guilt over Nathalie."

He looked at her bleakly for a moment, then nodded once. His mind latched onto something else that had been bothering him before events had taken over. The memory took the wind from his chest. "The MI5 man in the alley, Anna," he said breathlessly.

"Shit," she said, eyes widening. "I'd completely forgotten about that."

Images of the shock frozen in the man's eyes and his grisly throat were things McLeod would never forget. He remembered the man's finger taut on the trigger of the silenced gun. "Someone saved our lives in that alley, Anna. It can't have been a coincidence."

Doubt entered Wren's eyes. "Okay, Mac, but who? That whole thing makes no sense."

McLeod pondered her words. No sense. He thought about the most nonsensical scenario he could. "Here's an idea that makes no sense, Anna. What if it was the guy with the funny ear?"

Wren's look of interest turned to incredulity. "The man who killed Nathalie? Don't be going soft in the head on me, Mac," she said sharply.

"I know it sounds daft, but who else is there?" he countered.

"Two wrongs don't make a right, Mac." The train slowed further as it approached the station. "Anyway, we haven't got time to worry about it now. Better wake Penelope."

McLeod reached up for the rucksack, then placed a gentle hand on Penelope's thigh. She blinked and stretched and sighed. Then she looked at the faces of Wren and McLeod and groaned. "We're still in the shit, right?" she murmured.

"I've had a thought about that," said Wren. "We need to get our hands on an English newspaper."

McLeod tried to picture the layout of the station the last time he'd been through a couple of years earlier. "There should be a tabac on the left near the entrance," he said, helping Penelope into her gilet. "Why?"

Wren was touching up her lipstick and checking her appearance in her mirrored compact. "If there's anything about any of this in the paper, it'll mean the French authorities will be looking for us. If there isn't, MI5 will be trying to keep it in house." She put her bits back in her bag. "Okay," she said, "this is how we're going to do this."

The train hissed to a halt. "Mac, I need you at Penelope's back." She turned away briefly and surreptitiously slipped her pistol from her bag into her right trouser pocket. "Penelope, you carry the rucksack on your front. You keep your right hand on my left shoulder until I tell you otherwise, okay?"

"Whoa, Anna," she said, suddenly wide awake, "what is this?"

"Just sensible precautions, Penelope," she said, zipping her handbag.

"But we're all in equal danger here. Why the sudden emphasis on me?" She cast a worried glance at McLeod and saw a slightly plaintive look in his eyes.

"Damn it, Penelope," Wren snapped. "Just do as I say, okay?" She huffed out a breath. "I don't know what we're walking into here and Mac and I have been around longer than you."

Penelope didn't particularly care for the inference, but she let it go. There were some beeps and they heard the doors open. They turned their heads toward the sound. McLeod's heart began pounding in his chest like a heavy bassline.

Fifty-Nine

Saturday morning

On an average day, Miles Gatuso ran four fast miles before
breakfast, spent half his lunch hour pounding a punch bag, and
then an hour in the gym or swimming pool in the evening. At
thirty-two, he was fitter than he'd ever been, fitter even than in
his army days. But he was still struggling to calm his breathing
after the mad dash across town and up six long flights of stairs.
To an empty room in a building at forty-five degrees to the front
of the Gare du Nord. It would all be for nothing if he couldn't get
completely still. He breathed deeply again and tried to keep the
scope steady on the head of an attractive brunette coming out of
one of the station's large glass doors. The crosshairs were in the
right area but not steady between the eyes as he required. He
cursed, stood away from the tripod and looked at his watch. Ten
fourteen. He hoped the train was late.

The watchers saw them. It wasn't exactly difficult. Even with
the hundreds of people milling in the huge concourse. Three
people clustered unnaturally close together. Strained eyes looking
all around. About as clandestine as a klaxon. "Targets moving
towards front entrance," Brennan said quietly into what looked
like a small brooch on the lapel of her lightweight camel jacket.
"About thirty seconds," she said in response to the question in
her earpiece.

Then the three people did something the watchers weren't
expecting. The slight policewoman with the shock of blonde hair
veered left, the other two tight on her heels. "They're heading for
a newsstand... Now they're looking at front pages of
newspapers," Brennan said, pressing off the wall near the station
entrance. "There's a lot of people in the way. I need to take a

better position." The other watcher saw her move and countered it.

Brennan leaned against the side of a glass and steel information kiosk. "Okay, they're on the move again. Not towards the front entrance. Repeat, *not* toward the front entrance." She quickly pulled out her earpiece to cut off an explosion of expletives. Replaced it tentatively after a few seconds. "Looks like they're heading for the escalators." They were lost to view as a group of Japanese tourists approached the kiosk. Brennan cursed and hurried to where she'd last seen them. Angry stares and remarks followed her as she pushed people aside. She peered down the stairs. "Okay, they've gone into the Métro. Permission to follow them?" She looked at the busy escalators and opted for the stairs, took them two at a time. The other watcher was ten steps behind her.

Some two hundred metres away, Gatuso angrily disassembled his rifle. This had been his call and he'd thought it was a good one. He stowed the individual parts carefully in his specially modified briefcase, wondering if he'd be needing it again for this assignment. He slammed the briefcase shut and hit call on his phone. It answered on the second ring.

"Tell me it's done, Miles." Hope in Urquhart's voice.

"Negative, sir," he replied. "They're in the Métro, line five. I made the wrong call."

"Shit," said Urquhart. Gatuso heard muffled voices before his boss came back on. "Okay, don't sweat it, Miles. That would have been my bet too. That Wren woman's got balls." Another pause on the line. "Line five means they're probably heading for Gare de Lyon. Not enough time to organise anything there. I've had a military helicopter on standby." More muffled words.

Gatuso caught 'Good work,' and then Urquhart was back. "Get yourself to Hôpital Lariboisière just north of you. Go to the desk and someone there will take you to the helipad."

They waited nervously at the farthest end of the platform. It was a warm spring day above ground. Down in the maze of the Métro, the air that whistled past them into the tunnel to their right was sultry, electric and imbued with the earthiness of millions of people. The faint whir of an approaching train deepened and erupted into a rattling clatter as it entered the crowded station.

Wren scanned the faces of anyone coming toward them, matching each against the dark features of the fiend from Nathalie's apartment and the grainy image of the man with half an ear. She didn't give the vaguely attractive, casually dressed woman with a small backpack a second glance. McLeod did. But then she moved away and was lost in the swarming mass of humanity waiting to board the slowing carriages. He searched his recent memory. Something to do with transport. Then it was gone in the struggle to keep with Wren and Penelope as an impossible number of bodies tried to cram into the carriage.

"Change at Bastille." Gatuso's voice was empty of emotion. "Line one, direction Château de Vincennes. Get off at Gare de Lyon." There was a pause in the feed in Brennan's ear. When it came back, Gatuso was shouting above the thumping din of helicopter blades. "CALL ME WITH THEIR DESTINATION, OVER."

"Roger that," she said as unobtrusively as she could. The wiry man standing behind her in the cramped carriage gave no sign of interest. Just tugged the brim of his cap lower.

The concourse of Gare de Lyon was half the size and not remotely as busy as the one they'd left thirty minutes ago. McLeod handed a wad of euros to the gruff man at the ticket counter. Then he looked twenty yards to his left and was waylaid by Penelope's serene beauty as she stood with Wren, casually scanning the hall. As though she felt his eyes on her, she turned her head toward him and smiled.

His heart lurched. He was overtaken by powerful emotions, as strong as anything he'd ever felt for Catherine. They were mixed in his stomach with a crippling fear. The fear of losing another woman he was beginning to love.

He clenched his fists and wished with every fibre of his being that things weren't like this. That they weren't being hunted like dogs. That they were just like any of the other carefree people in the short queue behind him. The middle-aged man smiling and waving at someone. The young couple who couldn't keep their hands off each other. The Irish woman from the London bus last night and the Métro station fifteen minutes ago. Her hair was a different colour, but McLeod was sure it was her. Fear landed a mighty blow in the battle in his stomach.

Sixty

Saturday afternoon

"Sancerre," said Sir David, adamantly.

"Not with lobster, you old fool," replied Sir Francis with a pitying look across the immaculately laid table for two.

"The champagne here is pigswill," Sir David said. He leaned back in his chair and gestured disparagingly across the intimate dining room. They were tucked away in a corner by the window overlooking the robust architecture of St James's Street. The half dozen or so other diners were studiously ignoring them as Wagner's Tannhäuser Overture built tumultuously in the background.

"It's no better at your club and it's twice the price," Sir Francis griped, tapping a long finger on the white linen. The two men glowered darkly at each other for a spell.

Sir David angrily spooned sour cream and caviar on a blini from the tray between them. "It wasn't my idea to let them leave the country, you know," he said accusingly.

"Well it wasn't mine to send in Urquhart's unhinged psychopath," re-joined Sir Francis, tearing a bread roll.

Sir David looked up at the small patch of sky visible through the window as the room suddenly darkened. "Could be due a shower," he muttered.

"You're certainly due one," Sir Francis carped. "I'm surprised they let you in."

"Well, they allow you to be a member, so there we are." Sir David deposited another blini in his jowly chops. "And he's not a psychopath apparently, he's a sadist."

"What's the difference?" said Sir Francis, clicking his fingers at the smartly dressed sommelier who'd entered the small dining room.

"Haven't the foggiest, old chap. That's more your area of expertise, isn't it?"

The sommelier approached the table and stood respectfully, hands behind his back.

"There you are, Pierre," Sir Francis said and pointed at his companion. "Tell this imbecile he can't have Sancerre with his lobster."

The sommelier gritted his teeth and favoured them with a fawning smile. "Sir David can have whatever he likes with his lobster, Sir Francis, but I would perhaps consider something a little more substantial. We have a very nice Sauvignon from Marlborough that would…"

"Right, fine," Sir David said and waved a hand irritably. The sommelier half bowed and departed, rolling his eyes. Sir David looked after him thoughtfully for a moment. "Do you ever worry what people think of you, old chap?"

Sir Francis fixed him with a cloudy glare. "What a peculiar thing to say. What do you care?"

"I don't, of course. That's my point." He reached for another blini. "What does that make us?"

"Exceedingly wealthy and influential, old man," Sir Francis replied. "It's what separates us from ordinary people and has done for centuries."

"Hmmnn, I suppose you're right."

The sommelier returned, uncorked the bottle and poured a mouthful in Sir David's glass.

He swilled and swallowed. "Passable," he said. "Make sure the next one's colder, would you?"

"Very good, sir," the sommelier replied, wondering how much he needed this job. He poured the wine, deposited the bottle in a vacuumed holder and left it on the table.

"To a more fruitful day," said Sir David, raising his glass.

"It could hardly be otherwise," Sir Francis said, reciprocating. He took a large gulp and dabbed his mouth with a napkin. "So, Geneva," he murmured and rubbed his bristly chin.

"Hmmnn. Advantages and disadvantages." Sir David tipped a colourful array of pills from a plastic bottle into his wine glass to his companion's amusement. "What?" he said, emptying his glass and throwing his head back. "Makes 'em easier to get down." He refilled their glasses and leaned back in his chair. "They're further away from our situation here, but the Swiss authorities will be harder to manipulate. How friendly are you with whatshername, Gabber, is it?"

"No, more appropriate yet," replied Sir Francis. "Gasser, she's called. Only met her a couple of times."

"What sort is she?" said Sir David, taking his phone from a jacket pocket. He fired off a quick text to his P.A.

"Bloody efficient, but then they all are over there." Sir Francis took a couple of olives and chewed thoughtfully. "I think she'd be amenable were a sufficiently generous accommodation proposed."

Sir David's phone pinged. "How's your German?" he said, eyeing the approach of two long aproned waiters.

"Not as good as Fräulein Gasser's English," Sir Francis replied, stuffing his napkin into the collar of his shirt. The two men waited impatiently as one of the waiters ceremoniously took a variety of dishes from the tray held by the other and covered the small table with them.

"Right," said Sir Francis as the waiters departed, having given an exhaustive description of each plate, "let's get this over so we can dine in relative peace." He took Sir David's phone and hit call.

"Fräulein Gasser, this is Sir Francis Argyll... Very well thank you. And your good self... Sorry to hear that. Have you tried bearing down? ...You know, like when you go to the toilet... Ah, well you need to be on the toilet first... That's quite all right... That's sorted it has it? ... The pleasure's mine. Listen, we're having a spot of bother with one of our nationals... Thank you. Well, we believe they're on a train bound for Geneva... It couldn't be helped I'm afraid... No, no, we have that side of things in hand... Well, we'd like it kept quiet... That's the idea... Yes two others... No, just detained as suspects until our man comes for them... I thought you might... I'm sure that would be in order... If you could have a word with your head of intelligence, then ours will be in touch with the finer details? ... Excellent ...and a good day to you too."

"Well?" said Sir David, sucking on a lobster claw.

Sir Francis dipped a thrice-fried chip into white truffle-infused, free-range mayonnaise. "Banking it against a future situation."

A greasy smile appeared on Sir David's face. "Good work, old chap. This could be our lucky day."

Sixty-One

Saturday afternoon

"You're sure it was the same woman, Mac?" Apprehension tightened the corners of Penelope's wide green eyes.

McLeod was watching fertile French farmland recede from him at better than two hundred kilometres an hour. He switched his focus to her gaze in the window seat next to him and nodded. "Positive," he said.

"Then why didn't she get on this train?" said Wren from the window seat across their table.

"She must have realised I'd recognised her," McLeod replied. "Maybe she was just a pair of eyes. Probably why she took off in such a hurry when I was buying the tickets." Penelope took his hand and gave it a squeeze.

Fifteen hundred metres above them, Gatuso and Brennan sat in the cramped cabin of an adapted Lynx helicopter. They'd finally caught up with the train around Beaune and were now being helped by a tailwind. With the more direct course they were able to take, Gatuso estimated they'd be in Geneva twenty minutes ahead of their targets. The fact that the McLeod man had recognised his partner for this job made things more complicated. The Swiss denial to his request for access to a sniper's position didn't help matters. He thought about the station and brought up the layout he'd been e-mailed on his phone. Plenty of access points. Good for extraction. A nightmare for predicting movement. If only Brennan hadn't been made. Then he thought some more and felt a burst of adrenaline.

Saturday afternoon

Kurjac thought Penelope Lane was every bit as beautiful as his own sister. A similar sadness was in her eyes. She was walking toward him down the aisle of the train. The McLeod man was behind her. Their eyes met for a second before Kurjac turned his head and pulled his cap. Had he imagined McLeod pausing? Or was he just steadying himself against the train's slight move to the left? Either way, he carried on toward the toilets. Kurjac heard the doors being opened and let out the breath he'd been holding. Risked a look down the aisle behind him. No sign.

He stood and grabbed his backpack, and then hurried through to the carriage beyond the toilets and found a seat next to a middle-aged woman.

She flashed a smile at him. It vanished when she saw his eyes. "Entschuldigung," she said, rising hurriedly.

Kurjac made way for her as she took her small suitcase from the rack above and hastened away. He gave the incident no thought. He'd had the same effect on people for ten years or more. It was one of the many reasons he was still alive. Another was his default setting. Never plan in hope. Being exposed now risked everything. So he sat nervously waiting for the sound of the toilet doors.

"Nous arriverons à la gare Cornavin en deux minutes." The announcer's words were bookended with ding-dongs. People around them in the first-class carriage started stretching and reaching up for bags. Wren took the opportunity to vape furiously on her puffer. She'd given up trying to plan for the possible dangers ahead. They were heading into unknown territory. Her best guess was that they'd be watched at the station and followed. Therefore, the greatest threat would be from behind.

"Okay, Mac. You go ahead this time and I'll bring up the rear. Penelope, wear the rucksack on your back." She paused and looked at their sombre faces, willed a conviction she didn't feel into her voice. "It's going to be all right. Look how far we've come." She took a last puff and forced a smile. "We're going to be fine if we stay together and keep moving," she murmured. They stood up and shuffled toward the doors. Penelope turned McLeod around to face her. She reached her hands to his face and pulled his lips to hers. McLeod tasted the salt of her tears. He reached an arm between her back and rucksack and squeezed her tightly to him.

He broke the kiss and whispered in her thick black hair, "We're going to be fine, Pen." She nodded faintly and pulled back. McLeod wiped her cheeks and ran his thumb gently over her lower lip. Her eyes were searching his. He closed them and pulled her head to his chest. He scanned the platform through the window as the train slowed to a halt. Lots of smiling people waiting to greet loved ones. Some were waving and scampering after the carriages. Some held nameplates across their chests. An attractive woman in sunglasses was standing with her gloved hands together in front of her. McLeod's heart began thumping as she lifted one of them to her lapel and began talking.

"Okay, he's seen me," Brennan said into her collar.

"Good," came Gatuso's voice in her earpiece. "Now put your hand in your jacket pocket like you've got a gun in it."

"I have got a gun in it." She paused her commentary and watched the first people getting out of the car, then looked a hundred metres to her left to the escalators, her first checkpoint. Dozens of people were streaming toward them. When she looked back to the doors, McLeod was getting out, followed by Lane and Wren. He gave her a hard stare and took off at a quick stride, the others following closely. "They're heading the right way," she said and began walking quickly after them.

"Good. Keep them in sight."

Kurjac remained in his carriage further up the train. He wasn't tall so he was using his elevated position above the platform to scan the people milling toward the exits and transfers. He recognised McLeod instantly. He was working like a plough through the crowded platform. He saw the others as they passed him. Another disturbance a little further back caught his eye. He recognised the woman from Paris. She hadn't got on the train. How the hell...? His blood ran cold. He hadn't been expecting another attempt so soon. He took three quick steps to the door and hurled himself into the mass of people.

Wren struggled to keep her hand on Penelope's rucksack as they pushed through the river of bodies. People were coming towards them now as well, making the return journey to Paris. She looked behind her and saw the woman Mac had pointed out from the train. Her sunglasses were intermittently visible through the throng some ten metres back. Wren was nearly knocked off her feet by a heavy bag hitting her shoulder. She spun and staggered and was pushed forward. Stumbled on searching desperately for Penelope's rucksack among bodies and faces. She glimpsed it five metres ahead. Then she put her head down like a rugby player and used her wiry frame to muscle through.

Gatuso grinned as he was informed of their progress towards his position. He was gambling again, but this time, he had two chances. His excitement was making his heart quicken. "Where are they now?" he said, forcing himself to take slow, deep breaths.

"Still heading toward the escalators," Brennan's voice said in his ear.

He smiled to himself and attached the heavy silencer to his Beretta. It would reduce the bullet's velocity considerably, but then it didn't have far to travel. "Tell me when they're on it," he breathed. He closed his briefcase, flushed the toilet and headed to his position like a kid going to Disneyland.

"Is she still there?" McLeod shouted over his shoulder. He planted his left foot firmly and used his left arm to brush a large man aside, then surged forward again. Penelope's left hand firmly in his right.

"Ten people back." McLeod just made out Wren's barked words in the din of the station. Finally, he got a foot on the metal step of the escalator. People were standing still on the right. He pulled Penelope onto the stair below him and saw Wren behind her. He started moving slowly up the left half of the staircase, then looked back and saw the Irish woman five metres from the bottom of the escalator, turned back up and cursed as the people ahead were hardly moving.

"ALLEZ," he shouted in frustration.

"She's stopped, Mac," Wren called up to him. He spun around and saw her standing at the bottom of the down escalator. She was looking toward the exits but seemed to be talking to someone. He turned and gained another stair. "Shit, Mac," Wren hissed. "I think I see Kurjac. Small guy with a cap."

McLeod looked to where she was pointing, and stared in terror as the slight figure stepped onto the escalator. He turned and cursed again as there was nowhere to go.

A man rapidly descending the adjacent escalator caught his eye. He saw him bring something up in his right hand. A phone? Sun from the skylight above glinted off it. Something metallic.

Then it flashed once. Then he heard a loud pop. Then he felt a pull from Penelope below him and heard a loud gasp. He turned and saw her grasping her side. A look of agony and disbelief on her face.

"JESUS NO," he screamed. He bent down to where she'd crumpled, panting on the stairs, looked in horror at the blood pumping through the fingers of her left hand where she was holding her side. "IL Y A UN DOCTEUR LÀ?" McLeod yelled, looking around feverishly. He covered her hand with his right and put his left under her head. From her bag, Wren passed him a thick wad of tissues in desperation. People around them were watching in horror. McLeod looked fearfully at Penelope's eyes. They were squeezed tight in pain. Then they opened and he could see the light in them fading.

They were coming to the top of the escalator. He picked Penelope up under her knees and armpits. Her blood-soaked hand didn't have the strength to hold on. "ALLEZ, MERDE," he roared at the people ahead of him. Started running along the crosswalk, weaving through knots of people.

"Mac," he heard faintly. He slowed and stopped, gazed into her olive-green eyes. And knew.

"Mac...I...I...lo..." Then, in McLeod's arms, Penelope died.

Sixty-Two

Saturday afternoon

The man's face was familiar to Kurjac. Since the General's operation had become his country's de facto secret service, many files were kept on notable operatives in other agencies. The competition, the General called it. Miles Gatuso was the guy's name. Longest confirmed sniper kill by someone other than a serving member of the armed forces. Highly accomplished in small arms fire and beyond classification in hand-to-hand combat. So Kurjac was unsurprised by what he'd just witnessed. In the three seconds it took him to work out the most likely sequence of events following the shooting, he was more than half way up the escalator and Gatuso was heading rapidly for an exit.

He had a knife, but knew that was useless in a gunfight. He needed two things and he thought the woman walking briskly in Gatuso's wake might provide the first. He gritted his teeth and vaulted onto the shiny partition between the up and down escalators. Ran and skidded down its length and leapt off to his right. The woman was just visible in the shaded concourse forty metres ahead. Gatuso was gone. Kurjac took off at a sprint, had to dodge and weave between people screaming and scattering in fear. She was only twenty metres from the exit when she started to run. Kurjac cursed and dug deeper. Made a desperate lunge and managed to tap her right foot.

Kurjac was expecting to hit the ground. The woman wasn't. He turned his landing into a forward roll and pinned the sprawling woman by a knee in the small of the back and a hand against her right ear. He ground her head into the hard, concrete floor. The flailing of her arms and cries of help were in vain. Everyone in the vicinity was in panic, looking after themselves, fleeing from the awful events. Kurjac pulled the woman's head up and smashed it back fairly hard. She went limp and her eyes went blank. Her gun was a snub-nosed Glock. Not ideal, but adequate for his purposes. He took her wallet and smashed her phone. He found the little communication device on her lapel and bent close to it. "You're a dead man," he breathed.

McLeod's bloody hands were bound by plastic ties for the second time in as many days. He didn't care. About his tied hands or any other thing in the whole world. A part of him had hoped the heavily armed Swiss soldiers who'd rushed to the scene would riddle him with bullets. Release him from pain and grief as deep and visceral as anything he'd ever known. First Catherine, now Penelope. The thinking part of his brain was incapable of doing anything other than repeat 'No' endlessly. Like a mad monk's cathartic mantra without the relief. He could physically feel the hole in the core of his body. It ached and pushed against his ribcage, threatening to explode out of his chest.

On the edge of his consciousness, he was aware of people staring and voices around him. One in particular kept nagging at him. Every time his walking pace slowed, he felt the sharp jab of a gun muzzle in his back. He was walking toward a big bright light. He'd read about this. People who'd had near death experiences described it. He was dying and it couldn't come soon enough.

Wren recognised the deadly symptoms as they exited the station into bright afternoon sunlight. His eyes had lost focus as he stumbled next to her. His breathing was getting shallower. Sweat was beading at his temples. She was still reeling from the shooting and from being handcuffed and frogmarched through the station. But she was functioning fully and alert to her surroundings. Mac wasn't. He was in shock and she had to get him out of it.

Her repeated efforts to get through to him orally were having no effect. She was going to have to do something drastic or he'd be needing the ambulance that was making an ear-splitting approach to the front of the station. She knitted her fingers together and swung both hands into Mac's stomach. Bent him right over. She immediately felt two gun barrels in her back and one on her right temple and shouts of "STOP." One of the soldiers was hauling Mac upright. She looked desperately to his eyes. They were reddened and haggard, but they were focused.

"Are you there, Mac?" she pleaded. His eyes glazed again. "Jesus, Mac. STAY WITH ME," she shrieked.

"SILENCE," shouted one of the soldiers behind her.

McLeod began taking huge breaths as two paramedics with face masks unloaded a gurney from the back of the ambulance and wheeled it past them into the station. It had a long black bag on it.

An inhuman noise started up next to Wren and exploded into a bawled, "BAAAAAASTAAAAAARD."

The soldier who seemed to be in charge took a couple of paces and backhanded McLeod across the face.

"There's no need for that," Wren spat at the soldier. She looked up at McLeod uncertainly. He waggled his jaw, then shook himself all over. Looked down at Wren. "How're you doing?" she murmured.

"Getting there," he replied. The ice was back in his hooded stare. "What's happening?"

Two cars with 'Police' and 'Polizei' emblazoned on the side squealed to a halt at the kerb in front of them. Their sirens died, but their lights still flashed. "I don't know," she said. "They won't tell me anything. I've shown them my police ID and tried to tell them what happened. I don't think we're under arrest."

From his seat outside a café fifty metres away, Gatuso surreptitiously raised a small pair of high-powered binoculars and trained them on the developing situation.

The soldiers pushed Wren and McLeod roughly toward the first police car. McLeod turned his head to Wren. "That tells us everything, doesn't it?" he murmured. They were bundled inside. A grill separated the front and back. McLeod's rucksack was passed through the window to the two policemen in the front. He watched as the man in the passenger seat just put it on the floor between his legs.

"Very probably," Wren replied, eyes fixed on the soldier by the driver's window rummaging through her handbag. She'd taken the money from Penelope's bag and stashed it in her own.

Fifty metres away, Gatuso put down his latte and picked up his binoculars again. He saw the soldier inspecting Wren's puffer and put it back. Saw him look at both sides of the pen drive

259

which just had 'charts' written on it and put it back. Watched closely as the soldier removed and pocketed the small pistol and passed the zipped-up handbag to the driver who tossed it to his partner who put it with the rucksack at his feet. Gatuso recorded a quick spoken report of the last half hour to a file on his phone, left some Francs on the table and headed for the rendezvous.

In the back of the police car, Wren switched her piercing gaze to McLeod's eyes as the paramedics wheeled the gurney with its now filled black bag to the back of the ambulance in front of them and carefully loaded it. They remained hard as steel and his jaw was straining. "I'm so sorry, Mac," Wren gasped, a tear rolling down her cheek.

"Me too," he replied emptily.

"It was all about Penelope from the start." She paused and thought about her puffer with the magic juice inside it. "Nathalie was just in the wrong place at the wrong time."

McLeod just nodded slowly.

"There was nothing more we could have done, Mac," she said cautiously.

"No," he muttered and looked down at his hands. Wren could feel the torment coursing through him. The rage.

"I don't think this is a fight we can win, Mac," she said as the police car behind overtook them with sirens blaring. The ambulance followed, then their own vehicle pulled out and accelerated rapidly.

"No," he said again numbly.

Wren shot him a look. "Stay with me, Mac," she said sharply.

When he looked at her, resolve shone in his deep-set brown eyes. "No, Anna." His voice was flat. "I don't think I can do that. There are things I need to do that you don't want to be anywhere near."

In a quiet street a few hundred metres away, a futures trader in aviator shades was cruising slowly, looking for a parking space for his prized BMW. He'd bought it with some of last year's bonus. Kurjac looked at the long bonnet, spacious interior and generous boot as it glided past him and thought it would be ideal. He scanned quickly up and down the street, then sprinted after the car and gave it a fair kick on its back left panel. It came to an indignant halt. The driver's door opened and the livid trader leapt out. Aimed furiously for the slight man standing calmly at the back of his car. Kurjac used the same foot that he'd employed on the car to the man's balls. Did little more than stick it out as the man hurled himself in fury at him. A sharp elbow to the back of the neck put the bent-up man on the tarmac. Probably for a good while. Perhaps until he got to Italy. He smiled to himself as another brick in the impossible ziggurat fell into place.

Saturday afternoon

Wren searched the rugged face of the complex man she'd known for little more than a day. The quiet academic with a charismatic smile and a ready wit. The humble athlete with an intuitive sense of right and wrong. The placid martial arts expert who'd risked his life more than once for two women he'd never met before. Then she thought about the uncertainty facing them and looked out the window as they passed a large church bathed in late afternoon sunshine. No, she checked herself, the certainty. Penelope had been the target, but surely Mac and herself were facing the same fate knowing what they did.

But what did they actually know? That MI5, and therefore the British government, was responsible for the deaths of two beautiful young women. Possibly because one of them was about to expose a devastating financial scandal. More probably because the other was developing something that would wipe out a massive global market. Then she thought about her handbag in the front of the car and the two items it contained that could still bring about both outcomes.

McLeod was thinking hard too. About the world he thought he knew. The one in which you worked hard, did the right thing and minded your own business. If you could achieve those aims, then nothing more terrible than disease or the loss of a loved one could happen to you. As far as he could work out, that's all Penelope and Nathalie had ever done. They'd committed no crimes he was aware of. Neither had done anything to warrant the barbarity that had been visited upon them.

Except that they had. They'd both been brilliant. Each had devised a means of depriving a great many people of the thing they craved beyond anything else. They lay zipped up in black bags because there were too many people in the world for whom enough was an alien concept. Victims of a world desperately trying to consume itself to death.

The driver broke his reverie by swearing briefly and slamming on the brakes. McLeod and Wren weren't belted in and were thrown against the grill in front of them. Then they were rocked back into their seats as the car's momentum reversed. McLeod tried to peer through the windscreen. Ahead of their car was a silver BMW, its driver's side door and boot open. Then a small gun and a pair of hands appeared through their driver's window. McLeod couldn't see who they belonged to. The driver turned his head and opened his mouth to speak. He was prevented by the nozzle of the gun being shoved in it. His eyes widened and he gagged. One of the hands came off the gun and pointed to the policeman breathing heavily in the passenger seat.

"VOUS! Dans la coffre avec les sacs. BOUGEZ!"

The fact that he was speaking a different language couldn't hide the man's gravelly Slavic tone. Kurjac. McLeod's blood ran cold. The policeman without a gun in his mouth scrabbled at his feet for the bags, fumbled to open his door and ran a few paces to the back of the BMW. He threw the bags in the boot and then himself. McLeod looked desperately around the street for any signs of assistance. The few startled people he saw were recoiling in terror from the scene unfolding in front of them.

"SORTEZ," Kurjac shouted.

Gingerly, the policeman pulled his door handle and the gun came out of his mouth. He stepped out of the car and McLeod watched the gun go to his temple.

"LA PORTE," commanded Kurjac.

The policeman took a couple of steps and opened the rear passenger door. McLeod looked out of it into the wizened eyes of the man who'd killed Nathalie. They were dark, almost black. McLeod's breath caught in his throat. It was like looking into the eyes of a dead man. Then there was something else in them. A searching. Then Kurjac's thin mouth opened. "Come with me if you want to live," it snarled.

Sixty-Three

Saturday afternoon

"It's a steaming pile of shit is what it is, old man," said Sir David. His fervour caused one of the hot stones on his back to clatter to the floor of the womb-like treatment room.

"Let's not get carried away, old chap," Sir Francis replied from the adjacent massage table. "The woman's gone, that's the main thing. Urquhart's man will account for the others soon enough."

The room was filled with the sound of the sea ebbing and flowing over a pebbly beach. The only light came from scented candles in little recesses in the burgundy walls. The noiseless fan on the ceiling sent gentle wafts of air over the two men's backs. "The description would seem to point to the Bosnian fellow, what's he called, Kojak?" said Sir David, sleepily. A heavy lunch and a couple of bottles of wine were sloshing around somewhere beneath him.

Sir Francis lifted his head from the doughnut hole it had been resting in. "That's the chap from the Dirty Dozen, you arse. The Bosnian fellow's Kurjac. About as unstable as they come, by all accounts."

There was a discreet tap on the treatment room door and two therapists who looked more like air hostesses breezed in. They removed the stones, poured oils and got down to some heavy kneading. The two men groaned and wheezed.

"You think any of this is doing us any good?" Sir David murmured as the therapists departed.

"I don't think the thing that could do you any good's been invented, old chap," Sir Francis replied.

The music morphed into the eerie keening of humpback whales. "Jesus Christ," muttered Sir David. "Sounds like Lady Harris after one too many bottles of gin." He wriggled his considerable mass into a more comfortable position. "What d'you suppose that lunatic wants with 'em? Revenge?"

"That would have been my first thought," Sir Francis replied. "But surely that would have been best achieved by leaving them with the Swiss authorities?"

"Maybe he wants the satisfaction of despatching them himself. I have the feeling we're missing something here and I don't like it," Sir David grumbled. "Better get Urquhart on it."

"What about the media?"

Sir David expelled a deep breath. "Absolute fucking meltdown, old thing. All kinds of conspiracy theories. There's a video apparently."

"Hmmnn, I've seen it," Sir Francis replied. "Thank God you can only just make out the Bosnian fellow and the policeman. I gather Fräulein Gasser nobbled any footage from the station."

Something his companion said struck Sir David. He poked and probed at the idea and couldn't see a flaw. "What if we gave the press Wren and McLeod now? Mention that they're being sought by us for an undisclosed reason? That somehow they're in cahoots with this Kurjac chap?"

Sir Francis leaned up on a scrawny elbow. A smile threatened to break out on his haggard face. "And when they turn up no longer alive, we have a ready perpetrator in Kurjac. Brilliant, David. You're back to your best."

Saturday afternoon

Kurjac was a skilled driver of a variety of vehicles. Everything from motorcycles to tanks and even the General's helicopter. It took him a few kilometres through the busy Geneva streets to nail down the BMW's optimum cornering and acceleration capabilities, but now he was flying. In the back, Wren and McLeod could do little more than grip like fury to their respective door handles. Sirens started up in several surrounding streets. Kurjac shifted gears and pulled out to overtake a double-length lorry. McLeod held his breath as they headed straight at an oncoming car. Kurjac calmly pressed the accelerator further and swung the wheel right with centimetres to spare. Several horns flared.

"JESUS!" shouted McLeod. "Shooting us would be a lot easier."

Kurjac swerved past two more cars and pushed the needle up to one hundred kilometres an hour. "Believe me, Mr McLeod, that's the last thing I want to do." They were in the outskirts of town now, industrial and retail developments giving way to vibrant trees and the odd bit of flat cultivated land.

His words bewildered Wren. "Why are you doing this?" she demanded, glowering at the dark eyes in the rear-view mirror.

They flicked up to meet hers briefly, then returned to the road. "Have patience, Inspector. I need to get off this road and get rid of the cop in the trunk." He glanced at the SatNav that was indicating a right turn off the autoroute onto a minor road. A few kilometres through quiet residential streets with apartment buildings, parks and football pitches and they were onto a rural road. Kurjac hit the brakes and pulled onto the shoulder. He grabbed the Irish woman's gun from the glove box. "I'll be right back," he said and leaped out. Wren followed his movement around the car to the boot.

"ATTENTION, MONSIEUR!" Kurjac shouted and fired a shot into the ground near the boot. The noise was deafening. Then the lid popped and Kurjac was lost to sight. There were some muffled words, then Kurjac was climbing back into the driver's seat. Wren looked out the rear window again and saw the Swiss policeman departing rapidly back up the road. Kurjac tossed two guns on the passenger seat and passed McLeod his rucksack and Wren her bag. She rummaged immediately for her puffer.

Several kilometres later, Kurjac blasted through a pretty hamlet of alpine chalet-style houses and saw what he wanted up ahead. He slowed and pulled off the road onto an area of wasteland in front of a huge agricultural storage building. They came to a halt in a cloud of dust facing the road.

Out of his window to the south, McLeod saw the vast alpine plateau. The setting sun was pinkening the snow-capped mountaintops. Dark-green crops interspersed with even darker woodland to the foothills. Through the front windscreen was the broad entrance to the road they'd just left. It dissected a tired stone wall. Beyond the road stood a line of mature trees which backed onto a lush meadow. To the north, a wide mucky farmyard lay in front of a large cowshed. Several outbuildings and redundant pieces of farm machinery littered the yard. The farmhouse must have been beyond the shed. No living soul in sight. The only sound inside the car was relieved breathing. McLeod looked at Kurjac's lean, hard profile in front to his left. The nobbly stub of his right ear. He looked to be debating with himself. McLeod decided to take the initiative.

"You killed the MI5 agent in the alley last night, didn't you?" he ventured.

Kurjac looked down, then out of the window at the dust settling on the empty road they'd travelled stretching away north beyond the low wall.

"He was about to kill Miss Lane and then you, Mr McLeod." He paused and turned his head to look into McLeod's eyes. "Yes, I killed him."

"But why?" Wren almost shouted. "You were working for them. You poisoned Miss Lane's sister."

McLeod saw the pain enter Kurjac's dark eyes. He closed them and murmured, "Yes, I did."

Without warning, McLeod lunged for Kurjac's throat. It was difficult with the plastic restraints, but he managed to get a couple of strong fingers on the man's larynx. He pressed harder and knew that Kurjac couldn't breathe. The man offered no resistance. Didn't raise a finger. McLeod was confused. His grip faltered slightly. "Please," Kurjac gasped, "do it."

McLeod applied more pressure, then looked into the man's eyes. He saw the agonies layered in them like scarred rings on an ancient tree trunk. He released his hold in shock and sat back horrified. Kurjac took a few deep lungfuls and then a gun was in his hand. McLeod flinched and held his hands in front of his face, eyes tight shut, and awaited the inevitable. Cursed himself for being so stupid. One second passed. Then another. "Put your hands down, Mr McLeod," he heard Kurjac's guttural voice instead of the loud bang he was expecting. Slowly, he lowered his arms and opened his eyes. The gun was still in Kurjac's hand, but it was being held by the short nozzle, the handle toward McLeod. "Take it," Kurjac urged.

McLeod looked uncertainly at the gun. What the hell was the man playing at? He glanced at Wren beside him. She saw the doubt in his eyes and reached for the weapon, made sure the safety was on and put it in her lap. When McLeod looked back to Kurjac, there was an evil-looking knife in his left hand. "I need you to trust me, Mr McLeod," he said gravely. He pointed to McLeod's hands. "For your ties," he murmured.

266

McLeod thought about the MI5 agent, about Kurjac's indifference to being strangled, about the gun. Then he held out his hands to the man who was responsible for the nightmare he'd been living. Kurjac took McLeod's right hand and slid the blade carefully under the plastic. The knife was sharp and felt cold on McLeod's skin. With a quick deft cut, the tie was snapped. He did the same on the left and the ties fell to the foot well. Kurjac nodded once at McLeod who rubbed his wrists and glared back. "Will you do hers?" Kurjac said, flipping the knife, handle toward him.

McLeod looked from the knife to Wren. Then to his own hands. They were trembling slightly. "I don't think I can, Anna," he breathed. She closed her eyes briefly, then held out her hands to Kurjac. He looked a question at her.

"Yes, dammit. Quickly," she spat. She was struck by how warm and callused his hands were as they efficiently cut the ties. She let out the breath she'd been holding and narrowed her eyes at the hollow features of the killer's face. They gave nothing away. "What's this all about, Kurjac?" she said angrily. "One minute you're trying to kill us, the next you're saving our lives. Why?"

Kurjac was silent for a spell as he contemplated his plans. Then he looked from Wren to McLeod and pointed. "Him," he said quietly.

Sixty-Four

Saturday evening

A powerful smell brought Field Operative Brennan back to her senses. She immediately wished it hadn't. White-hot pain seared the left side of her skull. It resonated from there through her brain to a dull ache in her right ear. She opened her eyes to find the cause of the singing rawness in her hands. Saw torn skin on her palms. Dirt from the station floor was etched in the bloody wounds. She tried lifting her head from the ground, but her neck wouldn't allow it. She gasped as she felt like someone were plunging a knife in.

"Doucement, Mademoiselle," said one of the two red-jacketed paramedics huddled over her. He reached into his medical case and came out with a bottle of water and some pills. "Here, take. You feel better." The paramedics eased her into a sitting position and supported her back. Brennan felt even worse but held out her hand for the pills and swallowed them gratefully with a swig from the bottle. She looked around at the eerily empty station. Concrete and pillars and kiosks and escalators. To her left, a glass entrance was guarded by two sturdy policemen with automatic rifles. She felt for her phone, but it wasn't in her jacket pocket.

"You look for this?" said the other paramedic, holding up the smashed and crumpled remains of her phone.

"Shit," she said. She'd only seen his face for half a second before he knocked her out, but Brennan knew who it was. After all, she'd been the liaison between him and her boss. And not for the first time. She thought about the things the man was capable of and shuddered. Then she felt for the gadget on her lapel, and saw it in pieces on the floor. "Bollocks," she muttered. She had to get a message to Gatuso: there was someone even madder than him out there.

Saturday evening

"That's it," Kurjac breathed and hung his head. "I'm sorry."

McLeod let out a long sigh and cast his eyes to the moon-lit peaks through the right-hand rear passenger window. A thin veil of mist was forming in the fertile plain between. A battered tractor had passed their sheltered position half an hour ago, but nothing since. Beside him on the back seat, Wren was barely breathing, clearly struggling as much as him with Kurjac's incredible tale.

McLeod thought back to the phone conversation he'd had in London with the man silently rocking in the front of the car. He thought about Penelope and Nathalie. Then he thought about Kurjac's little niece. The worn, passport-sized photograph he'd shown them from his tattered wallet. The angelic face. The eyes that seemed to bore into your soul even from a two-dimensional image. The porcelain ears. Then he tried to imagine her with one of them missing. It brought a queasy feeling to his stomach. He thought again about Penelope. What would she have wanted?

He closed his eyes. "I understand," he said quietly and took a deep breath. "I understand," he repeated more forcefully. "But I don't forgive what you did to Nathalie."

He looked at Wren beside him, saw the battle being waged in her conflicted eyes as they stared daggers into the back of Kurjac's seat. She took a breath as if about to speak, then held it in and looked out the window.

The mother in her could only focus on Kurjac's little niece and nephew. "But why haven't you tried to break them out?" she barked and thumped the leather seat back in front of her. "If they're so important to you and you're clearly mad enough."

Kurjac's limp head shook gently. "They are and I am," he replied emptily. "I did try once, but it's impossible for one man."

"Why?" said Wren, taken aback. "What happened?"

There was a long silence from the front of the car. McLeod sensed the conflict raging in the tortured man's mind. His voice cracked when he finally spoke. "The General had seen me in one of the compound's cameras after I escaped my room. When I got to Lejla, the old man on the farm had a shotgun in her mouth." He paused and took a laboured breath. "Ten of the General's soldiers arrived and beat me unconscious. When I awoke…" His voice cracked again and he coughed. "I woke to find Lejla

269

hanging naked by her wrists from a rafter in the barn. The General...forced me to watch him...beat her with an iron bar." He choked on the word. McLeod saw him screw up his eyes. "She was pregnant, Inspector," he almost whimpered. "He beat her swollen belly over and over..."

McLeod stole a horrified glance at Wren. Her eyes were wide in disgust and glistening with grief. Then they were shocked as Kurjac threw his head against his seat back.

"Lejla's broken body couldn't keep the baby. The General made me catch it when it came, even while Lejla was screaming in agony above me." Sobs were clearly audible now from the tormented Bosnian. "It would have been a girl...but it was just a tiny, broken...bloody ..."

McLeod watched as he smashed both fists on the steering wheel and put his head between them. His whole body racked and heaved.

Wren was breathing heavily beside him. She wiped her eyes, took a deep breath and nodded. "Fuck it," she said. "What will this General do now?"

Another long silence, broken only by Kurjac's keening. Somewhere out in the night, a dog started barking. Perhaps in a farm outbuilding, disturbed by a wandering deer or fox. Then it stopped. Heavy breathing came from the front of the car. "He will be trying to find me," Kurjac said morosely. "He will try to make me go back."

Wren nodded thoughtfully. "You're his most valuable asset...and if you don't?"

Kurjac's breath hitched. "I can't think about that."

McLeod thought about it. "He'll kill them," he said quietly. "He'll give you a set period of time to reconsider. Maybe a week after you broke contact. Time, the great healer. But when you don't return, he'll kill them." He went quiet for a moment and turned over in his mind what Kurjac had related. "Not Lejla, though. He'll keep her alive to sire children, if she's still capable." He paused and saw Kurjac staring straight ahead, unblinking. "Ones he's certain are his own."

Kurjac turned his head quickly. "Enough...please," he begged.

McLeod thought back to Wren's original question. "You pointed at me when Inspector Wren asked why you'd saved us?"

As good as his English was, Kurjac was struggling to find the right words. "I can't tell you who ordered Miss Lane to be killed or why," he said emptily. Then he turned in his seat and looked at McLeod straight on. "But the General can." He waited until he saw McLeod's eyes go hard, then continued. "I was sent a video of you kicking that big man's ass. In the men's room…at the bar. The movement…it was impressive. Then you took out my men." He paused and mused on their violent histories. Each would have killed their own mother for the right price. "They were all ex-secret service. Highly trained killers. Now they are all in the hospital."

He reached for his backpack on the front passenger seat, unclipped it and took out a clear plastic wallet. From that, he extracted a single sheet of A4 paper and handed it to McLeod. "The General's compound," he said portentously and clicked on the roof light.

McLeod didn't look at the paper. Instead, he searched Kurjac's eyes, saw hope burgeoning in their haunted darkness. "Why are you showing me this, Kurjac?" He watched the eyes closely for any sign of duplicity. Saw none.

"I think you know why, Mr McLeod," an ominous note in Kurjac's gravelly reply.

McLeod looked at him for a long moment, then nodded and held the paper to the light between himself and Wren. It looked like a hastily printed satellite image from Google, taken on a sunny day around noon as the shadows were very short. Late spring or early summer. The image was centred on a large rectangular building. A long grey drive led to it from what looked like a straight, single-track, east-west road. The drive ended in a wide turnaround just in front of the north face of the main house. It surrounded a vivid green, lawned area, dotted with what looked like small conifers. Italian cypress maybe.

Kurjac pointed to the building. "The bastard lives there," he snarled. "A suite of rooms on the top floor."

"What's this here?" asked Wren, pointing at a small structure on the drive, maybe two hundred metres north of the big house.

Kurjac squinted. "The main gates. There is a smaller one to the south." He moved his finger over the house. Over a large, grassy, landscaped area, complete with pool to its rear and stopped what looked like the same distance further south. "Here," he said. "A fence connects both gates all around the compound."

271

McLeod could just about make out the fence from the faint shadow it cast. There was no break in it other than the north and south gates. McLeod pointed to a little white building about one hundred metres north and west of the big house. "Is this Lejla and her children?" he said.

"Yes," Kurjac replied. "This picture must have been taken before the wall around it was built. It's high and topped with razor wire. Like a prison."

Wren pointed to a couple of larger buildings to the south-east of the big house. "And these?" she murmured.

"Smaller one is a garage and armoury. The other is staff accommodation. Eighteen bedrooms on two floors. Shower block, living area and kitchen downstairs."

McLeod fixed Kurjac with a hard gaze. "How many of those eighteen bedrooms are occupied?" he said coolly.

Kurjac raised his dark eyes and returned a steely glare. "All of them," he said. A heavy silence descended on the car. A half-moon peeped over the mountains to the south.

"Not by gardeners I take it?" said Wren.

Kurjac leaned further around in his seat to look at her. "No, Inspector. They come from outside once a week except in winter." He turned and looked toward the distant glistening peaks. An idea began to take shape in his mind. "Two of the rooms are for the cook and his assistant. The rest are for the General's private army."

McLeod and Wren exchanged silent, solemn glances. Kurjac continued to stare at the mountains.

"Sixteen soldiers, Kurjac?" said McLeod quietly.

"Seventeen, Mr McLeod," Kurjac replied, without turning round. "The unit's Commander, Goran, lives on the first floor in the house with two technicians and the General's personal assistant."

McLeod's final hopes faded. "It's impossible, Kurjac."

The wiry man turned round urgently in his seat again. "No, Mr McLeod." A wild gleam entered his eyes. "You were sent to me to do this."

Sixty-Five

Saturday evening

Sir David dabbed at his forehead with his handkerchief, took a deep breath and pushed the door. A hundred cameras flashed and he couldn't help raising a hand against them despite being advised not to. He took a couple of wobbly steps to the platform and sat down weightily between the Head of the Foreign Office and the Commissioner of the Metropolitan Police.

This was the umpteenth press conference he'd faced in his life, but they never got any easier. Catastrophe was always only a word out of place away, or an error in timing or emphasis. He took a sip of water from the glass on the microphone-strewn table and tried to massage his features into a look of deep concern.

"Home Secretary," barked the snivelling twerp from the BBC, what was his wretched name? Mark, yes. What the hell was he smiling about?

"Could you tell us why we have you and not the Prime Minister with us this evening?"

Good fucking question, thought Sir David before engineering a fawning smile between his saggy jowls.

"Let me assure you, Mark…and the whole country…that the Foreign Secretary and I have this extremely sad and worrying situation under our complete control." He nodded briefly to Sir Francis on his right. "Whilst the death of Penelope Lane and the circumstances surrounding it are of grave concern, the G20 summit is the Prime Minister's most pressing responsibility at this time." He scanned the crowd and nodded to the ITV woman wearing a ridiculous amount of make-up.

"You mentioned the circumstances, Sir David," she said in an impossibly prim voice. "I assume you're referring to the video showing the apparent kidnapping of the suspects for Miss Lane's murder?"

273

Sir David turned expectantly to the Police Chief who returned his look blankly for a second before catching on. "Um, yes," the Commissioner blustered, "that's a procedural issue. Ahem...all we know from the Swiss authorities at this stage is that the suspects were likely British. One adult male, one adult female. The Swiss hadn't managed to acquire their identities before their abduction and the CCTV system at the station was apparently down for repairs." A hubbub started up in the room followed by more camera flash. He paused and consulted the crib sheet that had been forced into his hand five minutes ago by the Home Secretary. "No one else is being sought at this time over the death of Miss Lane. Her body is at the hospital in Geneva. The British Ambassador is overseeing matters and will arrange for repatriation of Miss Lane at the conclusion of the medical examination."

"But what about the kidnapper?" an unidentified voice called from the throng.

Sir Francis saw an opportunity to push the thing into more febrile waters and clacked his tongue. "Our understanding at this time is that the man was a foreign agent, possibly Eastern European." A louder rumpus erupted among the gathered media. Sir Francis waited for it to subside before continuing. "A major manhunt for the individual, his silver BMW and the two suspects has begun. Let me make one thing absolutely clear," he paused and exchanged a po-faced glare with Sir David. "The British Government takes the assassination of its nationals with the utmost seriousness. I assure you that we will not rest until the person or people responsible for Miss Lane's murder are brought to swift justice."

"Which murdered Miss Lane are you talking about, Foreign Secretary?" the man from the BBC called out.

Saturday evening

"He's called Gatuso," said Kurjac in reply to Wren's insistent question. "Miles Gatuso." He went quiet for a moment. Wren saw genuine apprehension in his eyes when they returned to hers. "He's possibly the most dangerous person I've ever come across. And believe me, Inspector, I've known a great many."

The reality of the situation they were talking about suddenly hit McLeod, sitting hunched in the back of the car, like a freight train. He was in a stolen BMW for Christ's sake, discussing ways of storming an unassailable fortress with a half-baked lunatic. All the while being hunted down by some kind of demon. An agent of his own government, no less. His whole body shook. "This has to stop," he said brokenly. A sudden brightness caught his eye out of the window to his right. "Shit," he said urgently. "Something's coming." He killed the ceiling light.

Kurjac saw it, turned back to the wheel and hit the ignition. He slammed the car into reverse as the headlights to the south grew brighter. Accelerated hard backwards into the mouth of the agricultural warehouse, parked it tight up against stacked sacks of animal feed or something, then killed the engine. The three figures in the car breathed heavily and watched the road, praying for the dust they'd churned up to settle. Sure enough, ten seconds later, three French police cars streamed past at breakneck pace. Breaths were held until the lights dissipated among the little houses and dark trees to the north.

Kurjac turned round in his seat once more. "Don't you see, Mr McLeod...this doesn't stop for you. It won't ever. Not unless you expose the people responsible and bring them down. It's the only way."

Wren took a thoughtful pull on her puffer. "No, Kurjac," she said with quiet determination, "I think there might be another." She hit the ceiling light and held her device up to him. "We think this whole thing's to do with the stuff that's in here." She saw bewilderment, then derision fill his eyes. "I'm serious, Kurjac." She paused and thought for a second. One question would confirm it. She closed her eyes and summoned the courage to ask it. "Who did the General send you to kill?"

He looked nonplussed for a moment, then ashamed. He turned away and muttered, "Penelope Lane. Her sister was a mistake." His head dropped. "One that will send me to hell." He banged a fist into his thigh.

Wren nodded slowly. "So I was right. It's all about money."

"I know that, Inspector," Kurjac replied irritably. "What I do for the General always is. What it's got to do with your...thing...I don't..." His voice trailed off.

"Everything, Kurjac," she said slowly, as if to a child. "Penelope developed a juice for it that's so good, Big Tobacco will be out of business as soon as it hits the streets." She let her words hang in the small space, saw realisation hit Kurjac's eyes as they swung wildly toward her.

McLeod suddenly became animated beside her. "How much of the stuff have you got left, Anna?" he asked anxiously.

Wren held it to the light and frowned. "Not much. Why...what are you thinking, Mac?"

"I don't know," he replied quietly and sighed. "What if that's all there is? I know Penelope would have wanted..." A fresh wave of grief hamstrung his train of thought.

"You're right, Mac." She put her puffer back in her bag and took a deep breath. "I won't use it again. There may be enough in it to take to a manufacturer." She looked earnestly at McLeod. "Maybe they can analyse it...reproduce it somehow." She smiled thinly at him and saw a faint gleam of hope enter his hooded eyes. Then her smile faded. "I'm going to need a tabac at some point," she mused.

"Okay," said Kurjac brusquely. "We know why Miss Lane was killed, but we don't know who's behind it."

Wren saw McLeod's jaw muscles tense. "Then I think it's time we paid your General a visit," he said coldly. "We make it to Italy, we disappear."

"But how, Mac?" Desperation in Wren's throaty voice. "All routes out of the country will be blocked by now."

Kurjac pointed south to the distant peaks bathed in pale moonlight. "One won't be," he growled darkly.

Sixty-Six

Saturday evening

"Would there be anything else this evening, sir," asked Andrews, the club's pencil-necked senior steward.

"No, that's all right," Sir David replied, "just leave the bottle, there's a good chap."

The steward retreated ceremoniously and closed the door silently. The fire cast eerie shadows across the haggard faces of the two beleaguered old men in the sombre room. The accusatory faces of their forefathers watched over them from where they hung on the dark walls. Heavy curtains had been closed and leather armchairs drawn up to the fire. The two knights of the realm exchanged bitter glares.

Breaking the pregnant silence, Sir David said caustically, "We should have been prepared for it, Francis."

"Hmmnn," his companion mused, "we hardly covered ourselves in glory in there. Where the hell that BBC toad got the griff on the other Lane woman…?"

"Urquhart says it was the upstairs neighbours," Sir David weighed in, selecting a juicy olive. "Called the creep directly when they perceived a lack of police action. There's your damned free press," he exhorted and spat a stone into the fire.

"Good job the Commissioner towed the line," said Sir Francis, raising an untamed eyebrow.

"Yes," said Sir David, rummaging in pockets for his pills. "Rather saved our bacon falling on his sword like he did. Ought to shove something his way I suppose."

Sir Francis nodded slowly. "CBE, d'you think," he murmured, clearly bored with the subject.

Sir David emptied the little plastic bottle into his brandy and chucked it back. "Yes, I think that would be in order," he replied.

The two men exchanged wary glances as each grappled with the real reason behind their late-night communion.

"It was a very minor detail in a very thorough report, Francis," said Sir David finally, fatigue getting the better of him. His companion's glare intensified to a grimace.

"A detail, you'd be prepared to ignore, old man?"

Sir David passed a shaky hand over his broad mouth and sighed loudly through his bristly nose. The second worst day of his life was drawing to a close with little prospect that the next one would bring about any improvement.

"We don't even know whether the Wren woman has any of the bloody stuff," he said, raising a meaty hand and letting it flop back on the arm rest.

"It's a possibility we surely can't afford to ignore, old chap. Look at the facts, man." Sir Francis poked the arm of his chair indignantly. "She was observed using one of the bloody things and she spent most of the day with the wretched Lane woman." He paused before delivering the coup de grâce. "Imagine if she does have some and she got it to a laboratory…"

Sir David did the imagining and immediately reached for the brandy bottle. "Shit," he muttered and looked disconsolately at the meagre amount of amber liquid left in it.

"My thoughts exactly," mused Sir Francis.

The ancient clock chimed twelve times and a log in the grate hissed and whined. "We're back where we started, old chap," Sir David muttered irritably. "All that's changed since we began this bloody enterprise is that we have three dead people on our hands and a media firestorm." He slurped needily at his brandy. "And no idea where Wren and McLeod are or where they're going, or what that lunatic Kurjac's doing with them." He set down his glass and undid his bowtie.

"Be patient, old thing," Sir Francis counselled. "They'll surface again soon enough and there'll be no pussyfooting around this time. The media can make whatever they want of it now." He eyed his friend's stony countenance. "Putting an end to this for the good of ourselves and our friends is all that matters," he said heavily.

Sir David tugged his jowls for a moment before reaching for his phone. "No holds barred, then," he murmured ominously and pressed Urquhart's number.

Saturday evening

"We're going to need fuel and we can't risk a gas station," Kurjac said anxiously.

McLeod looked out of the BMW's windows but could make out little in the darkness of the warehouse. "This car's diesel, right?" he said.

"Feels like it," replied Kurjac. He reached into the glove box. Found the manual. "Yes, diesel…why?"

McLeod eyed the gun in Wren's lap and said, "I'm going to scout out the farm." He pulled the door handle. "Back in a minute," he said and took off into the cool night.

McLeod's departure left an awkward silence between Wren and Kurjac. Strangely, she felt no menace from the deadly assassin sitting only a couple of feet in front of her. More like contrition. He seemed to be agonising with himself again. "There's something I need to tell you, Inspector," he muttered eventually.

"I'm all ears," she replied cagily.

He took a breath. "At some point on Friday evening, your status changed." He looked nervously toward the sound of a distant clunk. Listened hard for a moment before continuing. "Up to that time, no harm was to come to you. Then around nine on Friday evening, I received a mission update that included you as a named target," he murmured in a low monotone.

"I see," Wren replied quietly. Her chest tightened and her heart raced.

Kurjac blew out a loud breath. "I smashed my direct phone to the General and my MI5 liaison went dead."

Wren sensed rather than saw his head hanging. "I'm sorry, Inspector." His voice was reminiscent of a judge passing sentence. "I don't think your status has changed since."

"No," she said emptily, "I don't think it has either." She banished the unwelcome thought and focused instead on something that had been bothering her. "I don't know what you're expecting from McLeod, Kurjac. He was disregarded by our secret service as not being ruthless enough." She paused and wondered about the icy look she'd seen in his eyes recently. About the fact that he was out there in the night on some foolhardy venture. "I don't think he's capable of killing anyone," she said without much conviction.

"I'm not so sure, Inspector," Kurjac replied. In his experience, almost anyone had the capacity for murder given enough motivation. "Maybe, maybe not. But I don't need him to kill anyone. Just hurt them badly. And he's proven how good he is at doing that." He paused and glanced at the Swiss policeman's gun on the front passenger seat beside him. "You're with an anti-terror unit, yes?"

Wren moved to the other side of the rear seat so she could see his profile. "I am," she replied guardedly.

"You ever shoot at anyone?"

The question transported her instantly back to an unnervingly empty shopping centre in Shepherd's Bush just over two years ago. She'd warned the man with the feverishly hypnotic glare standing twenty metres in front of her to take off his explosive laden belt, told him she'd shoot him if he didn't tell her that was his intention. Flanked by four other armed officers of her unit, she froze momentarily as she saw the man's hand go to his belt. Then she pulled the trigger. She'd been aiming for central mass but hadn't accounted for muzzle lift. The shot missed the guy completely. Wren cursed herself and watched in horror as the bomber pressed the detonator. Nothing happened. His device couldn't have been properly wired. Then he was feverishly pressing it over and over. Wren fired again. This time, her bullet found its mark. Lower left shoulder. All sorts of smashed bones and tendons and cartilage. Put the guy on his back on the floor, writhing in agony. Then his belt went off and Wren was blown backwards and soaked with the man's body parts.

She closed her eyes on the horrific memory. "I can handle myself, Kurjac," she said coolly.

Kurjac turned and looked in her eyes, saw what he wanted. "Good," he murmured. "If this thing plays out how I want it to, you'll be the only one needing a gun."

His words caused Wren to think on something else about this inscrutable man that rankled. "How come your English is so damn good, Kurjac?" she said, aggrieved. Years of French and Spanish lessons had left her barely able to get by in either.

"I've spent most of the past five years in the States, Inspector," he replied thickly. "The CIA is one of the General's biggest revenue streams. He gets me to do jobs for them and they turn a blind eye to his vice rackets."

Wren nodded thoughtfully. "What sort of jobs?" she asked, curious to know what pies the CIA had its grubby mitts in.

"Don't make me relive them, Miss Wren," Kurjac murmured darkly.

The sound of quick footsteps caused them both to sit up poised for action. But it was McLeod who entered the warehouse. He rapped on Kurjac's window. "Follow me with the car," he said, breathing heavily.

He ran ahead of them through the farmyard, a hundred metres along the warehouse and past a huge slurry container to a large, cylindrical red tank twenty metres shy of the dark farm house. He motioned for them to stop and put the window down. "Pop the petrol cap," he breathed. He'd stuck a length of hose in the nozzle in the middle of the red tank. He sucked on the unattached end until he felt the liquid flowing toward his mouth. Spat, coughed and shoved the hose in the BMW's tank. "Probably agricultural grade," he spluttered, "but it'll do."

Kurjac smiled faintly. "Good work, Mr McLeod. You're as resourceful as I thought you'd be."

McLeod got deep gulps of oxygen in his lungs as the fuel continued to flow. "Whatever, Kurjac," he replied curtly. "And you can knock off the Mister, okay?"

"Sure, McLeod," Kurjac grunted.

The fuel started bubbling near the top and McLeod pulled the hose from the big red tank. He held it aloft to get the last of it and jumped in the back of the filled-up BMW.

"Okay…where we headed, Kurjac.?"

The wiry man grimaced in the driver's seat, hit the ignition and said, "The highest mountain in Europe." They didn't see the angry farmer come out of his front door as they blasted out of his yard.

281

Sixty-Seven

Sunday morning

Field Operative Brennan took the call in their twin hotel room in Geneva, just south of the city centre. It was sparse and camel-coloured with crisp white linen on the beds. She sat up on an elbow on her pillow and yawned, Looked warily over to her unnerving partner rubbing his eyes in his own bed. At least he was attractive, she mused. The caller ID was anonymous as she surmised it would be on her hastily purchased phone. "Brennan," she breathed.

"Urquhart," came the curt reply. Jesus, didn't the guy ever go to bed, she thought. He continued in a clipped tone, "We've just received a report that the occupants of a silver BMW stole some diesel from a farm several kilometres south of Geneva. Just off the D1205."

That woke Brennan up. "That would explain why we haven't picked them up yet, sir," she said and cursed the hastily hatched plan. They'd thought the fugitives would want to get as far away as fast as possible and hadn't considered minor roads as being conducive to that aim.

"Hmmnn," Urquhart murmured, "it would seem the Kurjac feller is a little too wise to our ways. Still, if their aim is to get into Italy, they'll have to use either the Mont Blanc or Fréjus tunnels. There is another way from Bourg Saint-Maurice, but it's closed at this time of year. With the road they're on, I'd say Mont Blanc was most likely, but then...they've yet to make any damned obvious move." He went quiet, but Brennan could almost feel him churning over the last fact.

"What do you want us to do, sir?"

Brennan heard only laboured breathing for a moment. "I think it's time we divided our resources. You drive to Fréjus and send Gatuso to Mont Blanc. That way, one of you will get them.

Leave as soon as practicable. Make contact when you're in position."

Brennan motioned for Gatuso to get up. "Aren't they too far ahead of us, sir?" she replied.

"Only ten kilometres and you'll be on a much faster road."

"Very good, sir," Brennan said finally and hit 'end' on her phone.

"Well?" said Gatuso, hauling on a pair of jeans. He cast a dark eye over Brennan's round and soft-looking behind as she got out the far side of her bed.

"Spotted heading south on the D1205. You're to go to the Mont Blanc tunnel."

Gatuso found the road on his phone. He pinched the map out, followed the road and smiled grimly. "Looks like it's my lucky day," he said, dark eyes gleaming. His smile faltered slightly. "Is the order still to terminate them?" he asked.

Brennan heard the slight anxiety in his voice as she struggled into her skinny jeans. "The old man said nothing to suggest otherwise." She was pretty sure that if she looked over now, there'd be a bulge in his pants. She reddened as the sudden thought turned her on for some reason. "Anyway," she said hurriedly, "I wouldn't get your hopes up. They've done nothing we've expected so far. By now, they're probably half way to Spain on a tour bus or canoeing down the Seine."

"We got the girl, didn't we?" he said. The obvious pleasure in his voice increased the urge in her groin. "And tomorrow the others will meet the same fate," he murmured excitedly. Brennan could have jumped him there and then.

Sunday morning

A gentle tap on his shoulder woke McLeod from his slumber. His first thought was a flashback to what had happened to Penelope and his sense of loss was no less intense than after the brutal shooting. "We're nearly there, Mac," Wren said.

He stretched and looked out the front window. It was still dark outside, but the sky above the mighty peaks surrounding the car was brightening in the east. "How long was I out?" he asked sleepily. In the BMW's bright headlights, McLeod could make out a roundabout looming ahead.

"Only a couple of hours, Mac. That's a pretty useful skill to have."

"Not when it's me behind the wheel, it's not," he replied, rubbing his eyes. Now they were on the roundabout. Kurjac didn't take the first exit toward the tunnel. He did take the next one signposted Chamonix Mt Blanc. McLeod remembered Kurjac's crazy scheme and found it even more hare-brained than when he'd first heard it. He recalled the last time he'd been here in his student days. It had been quite a party town back then, fuelled by the increasing popularity of snowboarding and the kind of characters that pursuit attracted. Wren broke into his abstract thoughts.

"There's no possibility that MI5 could have suppressed what happened in Geneva, Mac," she said, worry etched in the frown on her shapely forehead. "I think it's highly likely we've made the news and could be recognised."

McLeod pondered her words and agreed with the first part. "I'm not sure, Anna," he said hesitantly. He thought on it and became more convinced. "People over here are far more regional in their outlook than we are. They're not blind to national or international events, but they don't pay them nearly as much notice as we do."

"McLeod's right, Inspector," Kurjac's voice rumbled from the driver's seat. "You British have an almost unique, how do you call it...fixation with events."

"Hmmnn, maybe," Wren murmured, "but I still don't think we should be seen together. One of us should get the equipment, one of us should hire the guide and the third should buy the tickets."

Three hours later, after a short sleep in the car and a carb-rich breakfast in a café, that was what they'd done. The BMW was left abandoned behind a derelict building in Les Houches, a village just west of Chamonix. They rode the first bus up to town and now formed separate parts of a queue waiting to board the Aiguille du Midi cable car in full skiing rig.

McLeod stood awkwardly next to Dave, their colourful, and expensive, kiwi guide. In his own country, he'd probably have been labelled a streak of piss. McLeod surmised the guy couldn't be more than nine stone wet through and a good six inches shorter than himself. He eyed the man's rucksack warily. Didn't care much for the ropes and ice axes and extendable poles attached to it. He was rueing his decision as a teenager to try the trendier snowboarding rather than stick with the less glamorous skiing. He'd heard that getting back on skis was like going from driving a car to riding a unicycle. "Why can't you do this on a board, Dave?" he asked the mahogany-skinned ski bum.

Dave favoured McLeod with a 'you crazy?' look and shook his messy blond locks. "Oh, mate!" the guy replied, "anything's possible, dude. You just wouldn't wanna walk all that way through spring snow, man. Stuff's like bloody treacle." He pointed at the season-old skis propped against his shoulder. "These modern planks that you can unclip at the heel, dude? Let's you make like them cross-country freaks? Makes it easy-peasy, bro. 'S gonna be a blast, man." The guide's voice ascended annoyingly at the end of each sentence. McLeod decided against asking anything else.

They rode the two sections of the boxy cable car in divorced corners. It got brighter and brighter the higher they got until, when they struggled out at 3,777 metres, they did so in full spring sunshine. McLeod felt clumsy compared to the more accustomed Wren and Kurjac. She'd apparently skied her whole life and Kurjac had learned during his years hiding in the mountains. McLeod felt like an octopus carrying skis and poles and helmet and gloves, and he missed the comfort of snowboarding boots. At least Kurjac had offered to carry the rucksack.

Then his breath was taken away by the cold and the stiff breeze as they exited the lift station, crossed a wobbly bridge and headed through an echoing tunnel of turquoise ice. They came out in the dazzling sunshine surrounded by a cathedral of glistening rocky peaks piercing the ice-blue sky. Then McLeod saw a narrow ridge in front of them with vertiginous drops on either side and his legs went weak. He hated heights. He raised a suddenly shaking gloved hand to Dave at his side and pointed. "We're not...?" he began weakly.

Dave beamed back at him. "Full steam ahead, mate," he replied.

McLeod lost a fair portion of his breakfast into the chasm beside him, looking down at the tiny buildings of the town nestling in the valley floor far below.

Sixty-Eight

Sunday lunch

"No news, I take it?" said Sir Francis, scooping horseradish onto a slab of rare roast beef and depositing it in his wide, gaunt mouth.

Sir David rolled a feisty Brouilly round his mouth and cast a malignant eye over their distant fellow carnivores in the ornately decorated dining room. Midday sunshine brightly lit half of the far wall, part of which was taken up by a cavernous hearth with elaborate sconces either side.

"Which is neither good news nor bad, old chap," he replied and took up his fork again.

"Eh? What's that supposed to mean?" Sir Francis retorted, sauce dribbling from his thin bottom lip.

"Well," said Sir David, taking aim at his companion with his fork, "it's bad that we haven't the first clue as to their whereabouts…"

"How that's even possible in this day and age…" Sir Francis interjected angrily.

"It's only a big story here, old thing. Barely made a ripple internationally." He paused and grappled with a Yorkshire pudding. "Yet…" he said thoughtfully. "And I imagine they'll be using minor roads or they'll have changed cars or something."

Sir Francis looked askance at a beetroot foam on his plate and moved his beef away lest it became infected. "What's good about it then, old man?" he re-joined.

Sir David targeted his friend with a chunk of dripping pudding. "We've not heard of any requests from any lab to start making a new product." He paused and munched the confection. "Best case, they don't have the liquid. Worst case, they've got some, but haven't worked out what to do with it yet."

Sir Francis pushed a roast potato half-heartedly through some species of reduction. "What if they do get it to a lab, old chap? What if they get the bloody stuff made? What's to stop us, or whatever country they tip up in, banning its ruddy production?"

Sir David stared open-mouthed at his friend. "I blame that dodgy crab sandwich you had back in seventy-eight, old thing. It's been downhill for you ever since."

"What fresh rot is this?" replied Sir Francis heatedly.

"We ban the stuff, we become unelectable pariahs, old man," Sir David said, wiping his jowls vigorously with a thick napkin. "Preventing the manufacture of a product that stops millions of people doing something extraordinarily dangerous?" he opined, tapping the table with an indignant forefinger. "Think of the stink the whole health racket would kick up. The cancer lot. The anti-smoking zealots. Even people from Alan's department. It'd be carnage, old thing."

"Hmmnn," Sir Francis mused, "I suppose production would move underground at some point anyway."

Sir David warily inspected something green on his plate and decided not to risk it. "Our priority remains to locate Wren and McLeod. They're all that stands in the way of the status quo and the financial bounty we've enjoyed for hundreds of years."

"You're not concerned about the other players in the market then?" Sir Francis asked, pushing his plate away half eaten.

Sir David shook his head emphatically. "Not at all, old chap. That's a different market altogether. What they make is more of an aid to quitting rather than the direct bloody replacement the cursed Lane woman stumbled upon." He paused and caught sight of his friend's plate. "Are you ailing, old man?"

Sir Francis waved a limp hand and reached for the wine. "Leaving room for the excellent cheese they do here, old chap. Oughtn't we get another bottle?"

"Mmm hmm," said Sir David, scooping his companion's discarded meat and potatoes onto his plate.

Sir Francis eyed the other's continued glutton with disdain and said, "What's Urquhart's latest theory?"

The question caused Sir David to choke for a moment on a lump of beef. "Hell's teeth, old man," Sir David wheezed, "I wish you'd get your bloody meat cooked." He took a hearty draught of wine. "Where were we? Mmm...Urquhart." His brow creased in a heavy frown. "I'm beginning to wonder whether his judgement isn't what it was, or whether Wren and McLeod are insanely lucky."

Sir Francis rubbed his pointy chin with a shaky hand. "Or maybe the Kurjac fellow is more of a factor in this than we realise," he murmured.

"I think it may be a combination of all three," said Sir David, nodding sagely. "In which case, they could be heading anywhere. Urquhart's best guess of Italy given their last known vector could be complete claptrap." He paused and emptied his glass. "I think it's time we deployed Section Six as well, old chap," he murmured.

Sir Francis drew back from the table slightly. "The Circus? That's a bloody big step, old man," he said warily.

"Well, it's a bloody big mess," Sir David seethed and settled back in his chair. "Urquhart mentioned something else that might be important. Apparently, the Bosnian chap's controller contacted him directly on his private phone. Highly irregular."

Sir Francis' eyebrows shot up. "How on earth did they get Urquhart's number?"

"No idea, old chum," Sir David replied pensively. "Apparently, the controller is this Serbian General character we've had dealings with in the past."

"That would explain it," said Sir Francis, motioning to a waitress. "That lunatic's reach is bloody outrageous." He was struck by a grave realisation and held up a wizened forefinger to the approaching waitress who paused mid-stride. "If the General's by-passed the Irish liaison girl, how much further does he have to dig to get to us?" he hissed.

"Relax," said Sir David, glancing behind him. "There are still plenty of buffers in place."

"Alright," said Sir Francis, cautiously beckoning the waitress once more. "What the hell was the General calling Urquhart about?"

Sir David mopped up the last of his plate's juices with some soda bread. "To see whether Urquhart had been in contact with the Kurjac feller."

"Yes, sir," said the pretty young waitress.

Sir Francis wafted a dismissive finger toward the empty bottle. "More of that and the list of cheeses, if you would," he said haughtily. The waitress departed red-faced. Sir Francis was pondering his friend's words. "What, does Urquhart think the General's lost control of his agent?"

"Hmmnn, and there's more," said Sir David, closing his knife and fork. "When Urquhart said he hadn't had any contact, the General said something horrific sounding in Serbian and hung up."

Sir Francis eyed his companion keenly for a moment. "Shame Urquhart doesn't speak Serbian," he sighed.

"Well, his phone automatically records his calls. He bunged the General's words into an online translator." Sir David looked out the tall window as the sun suddenly dimmed.

"Go on then, man," said Sir Francis, agog.

Sir David turned his baleful eyes directly into his friend's and murmured darkly, "The translator came back with 'Oh my God.'"

Sixty-Nine

Sunday morning

The kiwi guide led Kurjac, McLeod and Wren through a tiny gate toward the knife-like arête. McLeod peered hesitantly down to the right and the sheer drop between the craggy black rocks made his legs even weaker. A bright red helicopter was drifting slowly over a glacier in the valley way below. The sound of its rotor blades ripped the air and echoed around the mountain spires. Then McLeod looked over the left edge and he recoiled in terror. There didn't seem to be any tangible land between him and the town nearly three thousand metres directly below. Kurjac had walked up a little ridge behind, and to McLeod's right, directly above a void, his head framed by cable car lines. "HEY," he called out to the guide.

The kiwi turned and his deep tan paled. "The HELL you doing up THERE, bro?" he shouted above the wind.

"I don't like the look of that arête," he shouted, then pointed to a distant peak. "We're headed there, right?"

"Sure are," the guide called back.

"Then I'll meet you there," Kurjac replied. "I'm going down here."

The guide looked where Kurjac was pointing. "That's Couloir POUBELLE, dude," he practically screamed. "It's a FIFTY-degree slope. People DIE in there. 'S like a descent into HELL, man."

"Yeah…well that's somewhere I'm going to have to get used to," Kurjac shouted back grimly and clipped into his skis. He made a couple of shuffling sideways steps to his right, poles steadying him, then he vanished.

"JESUS!" Dave shouted at the space where Kurjac had been. "Is your friend insane?" he said turning to McLeod.

"You could say that," McLeod replied, before adding, "but he's not my friend." He looked to the distant rocky peaks thoughtfully. "He is my enemy's enemy though," he murmured and looked at Wren.

She nodded and said, "Let's get going before we freeze to death."

The guide had walked this arête countless times, but he still needed his poles to steady himself in the blustery wind. McLeod followed him on to the ridiculously narrow path and Wren brought up the rear.

A shallow groove in the snow, maybe six inches deep and a foot wide was the only safe place to put your feet. So that was what McLeod did, focusing solely on that tiny strip of compacted snow, he placed one careful ski boot in front of the other as close to the middle of the groove as he could manage. His skis were biting into his shoulder and causing him to lose his balance. He tried to block out the horrendous drops to certain death just a few feet on either side. Stopped every few tortuous paces to try to steady the shake in his legs. The cold had taken the feeling from his hands despite his thick gloves. This was by far the most afraid he'd ever been in his life. He stared bleakly at the ridge as it stretched ever onwards. At least it was a fairly level knife-edge.

Then, after a hundred terrifying metres, to McLeod's horror, it wasn't. He saw ahead that the arête plummeted sharply downward and to the left. The drop to the north of the ridge was even more visible. It went straight down, several hundred metres to contorted black rocks. A group of six climbers fifty metres in front of them were roping up and then using ice axes as they descended the stiletto. McLeod looked desperately behind, but the way back was blocked by knots of skiers and climbers on the path. Impossible to go around. He couldn't go back and he daren't go on. He froze, unable to move a muscle. His mind went numb with terror. He was crag fast.

"Shit," said Dave, as he turned and recognised McLeod's stance and registered the fear in his eyes.

"What is it?" Wren called down from behind McLeod.

"Your friend's gonna need a lot of help to get down, mate," the kiwi called back. "There's only so much I can do."

Wren looked at McLeod's back. It was completely motionless. "What's wrong, Mac?" she cried. Nothing. "Mac, are you all right?" she pleaded.

"No, Anna, I'm not," he replied. His head didn't move. "I'm stuck," he said in a shaky voice carried away by the wind.

"Listen to me, mate," said Dave in front of him. "I'm roping you to me, okay? It's not as bad as it looks from here. There are little steps on the path as it goes down." He secured the rope to his own carabiner. "Look at me, mate," the kiwi said urgently, lifting his ski mask and blinking against wind-blown snow.

McLeod did so and saw an intense look in the man's eyes.

"I will *not* let you fall, mate," he said fervently.

McLeod nodded his head almost imperceptibly.

Wren was struggling to understand Mac's fear after everything he'd been through the last couple of days. She mused on her own feelings about their situation. Okay, it was scary, but nothing compared to delivering a nine-pound baby. Nothing would ever faze her again after that.

Then she thought about the heroic things Mac had done and realisation struck her. Everything had been a reaction to events. This was different. It was something he had to think about and positively engage with. She thought about what might snap him out of his paralysis, then took a deep breath. "Think of how much you've come through, Mac," she called behind him. "Think of *why* you're doing this. *Who* you're doing it for."

The wind howled and swayed him closer to the edge as McLeod cast his mind back to his quiet life in London before all this. Ruefully, he recalled the decision he'd taken in his flat: whatever it took. Getting down this ridge and out of this nightmare had become just that. He'd never have dreamed it would be so hard. Then he thought of Penelope and a powerful wave of outrage flooded him again. He flashed on Nathalie's face in his bed and another wave coursed through him. Suddenly, his crippling dread vanished and was replaced by a sense of abandon. His body unlocked itself and he felt strength return to his legs. He took in a few deep breaths of the cold alpine air. Way below, the helicopter disappeared behind a ridge.

"Let's do this," he said.

Behind him, Wren smiled at the iron in his voice.

Kurjac slid to an agonising stop and heaved air into his gasping lungs. He massaged his burning thighs, looked back almost vertically to where he'd come from and smiled with grim satisfaction. Thirty agonising jump turns had brought him halfway down the two hundred-metre chute of snow encased in claustrophobic rock. He took a swig of energy drink between gasps and surveyed the lower section. It narrowed just below him then broadened out toward the bottom where ragged rocks were exposed, then the slope eased considerably before joining the glacier in the broad valley.

He looked across to the rendezvous, Pointe Helbronner, way to the south and judged he was still a fair bit higher. But the vast white plateau between the bottom of the couloir and the distant peaks appeared somewhat bowl-shaped. He hated trudging through snow. He decided to take the rest of the couloir as straight as he could and let his speed carry him as far as possible across the plateau. Aim to stay high to the right and pray that there were no hidden crevasses. He looked warily at the rising sun then at the condition of the snow. It wouldn't hold up for long.

Kurjac took a final swig and put the bottle back in the rucksack with his stuff and McLeod's clothes and Wren's handbag. He planted his poles and made a couple of jump turns and a huge slab of snow detached from the mountain. It took him half a second to realise it was going to avalanche and take all the snow out of the couloir, making it impossible to descend. He couldn't stay above it. The only way to get to the General was to ride the avalanche. He turned his skis toward the cascading snow and creased himself up, chest against juddering knees. A second later, he was in the churning mass of falling snow. It assaulted and buffeted him from all angles so that all he could see was a white blur.

The snow roared in his ears and his whole world was a shuddering white mass as he tried to picture where the exposed rocks were. Then suddenly, he emerged from the wall of raging snow and saw the rocks dead ahead and impossible to avoid with the avalanche hard at his back. He was travelling at a crazy speed and his eyes were blurring. In desperation, he drove every ounce of energy he had into the ground and pushed off with his skis. Then all the noise and turmoil disappeared as he flew. All he could feel was the air whistling over his face.

The twisted grimace on McLeod's face dissolved into the biggest grin it had ever worn as he saw he was metres from the end of the ridge and salvation. He wasn't going to die plummeting off a cliff onto jagged rocks, a smashed pile of bones and blood on the north face of the Mont Blanc. The catastrophic drops to his left and right magically transformed into a manageable tumble and then, after a few more steps, became eminently skiable.

He unclipped the rope from his carabiner and surged past the guide. He took his skis from his shoulder and planted them and his poles in the soft snow and dove into it. Hugged the white stuff, half laughing, half sobbing as sweet relief flooded and racked his body. He rolled on his back, making a snow angel and looked up at the impossibly blue sky and let out a cathartic "YES!" Then he took huge gulps of air, closed his eyes and felt the warm sunshine on his face. When he opened them again, Wren was standing over him.

"I guess I understand now how hard that was for you, Mac." She bent and put a gloved hand on his forehead. "You did it, Mac. Well done."

Her words reminded him of something Penelope had said. The initial rush of relief over, a hard look of determination entered his eyes as he sat up. Nothing was going to prevent him from finishing this now. "Thank you for your help back there, Anna." He stood and put his numb hands on her shoulders. "Really, without saying what you did, I'd have needed a helicopter to get me off that fucking ridge."

Wren smiled back at him. "Mind your language, Mac," she said, raising an eyebrow.

He grinned and turned to the guide. "You too, Dave," he murmured. "You're a good man under all that shtick."

"No worries, mate," the kiwi replied warmly, "just keepin' it real, bro."

Seventy

Sunday afternoon

Kurjac roared in triumph as he cleared the rocks and careened out of the couloir. He could hear the deep rumble of the avalanche behind him. A wide slope was extending in front of him and he risked a backward glance. A seething mountain of snow was pounding at the heels of his skis like a herd of galloping white horses. But now he knew he could escape its path. Without taking off any of the enormous speed he was carrying, he leaned hard on his left ski and carved a wide right-hand turn into the smooth slope. He looked over his left shoulder and watched the hurtling torrent of snow sweep past on its way to the valley floor. He slowed to a halt and collapsed against the gentle slope, panting prodigiously. The boom of the avalanche reverberated around the stadium of gigantic pinnacles.

When his breathing regulated somewhat, he leaned up to get his bearings. First, he looked back to where he'd come from. He could barely make out where the narrow couloir had been now that all the snow had come off it. He would have been catastrophically stuck on a sheer rock face if he hadn't taken on the cascading snow. It had fanned out from the bottom of the couloir, leaving a shattered trail on the steep mountainside. Then he looked to where he needed to get to and cursed. He'd lost a lot of height. Even with a slow traverse, he was probably going to have to push.

He got a drink from the rucksack and caught sight of McLeod's clothes with Wren's handbag sitting on top. Maybe it was his heightened senses or the stress he was under, but either way, inspiration struck. It would cost him a bit of time and a lot of pushing, but it might just save their lives later on. He nodded to himself and took off toward the bottom of the avalanche.

He slew to a halt against the piled-up snow, took off his thick outer gloves and got to work with his thin base gloves. He opened Wren's handbag and removed a few bits of make-up he thought she might need, her puffer, pen-drive and a startling amount of euros, pounds and dollars. Stashed them in a side pocket of the rucksack. He left her purse and a few other unimportant-looking items in the bag and chucked it onto the contorted pile of snow. Then he took some of McLeod's worn clothes and threw them back up the avalanche. They looked unnatural so he clambered to them and pushed them into the snow a bit.

Satisfied, he returned to the rucksack and started closing it when he caught sight of his wallet. He opened it to the photos of Lejla and her beautiful children. He winced as he saw Hana's beautiful, delicate ears and thought of her awful disfigurement in the picture on the phone he'd smashed back in London. He looked to Pointe Helbronner again and gritted his teeth. He'd be with them soon enough or never again.

"AAAAAHH," McLeod and Wren cried together. Dave the guide had told them they had to do windmills with their arms to get the feeling back in their hands or they risked frostbite. Neither had anticipated the excruciating pain that would accompany the return of sensation.

"Sorry 'bout that, guys," the kiwi drawled. "Folk won't do it if I tell them how painful it'll be beforehand."

"I don't fucking wonder," Wren snarled.

Then, as soon as it had started, the pain left their hands and feeling returned.

"Okay, folks, listen up," Dave said, unravelling a lengthy red rope. "I've only done this route a couple of times, but she's pretty sweet." He tied the rope to his carabiner and measured out about fifteen metres. "Nice bit of spring snow to start, gentle turns, then it levels off on the glacier. We need to keep high and right. Then we'll probably be poling through the Col du Gros Rognon between those two nuggets," he said, pointing with a ski pole to a gap through two masses of black rock. He attached the rope to McLeod's carabiner then measured out another fifteen metres and tied it off on Wren.

McLeod's mind focused on the word 'glacier.' He knew they were basically rivers of ice and that meant they were always moving, however slowly. "Aren't glaciers incredibly dangerous, Dave?"

The guide snorted dismissively. "Yeah, if you're a pillock or ridiculously unlucky, mate. Only real problem is crevasses and we'll be avoiding them like the plague, bro."

"How long will it take?" Wren asked curtly. The café they'd had breakfast in hadn't sold cigarettes and she was getting fairly edgy.

"Aaah, most of the morning, probably," Dave replied, clipping into his battered skis. "Depends on how long the climb at the end takes."

"It'll be quick," Wren said, adjusting her goggles, "don't worry about that."

"Let's go, then. I'll take her nice and steady, mate," Dave said to McLeod, "'til you find your ski legs. Remember, weight forward, lean left and right, not forwards and backwards, okay?"

"Got it," McLeod replied and took a last look around at the stunning panorama of majestic mountains and bright white valleys, trying to imprint it in his long-term memory, to bring out again on some happy day in the future. If there'd ever be one.

In the end, McLeod had only fallen once on the descent to the wide, gently sloping glacier and now was having no trouble keeping up with the little flying kiwi. There was no need to turn anymore as they traversed steadily between creaking crevasses following a few lonely ski tracks. The wind had disappeared as McLeod surveyed the peaceful, saucer-shaped valley. Apart from a few ravens, the three of them could have been the only life on earth. The sole sound in the enormous empty space was the barely audible swish of their skis on the crisp snow.

Then McLeod thought he heard something else. Like a tiny voice or something. Then the snow melted away beneath his skis and he started to drop slowly into thin air. The dazzling bright white of the valley disappeared and was replaced with dark greys and turquoises. McLeod was bewildered for a moment before awful realisation hit: I'm falling into a crevasse, for Christ's sake. But he was doing so incredibly slowly. Like he was being lowered gently down. Then he realised what must be happening in the valley above. Wren and Dave were acting like counterweights. Being slowly pulled by his greater bulk toward the widening hole in the snow above him.

Then he heard the voice that he thought he'd imagined before, but this time much louder.

"GRAZIE MILLE MADONNA! GRAZIE MILLE DIO! SALVEZZA, SALVEZZA!"

McLeod knew enough Italian to know there was a very God-fearing man in here with him who thought he'd been sent to save him. He peered into the gloom below as he continued to glide serenely toward the floor of the crevasse. Sure enough, he made out a beaming sun-worn face staring up at him. Then he heard a cry and looked up to see Wren's skis and then her legs appear in the hole above. McLeod's own skis hit the ice as he stared transfixed at Wren's waist dropping into the hole. Then she stopped. She was no longer being pulled by his weight. But she was in a highly precarious situation. Probably clinging desperately to poles driven into the snow, McLeod thought. Then he felt arms round his shoulders.

"GRAZIE MILLE SIGNORE, MERCI BEAUCOUP, MONSIEUR!" said the voice again.

"Sono inglese, signore," McLeod barked in annoyance.

"Bene? ... Thank you, my friend, THANK YOU!" the man said in a thick Italian accent.

McLeod nodded distractedly, then looked frantically at the form dangling by her armpits fifteen metres directly overhead. "You all right, Anna?" he shouted up.

"Not lost your sense of humour then, Mac," he made out from above and smiled.

Kurjac had seen the events unfold from his slightly elevated position half a kilometre away a little north and west and was now pounding his poles into the snow for all he was worth. He'd renounced God many years previously in the mountains above Srebrenica, but he was praying to him now. 'Please, God, don't let him be injured,' he recited over and over in his mangled mind. He reached the crevasse maybe five minutes after he'd seen McLeod vanish. The kiwi guide was holding desperately to the woman's right forearm with his left hand, his other held an ice axe driven into the glacier. The diminutive man glanced up and recognised Kurjac. "Give us a hand, will you, mate?" he called strenuously.

Kurjac looked about him panting but saw nothing to tie anything to. He marched toward Wren's head and arms where they protruded from the hole, bent over and saw the rope taut on her carabiner. "She attached to McLeod?" he barked at the guide who nodded back vigorously. Kurjac placed what he hoped was a reassuring hand on Wren's back. "Sorry about this, Inspector," he said, leaning carefully over the crevasse and grabbing her ski pants at the waist. He used his free hand, his strong, deft fingers, to undo the rope on her carabiner. Then she popped like a cork from the edge of the crevasse to solid snow. Wren sat up painfully and nodded her thanks to the guide and then to Kurjac who answered with a nod of his own. "Mac's down there." She pointed. "And I think there's someone with him," she said, heaving sweet air into her lungs.

Kurjac and Dave looked at her incredulously, then edged to the small hole in the glacier and peered over. Just enough light reached the bottom of the crevasse to make out two faces. "Are you all right, McLeod?" Kurjac called into the abyss. His deep voice echoed back at him as he held his breath.

"I'm absolutely fine," McLeod's urgent voice came back. "But there's a feller in here with me who needs to get out."

The guide had heard stories of this happening before. He'd heard once of ten people being discovered in the same crevasse a few kilometres from here, some of whom had been down there several days. "No worries, mate," he called down. "Can your friend use ice axes, d'ya think?"

"I climb, yes," a thick Italian accent called back. "I live in mountains," it added.

Dave tied two ice axes to Wren's redundant rope and lowered them slowly into the void. "Put your rope around the Italian dude, mate," he hollered to McLeod, "and we'll haul his ass outta there."

After half an hour of heaving of ropes and planting of ice axes, five bodies were strewn in the snow in various states of exhaustion. The midday sun was high in the sky. They'd seen or heard no one else in the vast white space. Dave got out a flask when they'd rested up and they shared hot coffee, ham and cheese baguettes and chocolate. It turned out the Italian guy, Germano, had become detached from his friends in a blizzard yesterday afternoon. He'd banged his right shoulder and knee a bit falling into the crevasse but had managed to keep warm with spells of jumping up and down.

McLeod noticed Kurjac standing several metres away, hooded eyes fixed south-east toward the col and Italy beyond. He sighed and stood up. Took the glove from his right hand as he approached the slighter man. "I make that three times you've saved my neck, Kurjac," he said quietly and extended his hand.

Kurjac looked at it perplexed. The General's was the only other he'd ever shaken and that had been many years ago.

McLeod thought he detected something approaching pride in the man's eyes as they looked up to meet his. "Thank you," McLeod murmured as Kurjac removed his glove and clutched his palm firmly.

"Thank me when we've finished this, McLeod," Kurjac replied. Then added sombrely, "You'll be more than repaying me...believe me."

The sound of approaching steps made them turn around. "If you two have quite finished," Wren scowled, "I have an urgent appointment with a tobacconist over the hill."

Seventy-One

Sunday afternoon

Lejla's exquisite body was splayed, naked on the iron rack attached to his bedroom wall, but the General's cock refused to show any sign of life beneath his black dressing gown. He stood in front of her, eying the fresh angry red marks dotted on her rounded breasts above a thick black strap and the dark bruises covering her thighs, but they failed to raise a reaction. The bitch's whimpering only grated in his ears. He contemplated fetching the flogger from his armoury of implements, but the thought didn't illicit the usual response. He sighed and stubbed his cigar out in a heavy crystal ashtray on the bedside table. "It seems you have ceased to please me, Lejla," he said emptily. "You know the consequences of that."

His monstrous words caused her to writhe in fresh agony against the leather straps at her wrists and ankles. "No, please," she wailed, tears welling in her screwed-up eyes. "I'll do anything you want…just …just please…don't touch Hana."

A gleam entered the General's black eyes. "Will you do…that?" he murmured darkly and felt something stir below.

Lejla's blood curdled at the horrendous act he was proposing. She stifled a sob and gasped, "Yes…anything. Just promise you won't touch her."

"Now Lejla," the General sneered, "you know I've never kept a promise in my whole life."

She was fairly sure she'd saved Hana from his clutches, for a time at least, and felt slightly emboldened. "My brother made a promise to me once," she hissed. "And he *always* keeps his promises."

He flinched at her words. He knew them to be accurate. "What promise?" he growled.

Lejla felt a tiny wave of pride creep back into her tortured soul at the haunted look on the General's face. "He promised that one day," she murmured fervently, "he and I and the children would be together." She stuck out her chin, her pupils dilated in hatred.

The General took a quick stride and savagely slapped her gaunt cheek. "The only place you'll be together is in HELL," he snarled and marched to his office and slammed the door. He took a few calming breaths, stabbed a button on his console and picked up the handset. It answered on the second ring as he knew it would.

"Urquhart," came the clipped reply in his ear.

"It's me," the General replied coolly. "Why have you still not found him?"

"Why are you calling me on this line? The liaison officer…"

"Because I CAN," the General barked into the receiver. "I demand to know what you're doing to locate him."

"Kurjac is not our responsibility, General." There was a pause from London. "And you still haven't told us why he's taken the other two."

The General had a pretty good idea, but he wasn't about to admit it to this man. He knew he had to offer something plausible or he'd get nothing more from MI5. "The man's psychotic," he replied, judging that such a condition could cover any eventuality. "He's probably playing sick games with them."

"Well, not any more, he isn't." The General detected a note of superiority enter Urquhart's voice. "As it happens, we've got them. That is, we'll have them very shortly. The BMW they took in Geneva has been recovered in a small village in the Chamonix valley. CCTV footage of all three of them has been obtained from a cable car in the area."

The pause on the line only increased the General's incredulity. "They've gone SKIING?" he bellowed.

"So it would appear," Urquhart replied calmly. "One of the routes from the top of the cable car enables you to get into Italy."

"ITALY?" The General almost choked on the word.

"Keep your hair on, you old goat, that's the good news. The only place they could be headed is a narrow valley and we have every way out of it blockaded." The General could sense the MI5 man smiling. "They'll not evade us this time, I assure you."

The General's broad features contorted in a grin. If what the man was telling him were true, Kurjac was as good as home. "Call me when my agent has been detained," he said coldly. "I will come for him myself." He smiled at the punishments Kurjac would soon be suffering, then his thoughts turned to his sister and the things she was about to do for him.

Sunday afternoon

Whether by accident or design, McLeod found himself in a death-defying race with Kurjac on the south-facing, steep descent into Italy. The snow was slushy in the warm sunshine and there were patches of rock and bare earth on the ungroomed, end of season piste. The kiwi guide and Wren were some way back, helping the hampered Italian down the mountain. McLeod's inferior technique didn't allow him to turn as often as Kurjac and he raced ahead, but then had to throw on the brakes when he was headed for bare patches and the Bosnian carved past.

They tore into the tree line neck and neck and shared an exhilarated grimace, snow spraying behind their skittering skis. Then Kurjac was pointing, alarm in his eyes. McLeod looked and, just ahead, made out a boulder filled stream crossing the piste. McLeod favoured his left leg, Kurjac his right. So they faced each other as they jammed their skis into the mountain as hard as they could and came to a juddering halt on the last bit of snow before the stream's bank.

The men collapsed together in a heap, laughing and gasping in the snow, their thighs burning. Then McLeod heard the tinkling trickle of the stream and it was like his wife were there, chuckling at him. He closed his eyes against the searing feeling and his heart hardened once more at the thought of the cancer that killed her. Then he thought of Penelope's juice in Wren's puffer and wished it had been around for Catherine. He looked urgently at Kurjac and, for the first time, it was with a feeling of kinship, not enmity. "Hey Kurjac," he called, "you still got Wren's handbag in the rucksack, right?"

"No, McLeod," he replied, detaching his skis. "I took some things out of it and threw it on the avalanche."

McLeod was gripped by a sudden anxiety. "Tell me one of the things you kept was her puffer device," he pleaded.

"Of course," said Kurjac taking off the rucksack. "And a pen drive," he said, fishing it out of the side pocket, "some kind of make-up stuff and a lot of pounds, euros and dollars," he finished off, holding up thick wads of notes.

McLeod frowned, then faint calls from the slope above made him look up. He could just make out the others negotiating a narrow gorge above the tree line.

"Listen, McLeod," Kurjac murmured deeply, "I've survived a long time in very dangerous circumstances."

McLeod eyed him warily, reminded once more that the man was a stone-hearted assassin, wondered again how he lived with himself. "Go on, Kurjac, I'm listening," he replied guardedly.

"The reason I've done so is because I never plan in hope. It's not very exciting...but it's kept me alive this far."

McLeod nodded and thought back to the wiry man's tale of his survival during the Bosnian Conflict. It brought to mind his grandfather's stories of the 'Long March' in the Second World War.

It had always been impossible to make him talk about it. Then reluctantly, one evening, after several glasses of red, he recounted a tale about emaciated prisoners of war forced to walk from France where they were captured to camps in Poland and Czechoslovakia with no food or water. Living off whatever they could find in hedges: insects and birds if they could catch them; berries and dandelions. Occasionally, a chicken would cross their path. Drinking from streams if they were lucky or puddles if they weren't. Rarely sleeping sheltered from the elements. Months of endless trudging. Shot if you failed to keep up or fell ill.

Then years of merciless toil in murderous mines or poisonous factories. Then at the end of the war, the survivors had to walk the now war-devastated path they'd previously trodden all the way back to France. Men from all walks of life, bankers, farmers, teachers and ditch-diggers, but all with one thing in common thereafter. None of them ever said 'no thank you' to anything that was offered to them ever again.

"What are you thinking, Kurjac?" McLeod asked sombrely, his eyes fixed on the rapidly approaching trio of skiers.

Kurjac followed his gaze and said, "I have to think that the car has been found...that they've worked out our movements." He paused and McLeod turned and saw the man's eyes darting from one point in the snow to another. Assessing one option, shaking his head. Looking at another, same outcome. Then McLeod's thoughts were interrupted by the clattering arrival of

Wren, the guide and the Italian man. The jovial soul was in much better shape than when McLeod had almost landed on him in the crevasse. His mouth was parted, a gleaming toothy grin on his snow-tanned, weather-beaten face. A shock of grey-black hair protruded from a colourful bandana around his forehead. He was quite short and though not fat, a fair amount of fine Italian food had clearly featured in his fifty-odd years.

"Bella Italia!" he cried at them, and turned, throwing his arms out wide with pride at the majestic landscape below them. Then he clipped out of his skis and flung himself at McLeod and held him in a fierce hug. "I thank you a millions of times, signore McLeod," he practically sobbed. From somewhere inside his puffy ski jacket, he produced a bottle of homemade grappa. "This keep me warm in the night," he beamed. "To the extreme beauty of life," he exhorted, before taking a prodigious gulp and hugging McLeod again.

Bewildered, McLeod struggled to speak in the man's tight grasp. "I didn't save you, Germano. These people did," he said, nodding to the others.

The Italian relinquished his grip, passed the bottle to Wren and held McLeod's arms, smiling benevolently, then wiping a tear. "But you find me, signore. You arrive…like an angelo. I never will…como si dice…ricompensare?"

McLeod shook his head. "You don't owe me anything, Germano," he protested.

The Italian looked puzzled for a moment. "Owe?" he repeated. "What is this mean, 'owe'?"

Wren wiped her mouth and gave the bottle to the kiwi. "Don't say another word, Mac," she hissed at him under her breath, a menacing look on her glistening brow. To the Italian, she said sweetly, "It means, 'is there something you could do for us,' Germano?"

He looked confused for a second, then beamed. "Bella donna, I do anything for you. I know many persons. I can do many things." He smiled and nodded enthusiastically at each of them, before tapping his nose and winking.

Four minds started whirring at once. Each contributed a component to the plan that was hatched five minutes later. Germano thanked them over and over for the opportunity to repay a tiny part of the life debt he felt he owed them. The little knot of people huddled on the mountainside held a collective breath as Germano fired up his phone. Then they grinned at the sight of the full signal bar.

Seventy-Two

Sunday afternoon

Capitano Gezza Maldini wasn't having a good day. It had started badly in the bedroom, an on-going row with his wife over his desire for another child. "You got any idea how painful it is?" she'd bawled at him for the hundredth time. That was part of the problem. He wished he did know what it was like to push a reluctant little bundle of life into the world. To produce a living thing from and of himself. In a brief moment of circumspection, he cursed the capricious God who he believed had engineered the anatomy that prevented half of mankind from experiencing the joy of creation. Then he'd argued with his tweenage daughter over her iPad addiction. Then he'd drunk eight strong coffees at the station house in town and eaten a lousy panini. Then he'd been ordered by the Colonnello to oversee an operation up the hill.

Now he was entering his third hour of inspecting vehicles heading south out of the sun-scorched valley at the end of a warm afternoon. Looking for three fugitives not even wanted in his own country, for God's sake. He eyed the ancient blue tractor clattering toward his gate position with ill-concealed contempt. He knew that probably half the taxes he paid went on maintaining people like the wizened old man hunched over the wheel in the cabin in front of him. He had on a once white, tank-top vest, filthy jeans and battered boots. A scrawny mongrel lay panting at his feet. Just when Maldini thought his day couldn't get any worse, the contents of the tractor's trailer assaulted his senses.

"Ma, che cazzo," he muttered to his younger colleague who nodded in agreement. Maldini held up a hand to the gnarled driver, clasped fingers to his nose and took a couple of steps to the trailer as the brakes hissed and the exhaust heaved great clouds of smoke into the clear mountain air. He poked the steaming contents cursorily with his state-issued stick, then nodded vigorously to his partner to raise the barrier.

The old man revved and the tractor wheezed and rattled through the checkpoint. He bounced down the pine-strewn valley beside the roiling river for another couple of kilometres before creaking to a squealing halt at the pre-arranged layby. He hadn't asked any questions of his cousin's son at the foot of the mountain half an hour ago, just stuffed the hundred euro note Germano had held out into his back pocket.

The old man had seen a Ferrari once, back in the sixties. Some film company was shooting scenes in the valley. One of the actors had been quite ostentatious. The door of the metallic red, elongated model parked in front of him now opened and a slight, tanned man wearing sunglasses, a crisp white shirt, blue jeans and expensive-looking shoes stepped out and looked casually around. Satisfied, he popped the boot and took out bath towels. The tractor driver frowned, wiped sweat from his brow and looked up at the breeze-blown trees on the hillside and wished it would reach the baking valley floor.

The white-shirted man talked briefly into a mobile phone then walked past his distant relation in the tractor cabin, exchanged a nod then banged his fist on the side of the trailer. "It's okay, friends...come out," he called in flawless English. He took a few more steps, dropped the back panel and reared away, wafting his hand in front of his nose.

Under their tarpaulin, McLeod, Wren and Kurjac removed the lengths of hose from their mouths, crawled to the back of the trailer and emerged like new-borns from the fetid pile of cow-muck. "Thank you," McLeod said, squinting at the white-shirted man who removed his shades and beamed back at him. Then he looked up and down the road and saw a police car round the hairpin a hundred metres below them. He motioned to the others and they ducked back behind the trailer. The car shot past and carried on toward the village. When it was clear it wasn't coming back, McLeod crossed the road with Wren and Kurjac in tow, hopped over the low stone wall and leapt into the crystal-clear waters of an icy river pool.

Sunday afternoon

Less than two hours later, a somewhat frazzled McLeod stepped out of the Ferrari into the blaring horns of Piazza Carlo Felice in south-west Turin. Germano's cousin in the white shirt had said, "Hi, friends," as they'd sat damply in his plush leather seats after their cleansing dip, "I am Stefano." He had then proceeded barely to pause for breath for the duration of the scenic drive as he recounted his family history, told outrageous stories and roared at his own jokes.

McLeod wearily retrieved the rucksack from the boot and put it on the pavement where Kurjac and Wren were standing somewhat uncomfortably. He started rooting in the side pocket for some euros. Stefano saw what he was doing, hurried round the huge bonnet of the Ferrari and raised his hands. "Please, Mac, don't even consider it," he said, affronted. "My whole family owes you a huge debt."

This is getting ridiculous, McLeod thought to himself. Out loud, he said, "You're very kind, Stefano. Thank you for a very, um, entertaining journey."

The Italian's broad face creased into a dazzling smile as he produced a card from his wallet. "Anything you need, you call me, eh Mac?"

McLeod took the proffered card and put it in his own wallet along with those of the kiwi guide and Germano. An aged woman levered herself off a bench a few metres away and approached the little group. Her burgundy frock was fastened in the middle with bailer twine. "Una borsa per lei," she croaked to Stefano, holding out a bag. She looked wizened eyes up at him, slapped his cheek gently and hobbled off. The Italian smiled after the woman.

"Grazie, mama," he called after her. The bent-over woman threw a hand in the air and waddled toward a bus stop. Stefano opened the plastic bag, extracted three train tickets, several hats, a brunette wig and a couple of fake beards.

"This stuff will get you to the border, my friends." His smile turned to a frown as he looked at the time on the tickets and checked his chunky watch. "Put these things on quickly…your train leaves in fifteen minutes."

They did as instructed and inspected each other before Stefano kissed them all liberally, took a last shifty look around the Piazza, strolled back to his Ferrari and roared off. McLeod slung the rucksack on his shoulder and eyed Kurjac. He looked a bit quirky in the salt and pepper goatee. At least the cap covered his distinguishing ear. "You go, Kurjac. We'll be right behind you."

The Bosnian understood, crossed the road and headed for the huge grey edifice of the station.

"I need clothes, Mac," Wren said, fumbling with a lighter.

"I'm sure there'll be somewhere inside," he replied, checking the traffic. "You make a good brunette," he added over his shoulder as they crossed the busy street. Wren smiled and trailed fumes as she danced between vehicles. They reached the vast building's apron and McLeod rooted in the bag for some euros. "Find whatever you need," he said urgently, "the darker the better, I guess."

Wren couldn't help grinning up at him. "Look at you, all special ops," she chided.

Her words caused him to still a moment. He knew his grandfather had served with the nascent SAS for a number of years after the war. Then he dismissed the thought. "It's hanging around with you and him," he said, jerking a thumb at the station entrance.

Wren smiled and tugged the brown bristles on his chin. "I'll meet you inside when I'm done out here," she said, flicking ash.

McLeod nodded and headed once again into the unknown.

Seventy-Three

Sunday evening

McLeod looked out of the window to his right and watched a lurid pink sun set over the calm waters of the Adriatic as the train approached the station in Trieste. The small city somehow managed to squeeze itself between the azure sea and verdant mountains in the extreme north-east of Italy. Many of the city's inhabitants spoke Slovenian or Croatian, the languages of its near neighbours. All he'd known previously about the place was that it was a fairly major port in the Mediterranean. Kurjac had since told him that it held a significant historical position as the meeting point of Slavic, Latin and Germanic cultures. Apparently, it also had a beautiful square on the seafront where they could get a late bite to eat.

McLeod found that he was famished. He salivated at the thought of a big bowl of seafood pasta with a fear-inducing quantity of garlic, a large cold beer and a glass or two of local Prosecco. Then a bath and a bed. The last one he'd slept in properly was his own, he suddenly realised. He hadn't got much in the hotel with Penelope, he remembered. The air was sucked from his chest and the guilt racked his bones once again.

Kurjac reckoned that they were fairly safe once the train had pulled out of Turin station and they'd dispensed with their crude disguises. Now though, he was looking about him warily as the taxi took them off to *Piazza Unità d'Italia*, a wordy title for a place locals merely referred to as the Big Square. He knew the General used the bustling port here to move people and shipments. Arms to North Africa and the Middle East; illegal immigrants from those places to Slovenia and beyond; drugs from South East Asia and Turkey everywhere. The General had a number of employees stationed in the town and Kurjac knew of several who might recognise him. He pulled his cap lower on his head as the taxi pulled up at the impressive three-sided square, the fourth formed by the darkening Adriatic on their right.

McLeod paid the driver and headed out with the rucksack across the beautifully lit *piazza*. Kurjac and Wren followed after a minute or so. The elaborate architecture of the imposing grey buildings and occasional statue held McLeod's interest as he followed his ears to the hotel and grill Kurjac had mentioned. The haunting melody of Matt Monro crooning '*questi giorni, quando vieni il bel sole*' in a luxuriant baritone echoed around the sporadically inhabited square.

The restaurant was full inside so they reluctantly took a table on the terrace and warily eyed immaculately attired locals and tourists taking their evening *passagiata*. They ordered what might be their last decent meal for a while from a friendly waiter who was more than happy to arrange their accommodation in the hotel above. McLeod raised his large Peroni. "To tomorrow," he murmured and downed half of it in a single, stress-busting draught.

Wren was struggling with her lighter in the salty breeze, gave it up and raised a glistening glass of Prosecco. "And an end to this madness," she said without conviction.

Kurjac looked at them, the tiniest glint of hope in his eyes. "One way or another, it will be the end of my madness. Either I'll be dead or the happiest man alive." He threw back a shot of vodka and poured a glass of mineral water.

McLeod held his eyes which seemed even more hollow in the candlelight. "I think you deserve a chance of happiness, Kurjac," he said quietly.

Wariness returned to the bristly Bosnian's face.

"I think he deserves the chance to die just as much," said Wren testily.

McLeod looked a wince over at her.

Kurjac was nodding slowly. "She's right, McLeod," he growled. "I've died a thousand deaths already. One more won't make any difference to me."

McLeod looked at him solemnly. "I know that's a figure of speech and I've got no idea how awful your life has been to say such a thing." He paused and took another refreshing gulp of beer. "But you haven't physically died, Kurjac. Tomorrow there's a very real possibility that any or all of us will." McLeod looked for any sign of doubt in Kurjac's eyes as he thought about his

312

next words. "Let's be clear here, Kurjac," he said and glanced at Wren blowing smoke pensively. "I don't speak for Anna, but I'm doing this for Penelope and for Nathalie." His light Scots accent became more pronounced with the force in his words. "Because otherwise, no one will ever be brought to justice for what happened to them. I think whoever is behind this is beyond the law. And we're beyond any help from it." McLeod looked across the darkening square, then glanced at Wren who nodded back, a faint gleam in her eyes. "Saving your sister and her children would be a good thing, Kurjac. But it's the information from the General that I need."

Kurjac glanced at a little knot of strollers and scanned their shadowy faces with twitching eyes. Satisfied for the moment, he returned his gaze to the man he was depending on. "You're as wise as you are brave, McLeod. And you're right," he said, eyes up and left to the next group of walkers, "it's not going to be, what's your expression...a walk in the park?" He paused and took several quick sips of water. "But I make you this promise, McLeod. If we free Lejla and her children," he said vehemently, a taut forefinger tapping the table, "I will help you find the people behind all this and I will bring my kind of justice on them." His gaze was firmly on the other man so he didn't notice the burly brute talking animatedly into a phone until he was almost level with their table. Something about the man's outline in his peripheral vision caused Kurjac to look up.

It was the General's head honcho in Trieste, a man he had seen often at the big house. He turned his head away quickly as the thick-set man stopped walking ten feet away.

McLeod saw Kurjac's reaction and glanced left to the large figure gesticulating wildly with his free hand. He was talking loudly in a Slavic language McLeod thought might be Serbian. "I don't think he's seen you, Kurjac," he murmured furtively. "Seems to be deep in an argument."

"He is, something to do with money," Kurjac muttered quietly and stood, back facing the sturdy man. "I'm going to the bathroom, okay?"

McLeod nodded and turned to Wren across the small table. "Who do you think the guy is?" he whispered, inclining his head. He seemed to be finishing up his conversation, his voice deeper even than Kurjac's, then he poked his phone.

"No idea, but Kurjac mentioned something about the General having an operation in this place." She glanced up and saw the giant beaming down at her.

"Enschuldigung Fräulein," he boomed. "Haben Sie Feuer?" Wren looked helplessly at McLeod.

He saw the alarm in her eyes and swallowed, looked at the enormous figure towering over them and reached for Wren's lighter. Held it toward the immaculately attired man extracting a cigarette from an obscure packet and depositing it in unseen lips beneath a bushy grey moustache.

"Danke," the man growled, his eyes not leaving Wren's.

"Bitte," McLeod replied.

The man handed the lighter back to Wren, then directed a thick plume and a withering look at McLeod. He turned back to Wren. "Bis später," he grunted deeply and walked weightily away.

Wren took a feverish drag, eyes following the man until he was out of earshot. "What the fuck was that, Mac?"

"Coincidence, I think," he replied, but watched the big man carefully as he conferred with two others a little way off by an elegantly lit fountain. "He mistook us for Germans, so I think we're all right." He went quiet for a moment, musing on the incident and passed a hand through his thick dark hair. "The guy said 'until later' as he left," McLeod murmured.

Wren looked worried briefly before her lips parted indignantly. "He was hitting on me, Mac," she said, searching for the guy over her right shoulder. She saw the big man and his associates recede into darkness beyond the fountain, then turned back to the table and used the ashtray. "But we need to be more careful," she said as a couple of waiters approached bearing large white plates. Kurjac emerged from behind them, his head turning slowly left and right. He retook his seat, nodded to McLeod and Wren and cursorily acknowledged the waiter who'd placed a large Steak Béarnaise in front of him.

"Who was that?" said McLeod, stabbing a plump mussel and twirling spaghetti.

"Stojković," Kurjac spat. "One of the General's top men. We need to get this done quickly." He cut his meat into bite-size chunks the way McLeod had observed Americans doing and scooped sauce with his chips. "First thing tomorrow, we hire a car."

"To do what?" Wren asked, her face hidden by a huge burger.

Kurjac's eyes darted from his plate to the people passing the terrace. "Get us to the General," he murmured.

"You haven't told us where he is, Kurjac," McLeod said, pouring more Prosecco for Wren and a glass for himself. Kurjac declined. "It wasn't clear from that map you showed us of the compound."

"Little valley in the hills south of Belgrade." He almost choked on the word. "About seven hundred kilometres from here. And I don't think we'll be done tomorrow now. More like the early hours of Tuesday."

McLeod used a chunk of bread to mop up the last juices from his bowl. "But isn't that only around seven hours by car?" he said.

"We can't drive there, Mac," Wren said and shot Kurjac a confused look. "We'd have to go through Slovenia, Croatia and Serbia. They aren't Schengen countries."

"The Inspector's right, Mac," said Kurjac sitting back, legs jiggling, eyes scanning the square. "What do you know about the Danube?"

"The river or the waltz?" Wren asked, struck by a sudden urge to see Finlay. She needed a phone.

McLeod's brow unfurrowed as he caught Kurjac's drift. "It's long...maybe the second longest river in Europe." He paused, thinking about a quiz question he'd had once. "Aren't there something like seven capital cities in its course?"

"That's a bit of a myth," Kurjac replied, fidgeting. "But one of the four capitals it does pass is in a Schengen country and another is Belgrade."

"I was right then," Wren said to McLeod, wondering if she had time for pudding and nodding at Kurjac. "He was talking about the waltz."

McLeod and Kurjac turned matching puzzled brows toward her.

"*The Blue Danube*," she said, smiling. "It's composer, Johann Strauss Jr? He was known as the Waltz King of Vienna."

Seventy-Four

Monday afternoon

The ancient spires and domes and the more modern bridges and office towers of the Austrian capital receded quickly in the wake of twin hundred-horsepower Mercury engines. McLeod hadn't expected the speedboat to be cheap to hire. He wasn't anticipating paying eight hundred euros for the day. After the extravagance of the hotel and all the first-class train travel, they were down to their last five hundred euros. Penelope's father's euros, McLeod corrected himself. He inspected the wad of pounds and dollars. Plenty of those left. He put them back in the rucksack and zipped it up. He imagined dollars would spend fairly readily in Serbia. If they made it past the river patrols.

He sniffed a hastily purchased sausage sandwich and reckoned it would probably give him only mild indigestion. Early afternoon sun mitigated the breeze in the open cabin of the sleek boat being driven as fast as Kurjac felt he could get away with. McLeod shook his head at the sight of Wren devouring a variety of Viennese pastries on the white leather seat beside him. He thought briefly about what the night ahead would bring, then, just as quickly, gave it up. He'd do what he'd always done. Deal with whatever was put in front of him to the best of his ability.

Wren was reinvigorated. The meal and the soothing bath in the hotel had helped, but it was talking to Finlay that was mainly responsible. She recalled her son's words on the phone and she felt warm inside. "Do the right thing, Mum. Like you always do," he'd said. She could tell he was crying. Tears welled behind her eyes at the realisation that she'd never known he felt that way about her. She stuck her head beyond the protection of the boat's windshield to dry her eyes, thought of all the miles they'd covered the last few days. Boats, Trains, cars, skis. And then the frantic drive this morning, from Trieste to Vienna, through the spectacular mountains. Their longest journey was the one they were embarking on now and who knew what was waiting at its end. Would they be up to it? Then a worrying thought occurred. What if they were? But the sound of her son, safe and well, had galvanised her and it was with fresh determination that she vowed once again to find some measure of justice for the Lane sisters.

Of the three of them, only Kurjac had the vaguest idea what lay in store sometime after midnight. But that was only if their lengthy river odyssey passed without a hitch. And only if they could secure a vehicle in Belgrade to take them the final thirty kilometres to the General's compound. Then there were the guards, with their assorted weaponry and possibly dogs. Then there were the cameras. Then more guards. Then the General himself. He thought back to the decision he'd taken in the hotel room in London and smiled. It had brought him further than he'd dare to dream. Could it take him all the way to his deliverance? He offered a silent blessing for the gift of his accomplices and prayed they wouldn't be harmed in his cause. Then he prayed that Lejla was safe in her little house with her sweet children. Nowhere near the carnage that he was bringing toward them at better than thirty knots.

When the dense forest began to thin on the right bank of the wide, slow river, he started to get glimpses of the ancient-looking Bratislava Castle, most of which only dated to the nineteen fifties. A squat white edifice with a clay-tiled roof and matching turrets set on a hill above the sprawling city.

Bratislava. The first of his many mental checkpoints on the long journey ahead. Budapest was the next. Novi Sad was another. The final one on his list was the lair of the Devil himself. He made sure nothing was in the way in the placid water ahead. Then he turned with glistening eyes and looked humbly at the questioning faces of McLeod and Wren. "Thank you," he said.

Monday afternoon

The General returned the handset slowly to its cradle. His searing wide-set black eyes were flecked red from lack of sleep. His hairy nostrils flared from a bulbous nose as he heaved a deep breath into his broad chest. He parted thin grey lips and ground uneven stained teeth. Passed a massive, trembling hand through wiry grey-black hair. "NNNNOOOOO!" he bellowed at the recently refurbished walls of his office.

How was it remotely possible that the best secret service in the world could lose three people so easily? He could locate everyone in his sprawling clandestine operation with the touch of a button. Except one, he rebuked himself. The one upon whose devastating skills the rest of it had been built. He thought over the MI5 man's words. Nothing since Chamonix. That had been over thirty hours ago. How could anyone exist for such a period of time and not be observed somewhere doing something?

The answer came to him and tore the air from his lungs. Because it wasn't anyone. It was Kurjac. Then he had another thought and cold fear locked his huge frame. He took deep breaths and tried to force all irrational ideas from his mind, focused on what had brought him this far in life, made him so powerful. So wealthy. Self-preservation. Then he pressed a button on his console. "Bring the woman's children to my suite, Goran," he seethed. "Put them in the end bedroom and guard it yourself." He clicked off the button and instinctively reached into a drawer for his sedatives. They were in a little brown bottle next to a nine millimetre and his favourite knife. The sight of it gave him another idea. He took out the knife and shut the drawer. Then he opened another one full of stimulants and pressed a different button on the console. "Bring Lejla to my room," he snarled at it.

318

Seventy-Five

Monday evening

Plans. They'd been made and reformulated by Wren and McLeod throughout the day's long river cruise and well into the late afternoon. Kurjac had tuned in sporadically from the driver's seat in front. He'd only really had one plan for the last fifteen years: react faster than the other guy to the unexpected.

The printed sheet of the General's compound was worn, the ink almost erased from certain areas. Arguments had been heated at times. Kurjac had got involved in the technical aspects. Drawn and redrawn the layout of the big house for them. Its dimensions, the furniture, the position of surveillance cameras. The inventory of items they needed had been scrutinised down to four things: Kurjac's knife, the Swiss policeman's nine millimetre, wire-cutters and earth. The majestic medieval skyline of the Hungarian capital lay before them, glowing in the evening sun. Their last chance to kit up.

Tuesday morning

Kurjac flicked on the wipers of the hijacked Audi coupé as light drizzle started to blur the windscreen. He felt little guilt over the man they'd taken it from. He'd been cruising the red light district in Belgrade, seen Wren strolling seductively and propositioned her though his open window. She'd smiled sweetly, flicked away her cigarette and hopped in beside him. The man went straight for her breasts. Then Wren made to reach for his fly, but punched him in the balls so hard, it was biologically unlikely he would ever be a father again.

The dense woods started to thin as the car descended south and then west into the little kidney-shaped valley. The General's valley. His compound occupied almost half of it. Kurjac slowed the Audi, pulled off the single-track road and parked up next to a dilapidated, roofless farm building. He killed the lights. The last echoes of engine noise and shuddering tyres died. Silence filled the car. Complete blackness surrounded it. The first rays of dawn were a couple of hours away in the moonless sky. Then three doors were opened and three pairs of hands smeared rain-splattered earth on three fixed faces. As their eyes became accustomed to the dark, they could make out faint light to the south. Kurjac turned his gleaming eyes to McLeod and Wren's barely visible faces. "Let's go," he murmured.

They walked the empty road for over a kilometre to the west. For most of the way, they could barely see it. But now its verges were clearly visible in the faint glow from the unseen compound half a kilometre to the south. The air was mild, there was no wind and the rain had stopped. A few stars were visible through the occasional breaks in the cloud. Just ahead and to the left was the cattle-gridded entrance to the General's drive which was more like a gravel track with a grassy ridge growing down its middle.

There was no sign or any other indication of what the track lead to. Powerful gatehouse lights were directed straight up the drive, flooding two-thirds of it. Kurjac took that as a good sign. If the guards were operating under the conditions of a live threat, the lights would be moving in arcs, seeking out intruders in the no-man's land between the road and the compound either side of the drive. Kurjac signalled for them to stop walking and nodded to McLeod. "Remember," he breathed, black eyes twitching. "All of these bastards are killers. The only difference between me and them is that they had a choice."

McLeod's stomach was filled with butterflies and he increased his grip on the handle of the solid wire cutters in his left hand. He swallowed and stuck out his right. "See you at the rendezvous," he murmured.

Kurjac swapped his own hefty cutters to his left hand and clasped McLeod's. "You can do this, Mac," he said, jaws clenched. He looked in the bigger man's eyes, saw the steel he sought. Then he turned toward the nondescript entrance, tried to slow his breathing to attain a measure of tranquillity, but it wouldn't come. This wasn't like a regular assignment. This was the rest of his life. He gave it up and crossed the cattle grid, entered the General's land and mentally ticked off his last checkpoint. Then he scaled the low, white wooden fence to the right of the dusty drive and vanished.

McLeod dropped his cutters as Wren threw herself into his broad chest and squeezed fierce arms around his back. "This is from me and Nathalie and Penelope, Mac," she gasped.

He closed his hooded eyes and nodded against the top of her head. "And this is from me to you, Anna," he breathed and planted plump lips on her forehead, then released her.

She looked at his face, still darkly devastating despite the low light and the smeared earth. With tears welling in her eyes, she said, "See you on the other side, Mac." She blinked a few times and took a deep breath. Then she put a hand into her dark tunic and checked the gun was safe, put it back and zipped the pocket. She nodded grimly at McLeod and took off to join Kurjac.

McLeod bent to pick up his cutters. Looked at the two distant lights and thought of Penelope and Nathalie. Then he raised his eyes to the sky and saw a bright star and thought of Catherine. Then he ground his teeth together and felt the familiar kick of adrenaline as he pushed off for the entrance as though from sprinter's blocks.

Kurjac and Wren made steady progress west of the gatehouse. The small building reminded Wren of the kind of toll booth you saw on motorways all over Europe, complete with raising bar between two concrete pillars. They came to the wood that Kurjac knew ran south and met the perimeter fence level with the big house. Though they were well beyond the reach of the lights, if they were swung by a guard in their direction, Kurjac saw no harm in using the added protection of the trees. Such extra measures of precaution were one of the reasons he was still around.

Wren had little difficulty in keeping up with the agile man bent low in front of her. The soles of the dark-brown trail shoes she'd picked up nine hours ago during a fuel stop in Budapest stuck like glue to the pine pitch. How bloody stereotypical, it struck her suddenly. The men had bought tools, she'd bought shoes. The roots in the narrow avenue of aromatic trees began to become visible as their eyes grew used to the intense blackness.

After ten minutes or so, they started to make out the tall wire fence through the trees. Two hundred metres directly east, dim lights downstairs in the big house were just visible. Kurjac looked instinctively a hundred metres north of the house and saw the dark silhouette of the razor wire-topped wall surrounding Lejla's little haven, got no gut feeling as to whether she was inside or not. Neither could he tell from his angle if there was a man guarding its entrance.

His own room in the big house faced south so he hadn't observed the outside guards' routine in this direction since he'd been incarcerated. He cast his mind back to when he'd had liberty in the house. If there were two guards on duty as was usual back then, one would do a lap of the long perimeter fence while the other would sit in the gatehouse, watching the camera feed if he was vigilant, dozing, looking at a magazine, or more recently, a phone if he wasn't. He could just make out the path worn by the patrolling guards inside the fence. He followed the line of it north and east toward the gatehouse, but the bright light up there made everything between one black mass. He turned his head right and looked south along where he thought the path went.

Wren followed his eye line but saw nothing in the blackness. Then she watched Kurjac dart out of the woods and bend low at the fence. She heard tiny snapping sounds, saw him still and then dart back toward her. "I think someone's coming," he said, breathing quickly.

She listened hard, hearing nothing but the call of a distant owl. Then she froze. The unmistakeable sound of a dog panting and straining at the leash grew and headed straight in their direction.

McLeod's progress on the opposite side of the compound hadn't been as rapid. Try as he might, he struggled to fathom any feature of the ground he was covering. He'd fallen several times and stubbed his toes on unseen rocks and roots in his lightweight trainers. Low thorny shrubs had grabbed his legs and he'd pitched head first into a number of craters created by tank shells during the war. But he'd made it to the small knot of pine trees that Kurjac had described.

It sat on a little hill ten metres from the perimeter fence to the east of the compound. About equidistant between the bright lights of the gatehouse to his north-west and the single weak light he could make out coming from the big house at ten o'clock on a clock face. He took deep breaths, trying to judge the distance to the rendezvous at the gatehouse. Maybe two hundred metres.

A pain on his forehead turned out to be a gash that was bleeding into his left eye. He tried to staunch it with the sleeve of his thin black polo neck but knew he was just smearing mud into it. He hoped it would dry quickly in the mild night air.

He strained to make out the path near the fence but could see nothing against the glare of the lights. He sighed heavily and thumped his thigh. Then he crept silently out of the trees and approached the fence, looked left and right along its length but could make little out. He kneeled down against the thick cross-hatched wire, put the blades of his cutters around a bit where it became buried in the ground and snapped them closed. It barely made a sound. But something behind his left shoulder did. "не мрдај," snarled a vicious low voice.

Kurjac had been hopeful that tonight might be one of the rare ones when the guards couldn't be bothered with the savage pull of the Rottweilers on their long leashes. He wasn't overly concerned with the General's soldiers. He knew of two or three that could pose him a problem but nothing he wouldn't be able to work out. The dogs were another matter. Badly wired and completely unpredictable, the result of being intensively bred and crossed with American Pit Bulls. They had misshapen skulls that caused pressure points to flare in their brains. Made them erratic and angry unlike the pure breed. Ally that with tremendous strength, sharp teeth and a powerful bite, and you had sixty kilos of pure, uncontainable savagery.

He heard it snarling and grunting as it passed level with their position in the dense trees. He hoped they were out of range of the beast's sensitive snout. Then he could make out vague movement maybe five metres behind the creature and heard faint footfall. He waited until he could no longer see nor hear either and motioned for Wren to stay put. She nodded unseen in the darkness. Then he took a breath and broke through the trees and headed for the line of cuts he'd made in the fence, squeezed through and jogged soundlessly in the direction the guard had taken.

He had no plan for the dog. Just try to deal with it as best he could. The guard would present little difficulty. Creeping up and striking from behind had been his bread and butter during the war.

A noiseless jog if he could avoid ground detritus to within five metres then a sudden burst. If the guy heard and turned, you slashed the throat out in front. If he didn't, you pulled the head back and did the same from behind.

This brute was big, maybe six-five. But he hadn't heard his approach. Kurjac had to leap to grab his forehead from behind and deliver the fatal blow. He fell down on the dying man's back and looked urgently for the dog. He saw nothing but blackness. He strained his ears, but all he heard was the gurgling of the man's throat beneath him. Then a low blood-curdling growl started up. He held his knife in front of him and raised his left arm as a further barrier. Then the growling stopped and he braced himself. Nothing came. He heard a loud sniffing sound. Then a keening he recognised, though he hadn't heard it in several years. "Sasha?" he called out in the direction of the noise. There was a curtailed bark and then the beast was on him, licking his cheeks and whining. One of the few requests the General had ever granted Kurjac had been to train the new puppies in his room. Sasha clearly hadn't forgotten him.

McLeod had no idea that the man had told him not to move. Had he understood, he still wouldn't have done so. Kurjac had spent an hour of the long river journey describing some of the basic rules of close combat. Number one was to do nothing predictable or slow. Kurjac had also described the physical attributes of the General's men. They were mostly Serbian survivors of the conflict. Mostly in their forties. They did little in the way of training anymore, although quite a number were bodybuilders. Plenty of pills knocking around the compound. Big, cumbersome men.

McLeod was bigger than average, but he could move like a leopard. He did so now. Judged where the voice had come from and spun low to his left, threw the chunky wire cutters with all his might as his spin unfurled, followed his momentum into a forward roll and looked up. The faint outline of a big man to his right, clutching something across his chest was what he saw. He also made out a pair of legs and threw himself at them low and hard. The huge man toppled slowly like an ancient oak. There was a loud crack when his head landed on bare rock and he went still. McLeod listened hard, poised above the inert man, a mighty punch in the solar plexus ready if needed. But it wasn't. The man

324

was not in a good way. A dark stain was growing on the pale rock behind his bald head. McLeod felt his neck and found only a very weak pulse. It was touch and go whether his steroid-hardened heart would keep him alive till morning.

McLeod took deep breaths and inspected the rest of the man. The thing he'd been clutching across his chest was some sort of rifle. The reason he'd been doing so was because a tear in his camouflaged jacket was directly over where McLeod had been planning to punch. He'd probably been winded immediately by the force of the cutters hitting his chest. McLeod prized the rifle from the barely breathing man and threw it into the trees. Quickly checked the guy's pockets and found a flick-knife, gum, some notes and coins, half a pack of cigarettes, a zippo lighter, an old mobile phone, a bottle of pills and a set of keys. McLeod put the knife in a back pocket of his dark jeans, the lighter and keys in his front right and recovered his cutters. He set a hooded glare at the fence, then north and south along it. Listened hard, then started off again.

Kurjac found something very unusual on the dead guard that made him reconsider his options. From a holster inside the giant's jacket he took a fully-loaded Sig S4 handgun and a heavy Trident silencer. He also found a small torch which he used to inspect the guy's pockets as best he could with the dog trying to lick his face off. He reminded himself to smear more mud on it. He found a set of keys that he trousered, a slightly dull knife that he didn't. Then he shone the torch on the holster and judged there was no way it would ever fit him. He checked the trigger pull, then shoved the pistol in a back pocket of his lightweight khaki trousers and the silencer in a thigh pocket. He extinguished the torch, took Sasha's lead from the dead man's hand and hurried back to the gap in the fence he'd made. Called to Wren, low and quiet. He saw her faint outline emerge from behind a trunk and he pulled the fence back for her. Sasha rumbled a menacing growl. Wren stopped dead in her tracks just short of the fence. "What the hell, Kurjac?" she hissed.

He grunted and thought quickly. "I'll put her somewhere safe. Wait there a minute." He stroked the dog's head and took off south along the fence for fifty metres then tied her to it. He scratched her ears. "Be a good girl and I'll be back for you later," he murmured to the panting dog. He turned and looked at the west face of the big house maybe a hundred and fifty metres east of him. It had a wide veranda along its side with wooden struts housed in matching decking. An opaque fluorescent lamp shone above a heavy door next to the security camera pointed almost directly down at the decking. On the ground floor, light spilled from the shuttered kitchen windows. It was the only lit room on the whole side of the house. That made up his mind.

McLeod made the owl call again, hands cupped together, blowing on the knuckles of his thumbs. Twenty metres shy of the gatehouse. Then he heard the answering hoot he'd been waiting for the past couple of minutes. He crept forward and threw the small stone in his right hand from ten metres east of the gatehouse at its fibreglass wall. Saw the door at the back of the small, brightly-lit cabin open, and a beefy, rifle-toting man in fatigues stride out purposefully toward him where he cowered behind a tree stump surrounded by tall grass. The guard was conscious for three seconds after Kurjac burst from the other side of the gatehouse and caught his heels with his wire cutters. Then delivered a blow with the same instrument to the back of the prone man's neck which may or may not have severed his spinal cord. Wren ran past Kurjac and the limp guard to McLeod. "You all right, Mac?" she breathed, peering at the blood beginning to cake over his eye.

He put a hand on her shoulder and gave her a quick look up and down.

"I'm fine, Anna," he replied between pants. "Ran into a real meatbag lurking outside the fence."

"What happened?" she said, alarm clear in her face backlit by the gatehouse.

"I was lucky," he murmured as Wren dabbed his forehead with tissue. "The man was a cheeseburger shy of a heart attack."

Wren nodded silently and flinched at Kurjac's approach. "Okay," he breathed, "so far, so good." He looked to the south-west. "We have to forget Lejla's house for now," he whispered, turning his feverish gaze to the big house. "Concentrate on the General." He took a few quick strides to one of the arc lights and shone it along the fence in both directions, then trotted back to Wren and McLeod. "I think we've taken care of all the security this side of the house," he said, attaching the silencer to the pistol. "If there's any to the south, we don't need to worry about it."

"What about all the other soldiers, Kurjac? We've only accounted for three of seventeen," McLeod whispered urgently.

Kurjac was silent for a moment, breathing hard through his nose, putting himself in the General's shoes. "There'd normally be one guard downstairs in the house and another in the brain room, possibly with a tech guy," he breathed. "I'm betting he's doubled that."

"But if we get caught in a camera, won't that bring the rest from the barracks?" Wren seethed.

Kurjac's taut lips contorted into a grim smile. "It would, but we won't be caught in a camera before we need to be and I have an idea about the General's men," he said, excitement shining in his dark eyes.

McLeod replayed the jittery man's words. "Wait," he said confused, "you want to be caught in a camera?"

Kurjac was checking the sights on the pistol. "It's vital if this is going to work," he murmured, raising the gun to shoulder height. He took aim at a point on a fence post ten metres away and fired. There was a loud 'clack' and then an immediate thud from the thick wooden post. "Fire's straight," he muttered, "but has a strong lift."

"What the hell are you doing, man?" Wren gasped, as the shot died to an echo in the low surrounding hills.

"Relax, Inspector," he replied coolly. "The General's men often take pot shots at animals in the night. Come here." He beckoned to Wren and handed her the pistol. "See my mark on the post?" he murmured, standing behind her. She nodded and assumed a marksman's stance. Breathed in slowly and fired. "Good enough," Kurjac said as the sound subsided. "Give the Swiss policeman's gun to McLeod, Inspector. Too loud to test it here and this thing's good." He nodded at her assured handling of the weapons. "Just aim a couple of feet low when the time comes, okay?"

"Okay," Wren replied tensely. "When will that be, Kurjac?"

"Soon enough, Miss Wren," he replied and cast menacing eyes toward the imposing façade of the big house.

Seventy-Six

Tuesday morning

The General was a light sleeper and the second of Kurjac's distant shots jerked him awake. He rubbed his eyes and peered at the luminous display of his digital clock. Three twenty-four. He heaved himself out of bed and shuffled to the bathroom, then to his study. He clicked a button on the console on his heavy mahogany table. "Everything all right?" he barked at it.

Two floors below in the first-floor brain room, head technician Zlatko reluctantly paused the game on his phone, sighed, scanned banks of screens and pressed the intercom answering button. "Everything's fine, General," he blustered, nervously checking the composite camera display to ensure that was actually the case. He was slight and gaunt, the result of years spent glued to a computer screen in his bedroom. His sallow, pock-marked face was thin. He had a crooked nose, greasy skin and his lank black hair flopped over a rounded forehead. "All cameras clear," he said flatly, "no reports from the patrol or the gatehouses."

The General released the breath he'd been holding. "You're positive, Zlatko? Something woke me."

The technician rolled his eyes at the swarthy guard reading a bodybuilding magazine in a swivel chair opposite. Something always woke the old bastard. He turned back to the intercom. "Positive, sir. Nothing to worry about," he yawned.

"All right, Zlatko," the General murmured, "stay vigilant." He crossed to the bay window, pulled the heavy curtains and looked two hundred metres north to the gatehouse and its twin lights shining up the drive. The grounds below were indecipherable apart from the slightly pale line of the gravel track terminating in front of the house in a circle dotted with squat driveway lamps. Everything seemed quiet. He closed the curtains and thought about going back to bed, but he knew he wouldn't sleep and thought about Lejla. Felt nothing. He cursed and picked up his phone that had refused to ring despite the Urquhart cretin's assertions. No messages. He grunted and hit 'call' again.

Outside of the west veranda on the far side of the huge building, Kurjac took careful aim at the security camera above the door ten metres away. Breathed as slowly as he could and when his hand was completely still, gently pulled the trigger. The bullet smashed through the device and took out the light for good measure. He ran a few steps to the left edge of the door and pulled back his right arm, knife poised.

The sound of urgent steps grew louder from within. Then the handle turned, the heavy door swung out and a raised pistol and a khaki-clad arm appeared. Kurjac slashed at it with the hunting knife. Must have ripped the radial or ulnar artery or maybe both judging by the amount of blood that sprayed. The arm dropped and then the man followed as Kurjac stuck out a rigid leg. The soldier managed to break his fall with his forearms, but that was the last positive thing he ever did as Kurjac smashed his head against the decking and twisted it. Ten feet away, pressed hard against the wall of the house, McLeod and Wren heard an unpleasant sound, somewhere between a snap and a crunch.

Then they were on the move, hard on Kurjac's heels. Speed at this point was crucial, he'd said. They had to get to the cellar door before the guard on the other side of the house downstairs came to investigate. Or the one from the brain room if there were two people on duty up there. They ran ten metres down a dark, wood-panelled corridor to where Kurjac was trying keys in an old rusty lock. Nothing fitted. They heard the thud of heavy feet on stairs above and from somewhere else on their floor. Kurjac was only halfway through the bunch of keys. In desperation, Wren reached past him to the ancient door handle and turned it. There was a sharp crack and the door opened. It hadn't been locked. Kurjac grimaced and gave the gun back to Wren. He switched on the small torch. "Follow me and close the door," he hissed. "There's another door at the bottom," he said, taking the stone steps carefully in the weak torch light. "Stand on the other side of it and shoot anything that comes through."

He opened the bottom door as they heard two pairs of feet clatter along the wooden corridor behind them, heading for the outside and the dead colleague they'd find on the veranda. Kurjac tried a light switch cobbled to the stone wall in hope, but nothing happened. He pushed into the low room following his narrow beam of light. McLeod was last into the cellar and closed the door. It didn't fit very well and it made a loud clunk as it shut. Kurjac shone the torch desperately on the walls of the pitch-black room, but it couldn't penetrate the dust.

Wren turned ten feet in the darkness back to where she thought the door was and put one knee on the cold floor and her elbows together on the other, gun pointing. She felt McLeod's leg and used her arms and gun to push him behind her as footsteps sounded on the stone steps beyond the door. She re-aimed the silenced pistol with quivering hands, heard the door creak and then a blinding light appeared. She fired at it and rolled to her left. The shot was loud in the low space despite the silencer. She looked up to see the light falling and another appearing behind. Then she fired twice in quick succession and rolled again.

The sharp cracks reverberated around the cellar walls as Wren held the gun ready to fire at any movement from the two dark shapes on the ground. But neither would move again any time soon. Wren's first bullet had probably killed them both. It had been aimed at the bright torch beam, but the gun lift had sent it through the first guy's right eye and it had then lodged in the following man's liver. The second of her two subsequent shots had pierced the following guard's right ventricle.

Cautiously, she took a few steps and reached a shaky hand for one of the two bright beams on the cellar floor. She picked it up and shone it on the grisly lifeless bodies and gasped. Kurjac reached past her for the other torch and shone it at Wren's middle. The spill was enough to see her strained eyes by. He was unsurprised to see the shock they registered. "They were scum, Miss Wren," he rumbled. "Believe me, you just did the world a big favour." He watched her eyes again and saw the return of her resolve, grunted and shone the powerful beam on the far wall, and saw what he was looking for. "Help me with this, Mac. Keep an ear out the door, Inspector," he said warily.

The fuse box was dusty and cobwebbed but relatively new. McLeod held the sturdy lid whilst Kurjac shone the torch on the twenty or more labelled switches. "We need to get into the brain room, so we need to get the tech guy out of it without raising the alarm over at the barracks. We also need the tech guy fully functioning."

"Why?" McLeod replied.

"Because I never plan in hope, Mac. The General's suite is self-contained, cameras everywhere. No way I can shut down his system from here." He ran his finger over the first row of switches, his frown deepening. "He's a terrible sleeper. We will be seen before we get anywhere near him. If he has Lejla, there's only one way I can make this work. For that, we need the tech guy unharmed but terrified."

McLeod looked doubtful. "How the hell are you going to manage that?"

"I'm not," Kurjac replied and flicked a fuse switch, "you are."

Seventy-Seven

Tuesday morning

Two floors up, silence suddenly filled the brain room. The hum of the server fans stilled. Zlatko looked up from his phone to see blank screens all around. The downlights were still on so it couldn't have been a power cut. He cursed as he realised what must have happened. The moronic guard who'd been with him and then went to investigate the camera malfunction must have tried to fix it himself, shorted the whole damned network. Just because they'd done a bit of engineering in the army, they thought they were qualified to meddle with his system.

He stood wearily and grabbed his keys and tool case from his desk drawer. Walked to the door and turned the key in the lock and pushed the door and felt a strong thumb on his right wrist, then another in the crook of his arm and then a lightning blow to his neck. Then his world went black. The last image in his mind was of a strange man's determined face caked in blood and mud.

His next was of another mud-stained face, but this time it was one he recognised. One that caused all the blood to drain from his already pale features. He'd never actually met the monster. Very few people in the compound had. He only recognised him from photographs for passports and visas he'd arranged.

The man was like a mythical diabolical creature among the compound's inhabitants. He wasn't referred to by his name. Just 'the killer.' And now he was here in his room holding a knife to his own Adam's apple. Zlatko lost control of his bladder. A dark stain grew on his blue jeans in front of him where he sat on his office chair. His hands were tied behind him with what must have been sticky tape. Hairs painfully ripped out of his wrists when he strained against it. His shoelaces bound his bony ankles. Then the creature's thin mouth parted above him. "If you do exactly what I want, when I want," it snarled in broken Serbian, "there's a chance you might see tomorrow."

"But, but…" Zlatko stammered, hopelessly.

"Okay, Mac," Kurjac murmured without breaking fearsome eye contact with the technician.

Zlatko heard a long breath being taken behind him and felt strong hands on his own. Then he heard and felt the little finger of his left hand snap. "AAAAAAHHH," he screamed as indescribable pain shot up his arm, through his shoulder and out through the top of his head. He writhed and whimpered as it refused to abate. Cold sweat broke out on his forehead and down his back.

"If you say 'but' to me again, or anything other than 'yes' or 'I understand,' my friend will continue to break your fingers," Kurjac said through grinding teeth. "Then I will take over with my knife on other parts of your body. Do you understand?"

"Yes, yes," Zlatko whined, "anything…please, I understand."

"Good. You've just taken the first step toward saving your life," Kurjac murmured coldly. "This is what I need you to do and Miss Wren over here with the gun will make sure you do it right."

The General rose angrily from his bed again at the insistent sound of the intercom in his study. He stomped toward it and stabbed the button. "What is it, Zlatko?" he blared.

Nothing could hide the terror in the voice that came back at him. "It's Kurjac, sir," it stammered, "with the other man. They got past the guards downstairs…overpowered me and took the spare keycard. They're headed for your suite…they'll be on your monitors now, sir."

The General cast disbelieving eyes at his large computer screen and waggled the mouse to wake it. There, large as life, captured by the camera at the bottom of his suite's stairs were the unmistakeable twisted features of his worst nightmare. Next to him, the British man strode calmly. He thought feverishly. Thirty seconds? "What about the woman?" he shrieked at the intercom.

"There's only the two men, sir, the woman's not with them," came the weak reply.

"Get onto the barracks NOW," he roared. "Flood the house with guards."

"Doing it now, sir," Zlatko lied as Wren nodded at him briefly and then looked to the door.

The General clicked off and pounded through his bedroom, then across a bit of landing to the one next door. He used his card on the reader, took a few fast steps and pulled Lejla naked and groggy from her induced sleep. Then he grabbed his favourite knife from the bedside table and dragged the limp woman to his own room and slammed the door.

The two men faced the wide solid door at the end of the dark hallway. Kurjac glanced briefly up at the hard stare of the taller man at his side, then took the spare keycard from his jeans pocket, swiped it on the little device next to the door leading to the General and took a deep breath. The heavy door sprung from its latch. "Everything that has happened in my life will be worth it if the next minute goes well, Mac," he said nervously. "All the blood. All the death. All the agony." He pressed the tiny button on his flick knife. "The rest of my life is right here."

McLeod didn't say anything. Just nodded once. Kurjac nodded back and took another calming breath. "Let's finish it," he growled and threw himself through the door and bounded up the carpeted stairs.

The broad landing was dark, but Kurjac saw light under the General's bedroom door. It wasn't going to be a quiet ending. He waited until McLeod was at his left side and with a trembling hand, swiped the card and pushed the General's wide bedroom door and was confronted with the worst scenario he could have ever devised. The one he'd been dreading.

The General was standing in black pyjamas in front of his iron-framed white bed in the large, sumptuously decorated room. A heavy crystal chandelier glittered above him and cast bright light on the scene. Clasped tight to the General's side, Lejla was naked and barely able to stand. Her eyes were almost closed. Kurjac's breath caught in his chest as he saw the fresh scars on her jaundiced body. Her hands were bound in front of her navel and blood oozed from a gash on her left breast. Kurjac felt physically sick at the sight of the bloodstained knife in the General's clenched fist against his sister's pale throat. He looked murderously into the General's snake eyes.

Bulbous veins stood out on the heavy man's thick red neck. Sweat was beading on his wide forehead and his breathing was ragged. Demonic black eyes flashed between Lejla's throat and

Kurjac. "So, Dragan, you came back," the General panted in guttural Serbian, ears straining for the arrival of his men. "Not quite in the circumstances I'd hoped, but things will be back to normal soon enough."

Kurjac felt his eyes harden. "No, they won't," he seethed back. "I will never do anything for you ever again, General. I would rather you killed me and my sister and the children." He watched the General's eyes carefully, saw them turn from feverish omnipotence to cold resignation.

"So be it," the huge man spat.

They were the words Kurjac was waiting for. The ones that meant an end to his life. "Here, General," he said, tears streaming down his gaunt cheeks. "Let me make it easy for you." He tossed his knife to the General's feet.

McLeod did likewise with the Swiss policeman's pistol.

The sudden uncertainty in the General's eyes disappeared and an inhuman snarl smeared across his face. "You fool, Dragan," he gloated. "You forgot the most valuable lesson I ever taught you." He pointed the knife at him. "Never plan in hope," he spat, stabbing the knife with each word.

"I never have, General," Kurjac replied, stonily.

Before the General understood the implication of his words, Kurjac took a step to his right. McLeod took one to his left and the General stared in horror at the slight blonde woman with a raised gun who materialised in the space between them.

Wren's fierce blue eyes stared down the long barrel of the silenced weapon. For the few seconds she'd been listening behind the two men who'd parted in front of her, she'd tried to gauge where the General's head was. She'd been dead on. She lowered the barrel to his chest, held her breath and squeezed the trigger. An eighth of a second later, the heavily-jacketed bullet from the gun smashed through the General's dense forehead. Half a second after that, it had carved a devastating swathe through his brain and embedded itself in the far wall. A few bits of bone and lobes and cortices, but mostly blood, sprayed the sheets of the bed crimson as the echo of Wren's shot reverberated around the room. The General's wide mouth parted in a hideous grimace as he crumpled like a cracked stone statue and crashed against the ornate iron bed frame. His broad, flat forehead had a third, black, unseeing eye in its centre. Slowly, his massive body slumped to the floor, palms up, chin on chest, twitching in the final throes of his abhorrent existence.

In another room in the General's penthouse suite, Colonel Goran Bogdanovic's eyes flicked open, his ears straining for the noise that had woken him. He caught its last echoes amongst the discordant harmony of early morning birdsong. He clenched his jaw, cast guarded eyes toward the children sleeping peacefully against the far wall and reached under the pillow for his gun.

To be continued...